Sir Walter Besant, Rice James

The Ten Years' Tenant

And other Stories

Sir Walter Besant, Rice James

The Ten Years' Tenant
And other Stories

ISBN/EAN: 9783744749749

Printed in Europe, USA, Canada, Australia, Japan

Cover: Foto ©Andreas Hilbeck / pixelio.de

More available books at **www.hansebooks.com**

THE TEN YEARS' TENANT

THE TEN YEARS' TENANT

Ballantyne Press
BALLANTYNE, HANSON AND CO.
EDINBURGH AND LONDON

THE
TEN YEARS' TENANT

AND OTHER STORIES

BY

WALTER BESANT AND JAMES RICE

LIBRARY EDITION

London
CHATTO AND WINDUS, PICCADILLY
1888

CONTENTS

THE TEN YEARS' TENANT.

SWEET NELLY, MY HEART'S DELIGHT.

OVER THE SEA WITH A SAILOR.

CONTENTS.

THE TEN YEARS' TENANT

THE TEN YEARS' TENANT

CHAPTER I.

HOW I MET HIM.

IT is now twenty years ago. I was staying at an hotel in Scarborough, one of the great places where they have a couple of hundred people every day at their *table d'hôte*. In the evening some of the company who had been long enough in the place to make each other's acquaintance had got up an entertainment for the rest in the shape of private theatricals, which was given, after the Elizabethan manner, without the accessories of scenery, in the dining-hall. I forget what the play was; but it needed no scenery, being a comedy of the last century, for which the actors were dressed in the fashions of the second George, stately and splendid, though rather stiff.

I am not very fond of private theatricals. It always seems to me that the best amateur actors are those who have most carefully studied the gestures and tricks of professionals in the same parts. Therefore my attention was gradually diverted from the performance to the audience, where were all the materials from which an old-fashioned moralist would have drawn his weary old moral, with a tag of "telle est la vie" about the group met together that night, never again, perhaps, to gather under the same roof. There was the doddering old gentleman; there was the bright and happy girl of seventeen, to whom life seemed made up of lovers and sugar-candy, a most delightful object of contemplation for men of all ages; there were the two elderly maiden ladies, who were enjoying the representation enormously, with a fearful joy, because they had been taught to regard the drama as wicked beyond all things: could, it was always asked, a serious person, with a regard to his soul, look even at the outside of a theatre without shuddering? There was a comfortable old widow, sound asleep with her mouth open; there was a group of children, in happy raptures; there were young men and maidens, half listening and half flirting; there were the usual superior young men from Oxford, who looked on with tolerant pity; there were the country cousins, half ashamed of enjoying the performance too much; there were the waiters and servants at the door, mouths and eyes wide open. Presently my eyes fell upon a listener who somehow compelled my attention, so that I forgot all the rest, even that sweet rosebud of seventeen, and gazed steadfastly upon him alone.

He was a man between fifty and sixty years of age; his hair was " greyed," but not white; his whiskers were greyer than his hair; his face was puffy and red; his nose was certainly swollen with good living and little exercise; his lips were rather thick; his eyes were bright; his forehead was broad; his chin was square. It was the face of a man who had lived and enjoyed all his fifty years.

He was listening to the performance with a curious intentness which the subject scarcely deserved. What did he see in the old-fashioned play? The dialogue was stilted, the sentiment was false. Lord Bellamour, Captain Lovelace, and Amanda were tedious to me, with their parade of musty epigrams and stale claptrap, though their dresses were fine. Yet to this man they seemed full of interest. Yet he neither laughed nor sighed; what pathos there was in the piece moved him not, nor did the low-comedy servant provoke a smile. There was a good deal of "business" with snuffboxes and fans: at this he shook his head critically, as if the by-play left much to be desired; when they performed a minuet he turned away his head despondingly, as if he must draw the line of endurance somewhere, and he could not stand that. Yet I thought the minuet gracefully danced.

He was, perhaps, an actor himself; or he might be a London manager on the look-out for talent. That, no doubt, was the meaning of it. Managers in strange towns always go to see the play, I believe, just as the attendants at one Turkish bath spend their little holiday in visiting rival establishments or conscientious mutes off duty haunt cemeteries. Yes, he must be a London manager.

After the performance some of the men found themselves presently in the smoking-room. Here, instead of gloomily staring at each other, we fell to talking over the evening's entertainment. Hither came my friend with the red face and thick lips. He took a chair next to mine, and, calling for a brandy-and-soda, began to talk. His utterance was slow and measured.

"It is always," he said, when his mixture was set before him, "advisable to fall in with the habits of the current generation. A hundred years ago—in 1760, for instance—gentlemen did not drink brandy-and-soda, nor did they smoke tobacco. Common people, country clergy, light porters, and the like took their pipes. But not gentlemen."

These propositions, thus baldly stated, produced on my mind much the same effect as two or three copy-book texts.

"I suppose," I replied, presently rallying, "that one cannot help adopting the manners of his own generation."

"Perhaps," he said, "it is difficult for ordinary people to avoid doing so. As for myself, I confess it is sometimes pleasant to live again in the past—sometimes to dine off peacock-pie at noon, to eat a larded swan, to order a plum-porridge, now and then to exchange claret for mead, and to breakfast off that neglected beverage, small ale."

Not a London manager: an antiquary, an eccentric of uncommon type. It would, perhaps, reward one to encourage him by a nod of approval, as if mead, larded swans, and plum-porridge were within the art of every plain cook at sixteen pounds a year.

"It gratified me to-night," he went on, "to witness an

attempt, laudable though unsuccessful, to revive something of the great and glorious eighteenth century. The dresses were fairly correct; it is difficult to go wrong in the matter of dress with so many pictures before one; at the same time the fashion of one wig was that of 1750, and of another that of 1770, while I think the patches in the year 1760 were worn quite differently. But perhaps I am thinking of 1745; one's memory sometimes plays one false in the matter of ten years or so. As for the language, it was, of course, that of the time; where they failed was in the tone, the pitch, the management of the voice. Good Heavens, sir!"—he turned quite red with emotion as he said this—"what would be your surprise and indignation were a modern actor to represent a young gentleman of the Victorian age talking in the cockney accent and the nasal twang of an omnibus cad? And the management of the fan and snuff-box! Deplorable, sir! Quite pitiable! And the minuet! How contemptible a failure! To think of that courtly dance being executed as if by clumsy boys and girls in a dancing academy!"

"But, my dear sir," I ventured to say, "it is not everybody who has studied the period so deeply as yourself. What, for instance, was wrong about the snuff-box?"

"They handed it so;" he imitated with exaggeration the offering of the box as rendered by our actors of the evening. "So. Did one ever see the like? Why, sir, a cit at Vauxhall, a London mercer trying to pass for a gentleman at Epsom Wells or Tunbridge, a country bumpkin thinking to put on the manner of St. James's at Bath, would have done better! The true way to offer the snuff-box, the courtly way, is—thus."

He stood up and assumed an attitude which, in his frock coat, seemed profoundly ridiculous. The body was slightly bent, the head inclined in an attitude of courteous and deferential invitation, the right hand held out the snuff-box with the lid open, the left was raised as if partly to protect the snuff-box and partly to emphasise the offering. The attitude of the legs was similarly studied, the right leg being advanced and slightly bent at the knee, the left being held in readiness for immediate action.

"That, sir," said the antiquary, "was the courtly method of offering the snuff-box, and, of course, with the lid open. I would I could by any attitude of mine figure to you the elegance and ease with which the charming ladies of the period handled their fans. Believe me, they as far surpassed the present age in their grace and beauty (which was the triumph of Art practising on Nature in her most generous mood) as the beaux of the time surpassed the uncouth moderns in carriage, wit, and politeness."

He sat down again, and drank off his tumbler of soda-and-brandy.

"A theory," I said very weakly, "which you would have to defend against a formidable array of facts."

"Facts! what facts?" he burst in. "Where are they? Can literature, books, letters, poetry, reconstitute a *salon?* Can we actually see Horace Walpole amusing old Madame du Deffand, for instance, or can we again hear the witty Mrs. Montague, or see the beautiful Peggy Banks, or cry over the fate of the lovely Miss Ray cut off in her prime? Can you even imagine the atmosphere, the light, the grace of an evening when men met ladies, not to rush round the room with them, but to *talk?* I say advisedly, *talk.* Why, sir, every sentence was an epigram; the meaner wits studied their phrases before they came; the ladies were as ready as the men—ay, readier sometimes—with their arrows, whose points were so sharp, though they were no longer than the point of a pin. A dance in such an assembly was a stately thing, in which every lady walked as if she were a goddess, and every man as if he were a great lord. Attitudes were taught and studied in those days; a proper carriage of the body was part of a gentleman's education, and the art of deportment, now lost, was a thing which could never be truly acquired save at Courts and under the wing of great ladies. This art alone, sir, marked the distinctions of rank, and taught the classes who work for their bread that between themselves and the nobility was fixed a gulf never to be bridged over. Why, why did the nobility of England and France resign that inestimable advantage?   Why has a school of manners been allowed to grow up which opens the *salons* of the greatest to every scrub who can boast that he does not jump a counter and can buy a black tail-coat?   A dress-coat! Saw one ever a more frightful, a more meaningless, a more levelling garb? Into what days are we fallen when our gentleman sit down to dinner in the same dress as the lacqueys and fellows who wait upon them!"

This was given with such earnestness, that one felt exactly as if the man were delivering himself of a personal reminiscence. Of course that was nonsense. But one felt so. The other men in the room were attracted, and chairs were pushed closer to the table at which we sat. Presently conversation ceased, and all listened.

"Every century," he went on, his eyes having a far-off look, "takes something away with it which can never be restored. I dare say there is something, if one knew it, in this dull and driving age of yours which is to be prized; but one by one the old things leave us. What I most regret in the eighteenth century is its politeness. What have you gained to compensate for the loss of politeness? Think what it means.   The attitude of body proper for every circumstance in life—can one ever forget the dignity with which, for instance, Lord Ferrers went to be hanged?—that is one thing; the tone of voice suitable for every kind of necessary or complimentary speech, such as that proper for a tradesman or a servant, that for a lady, that for a pretty woman. Lord Foppington in the play may show you what I mean. There is the true manner of estimating your own position and rank compared with those of other people. None of your accursed revolutionary levelling down; no freedom in print over a nobleman's name; a gentleman was a gentleman; rank had a real meaning; every younger son of a squire did not consider himself as good as an earl; and lawyers, doctors, chaplains, ushers, actors, artists, writers, curates, and such cattle, worthy enough in their way, did not pretend to be gentlemen. Think of the absurdity of any

man who earns his living by work calling himself a gentleman! When levelling began, politeness vanished. Where
are your manners now? How do you treat ladies? What
respect remains for rank? What have you got in exchange
for the good old rules which laid down the deference to be
paid to woman and the aristocracy? I saw, only a month
ago," here he shuddered, "I actually saw a common man,
whom I knew to be a person in the City, tap a Duke—a
Duke!—upon the shoulder!"

The men laughed. One of them replied conventionally—

"We have railways. We can travel."

"The better sort travelled then," replied the antiquary,
"and quite fast enough. As for the rest, they stayed at
home, did their work, went to church, died, and went to the
heaven set apart for the unbred and the illbred."

"Electric telegraph," proposed a second.

"Rubbish! what good to know bad news a minute before
you need?"

"Free-trade," said a third. "You will allow that——"

"That the farmers are on the high road to ruin."

"Universal education is fast coming," said a fourth.
"That alone——"

"Will complete the ruin of the world. Society will
dissolve into universal anarchy when you have taught even
your farm-labourers to read, write, learn, and compare.
Stick to your old Church Catechism: 'Learn and labour to
get your own living in that state of life'—ah, good and
honest teaching, how is it disregarded! Your own state!
You would like my state!"

"Come, sir," said a man who looked as if he belonged to
Birmingham—that is, he had an intensely practical and self-
satisfied air, so that one felt sure that, if he was not really a
native of that illustrious town, he must sympathise with the
opinions of the majority. "Come, sir, what do you say to
the spread of Radical ideas and the progress of national
freedom? What do you think of universal suffrage and the
ballot, which we are bound to introduce?"

"Tut, tut!" The learned antiquary put him aside with

a wave of his hand, and declined to reply. As no one else made any suggestion, he went on himself—

"Your steam has turned the working man into a machine. He is no longer an intelligent man; he makes a little bit of something, always the same little bit; away from his work he is a barrel for the reception of beer, which you have not the sense to supply unadulterated; he can read, but he cannot think, therefore he is a tool in the hands of any agitator. Your railways incite people to travel about and look for visionary joys abroad instead of finding substantial ones at home; your electricity threatens to upset everything left that we value—but never mind. Of all your boasted inventions, only two deserve to be mentioned with respect. One is the use of chloroform. This shows that when mankind begin to pay one-tenth the attention to medicine which they pay for the accursed arts by which accidents are multiplied and life made noisy and noxious, they will be on the right path. I believe the sewing machine is also a useful invention. And upon my word, gentlemen"—he rose and took a candle from the table—"upon my word, there is no other invention of modern days worth a thought, and your losses are greater than your gains. Politeness, rank, conversation, dress, dancing, cookery—all these are gone."

"Pardon me, sir"—it was a young fellow who had played in the piece—"you have forgotten one thing. Permit me to suggest that we have gained by the loss of the tallow candle."

The antiquary set down his candlestick, and regarded the speaker with a benignant admiration.

"That," he said, "is the most sensible speech I have heard to-night. You are the young man who made an exhibition of ignorance with a snuff-box just now, are you not? Come to me to-morrow morning, and I will teach you better, as a reward for this reminder. Yes; you have gained by the adoption of a composite candle. Everything which adds to the comfort of the upper classes is a distinct gain to humanity, if only because it promotes admiration of their happy lot. I allow, gentlemen, that the tallow candle was, in the last century, a serious grievance. No house, however rich, could afford wax candles for the kitchen; few, indeed, of the middle classes could afford a sufficiency of common dips. From the palace to the tavern we were cursed with the continual dropping of tallow. The servants smeared the loaf with it and poisoned the butter with it; they snuffed candles with their fingers, and then handled the white French bread for breakfast; the cook held a tallow candle with one hand while she fried a cutlet with the other; the tallow mingled with the hot bread-crumbs; you found a melted drop in the soup; it lurked in the sauce; it poisoned the gravy; it lay upon the browning; it corrupted the pudding; you smelt it in the air, especially when you passed a bevy of servant-girls on a Sunday; the smell of the candle-snuffing destroyed the illusion at the theatre, and shocked the flow of devotion in the church. The saloon, lit with wax candles and crowded with high-bred ladies and gentlemen who knew the value of manners, more nearly resembled heaven than anything you have to show; but to reach these sweet and pleasant places you had to pass through a purgatory of stinking tallow. Gentlemen, I wish you good-night."

CHAPTER II.

HOW I DID HIM A SIGNAL SERVICE.

BY the simple process of asking the waiter, who consulted the visitors' book, I discovered before going to bed that this remarkable lover of the past was named Mr. Montagu Jekyll, and that his room in the hotel was next to my own, both being at the end of a long passage on the first-floor. The name taught me nothing. I knew of no books written, so far as I could remember, by any one of that name; I had never heard of any great historian or scholar of the name. Possibly he was one of those little known but learned antiquaries who grub along among their books in the country, acquire immense knowledge, keep it to themselves, chuckling over the ignorance of mankind, and never write anything except, perhaps, a paper for a meeting of the Archæological Institute, should that rambling body pass their way.

We continued to talk of him after he went away at eleven o'clock. The reality and vividness which he had thrown into his talk concerning the past; the confidence with which he spoke of such little details as the snuff-box, whose lid was always to be open when offered; the attitude with which he illustrated his teaching; the way in which he spoke of us and our *gaucheries* as "you" and "yours," just as if he did not belong to the century at all—all these things pointed to an absorbing study of our period. Then we began to recollect similar instances from our own experience and from the pages of history.

"I knew a man," said one, "who never read anything which was not connected with the history of his own cathedral."

"I knew a man," said a second, "who never read anything that did not bear on the subject of infant baptism."

"I knew a man," said a third, "who was always engaged in finding out mysterious things about the Great Pyramid."

"I knew a man," said a fourth, "who was for ever occupied with the site of Solomon's Temple. He couldn't talk about anything but the Temple."

"I knew a man——," said a fifth; and so on.

They went on telling anecdotes about men they had known. I listened until two superior undergraduates began to relate marvels about the men of their college. Then I left them and went to bed.

I found the antiquary putting his boots outside the door. He looked up and nodded.

"Very interesting conversation to-night," I said, "thanks to you."

"About the last century? Yes, you know nothing, any of you—nothing at all, conceited though you are—of that most remarkable period."

"In what books," I asked, "can a man find those curious details which you presented to us to-night in the smoking-room?"

"Books! books!"—he spoke with great contempt—"I

never read. Men—and women—women especially—are the only books worth studying."

"Then how in the name of goodness—— "

"Good-night, sir. It is past twelve o'clock."

I went to my own room and sat down on the bed, pondering over this very singular person. Perhaps he was mad; perhaps he was only affected. Men have been known to study repartees and *bons mots*, which they afterwards bring out under the pretence of their being impromptu. No doubt this humbug had carefully got up the whole scene beforehand. Not read books! Of course he must read books. How else could he know things? To be sure it was possible, and perhaps not unlikely, that he invented. Anybody, with the necessary impudence *and a little practice beforehand*, could have invented the whole thing. Likely enough he was posturing before his looking-glass at that very moment in an eighteenth-century attitude. Or was he the Devil?

I went to bed with just that little touch of nervousness which always comes over a man when he seems to touch upon the domain of the supernatural; and I confess that I should have been better pleased had my room been at the other end of the house. There was a door of communication between my room and his; there was a bolt on my side, which I drew. The key was on his side, to be sure; but it was useless while my bolt held. With such reflections to soothe me, I fell asleep.

I was awakened an hour or so later by a suffocating smell of smoke. I sprang to my feet, rushed to the door, and looked into the passage; there the gas was burning tranquilly, and I could see no sign of fire. I ran to the end of the passage; all was quiet and safe. I returned to my own room; there was no mistake possible, the room was filled with smoke. But where was the fire? My candle had long been out. The fire, I said to myself, must be below me; the ceiling very likely was already on fire. At any moment the flames might break through the floor. At least, I thought, rapidly weighing the chances, the joists might hold out long enough to enable me to escape either through the door or the window.

One thinks quickly in moments of great danger. I bethought me, next, of my neighbour, the man in the next room. I ran to the door of communication, unbolted it, and tried to open it. It was locked on the other side. With one firm and judicious kick, I burst the lock open and rushed in. Good Heavens! the man was lying in a heavy sleep on the right side of the bed, while on the left, close to him, the curtains, sheets, mattress and all, were in flames. I threw myself upon him, dragged him, still half asleep, from the bed, and began to pile the blankets upon the flaming mass. There were a couple of cans full of water, for the bath in his room and my own. I poured the whole over the bed, pulled down the curtains, and succeeded, at the expense of a few slight burns, in rapidly subduing a fire which might have burned the house down. When I saw that there was no more danger, I opened the windows in both rooms, and lit a candle in my own. Then, and not till then, I remembered my friend the antiquary. He was sitting on a sofa in his room in the dark, shivering and shaking. He had taken no part in extinguishing the fire; he had said nothing; and now, when it was all over, he sat still in helplessness, terrified out of his wits.

"Come," I said, taking him by the arm, "you must not sit there any longer; you will catch cold. The fire's out, however; that's the great thing. Get up and come into my room, out of this horrible mess."

He followed without a word. His teeth were chattering, his face was horribly pale, his limbs shook with terror.

I had a spirit-flask containing brandy. I made him drink a couple of glasses, one after the other; then he looked up, gasped, and said incoherently—

"I lost it in the eighteenth century."

"What did you lose?" I asked, to humour his wandering wits.

"I lost my Religion. In a moment like this one feels to want it; but it is quite gone. I have not looked after it for close upon two hundred years."

"You had better get between my blankets and go to sleep,"

I said, wondering if the man was really mad, or only frightened out of his wits. "This business has upset you. Come."

I laid him in my bed and covered him up like a child. Then I stole to look at the extinguished fire—*what* a mess the place was in!—shut the windows, wrapped myself in my rug, and went to sleep on my sofa.

In the morning I awoke and found my guest still sleeping. I rang for the waiter and explained things; the manager was called; he came and saw the mischief and heard my story. He used bad words about the cause of the accident, still asleep, and good words about my promptitude in action. Truly, the house had had a most narrow escape.

After breakfast I found my antiquary still sleeping. In fact, it was not until past eleven that he awoke; then he sat up with lack-lustre eyes and looked round. If it was a remarkable face which I had observed the night before, the face of the morning was still more remarkable: it seemed the face of a very, very old man, older than any man one has ever read of, full of wrinkles, crows' feet, and lines; shrunken were the cheeks and feeble were the eyes. As I looked on, the sleep passed from him, a change came upon him; the lines rapidly disappeared, the cheeks filled out, the eyes brightened. The face became again that of a man of fifty or so.

"I know now," he said, nodding his head. "I remember now what happened last night. I was reading in bed. I went to sleep. (I shall never, never, never read again in bed, unless by daylight, as long as I escape accident.) The bed caught fire. You got in, somehow, and dragged me out. You saved my life. I do not know your name, sir, but I thank you."

"That is nothing," I replied. "Of course I did what——"

"You call it nothing"—he had by this time got one leg out of bed—"you call it nothing? Sir, the life you have saved is no common ephemeral existence. It is a most remarkable life, sir, although you know it not."

I bowed.

"It is a life to which history affords no parallel, one of which the world is ignorant."

" Really ! "

One naturally felt a little angry at this extraordinary boastfulness. Both legs were out of bed.

" Sir "—he stood upright with the blanket round him— " the life you have saved is a *unique* life."

He strode with the grandest air into his own room and closed the door of communication. Presently, while I was packing my portmanteau, he opened it again.

" In case I do not see you again to-day," he said, " would you kindly give me your card ? Thank you. I will do myself the pleasure, if you will allow me, of calling upon you in town. You have saved, sir, a life which is unique in history."

CHAPTER III.

HOW HE REWARDED ME.

AFTER my return to town, I thought little more about the strange old antiquary. Perhaps the adventure, with its hero, mad with too much learning, served for an after-dinner story more than once. But I hardly expected to see him, and nothing ever surprised me more that to receive his card, brought to my room by a clerk one afternoon in the following winter. He followed his card. He called, he said, to thank me again for the presence of mind and courage I had displayed, and begged me to believe that he was not insensible nor ungrateful. Having satisfied me upon this point, he invited me to dine with him that evening at a well-known private hotel in Jermyn Street. I accepted, and he went away. When he was gone I began to recall the many curious things connected with the fire; how old and worn he looked when he woke up in the morning, the strange words he used about his own life.

" A maniac," I said. " Probably a harmless one, mad on one point. One had better humour him."

He gave me an excellent dinner, with no attempt at emulating the ancients in the matter of larded swans and plum-porridge. On the contrary, the *menu* was as modern as could be desired, and the dinner as well cooked and as well put on the table as could be wished.

"Come," I said, "the eighteenth century could not beat a dinner like this, and there couldn't have been better wines."

"The century was greater at suppers," he replied, "than at dinners. As for wines, the claret and champagne and German wines were as good as they are now. The port, I admit, was generally too fiery. Many a quarrel has been caused, many a valuable life has been thrown away, by the ardent nature of the eighteenth-century port."

"We do not fight duels now," I urged. "You must give us credit for so much."

But he refused to give us any credit on that account. He said that a quiet and unpretending gentleman need never fight a duel; that the knowledge of its dangers made all men practise and acquire the noble art of fencing, which brought with it a dignified carriage; that polite manners were greatly assisted by the fear of being called out if you offended a man; and that public opinion was set dead against unnecessary duels and professional bullies.

I humoured him, and he enlarged at length on the eighteenth century. He seemed to know the beginning as well as the end, and was as familiar with Queen Anne's reign as with George III.'s. Yet it was a strange sort of familiarity. He showed no interest in political events, regarded Ministries with contempt, and such things as wars, alliances, sieges, and victories, or the growth of national liberty—about which modern historians keep such a coil—he had either forgotten or was ready to forget. Nor did he care at all to talk about poetry and literature, evidently holding authors and poets in the greatest contempt. Indeed, he professed not to know who Oliver Goldsmith was, and called Dr. Johnson himself a dictionary grub. He loved, however, to talk about dinners, society, the coffee-houses, amusements, theatres, actresses, young lords, gambling hells, and so forth; and he told me some excellent stories about Cupid's Gardens, the Folly, Ranelagh, the Marylebone Bowling Green, and Vauxhall. One thing presently struck me : he seemed to have collected and to remember quite clearly every story he could hear connected with accidents.

"It was not nearly such a time for accidents," he said, after telling me some of them, "as the present. To be sure there were a good many fires, and the service for extinguishing them was next to useless; but there were no railways. There was a great thing to begin with. There were no hansom cabs, no mail-carts, no galloping butchers' carts, no enormous vans thundering down the street. Things everywhere went slow. There was no hurry. Only think of the safety to life and the immunity from accident involved in that single statement. Things went slow. Then there was no steam-engine of any kind; not a locomotive yet built, not a paddle-wheel boat yet devised, no machinery, no boilers, no driving-wheels, no explosions, no bursting of pipes, no scaldings by escape pipes, no collisions. Think of there being no fear of accident on the line or on the river. To be sure, one could not wholly escape the danger of accident. If you rode, your horse sometimes ran away with you and killed you; but you might easily get a quiet pad. In the streets there were sometimes mad bulls; a friend of mine—that is, a man of whom I have read—was once killed by an escaping bear; there was once a highly respectable merchant of the City, also a friend of mine—that is to say—well—such a man was once killed by the fall of a shop sign upon his head; another, I remember to have read, was knocked over by a crowd chasing a pickpocket, and trampled on so that he died; or a man might be bitten by a mad dog, or he might be run through by mistake, being supposed in the twilight to be quite a different person. Then there were such things as occur everywhere, such as the fall of things from roofs upon your head, or slipping and breaking your ribs, or being upset in a coach, or—in fact, one can never escape the chance of an accident. But in quiet and slow times one has comfort in taking precautions, and I say that the precautions one had to take a hundred years ago were as nothing, merely nothing, compared to those one must take now."

He spoke with heat, and as if labouring under the sense of

some personal injury. I said that everybody must run his chance, and that if we did nothing but look out for accidents, we should have no time to look after our business. The observation was weak.

"Ay," he groaned, "you are right. That is what I find : looking out for accidents absorbs the whole of a man's time."

At eleven o'clock I left him. He very kindly hoped that we might meet again, and spoke of calling upon me when next he should be in London.

In the morning I received a small parcel with Mr. Montagu Jekyll's compliments. It contained a splendid gold watch and chain. This was very handsome. I wrote to thank the donor, but received my letter back. Mr. Jekyll had left the hotel, given no address, and ordered that letters were not to be kept for him.

It was in the year 1870, ten years later, that I saw my friend again. He called at my office as before, and asked me to dinner as before. I congratulated him on his excellent health. In fact, he looked younger than he had some ten years before, yet he must then have been considerably over sixty. He said he had been at some German baths, and had found great relief as to gout.

"We old fellows," he said, "like to look as young as we can."

In the course of the evening he informed me that he had married since he saw me last, but had lost his wife. I condoled with him, but found him singularly cold on the matter, or perhaps he affected a coldness which he did not feel.

"It is the way of life," he said. "We desire a wife ; we take a wife ; if she is a good wife she dies, to disappoint him ; if she is a bad wife she lives, to torment him. My dear friend, if I could only tell you my experiences ! Are you married ? "

"No ; but I am engaged."

"Ah ! "

The expression he threw into that interjection was wonderful, but he did not pursue the subject.

The day after the dinner he came to my office and desired to confer with me on professional matters. He proposed, he said, to buy a certain house standing in its own grounds about ten miles north of London.

I managed the business for him and drew up the conveyance of the property. After he had bought it, however, something disgusted him—I think it was the fall of a slate from the roof, which he said might have come upon his own head and killed him—and he begged me to sell it again. I managed that, and my friend disappeared without telling me he intended to leave London.

I saw him no more for ten years. It was in May of this present year of grace eighteen hundred and eighty, while the young spring days were still like January for rigour, that he came to see me once more. For the third time I went to dine with him, and he looked positively younger than ever, yet he must have been seventy-five at least. He was very friendly; produced a pretty set of presents, which he begged me to give to the wife and children, made a little speech about that fire business, and offered me as good a dinner as the heart of man could desire. I asked him where he had been during the last ten years. He said that he grew restless from time to time; that England, France, and other civilised countries became during these fits insufferable to him, and that, under the influence of one of these fits, which were a kind of melancholy, or, as he boldly put it, due to the extraordinary isolation of his position, he had thought that a few years in some quiet place, reasonably free from the chances of accident, quite removed from western civilisation, would act as a beneficial change, and probably restore his mind to its usual groove of contentment. The place which he fixed upon, after very great inquiry and search among gazetteers and consular blue-books, was a small island in the Greek Archipelago.

"The wine there," he said, "is rough, but remarkably good; it keeps a long while, like Commandery, and when you get it old it has a luscious fragrance, quite peculiar; the climate is delightful; the fare simple, it is true, but wholesome for a few years. No carts, no horses, no railways, because there are no roads ; none of the ordinary causes of accident. There were dangers in getting there, to be sure, and I meditated long whether I should go on grumbling over the dulness and stupidity of this century, of which thirty years more had then to be got through before we began a new period "—did the man expect to live another thirty years ?—" but I turned everything over in my own mind, and at last resolved to pluck up courage and brave the dangers of the journey. You will probably laugh when you hear me speaking of danger which common men, ordinary men of the groove, so to speak, recklessly meet every day and think nothing of them. But you do not know, my friend, you do not know what risk I, alone among men, have to face. You, and the rest of you, may lose the short remainder of your contemptible lives . . . bah ! ten years, twenty, thirty, forty at the outside . . . while I . . . but you do not know. Horrors! I did face the danger. I went across the continent in an express train, and a tumult of terror ; had three days of gale and peril in a steamer, with four and twenty hours of risk in a half-decked boat ; and finally landed with all my stores and with my French valet on the island. Ah !" He breathed a long sigh. " Here I lived for nine years and a half. I married a wife "— good Heavens ! he had actually married again—" found that the place suited me remarkably well, and, in fact, was for a short time perfectly happy. They murdered my valet ; but as I found that the Greeks of that island only stick knives into each other when they are jealous, I did not consider myself in any peril. My wife was, at first, a most remarkably beautiful girl, with such eyes as one dreams of when one is young. She fell off, however, terribly, and— and, in fact, the reason why I came away was that I made the dreadful discovery that Greek women are sometimes jealous without a cause. There was not a creature of her sex upon the island on whom I dared to cast an eye, on account of their brothers' knives. Yet she was jealous. And her temper was violent, and I love a philosophical calm. So

I ordered a steam-yacht; gave instructions to the skipper to pretend it was his own; went on board to see the craft when she arrived, and ho—ho! ho! steamed away."

"And your wife?"

"She will, I dare say, think that I was drowned. No doubt by this time she has dried her eyes. Do not let us trouble ourselves about her."

It seemed afterwards, when I came to think of it, a tolerably cold-blooded thing to do.

We drank a good deal of wine during dinner and after. My friend's red cheeks became redder and he began to talk faster. When we were in the middle of the second bottle of claret, he laughed oddly, and said—

"And who do you think I am?"

"I have not the slightest idea. You are an enigma to me."

"And to every one else who knows me: that is the reason why I am unhappily compelled to change all my friends every twenty or thirty years."

"Of course I do not understand a word you say."

"I have a great mind to tell you. Yet I fear. Are you sure that you can keep a secret?"

"It is part of my profession to hear and to keep secrets."

"True, true; and it would be comfortable to have a man like yourself to advise with on matters. You see, my position is a lonely one: I have never confided my history to a single person, not even to any of my wives."

"*Any* of your wives?"

"I have had seventeen," he replied calmly. "Now, to you I think I might, perhaps, communicate part of my history. People are no longer burned for possessing knowledge, even if you should break confidence. And besides, I may sometimes want an adviser."

"Pray go on."

I was by this time extremely curious and interested.

"I was born," he said solemnly, "in the parish of Malvern, being the eldest son of a gentleman of good family, on the fourteenth day of August, in the year one thousand six hundred and fifteen."

"What!" I pushed the chair back, ready to fly from a madman. "In what year?"

"In the year one thousand six hundred and fifteen. Sit down again, my dear sir; I am no more mad than yourself. Shall I repeat the words? In the year one thousand six hundred and fifteen."

CHAPTER IV.

HOW HE CONFIDED IN ME.

"I WAS born," he continued, "in the year one thousand six hundred and fifteen. Ah! a long time it seems to look back upon, but nothing when it is gone. The Jekylls are an old family, although ours was a younger branch. They sent me to Cambridge, and thence to Lincoln's Inn, where I studied such law as is useful for a country gentleman and a justice of the peace. There came a time, however, when I exchanged the pursuit of the law for one more fascinating and useful. After profiting by the result of those studies for two hundred and fifty years, it would be ungracious to join in the ignorant outcry which your men of science (poor blind mortals, most of them) carry on against the search which we of the seventeenth century made after the philosopher's stone and the elixir of life. I allow that you know more about electricity, with which, if you used it rightly, you could——" here he stopped short and paused for a moment. "What we sought was effect; that is the only thing in this world worth looking for; what you seek is cause. You consider that when you have formulated laws, you have found a cause; you think that when you have classified facts and deduced a rule, you have laid your hand on the final cause; you escape from God by substituting an equation; you think it better to live under the reign of law than the reign of love. Cause! Can any one among you all tell me why the sun puts out the fire, why the poker placed in front of it gets it up again; or why the moon causes the rain to fall? Yet these are little things. How, then, can you explain birth, growth, and decay? We did not try to explain. We sought to prevent decay, to find out, not the secret of life, but the preserver of life, the universal specific to cure all things, even the slow decay of man's strength. Glorious and noble pursuit.

"You never heard, I suppose, of John Rowley, reputed necromancer and astrologer? Yet history preserves the smaller names of Cromwell, Milton, and Hampden, who lived about the same time. Rowley was no astrologer, though he did not doubt the influence of the stars, a thing no reasonable man who has weighed the evidence can for a moment doubt. He was a searcher after the secrets of Nature; he worked upon the properties of matter; he looked to find the primitive metal from which all the common metals have descended; he wanted to make gold for himself, because the possession of gold gives power to conduct experiments; and he worked at the discovery of this universal medicine.

"I made the acquaintance of this remarkable man, it matters not how. I was admitted to his laboratory. I acquired his confidence; I worked with him. In those days I was young, hopeful, and enthusiastic; I worked with an ardour the contemplation of which at this moment appals me: sometimes our labours were continued without remission for two or three days and nights continuously, one of us taking turn now and then to snatch an hour's slumber while the other watched at the fire. All other work was thrown aside, all other friends were neglected, and from my twenty-second to my twenty-eighth year it was hardly known whether I was living or dead. Yet during this long period I was but on the threshold, working for the master as his apprentice, by whom all kinds of work must be done, while his master teaches him by slow degrees the mysteries of the craft.

"After serving John Rowley as long as Jacob served Laban for Rachel (which is an allegory for the patient working after the Elixir), and received Leah (which means that he got that lower, yet most excellent gift which came to me), the master called me apart and spoke to me very gravely.

"It had given him, he was good enough to say, the greatest pleasure to watch the zeal and patience with which I had worked for seven years, and it cut him to the heart to discourage any student in our glorious science, the only science worthy of the name. Yet I must understand and be under no illusions, that the highest prize of philosophy is given to none but those who possess, to a degree beyond that of my own gifts, an insight almost prophetic, and the power of reaching out, as it were, into the darkness and depths of ignorance which enables the truly great man to walk blindfold among pitfalls and traps. Therefore he would not encourage me to persevere in researches which would lead me to disappointment. Let me leave them to others more favoured by Heaven than myself.

"I was greatly dashed at hearing this advice, for I was already so far advanced as to know something of the infinite possibilities of chemistry. Yet the master spoke with so much wisdom, and with such evident sorrow, that I could not choose but be persuaded that he spoke true words.

"'Those,' he continued, 'to whom it is given to discover the Great Secret of Life, hidden away by Nature till the time shall come, must keep that secret jealously and hand it down to few. No greater misfortune to humanity could possibly happen than a general immortality with all their sins and vices still upon them. Think of an immortal Nero! Think of an immortal Grand Inquisitor! It is the prospect of dissolution alone which prevents men from committing the most frightful crimes. Thanks to death, there is a limit to suffering as well as to sin. The tyrant must die as well as his victim ; the torturer must lie down beside the tortured.'

"I asked him, were there many who knew the secret?

"He replied that, so far as he knew, there were but two or three to whom it had been given to discover it, and that they had communicated it to none. He was himself, he said, one of those who had arrived at it after a long life of research. 'I hold it in my power,' he said solemnly, 'to live as long as I please; to die when I please; to ward off all diseases; to suffer no pain; to return to youth if youth should seem desirable to me. If I please I can go on enjoying the pleasures of life, or I can spend a deathless period, as long as the world endures, in research and contemplation. I can follow the slow growth of true religion, and mark the onward march of mankind, a man among men. Or, by a simple effort of the will, I can stay the beating of the pulse, and pass away painlessly to an unknown and unknowable Eternity.'

"I asked him, then, if his studies gave him any glimpse or vision of the other world.

"He replied that Nature can only yield up her own secrets. As to the mysteries of the hereafter, they were hidden from the search of man, and could only be seen and apprehended by the eye of faith. And here he changed the discourse, and informed me with further expressions of goodwill that he was resolved upon giving me such a proof of his affection as the world had never before heard of.

"It was, in fact, this. He offered me nothing short of the absolute power of living as long as I pleased. There were certain conditions which, he said, were necessarily imposed upon the gift; otherwise I should grow to regard myself as an Immortal. The mention of conditions, I confess, troubled me; but as he proceeded to unfold the plan, I found the conditions light indeed compared with the magnificence of the gift.

"Briefly, because it would be tedious to relate all the discourses we held and the instructions I received, I learned that by following a simple course in which he instructed me I could arrest my age for ten years—that is to say, supposing I began at thirty, I could for ten years remain thirty, and then after ten more years I could again remain thirty for another decade; but that should I pass beyond the ten years without renewing the term, I should at one leap become forty; and if I did not choose to continue, the ordinary lot of human life would be mine, and in course of time decay of strength and gradual decline would follow. During each period of ten years I was to be subject to no other disease than any which might be upon me or in my constitution at or before the beginning of that period; so that if I were subject to rheumatism, gout, cold, or fever, I should remain subject, but yet not be killed by any attack. The rules, further, did not hold me free from accident. A drunken man's club, a quarrelsome man's knife, a chance gun-shot, the kick of a horse, anything might bring upon me the death which otherwise I had no occasion to fear. When, in cold blood, I came to think of this danger, it became certain to me that some day or other I should fall a victim to accident. For though a man may possibly pass through the wretchedly short tenure of life allotted to the common herd without accident; and although one may, as I have done, pass through two centuries and a half in perfect safety, yet the time may come—nay, sometimes, I think it must come—when the inevitable accident will happen, and I shall perish."

He paused again, overcome by this apprehension. It was not till much later that I realised how differently the chance of an accident would appear to him. For to us, though a hansom cab may run over us or a train may have a collision, yet there is always the feeling (in anticipation) that we are all of us in the same boat; whereas to my friend, Mr. Jekyll, the feeling was always that he was alone. He would live for ever; he had lived already for a quarter of a thousand years; and there was only this one danger to fear; no disease, no decay could kill him—only the danger of accident. Presently, he went on again, with a long sigh.

"The conditions once understood, and the instructions learned, we had next to decide upon the age of commencement. This, on reflection, proved a much more difficult matter than would at first be supposed. The master was for my waiting until I was seventy, and then beginning life. 'For,' he said, 'at seventy one is free from the passions of youth and the ambitions of middle life; one is full of wisdom, reflection, experience, and learning. There may be, it is true, a few of the inconveniences of old age, but think of the advantages of beginning with the stock of a lifetime of work!'

Now a singular change had come over me from the very first moment that the master communicated his design to me. My thoughts flew away from the dingy and smoky laboratory to the joys of the world. 'Let me,' I cried, 'be twenty-two?' 'Fie upon thee!' said the master; 'wouldst remain ever a boy? Well, I see that the last and greatest gift could never have been thine. Choose rather some ripe age, when the passion of youth is over, and the strength of the brain is at its best; an age which commands reverence, but not as yet pity.' I had, however, no taste for grey locks, and pleaded at last to begin at once, being then about twenty-eight. To this, however, he would not accede. Finally he consented to my beginning at thirty-five, provided that I should wait in patience and take my chance with the rest of mankind until then. Thirty-five, he reminded me, is an age when one should be strongest in body and fittest in brain for undertaking any kind of work, and most ready for any kind of enjoyment. I have always thought it a happy thing that I consented to wait for seven years in order to begin the long period during which I remained steadily at thirty-five. Fool, insensate fool that I was, ever to pass that limit!

" Further, the master promised me that just as my health and vigour should continue unabated, so my fortune should be unimpaired. Both were to remain unaffected by time or waste. Therefore he urged upon me to live with economy and thrift, as well as with great moderation as regards eating, drinking, exercise, and so forth, for the seven years between me and full fruition. Then he took a solemn farewell of me. We should never more, he said, meet in this world; he was about to retire to the wastes of Arabia, where, removed from the clash of arms and the struggles of men, he could work on until he felt tired and satisfied, and content to fall asleep. As for me, he wished me a happy use of the gift which he had placed in my hands, and hoped that I should find this limited tenure of life so satisfactory that I should be induced to prolong it indefinitely. He exhorted me to use it well, and for the benefit of mankind; to work on, accumulating know-edge, extirpating diseases, discovering new modes of increasing happiness, preventing famines, and spreading wisdom. 'Then,' he said, 'you will be a benefactor to the human race such as the world has never yet seen. We who learn and meditate can assist you who will learn and work. My friend, you may become the greatest of mankind.' He added cautions about certain temptations which might draw me aside, but I will not repeat these. 'Farewell!' he said. 'I have hopes, but I have misgivings. Take the gift and use it as you will. When you are tired of your work or dissatisfied, let the years go on unheeded; take your chance with the rest; lie down and die with the common herd.' He left me, and I sat down, wondering, overwhelmed at this great and wonderful fortune. Now consider my situation. I was twenty-eight years of age; I owned an estate of five hundred pounds a year in Warwickshire (what was then five hundred has since risen, by increase in the value of money — for I have long since sold my land—to five thousand a year). I had seven years to wait, during which my life was exposed hourly to the same dangers which threatened Tom, Dick, or Harry. I might in quiet times have gone to live on my estate, content to wait there in comparative safety. But the times were not good for quiet men. Everybody in the year 1643 was taking a side : a man had to. be Cavalier or Roundhead, and to fight for his cause. Was it likely that I, with so great a gift, was to imperil my precious life, my unique life, for the sake of a party ? Why, from that very moment I ceased to take the least interest in either side or in any politics. Men who had only a few trumpery years to throw away might go and fight for King or Parliament. Was a man who had hundreds, nay thousands—perhaps—to hazard them for any cause whatever? I made up my mind, therefore, to withdraw. I put my affairs into such order as was possible, and I retired to Leyden, under the pretence of studying at the newly-founded University.

"Few places in Europe were better suited to my purpose than Leyden. It was retired; it was not a great city; it was peaceful, it was healthy; the students were not brawlers or strikers; one might reasonably expect there, if anywhere, to escape accident and disease. I entered my name as a student, and I began the seven years—a longer seven years than any captive ever passed—with an anxiety which made me, who had previously been as brave a man as my neighbours, nothing short of a coward. I passed for one who was entirely absorbed in study. Alas! I read but little, being continually pondering over the chances of accident. I had narrow escapes, too, which made me more anxious. Once there was a rumour of the plague; once a neighbour's house took fire in the night and was burned down; once, when I was walking with a companion, a drunken fellow ran past us with a knife and stabbed him to the heart, so that he fell dead. It might just as well have been myself. They accused me of cowardice because I did not run after the flying madman. Why, what would have been the sense in pursuing a man who would have finished the race with a stab in the vitals? Was such a life as mine to be fooled away in an attempt to revenge the death of another? And another time I was run over by a trooper on horseback. It seemed as if sudden and horrible accidents were around and about me on every side.

"The years passed slowly on; there came a time when twelve—six—three months only remained to complete the time. The three months became one; the four weeks became one week; and then, because I would be alone when the time arrived, I left Leyden and sought a lodging in a farmhouse some four or five miles from the town. The farmer, who lived there with his family of two or three sons and a daughter, gave me his best room, thinking that the grave and serious scholar from the University would benefit by the country air.

"Then came the eve of the day, my birthday, my thirty-fifth birthday. I spent the day in the fields, meditating. The words of the master returned to me. I was to be a benefactor to the human race. I was to use his gift in the acquisition of knowledge. I resolved that I would do so. I would master all knowledge; I would confer such benefits on mankind as they had not dreamed——"

"And have you done so?" I asked eagerly.

"Not yet," he replied; "all in good time. Why, man, it is only two hundred and fifty years since I began to live. Give a man a little rope——"

He grumbled and growled for a few moments about the hardships of expecting a man to begin work at once before he had had his fling. Presently he resumed his narrative.

"In the evening I went early to my room. Now I suppose I could have considered the day as beginning at midnight. I would not; it should begin at sunrise. All night long I sat up waiting. The casement was closed; I would not begin the new life with a cold in the head. Then I considered myself carefully. I was well-made, strong, and had no complaint, weakness, or defect of any kind. Every function of mind and body in perfect working order. What a future lay before me!

"As I waited and watched, full of fears, calculations, and doubts, it seemed, just at the darkest hour, about two in the morning, when the whole world is sleeping, as if the room became suddenly filled with ghosts. I saw nothing; but I knew they were there, and that they had come to reason with me. First it was the voice of my mother who spoke to me. 'Son,' she said, 'I looked to see thee soon among us in the Islands of the Happy Dead. Now must I wait—and how long? Yet forget not that, soon or late, Death will come even to you, and the past shall be but as a dream of the night, even if thy days be as long as the days of Noah. Forget not this; and remember that men do not live until the after-life.'

"Then spoke the voice of my father. ''Twere better, son, to fight the good fight and then to die like thy forefathers. Thou hast turned aside from thy country and thy kin in their sorest need. Turn not aside from the Faith. We watch and wait for thee.'

"Then spoke the voice of one whom I had loved in my youth and forgotten. 'Sweetheart,' she said, 'bethink thee. There is no life without love; there is no love between our generation and those which follow after.'

"Then it was the voice of my little sister. 'Brother,' she said, 'come to us before you have forgotten us all; do not quite desert me. Come soon and play with me again.'

"Strange. It is two hundred and fifty years ago. I have indeed forgotten them. During all these years I have never thought of them again until now. Can it be that they wait for me still? My sister must long since have grown up— grown old—do they grow old there?"

His face changed as he said these words; his eyes softened, but only for a moment. Then he went on again—

"These appeals annoyed me. Just at the last moment, when I was entering upon my glorious career, to be thus addressed by my own people, who should have been proud of their son's distinction! I thought of the future, and hardened my heart against the past. Then the voices ceased, though I heard a weeping and sobbing as of women over the death of one they love. Yet this moved me not; for I was mad to begin the new life free from fear of death, disease, want, and age. The weeping of the spirits ceased, and they left me. Then another vision began, and it seemed as if the world with all its pleasures lay at my feet, waiting for me to enter upon my inheritance and enjoy.

"A long night, but it came to an end. I saw the streak of light in the east; I saw the grey grow into red, the darkness into dawn. Then up sprang the glorious sun, bright, warm, clear; the sky was blue; the birds burst out a-singing. Nature rejoiced with me as I rose and followed the instructions I had so long known by heart.

"Why, I was filled with a new life; I was like one intoxicated with the joy of breathing; I was strong with a strength you cannot dream of. Heavens! what a splendid man I was; what a splendid man I remained for two hundred and sixty years! You shall hear, presently, by what mad folly I threw away that glorious manhood."

CHAPTER V.

HOW HE USED HIS MOST EXCELLENT GIFT.

"I REMAINED in my room," he went on, after a pause, "while the sun rose higher in the heavens. With every moment my pulse beat stronger, the blood coursed more freely through the veins, my heart sounded the note of stronger, eager, and impetuous manhood. I was more than a king—I was a demigod, because Death, the slayer of all, and Time, the slow subduer of all, had no power over me. I, alone of created things, was free from the law of decay. In the fields below me I saw the farm drudges creeping about their day's work; I heard the song of my landlord's daughter as she began her work in the dairy; I watched the birds in the trees, the cattle in the meadows, the horses being led from the stable, all alike, at first, with that pity which naturally seized the mind in thinking of the pitiful condition from which I had myself only that moment emerged."

"And you still feel that pity?" I asked.

"Not at all," he replied promptly. "I feel no more pity for those who are beneath me—in fact, for all humanity—than you feel for the menial condition of the waiter who has just brought in the soda-and-brandy, or for the abject state of any wretched beggar in the street, or for the sufferings of any unknown patient in an hospital. It is Fate. We have nothing to do with Fate. When I think of my long life behind me and the long life before me I am glad, that is all."

I was silent, and he proceeded—

"I went downstairs, presently in a dream, and my landlord's daughter, a blue-eyed girl of eighteen, gave me a cup of milk, for which I thanked her with a kiss. She laughed and said she did not expect that of the grave scholar from Leyden schools; and then she blushed and started, and wanted to know what I had done with myself; for my feet seemed to dance as they went, and my eyes were bright with life and love; my lips were ready to sing, or to kiss, or to drink; my cheek was ruddy and healthy, and dotted with a couple of dimples; and my arms were swinging so loosely that it seemed the most proper and seemly thing in the world for them to seize the girl by the waist and kiss her again. Poor Lisa! Well, she has forgotten her troubles this many a day.

"After a few weeks I began to think it was time to devise some plan for the future, and without saying farewell to the poor fond creature — indeed, I found consolation in the thought that a short forty or fifty years would bring her to the end of any sorrow my departure might occasion. I therefore returned to Leyden, where I sat down, resolved to draw out a fixed plan for work.

"First, I recalled the words of the master, how I was to use my gift so that it might become a boon to the whole of mankind. How was this best to be effected? Not, I thought, by conferring the same gift upon the whole of humanity. Why, if there were no end to life, there would be no need of religion, to begin with. Why, if there were only two such men in the world at the same time as myself, very serious difficulties might arise.

"I would not make men immortal; but I would free them from disease.

"I conceived the most beautiful dream—some day I mean to work it out thoroughly, if it takes me a thousand years to do it; but not just yet, not yet. To remember that dream causes me the greatest satisfaction, because it shows how fit and worthy a man I am for the confidence bestowed in me. I thought that if a man situated as happily as myself were to devote himself, taking one disease at a time, not only to its alleviation and cure, but also—a very much more important thing—to its complete and entire suppression, he would become in very truth the greatest benefactor to the human race that has ever appeared upon the world. It would take time to collect statistics, facts, figures and accounts; but what was time to me? Nothing. If each disease were to take me a century of uninterrupted labour, consider what that would mean to mankind if it ended in its entire abolition.

"You see, there are the big things first: fevers, plagues,

small-pox, consumption, rheumatism, gout; then the smaller things, for which surgeons use the knife; then the many little ailments of life which cause so many grievous moments, such as toothache, earache, headache, and all the pains. I would begin with the great things, and after destroying them from off the face of the earth I would attack the smaller, and finally the smallest diseases. Acknowledge that this was a great—a noble dream. I pictured myself at work in my laboratory for generation after generation, discovering why this or that disease existed, and what should be done to meet it and prevent it. What, to me, were centuries of patient labour? I pictured to myself at last a strong and grateful humanity plagued no longer with diseases, or, if the symptoms showed themselves in punishment for excesses, able to meet them at once, and, with little suffering, to subdue them. My friend, I declare to you that this dream, while it lasted, filled me with an ineffable rapture; my old religion, which seemed to have deserted me, came back and filled my soul; I was able to thank God solemnly for His great and wonderful gift, and to implore His blessing on my most beneficent enterprise."

He was silent, and shook his head sorrowfully.

" Why did the dream leave you ? " I asked.

" There is always between the conception and the realisation of a dream," he replied, " the interposition of something from the outside. This time it was the arrival at Leyden of Lisa's brothers. I fled with such precipitation that the dream was for the time shattered to atoms.

"I repaired to Paris, whither I was quite certain those young Hollanders would not follow me. Here, as an English gentleman of fortune, I was hospitably received, although I was fain to assume the disguise of a Roman Catholic, as an excuse for not having fought for the king.

" Paris, in the year 1650, was a much less desirable place of residence than London, except that there were fewer theological controversies. The streets were narrow, accidents were fearfully common, the people were rough and rude, gentlemen were given to duelling on small provocation, and there were always the dangers of the Bastille. Suppose, I thought sometimes, that I was to incur the misfortune of being imprisoned for life on suspicion of some libel. How long would it be before my goalers would have their suspicions aroused by the youthfulness of their prisoner? And what would the Church say if the problem were set before it? And with what face could I tell the story and bear the tender mercies of the secular arm, which was heavy indeed upon magicians? Had it not been for disquietude on these accounts, I should have been happy in Paris. It was a city which possessed (should my dream of labour come back to me) the best library of medical books in the world, and when I was inclined to enjoy the pleasures of life, give me such boon companions as Chapelle, Bachaumont, and Bois-Robert; such evenings as none but well-bred ladies of Paris could offer; and such talk as was to be heard nowhere but among the scholars of Paris.

"After a year or two of Paris, when it seemed as if things were becoming more settled in my own country, I returned to Warwickshire. In the calm retreat of my estate, I thought, I could carry out undisturbed those projects which I had only laid aside for a while, and proposed to undertake in earnest."

"And what prevented you?"

"The usual thing—a woman. I fell in love. She was a girl of twenty-four, handsome, well-born, with a considerable fortune, and was reported to have a good temper. I have nothing to say against her at all; she was a most excellent housekeeper. At making of strong waters, brewing, baking, pickling, preserving, and the knowledge of herbs, there was never any one her equal. We married, and for the first twenty years of my married state I was perfectly happy. But in each experiment made in a life like mine there are new dangers and difficulties which were unforeseen. The danger which I had overlooked was that my wife would grow old while I should not. In fact, when she was forty-five and I was, in the eyes of the world, fifty-five or so, I was freely congratulated on my wonderful preservation. This, which was only matter for laughter then, became, ten years later, when

I should have been sixty-five, a thing of unwelcome notoriety. To be sure it is not every day that one sees a man of sixty-five with the crisp beard and brown curls, the clear eyes and the elastic tread of thirty-five. To avoid this kind of talk I once kept my bed for a week, pretending illness, and came out of it with a stoop in the shoulders and a shaking at the knees. I also adopted an old-fashioned peruque, and painted every morning crows'-feet and lines about the eyes.

"It is very well to make up (being five and thirty) into five and sixty. But what about five and seventy, five and eighty, five and ninety? My friend, the most unforeseen thing happened. The life of my wife was prolonged so far beyond the usual span that she actually reached the age of ninety-eight. Now consider what that meant to me. First, there was the discomfort, which lasted for sixty years and more, of being married to a wife older than yourself. How should you at thirty-five like to be married to a woman of ninety-five, eh? Then there was the inconvenience of having to look as if age was telling upon me more and more. It would be positively indecent for a man at a hundred to shake a leg as merrily as a man at thirty : he may not laugh, nor sing, nor ride, nor dance, nor talk cheerfully, nor even drink. Now when she had got to ninety-eight, I, though still only thirty-five, was actually supposed to be a hundred and nine. You may walk bowed and bent; when any one is looking, you may shake in every limb; you may pull an old-fashioned wig over your ears, or sit muffled up in a night-cap; yet your *eye will look young*. You cannot pretend at five and thirty to get along on the same amount of food as does for an old man of a hundred; you cannot disguise the fact that you have all your teeth; you cannot wholly dissemble your vigour. Therefore it became the fashion in my neighbourhood to see, and bring strangers to see, this wonderful old fellow, who, at a hundred and eight, was so vigorous. 'Look at him,' they would say, as if 1 were a prize ox; 'there is health for you at a hundred and eight. Look at his eye, full and clear and strong. A hundred years, gentlemen, and eight! This is marvellous!

He ate two mutton-chops yesterday to his dinner, and a dish of hot sausages to his supper, and drank a quart of October. Saw one ever the like? His teeth, too, look at them! And your memory, good sir?'

"'Alack,' would I reply, in feeble pipe, 'there my age finds me out; for my memory, gentlemen, save for things of my childhood, when Charles I. was king, is but a poor thing.'

"Clergymen preached about me, books were written upon me; and I sat still in my chair opposite the poor old lady, who was now bent double, wondering what would happen, and how to get out of the difficulty. A cruel thing to desire the death of a wife, yet what else could I wish for? And in the end I killed her."

"You murdered your wife?"

"Not exactly; yet I killed her. Thus it was. On one Saturday afternoon in June, the year being 1724, I felt an uncontrollable desire to leave the arm-chair, in which after dinner at noon I was left for my afternoon nap, and to move about somewhere. The maids were in some distant part of the house. I took my sticks and hobbled slowly along, intending to creep into the garden, where, if no one were about, I might straighten my back and stand upright for a bit. On the way I passed the cellar door, and thought I should like for once a full tankard of ale. I descended and throwing away the sticks, I sat on a stool and poured down the strong October tankard after tankard, till it mounted to my head. Still, I did not so far forget myself but that I returned to my own room on the crutches, stooping and staggering, so that the maids whispered that the old gentleman was failing fast. When I found myself alone, as I thought, I contained myself no longer; but, locking the door, I threw my wig up to the ceiling, my crutches on the floor, and I began to dance, the jolly old ale in my heels.

"Ouf! It was a relief. For many days I had been so carefully watched, that there had been no chance of any exercise. The quiet house, in which the only noise was the slow ticking of the cuckoo-clock; the aged lady who sat opposite to me all day long, bowed and bent, meditating on the past and future—for to the old there is no present—the old servants, the old dogs, the old furniture, amid which our married life of seventy-five years had been spent—all these things fell upon my spirits like lead. So that, warmed by the strong ale, believing myself free from observation, I shook off all disguise, and danced with the agility of a man in his twenties.

"A loud shriek interrupted me. I had made a mistake in the room, the beer being in my head: instead of my own bedroom, I was in our common sitting-room. My poor old wife stood before me, pointing with her shrivelled finger, gasping for terror and amazement. Then her head turned, and she fell headlong to the ground. The shock and affright were too much for her, and she never spoke again."

"After that," I said, "there would be nothing to prevent your beginning the Grand Research?"

"Stop a moment. Think. Another difficulty began here. How was I to get rid of myself? An old man of a hundred and eight could not suddenly leave his house and go away by himself. How was I to make the old man disappear? This difficulty occupied my thoughts continually. Sometimes I thought of escaping at night; but I wanted to keep my estate, which, when I disappeared, would fall to my heirs. Now, here an accident happened which proved of the greatest use to me. My eldest son (cut off at seventy) had left a grandson, his own son having also died, who was at the time living quietly, being a young man of twenty-two, and of studious habits, in a lodging at Westminster. Here he contracted a fever of some kind, which quickly carried him off. No one of the family, except myself, knew his place of residence; none of his cousins or great uncles (my sons) had ever seen him; for an obscure country lad to die in an obscure London lodging makes but little stir. Therefore I made use of his death to my own advantage. I instructed my lawyers that my heir, Mr. Montagu Jekyll the younger, would shortly call upon them. He did call: he had a long talk with them about the estate and the failing health of the old squire; but when he came to pay his respects at the Hall I was nowhere to be found.

"It was strange; I had disappeared. They dragged the rivers; they searched the woods; they found my crutches; they found my clothes, my wig, and my hat. But my body was never recovered. I need not tell you that the young man, the heir, was no other than myself.

"That difficulty surmounted, I resolved that it should not occur again. The estates were not entailed, and I sold them, reckoning on the promise that I should always have the equivalent to what I started upon in an annual income."

"And the rest of your children and grandchildren?"

"I do not know. It is absurd to suppose that I could keep the genealogical tables of so large a family as mine. Why, at the estimate of four children apiece, I have reckoned that my present descendants amount to over a million and a quarter; and, of course, many of them must have had more than four children. It is long, however, since I cared about following the fortunes of my grandchildren. I start the sons and portion the daughters; then they go out into the world, and I know nothing more about them. Long before the grandchildren begin to get troublesome, I am away and forgotten."

"Do you, then, change your name?"

"Sometimes, for a generation or two. Then I take it again, and display a curious acquaintance with the family history of the Jekylls of Worcestershire. At present I am bearing my own name."

"Then, having got rid of your estate, I suppose the Research was fairly begun? There were no longer any obstacles."

He laughed gently.

"No obstacles? Why, I was beginning the world all over again. I, who had for forty years pretended to be an old man, I was a young fellow again of five and thirty. My heart was young as well as my body; I quickly forgot the poor old lady with whom I had for so long been unequally yoked; and I burned to make a new departure."

"But your studies, your resolutions — did you think nothing of them?"

"Yes, at times I thought of them; but they would always

wait; meantime, I wanted to enlarge my experience of the world.

"I went to London this time; the glorious eighteenth century was well begun: when shall we see its like again? I found myself among wits of whose talk you can have no conception, among ladies whose beauty was only equalled by their incomparable grace, and in a school of manners the like of which the world has never seen. It was only in the eighteenth century that men and women succeeded in defeating age. By means of wigs, powder, paint, stays, and other artificial adornments, they kept up the pretence of always being young. When they failed, as sometimes happened through an unmannerly palsy or a disconcerting blindness, or anything of that sort, the rest of us pretended that nothing was wrong. But, short of their afflictions, men and women —I mean gentlemen and ladies, of course—went on with their suppers, their cards, and their dice, until they fell down and died. To me, of course, who dreaded nothing but an accidental knock with a chairpole, or the upset of a coach, or the falling of something on my head, there was no merit in this kind of acting; but I confess that I was then, and am still, lost in admiration of the admirable way in which these poor creatures of a few short years behaved as if centuries at least were before them."

He sat still and stroked his chin reflectively.

" How well I remember it, that century of gaming, drinking, suppers, and what preachers call unreality! Unreality, indeed! when men and women took all there was to be had in life, and said: 'Thus will we live while we are in health. Sufficient for the present the wax-tapers, the supper-table, the wit and conversation of well-bred men.' Ah!"

He heaved a profound sigh.

" We might have been going on still in the same way, making a little Paris in every capital, the rich enjoying life, and the poor—I suppose the poor were no worse off then than they are now. But the French Revolution came and spoiled everything. I never before thoroughly realised the selfishness of mankind. The most beautiful society that the world had ever seen, smashed and destroyed; a whole continent in flames; and all because a few demagogues persuaded the people that they were unhappy. For the first time I was disgusted with my epoch, and for the first time for a hundred and fifty years I was contented to think that I had not spent my time in toiling for them.

"Long, however, before the crash of the Revolution, which altered and upset so much, I left London and retired to the country, where I met with that great misfortune which——"

"Which retarded the prosecution of the Great Research?"

"No, sir, worse than that—which added ten years to my life. It began, naturally, with a woman. I formed for her the most serious passion of my life. Can you wonder if I postponed, for the sake of her society, the prosecution of my stupendous design, which could always wait, and might be commenced when she grew old?

"She was eighteen when I married her. She was the daughter of the old vicar of the parish. She was innocent and true; her temper was of the sweetest; her face was the loveliest; she loved me"—here he paused and sighed again. "Never, never shall I meet again any one like her. We lived together in perfect bliss for eight years; at the end of that time a fever carried her off.

"I was entirely cast down at this sad misfortune: her religion had softened me; her faith at the end subdued me; I made a resolution that, come what might, I would give up my immortality for her sake, and take my lot among my fellow-creatures. I kept that resolution with firmness. I saw the hour approach when I must either go back ten years again, or take the irrevocable step of going on ten years. Life was so dreary without my Susan that I did not care to face it again; and on the last night of the tenth year, when I should have become five and thirty for the fifteenth time, I went to bed heroically resolved to pass straight on to forty-five, and after that to endure the rapid advance of time, and sink to the grave with my seventieth year. I would live, I said, always in the country; I would know no joys but those of meditation and retrospect; I would recover, if I could, the consolation of religion; my future years should be spent in making me worthy to join my Susan in heaven, where she awaited me.

"Nothing could have been more laudable than my resolution; but there was one thing which I had forgotten. There was a clause in our agreement that should I slip a decade, and therefore carry on my age for ten years, I should be, like other men, liable to punishment in the flesh for the sins of my past life. Now before I fell in love with Susan I had been drinking in the company of the hardest livers of the time—with perfect disregard of the future, as I had a right to do—port, punch, and strong waters of all kinds. I had gone to bed in the most beautiful, resigned, and religious mood possible. I felt, for the first time since many a long year, repentance for the past follies, and a sincere desire to amend during the brief future. I would, I was resolved, die when my time came, and join my Susan in heaven. And at that moment I even remembered my mother and sister departed so long before, and forgotten since that night in the Dutch farmhouse.

This peaceful and holy frame of mind was to be rudely disturbed in a way quite unexpected and most disagreeable. I fell asleep. At midnight I awoke suddenly to find that not only was I forty-five years of age, in itself a fearful misfortune, but also that I was afflicted with the most violent attack of gout in the great toe that ever unfortunate man experienced. What can withstand gout? Not love, not religion, not regrets. All these vanished, and I cursed the hour when I was fool enough voluntarily, actually without being obliged, to surrender the best part of my manhood.

"I got through the gout; but, my dear friend, forty-five is not thirty-five. The elasticity of life is gone at forty-five; the muscles are no longer young; the stomach is beginning to be used. They say that a man of forty-five is in his full vigour. I deny it; he is not. He has already begun to feel the prickings of time; he has passed the first fresh rush of feeling and enjoyment. The world has no more to give him; and to think that I might have continued my vigour and enjoyment but for mere boyish, weak, mawkish, sentimental regret over a girl I loved!"

He paused again, this time deeply moved.

"That was," he resumed, "about the year 1795, more than eighty years ago. I confess that my life since then has been a wandering and uncertain life. You, as a moralist, might condemn it——" He hesitated, and looked at me with uncertain eyes.

"I am your confidant first," I said, "and a moralist afterwards. Let me hear such particulars as you wish to tell me."

"I told you before," he went on, "that I have had seventeen wives. I have only as yet accounted for two. That leaves fifteen for eighty-four years, an average of less than six years apiece."

"You don't mean to say, man," I cried, "that you have murdered fifteen wives?"

"Nay, I am not Bluebeard. I did not murder them; I only deserted them."

"You—deserted—them?"

"Yes." He was quite calm, and looked as if he was confessing an action neither virtuous nor the opposite, but just of the commonplace kind. "Yes; you see, after my last experiences of marriage, I was difficult to please. If my poor Susan, blameless herself, was the cause of my gout, my forty-five years, the loss of my youth, the appearance of crows'-feet, fatness, puffed cheeks, thin hair, and a red nose, she had also instilled into my mind an ideal of womanly perfection which, while it was delightful to possess and to reflect upon, stood greatly in the way of conjugal happiness. I passed in review one maiden after another; I considered, but without profit, the widows: I failed anywhere to find my ideal. I did not, perhaps, consider that most unfortunate rule of human life, that, as a man grows older and knows women better, he becomes more difficult to please, because his imagination is duller; while it is more difficult for him to please, because he is no longer a young man and comely. To be sure, I was less comely just then than I am now, having upon me the effects of a hundred years' suppers.

Still, with a courtly manner, good means, and such experience of the world as was mine, one might have hoped for something better than what I found. Eight of my wives lasted for an average of two years each. Then they became insupportable, and, after making due provision for their welfare, I left them."

"Children and all?"

"Children and all. I never did care greatly for children, and latterly I have cared less than ever. They are the most selfish creatures in existence. To be sure, women are not much better."

He was silent again, and reflected for a few minutes.

"I did not expect much; but a little honour, a little respect to my extraordinary attainments, I did look for. Yet—would you believe it?—they treated my science as if it was so many old women's tales, and my stories of the past as if I had made them up, and the halo of romance, which I could not help wreathing round my own brow, they laughed at. Women have no poetry, no imagination! And then they annoyed me by always wanting to know about my parents and connections; searching among my papers when they thought I was out of the way; putting leading questions about the origin of my fortune; giving me, all round, no peace.

"It was this intolerable curiosity which caused me to desert my vows, not, I assure you, any roaming disposition, nor any selfish desire to seek for greater beauty. Selfishness is a vice of which I have never, I am happy to say, been guilty, though my wives have frequently brought it against me as a charge. The difficulty in each case was to get rid of them quietly and without fuss. The best way seemed to make them widows. You can't call a man selfish who makes away with himself in order to benefit his wife—come. Once, when we lived by the seaside, I pretended a violent passion for boating, kept a sailing boat, and one evening set the sail, stove a great hole in her side, and launched her. I then walked away. The boat was found, capsized, and of course they concluded I was drowned. On another occasion, later

on, when we were in London there was a great accident on
the river—a steamer run down, with two or three hundred
people drowned. I did not go home that evening or ever
after, and had the satisfaction, a few days later, of seeing my
own name among the list of the supposed victims. One cannot, however, always find an accident ready to one's hand,
and different means had to be devised. In these I think I
showed considerable ingenuity. On one or two occasions,
however, I was compelled to adopt a common and even a
brutal plan, as when, after a more than stormy scene with
a very bad-tempered and long-tongued wife (although a
beautiful creature), I left home, and sent her a letter to say
that I was going away and should return no more. This
was in 1808, I remember. She was living in Edinburgh,
but I suppose she lives nowhere now. Ah! she promised
well at the beginning. But they all fall off—they all fall
off after the first month or two. Selfishness, morbid curiosity,
and inability to appreciate my exceptional qualities! . . . .
But these details tire you. Of course I had to leave the
place and move to quite another part of the world after every
such little change.

"They have been, one with another," he went on, "a good-
looking lot of women; fair, dark, brunette, blonde; eyes of
every shade, blue, grey, brown, black, violet, hazel; tall and
petites; majestic, like Juno, or *gracieuses*, like Venus. I
have had little to complain of about their beauty. Their
tempers have, of course, varied from 'set stormy' to
'change.' They could all be coaxed into good temper, and
most of them would believe anything, unless they were
jealous. One of them, whom I could only stand for three
months, was extraordinary in her jealousy—gave me no peace
at all."

"And about your friends?"

"My—my friends!" He lifted his voice a little, and
smiled. "You are comparatively young; you think there
are such things as friends in the world. Perhaps some day
you will know better. Friends! I never had any. Nobody
ever has any. A few men become close acquaintances, and

are fools enough to tell them all their private concerns; but I was never that kind of man. No; we were acquaintances in the dear delightful eighteenth century who conversed with each other, gambled, drank, and banqueted, at arm's length; ready at a moment to draw the sword upon each other, distrustful and distrusted, anxious to get the best for ourselves, and careless about anybody else. Friendship means the association of men for the purpose of making the best out of life; marriage means a compact in which either party expects the other to work for him or her; children love their parents for the good things they get——"

"And parents love their children—for what?" I asked.

"You forget," he answered coldly, "I told you I did not like children."

He went on talking; but I fell into a sort of reverie, and only half heard what he said. He was describing his different wives, I believe. I was thinking what a strange effect this man's wonderful gift had produced upon his moral nature; of his cold and callous crust of selfishness, which made him insensible to any of the ordinary feelings of human nature; how the sight of so many generations dying around him had robbed him of sympathy, power of love, friendship, humanity—all the qualities which draw men together, and make them seem less lonely. He could no longer love woman, man, or child; he could no longer shed tears for bereavement, or feel the sorrow of the hastening years. He could no longer feel for the sufferings of others; he pretended to perish suddenly, thinking only how to get rid of a woman of whom he was tired; he walked away, deserting a creature who loved him, with children who looked for his love, in cruel, heartless, unheeding callousness. It seemed to me as if, were that the inevitable result of such a gift, it would be better to take one's chance with the rest, and live out the threescore years and ten.

When I listened again he was still talking.

"On leaving her, my fifteenth wife, a truly dreadful thing happened. I had been so continually occupied for a whole year in devising this notable scheme of separation, that I actually forgot that the fatal ten years was once more drawing to a close. The time arrived in the middle of the night, when I was still walking away from the house, on the hard and frosty road, rejoicing to be once more free, and resolving that it should be indeed a long time before I would again run the risks of matrimony. Suddenly I heard the clock strike twelve; in a moment I remembered, with horror and agony, what had happened. A sudden loss of vital force, a curious feeling of comparative weakness. I had forgotten to renew my forty-fifth year, and I was fifty-five.

"That, my friend, I am still; that I intend to remain. It is not a bad age. My gout is with me still, but it is not so troublesome as it has been. I have contracted no fresh diseases. I lead a regular life, drink little, go to bed early, and enjoy things in moderation."

"And now," I said, "that you have given up marriage, you will be able to commence the Research."

"Oh, the Research—the Research!" he spoke impatiently. "Yes; no doubt some day I shall begin it. Meantime, is my experience complete — *have* I done with matrimony? Truly, I cannot say. Stay; I will show you some of my manuscripts."

He opened a desk, and took out a volume bound in leather, fastened with brass, and put it into my hands.

"Sir," he said, "one of my old volumes. This contains all the chemistry of the sixteenth century."

I opened it. The volume was closely written in a small and crabbed handwriting, on paper gone yellow with age, and in ink still black and clear.

"All the chemistry of the sixteenth century. I have only to read that book again, to read the discoveries of modern science, and I am furnished with the materials for the Grand Research. Yes, I am resolved to begin it. Sometimes, though, I confess, my desire to benefit my fellow-creatures is much less than my desire to live comfortably and beyond the reach of accident. And, to live quite comfortably, I want the right kind of wife. Find her for me, my friend, and I will show my gratitude to you in any way you prefer."

We had more talk, but it was of no further importance; and presently, as I saw that my host was growing silent, and besides, as it was already half-past eleven, I took my leave. He promised to call upon me the next morning about some business, the nature of which he did not state, and, shaking my hand, he said—

"My friend, I am in earnest about a wife. Find me a sensible, kind, good-tempered girl, who will put herself out a little to please a man—no longer young."

"But you would grow tired of her after a little and leave her."

"Not till she grew tired of me," he replied. "Believe me, my wives were as glad to get rid of me as I was to be free. 'Selfish, thoughtless, except about my own pleasures'—such were the epithets they used to hurl at me! What a benefactor I have been, to make so many widows—and all so young!"

"What a benefactor," I said, "you might have been, had you stuck to your Grand Research!"

"Perhaps," he replied airily. "Patience: your great-grandchildren will reap the benefit of my work. I shall begin—say in thirty, forty, fifty years. Who knows? I am now two hundred and sixty-four years of age. During nearly the whole of that time I have lived for my own pleasure. What a life I have had! And how I wish the eighteenth century would return with my five-and-thirty years! Oh, to sit at the play in wig and satin coat, with your hat under your arm and your little telescope in your eye, ogling the women behind the wax-candles! Oh, for the little suppers after the play, with songs and the wine and the punch! Oh, for the faro-table and the sweet rapture of winning a *coup!* Oh, for St. James's Park in the afternoon and Ranelagh in the evening, and the dominoes and the hoods and the chase of the fair *incognita!* But the century is gone, and with it half the grace and pleasure of life. Good-night, my friend!"

I was very busy next day, and forgot all about his appointment, which was for half-past twelve. At about two o'clock in the afternoon, however, a policeman came to see me, with a letter addressed to me. I opened it. The lines which were written were illegible. The signature alone remained, "Montagu Jekyll," with the address.

"Sad accident, sir," said the policeman. "The gentleman slipped in the road and was run over and instantly killed. It was a hearse as did it."

A sad accident, indeed. I went to the hotel. My poor friend was laid out, quite dead, ready for his funeral. The odd thing was that his face had grown already quite old, incredibly old; a thousand lines were round the eyes and mouth, the skin looked like parchment, the fingers were lean and shrivelled.

"He made up wonderfully well," the head-waiter whispered. "Who would have thought he was such an old man? He looks like ninety."

"He looks, John," I said, "like two hundred and sixty-four—or," I added, because the number might seem strange, "like any other age you like. I was his lawyer once, in some business matters. I will, if you please, open his desk, and ascertain, if possible, the address of his present advisers."

We searched the desk. There was money in it, but no more than enough to pay his hotel and funeral expenses, and a number of papers, but all of them illegible. Nor have I learned anything since then about this wonderful client.

SWEET NELLY, MY HEART'S DELIGHT

SWEET NELLY, MY HEART'S DELIGHT

CHAPTER I.

IN SACKCLOTH AND SLAVERY.

IN a trackless country, through a forest stretching away for hundreds, and perhaps thousands, of miles — for no traveller has ever yet crossed the great continent of America and measured its breadth—there journeyed, slowly and with pain, a woman who sometimes carried and sometimes led a little girl four years old. The woman wore no hat nor hood, and her clothes were torn to shreds and tatters by the thorny briars through which she had made her way. Her eyes were wild, and her face, save when she looked at the little child, was set stern: her lips moved as she went along, showing that she was engaged in some internal struggle. The forest since she first plunged into it had changed its aspect. Everywhere now were pines, nothing but pines, growing in clumps, or in belts, or in great masses, in place of the oaks, maples, hemlocks, and birches through which she had passed. There were no longer any wild vines; the air was resinous to the smell; the ground was soft and yielding. In some places the fugitive drew back her foot in dismay, because the soil sank beneath her weight.

The sun was making rapid way down to the west; the shadows were long ; the child dragged its steps, and presently began to burst into a little crying; the woman soothed her. Presently the little cry became a great sobbing. " Nelly is hungry," she sobbed.

Then the woman sat down on a fallen trunk, and looking round her, wrung her hands in despair, for she was quite lost, she knew not where to go, and she had no food.

"I thought to find revenge," she cried, "and I have found death and murder. Heaven is just. I shall sit and watch the little one starve to death—the child will go first—and then I shall die. O wretched woman! why wast thou born? Child, child"—she burst into tears of despair, and clutched the little one to her heart—"curse me with your dying breath. Oh! my little innocent, my lamb, I have murdered thee; for I have no food, no water. Hush! hush! Try to sleep."

She soothed and rocked the little one, who presently, weary with the long day's march, dropped asleep, hungry as she was.

Then the sun sank lower: a little more, and he would have disappeared altogether, and the woman would have been left alone for the night with the starving child: but while the red colour was beginning to spread in the west, she saw emerging from a clump of pines before her an old man.

He was a white man, but his skin was now dark with exposure to the sun and air; he was clad in skins; he was very old; his hair and beard were long and white; he leaned upon a stick as he went; his steps were feeble; his eyes wandered up and down the glades of the forest, as if he were afraid of being watched. Presently he saw the woman and the child, and after a moment's hesitation he made his way, in a curious and zigzag fashion, across the green space which lay between himself and the woman, and accosted her.

"Who are you?" he asked.

"A runaway,'" she replied.

"Show me your hand."

She held out her left hand; he held out his; on both was the same mark—the brand of a convict.

"I am a thief," she said; "I was rightly punished."

"I am an Anabaptist," he replied. "I was punished by the law of the land. Who is the child?"

"I stole the child. It is my master's. I stole it for

revenge, because they were going to flog me. I have brought it all the way. My food is exhausted, and so she will die. And now," she added, with a despairing cry, "I am a murderess as well as a thief and the companion of thieves, and there can be no more hope for me in this world or the next."

The old man shook his head and looked at the child, still asleep.

"Come with me," he said; "the little one shall not die. I have a hut, and there is food. Both hut and food are poor and rough."

He led her with the greatest care across the treacherous quagmire by steps of which he alone knew the secret. "Here I am quite safe," he explained, "because no one except myself can cross the place. Safe, so long as I am in hiding. This place is an island of firm land in the midst of a bog."

There was a hut standing beneath pines which grew on ground a little elevated. It was furnished with a few skins and an earthenware pot of the rudest kind. There was, besides, another earthenware vessel containing water. In the pot was meal. The old man mixed the water with the meal.

"When the child wakes," he said, "give her some, and take some yourself at once. Now sleep in hope: to-morrow I return."

"Oh! do not leave us alone," said the woman.

"You are quite safe. I go to fetch more meal; there are some friendly blacks who will provide me. Sleep in peace."

Then he disappeared, and the woman, laying the child upon one of the skins and covering it with the other, sat beside her, wondering, and presently fell fast asleep. In the morning when she awoke the sun was already up, and her host was standing in the doorway. Then the child awoke too, and presently sat up and ate her breakfast with a hearty good will. The old man, leaning upon his stick, thereupon began a very serious and solemn discourse. He told the woman what a wicked thing she had done in carrying away a helpless child to the great Dismal Swamp, a place inhabited by none but runaways, and those scattered about, difficult to find, and poorly provided. "Here," he said, "the whites who have exchanged slavery for this most wretched freedom live separately, each by himself; they are jealous of one another, they suspect each his brother; and the blacks, who live together in communities, change their quarters continually, for fear of being caught by the planters, who come out with guns and dogs to hunt them down. I have had to lie hidden here without fire or food for days, while the hounds followed my track until the morass threatened to swallow them up. You, who might have courted such a life yourself—did you think what it meant for a child?"

The woman shook her head.

"I have been here twenty years and more. I have lost the count of time; I know only the seasons as they follow. I think that I am over seventy, and when I can no longer beg meal of my friends, I must lie down to starve. I have spoken to no white person except to you during all this time. When I came I had a Bible. That was lost one night of storm. Since then I have had nothing but my meditations and my hopes; and you—what would you have had? The continual memory of a murdered child."

"What shall I do? what shall I do?" she cried.

"Take back the child; whatever happen afterwards, take back the child."

The little girl looked up in the woman's face, and laughed and clapped her hands.

"I have sinned," said the woman. "Let me take her back. God forgive me! She shall go home to her mother."

She rose at once, as if there was not a moment to be lost. The old Anabaptist put up some meal in a bag of skin, and led her again over the treacherous path.

"You have lost your way," he said. "I will be your guide."

He led her by paths known to himself across forty miles and more of thick forest. When they came near any cleared land, they rested by day and travelled by night. After four days of travelling, they came to their destination.

The old man took the child in his arms and solemnly blessed her in all her doings. Then he prayed with the woman for a while, and then, grasping his stick, he disappeared in the forest.

The woman, left alone, began to tremble. Before her were the broad fields of tobacco belonging to the plantation. On the fields she saw the gangs of men and women at work, the overseers going about among them armed with their heavy whips. Some of the labourers were white, like herself; some were black. Far away, beyond the fields, she saw the house. It was afternoon. She retreated to the forest and sat down, thinking. Finally, she resolved to delay her return until the day's work was done and the gangs had left the fields.

It was past seven o'clock and already dark when she came to the house. She told the little one to be very quiet. There was no one in the portico, but there were lights in the state room.

The woman opened the door and set the little one down.

"Run to your mother, child," she whispered.

A pattering of little feet, and a wild cry as the mother snatched up her lost babe, and then the woman, leaning against the door, sighed heavily and sank to the ground. They found her there—those who came running at the cry of the mother—and brought her within the room.

"It is the woman Alice Purview," said the master.

"Leave her to me, husband," said his wife. "If she carried away the child, she hath brought her back again. Let me deal with her."

Madam dealt very gently with her. Her past offence, whatever that was, received pardon; her wounded and torn feet were bandaged and cared for; her broken spirit was soothed. When she recovered she was taken from her former office of nurse to the sick ward, and made nurse to the little girl; and, as the sequel will show, no girl ever had nurse more faithful, loving, and true.

The woman was my nurse; I was the little girl; that journey to the Dismal Swamp is the first thing I can recollect; and when I read of Elijah, I think of the poor runaway Anabaptist, whose face, I am sure, was like unto the face of the prophet.

It was my fortune to be born in his Majesty's Plantations of Virginia. I am persuaded that there is not anywhere upon this earth a country more abundantly supplied than this with all God hath provided for the satisfaction and delight of man. It is not for me, a simple woman, to undertake the praise of this happy colony, which has been already fitly set forth by those ingenious gentlemen whose business or pleasure it is to recommend the place for the enterprise of gentlemen adventurers, planters, and those whose hearts are valiant, though their fortunes be desperate. Yet, when I contemplate the hard and cruel lives led by so many poor people in the great city of London, I am moved to wonder that his Majesty the King, who with his council is ever considering the happiness of his subjects, doth not order the way to be made plain and easy for all who are in poverty to reach this happy land. Who, for instance, in the hope of a few pence earned with trouble and sometimes with kicks and blows, would cry up and down the street dry faggots, small coal, matches, Spanish blacking, pen and ink, thread, laces, and the like, when he might with little toil maintain himself in comfort on a farm which he could get for nothing? There is room for all on the banks of the Potomac, the Rappahannock, and the James Rivers. Yet the crowd of the city grows daily greater, and the forests of Virginia remain uncleared. Or when learned men demonstrate that, at the present rate of increase, our own population long before the end of this eighteenth century will be so vast that there will not be enough food for all, and thousands, nay, millions, will yearly perish of starvation, I am constrained to think of those broad tracts which are ready to receive thousands upon thousands of Englishmen. Sure I am, that if those at home knew the richness and fertility of the American colonies, every newly-born English child would be regarded as a fresh proof of Heaven's benevolence to this country, and another soldier in the cause of liberty and the Protestant faith.

I was born in the year one thousand seven hundred, on my father's great Virginian estate. It stretched for six miles and more along the banks of a little river, called Cypress Creek, which runs through the Isle of Wight County into the James River. My father, Robert Carellis, Esquire, was a Virginian gentleman of old stock, being a grandson of one John Carellis who came to the Province in the ship which brought the first company of Gentlemen Adventurers. There were, alas! too many gentlemen on board that vessel, there being fifty of that rank to a poor three of labouring men. They were too proud to dig, being all armigeri and esquires, although younger sons. Some of them in consequence proudly perished of starvation; some fell fighting the Indians; a few, however, of whom John Carellis, was one, survived the first disasters of the colony, and became lords of vast territories covered with forest, in a corner of which they began to plant tobacco. It has been said of the Virginian gentlemen that they would all be kaisers, and obey none. In sooth, they are all kaisers, inasmuch as they live each on his own estate—the lord and seigneur whose will none questions; the owner and absolute master of slaves whom they reckon by hundreds. When I read the narratives of those unfortunate men who have served in captivity to Turk or Moor, I think of our slaves in the plantations; and the life of the Turkish bashaw, in my mind, greatly resembles that of his honour, Robert Carellis, save that my father was ever a merciful man, and inclined to spare the lash.

Those who worked for us were, of course, all slaves. They were of many kinds, white, black, and copper-coloured. They were English, Irish, Scotch, French, Africans—men of every country. First, as regards the negroes. There are some, I know, who doubt the righteousness of this trade in men. Yet it cannot be denied that it must be a laudable thing to bring these poor creatures from a land, where they live in constant danger of life, to one where they are maintained in security; and from the most brutish ignorance of religion to a knowledge of the Christian faith. I am aware that the Reverend Matthew Marling, Master of Arts, our late learned rector, held that it is uncertain, the Church not having pronounced upon the matter, whether black negroes, children of Ham and under his curse, have souls to be saved or lost. Yet, I have seen so many proofs of intelligence, fidelity, and affection among them, that I would fain believe them to be in all respects, save for their colour, which for this life dooms them to a condition of slavery, like unto ourselves.

Side by side with the negroes worked in our fields the white slaves, sent over to the plantations from the London and Bristol gaols—the forgers, thieves, foot-pads, shoplifters, highway robbers, passers of counterfeit coin, vagabonds, and common rogues, who had, by their ill-doing at home, forfeited their lives to the law and lain in prison under sentence of death. They had been respited by the King's mercy, some of them even rescued at the very last moment, when the noose that was to kill them was already hanging from the fatal beam, and the bitterness of death was already tasted, and the dismal funeral service had been already commenced by the ordinary. The Royal clemency gave these fortunate wretches a reprieve, but they were pardoned only on condition of being sold for a term of years, to work on the plantations of Virginia, whither they were conveyed after being branded in the hand, and sold on their arrival by public auction to the highest bidder.

It might be thought that desperate creatures such as these, the offscourings of the country, would prove troublesome, mutinous, or murderous. But the contrary was the rule. No one, seing their obedience, their docility (to be sure, the overseer's terrible whip was always present before their eyes), would have imagined that these men and women had once been hardened criminals, common rogues and vagabonds. For the most part they worked cheerfully, though they lived hardly. Some of the more prudent of them, when their time was out, took up small plantations of their own, grew tobacco, and even advanced so far as to become themselves the owners of slaves, as well as of lands. Then would they fain forget the past, and, in company, when they thought themselves unknown, would even try to pass for Gentlemen Adventurers.

There was a third class of plantation slaves of whom my father would have none. I mean the men sold into captivity for religious opinions or for political offences. It was a most dreadful thing, my father said, that men whose only crime was a lack of reasoning power should be driven to work under the lash. Therefore he would never buy any Papists, Anabaptists, or Quakers, although on other plantations there were plenty of these gentry. And while other planters had servants who had been out with Monmouth, or were concerned in some of the little conspiracies of that unquiet time, my father would have nothing to do with them. Once, indeed, in the year one thousand seven hundred and sixteen, he bought and brought home with him half-a-dozen gallant gentlemen (though they were at the time greatly cast down and unhappy in their appearance) who had been engaged on the wrong side in the rising of the Pretender. These, I say, he brought home to his house, and then, calling for wine, he made them a speech. "Gentlemen," he said, "it grieves me to see you in this piteous case. Yet believe me it might have been worse, because, although I have bought you, and for so many years your services are mine, yet I cannot find it in my heart to subject persons of your consideration to the rigours contemplated by your judges. I cannot, however, break the law and give you your freedom. I propose, therefore, to establish you altogether on a piece of land which you will cultivate for yourselves, according to such rules as you choose to establish for your own guidance. There I will help you to what you want for necessaries. And now, gentlemen "—for all began to cry aloud for surprise and joy—"here is wine, and we will drink to the health of the King—and on this side of the Atlantic we must all, whatever our opinions, add—' over the water.'"

We lived in a large house built entirely of wood, like all the houses in the country, and embellished with a wooden portico after the Grecian style, erected in front; this served instead of the verandah which most Virginian houses possess. The great chimney, which served for all the rooms, was built of brick outside the house. The room of state where my mother sat was a low room, forty feet long, lit with five windows, opening upon the great portico; in the summer the glass windows were replaced by green jalousies; the ceiling was plastered white; the walls were painted of a dull lead colour; the fireplace and mantlepiece, which were very grand, were made of walnut-wood richly carved by a London workman, in flowers, fruits, and the arms of the Carellis family, gilt. In the winter there was a screen and a carpet before the fire, but in the summer these were taken away; the tables and chairs were all from London; there were portraits of our ancestors on the walls; there was a genealogical tree carrying back the family of Carellis to a patriarch who lived about the same time as Abraham (it was so stated on the tree), but who is passed over in the sacred narrative because, as I always supposed, his estate was far from that of Abraham, and they never met; and outside, in the portico, were chairs made of hickory wood with sloping backs, where, in the summer evenings, my father sat with his friends and smoked a cool pipe of his best Virginia.

One does not look for books on a Virginian estate, yet we had a goodly library, consisting of Captain John Smith's History of Virginia, Speed's English History, Livy done into English by Several Hands, the History of the Turks, the History of the Spaniards' Conquest of Mexico, and the True Relation of Bacon's Horrid Conspiracy. These books served for lesson books for myself, though I do not remember that any one else ever read them. As for our overseers and people, my father was ever of opinion, in the which I agree with him, that the arts of reading and writing should only be taught to those who are in a position of authority, so that they may with the greater dignity admonish unto godliness and contentment those placed under them. The Church Catechism warrants this doctrine, to my thinking.

Our house was, in fine, a country seat which any English

gentleman would be proud to call his own, furnished with guest-chambers, dining-rooms, and every sort of convenience and luxury. Behind it lay a great garden planted with fruit trees, vegetables for the table and herbs for the still-room. Before it was the square, a large cleared ground, on the three sides of which stood the houses of the overseers and the slaves. All these houses were alike, built of logs, the windows without glass, the brick, or mud-built chimney standing at one end; each with a little projecting verandah or lean-to, and some with a small garden, where the people grew what liked them best. There were stables, too, and coach-houses, with horses, mules, cows, turkeys, ducks, geese, fowls, and pigs. A running stream ran through the square, and after providing drinking-water above the clearing, became, below it, a gutter to carry off refuse. The pigs ran about everywhere, save in the gardens of the house; and here and there were enclosures where fatting hogs lay grunting and eating till their time arrived. It was like a great farmstead, only there were no corn ricks; the barns held meal (but it was not grown on the estate) and home-made pork and bacon: the pigs and cattle, like the slaves, belonged to his honour; all was for him.

Beyond the house and square lay the tobacco-fields, and beyond them forest, everywhere forest. Save on that side where you rode down to the banks of the great James River, running into Chesapeake Bay, you had forest on all sides, boundless and without end. Unless you knew the forest very well; unless you knew the Indian compass, the hemlock-tree which always inclines its head to the east; and unless you could read the blazings of the trees which pointed to the homestead, you could lose yourself in the forest in five minutes; and then wander round and round in a ring of twenty yards, thinking you were walking straight ahead for miles, till starvation seized you and you fell down and presently died.

The Virginian manner of life was simple, yet plentiful. It becomes not a woman to think overmuch about eating, yet I own that the English breakfast-tables seem to me but poorly provided compared with those of Virginia. Here, indeed, you have cold meat and small ale in plenty, with bread and cheese, and, for the ladies, a dish of tea; there you had daily set forth fried fowl, fried ham, bacon and eggs, cold meat, preserved peaches, quinces and grapes, hot wheaten biscuit, short-cake, corn-cake, griddle-cake soaked in butter, with claret or small ale for the gentlemen and milk or milk and water for the women and children. Our wine, our malt for brewing, the best sort of our beer, our spices, our sugar, our clothes, our furniture, all came from England.

Virginia has been divided into parishes — not like your little London parishes, which consist of half an acre of houses, but great broad districts half the size of an English county. To each parish is a clergyman of the Established Church. No dissenters are allowed, nor any meeting-houses, save one of Quakers. Our clergyman was paid ten thousand pounds of tobacco for all his stipend; and as he could sell it for threepence the pound, you will perceive that the clergy of Virginia are better paid than those of England. In addition to their stipend, they received two hundred pounds of tobacco for a christening, three hundred pounds for a wedding, and four hundred pounds for a funeral. Add to these advantages that the clergyman was not expected, as is too often the custom here, to rise from the table at the third course, or to drink less wine than his host and the other guests.

Thus, then, and in so great state, did we live, in the enjoyment of every luxury that can be procured in England, together with those which are peculiar to America—notably, the soft sweet air of Virginia. We were, on our estates, our own builders, carpenters, gardeners, graziers, bakers, butchers, brewers (only we used English malt), pastry-cooks, tailors, and bootmakers. We had every variety of fish, flesh, and game; we drank Madeira, Canary, claret, cider, peach brandy, and apple wine; we formed a society of gentlefolk, separated and set apart from the settlers who had been our bought servants, and who bore in their hands the brand which no years can ever efface. We had been Cavaliers in King

Charles's time, but we stood up for Church and State, and welcomed the Protestant hero, great William the Deliverer. We had scant sympathy with those who would trouble the peace for the sake of a Papist Pretender, who if all reports were true, was no son of King James at all, but had been brought into the Queen's chamber in a warming pan. Open house was kept for all comers—all, that is, of our own station, for no peer in England was prouder of his rank than we of Virginia were of ours—and should there be a decayed gentleman of good family among us, he might still live at ease and gallantly, by journeying from one plantation to another, only taking care never to outstay his welcome. And this, provided he were a man of cheerful disposition, or one who could sing, shoot, drink, and tell stories, would be difficult, or wellnigh impossible in a Virginian house.

So we lived, and so I grew up; bred in such courtly and polite manners as were familiar with my mother, the most dignified gentlewoman in Virginia; taught to read, write, cypher (but indifferently); to work samplers, to make puddings, pies, and preserves, to distil strong waters, to brew home-made wines, to say the Catechism and respect the Church, and naturally, to believe that there was nowhere on the surface of the earth, except, perhaps, the King of Great Britain, a man of nobler birth and grander position than his honour, Robert Carellis, my father.

But at the age of nineteen a great misfortune happened to me. The overseers brought from James Town, where they had purchased them, six men who, though we did not know it, were suffering from gaol-fever. They all died; two of the overseers died; many of the people died; lastly, my father and mother caught the infection and died too.

Then I was left alone in the world.

I had many cousins to whom I could go, but by my father's will—made while in full expectation of death and in true Christian resignation—I was to be sent across the Atlantic to our agent in London, there to remain as his ward until I was twenty-one, when I was to be at liberty to do what I pleased with my inheritance.

CHAPTER II.

ON TOWER HILL.

WE had a favourable voyage of five weeks and two days, with fair weather and no adverse winds until we arrived off the Nore, where we were compelled to lie to and anchor in the Roads, together with over a hundred other vessels, small and great, waiting for the wind to change, so that we might beat up the river to the port of London. If I was surprised at the sight of so many ships gathered together in one place, you may think how much more I was astonished as we slowly made our way up the crowded river, and finally dropped anchor in the Pool over against the Tower of London, in the midst of so many masts and such a crowd of ships as, in my ignorance, I had never dreamed of. There were East Indiamen; dusky colliers; brightly painted traders with France and Spain: prodigious great ships in the Levantine trade, armed with long carronades; round Dutch sloops; with every kind of pinnace, tender, smack, hoy, brig, schooner, yacht, barge, and ferryboat. On all these ships men were running about, loading, unloading, painting, repairing, fetching, carrying, and shouting. There, before my very eyes, rose the White Tower, of which Speed speaks so much; London Bridge was on the left; beyond it the Monument to the Great Fire; then the dome of St. Paul's, and innumerable spires, steeples, and towers of this rich and prosperous city. I remembered, standing on the deck of the ship and seeing all these things for the first time, how we colonists had been accustomed to speak in our boastful way of America's vast plains. Why, is the greatness of a country to be measured by her acres? Then should the Dismal Swamp be more illustrious than Athens, Virginia more considerable than Middlesex, and the Potomac a greater river than the Tiber or the Thames. What have these new countries to show with the old? Why, the very stones of the old Tower, the narrow arches of the bridge, the towering cathedral, even the roofs of the houses, cry aloud to the people to remember the past, how they fought for liberty and religion, and to be jealous for the future.

It was late in the afternoon, about five o'clock, when we finally came to anchor in the Pool, and I began to wonder what was coming next. My guardian's name was Alderman Benjamin Medlycott, and he lived on Tower Hill. He and his had been agents to the Carellis plantation since we first settled there. They were far-off cousins, John Carellis the Gentlemen Adventurer having been a first cousin of Carellis Medlycott, the alderman's great-grandfather; so that I was not going among strangers, but my own kin.

What was he like, this formal merchant whose letters I had read? They were full of the prices current; they advised the arrival of cargo, and the despatch of wine, spices, furniture, clothes, wigs, saddles, guns, swords, sashes, and all the things which were required in the settlement of a Virginian gentleman of rank. But nothing about himself or his family.

I had not long to wait in suspense. Presently, standing on the quarter-deck with Nurse Alice, I saw the captain shake hands with a young man soberly attired in a brown square-cut coat, with long calamanco waistcoat down to his knees. I had time to look at him, because he conversed with the captain for a few minutes before the latter led him aft and presented him to me. I set him down at once as a messenger from my guardian, and I made up my mind that his dress, which was by no means so splendid as that which my father habitually wore, was in the fashion of London merchants. There was no finery; the cuffs were wide and large; steel clocks adorned the shoes; the stockings were silk, but of a dark colour; his peruke was long and curled, but not extravagant; a black silk cravat, of the kind they called a steenkirk, was round his neck, and his laced linen cuffs were of a dazzling whiteness. This splendour of linen, I learned afterwards, was thought much of by London citizens. On his hands, which were white, he wore a single signet ring. He carried no sword, but a short stick was under his arm. His hat was trimmed with silver galloon. As for his face, I could only see then that his features were straight and handsome. Was he, I thought, a son of my guardian?

After the exchange of a few words with the captain, and receiving a packet of papers, he climbed the companion, and, taking off his hat, bowed low.

"Mistress Elinor Carellis," he said, "I have the honour to present myself as the alderman's chief factor, though unworthy of that position, and your most obedient servant. My name is Christopher March."

I made him a curtsey.

"I hope," I said, "that my guardian is in good health."

"He suffers from gout, otherwise he is well. I trust," continued the chief clerk, "that you have had a favourable passage, and as much comfort as is possible on board a ship."

These compliments exchanged, Christopher March—I call him so henceforth, because he never received any other style or title—informed me that he had waiting alongside a boat to carry me ashore, and that the ship's officers would see all my boxes brought up to the house as soon as convenient. Upon that I took leave of my friend the captain—an honest, brave sailor, and less addicted than most seafaring men to the vice of swearing—and so into the boat with Alice, my nurse.

The little voyage lasted but a few minutes, and we were presently landed at the stairs. Our conductor led us through a narrow lane, with tall warehouses on either side, and paved with round stones, which were muddy and slippery; then we turned to the right, and found ourselves in a broad and open space, which was, he told me, Tower Hill, the place where so many unfortunate gentlemen's heads had fallen. On the other side I saw the beefeaters in their scarlet embroidered uniform. But I was so bewildered with the noise and the novelty of everything, that I hardly saw anything or heard what was said to me. But we had not far to go. We passed a warehouse four storeys high, and from every storey a projecting beam with ropes, which made me think of the gallows. But the beams were only for the pulleys and ropes by which bales were lifted up and down.

"This," said Christopher March, "is Mr. Alderman Medlycott's warehouse, and this"—he stopped at the door of a private house next to the warehouse—"this is Mr. Alderman Medlycott's residence."

He spoke of the alderman in tones of such great respect, that I began to feel as if part of my education had been neglected—that part, I mean, which teaches respect to the aldermen of London. A thought also crossed my mind that this excessive respect for his master was useful in exalting his own position.

However, there was no time to think, because the door was presently opened, and we found ourselves in a large and spacious hall, containing chairs and a fireplace, with a stand of strange weapons. Horns, heads of buffaloes and deer, and curious things of all sorts, brought to Tower Hill by the alderman's captains, hung upon the walls. Then the maid opened a door to the right, and I found myself in the parlour of a great London city merchant.

The room was lofty, and had two windows looking upon Tower Hill; the walls were wainscoted and painted in a fashion strange to me and unknown in Virginia. A soft Turkey carpet was on the floor, a bright sea-coal fire was burning in the fireplace, though the air was not cold to one fresh from the sea-breezes; there was a high mantel-shelf, on which were displayed more curiosities from beyond the seas, and above them wonderful specimens of ladies' work in samplers, representing peacocks, birds of paradise, landscapes, and churches all in satin. Seated at one window were two ladies and a gentleman, who rose to receive me. Christopher March, I observed, left me at the door with a profound bow. We made deep reverences to each other, and then I blushed, because, although Alice had dressed me in all my best, I felt how countrified and rustic was my appearance compared with the fine new fashions of these London ladies.

The elder lady, who was about forty-five years of age, and had a most kind face, with soft eyes, held out her hand.

"My dear," she said, "I am Mistress Medlycott, the wife of your guardian, the alderman, who is now ill with the gout, but will see you shortly; and this is my daughter Jenny, who desires your better acquaintance."

Jenny here in her turn took me by the hand. She was a little thing, and so pretty and agreeable was her face, with bright laughing blue eyes, light brown hair, a dimple in her chin, and saucy lips, that I thought I had never seen the like.

"Good heavens!" I thought: "what must they think of me—ill-dressed, tall, and ungainly?"

"Mistress Elinor," said Jenny, "if I were tall enough I would kiss you. As I am not, I hope you will stoop down and kiss me. We shall be very good friends, I hope."

"I may present my Lord Eardesley," said madam, with dignity. "His lordship, being here upon business with the alderman, hath requested permission to see—" here she stopped and smiled very kindly—"to see the Princess Pocahontas of Virginia."

At that little joke we all laughed. His lordship was a young man, about the same height as Christopher March, but very much unlike the chief factor. For while Christopher had a way of dropping his eyes when he met your own, and of hanging his head, and in many other ways of showing that he was not perfectly at his ease with ladies, the young lord looked you frankly in the face and laughed, and was not only happy himself in being with two girls, but also made us all happy as well. Only this knowledge came later.

"I must call you Nelly," said Jenny, pressing my hand. "Elinor, or Mistress Elinor, is too long. How tall you are! And oh!" she broke off, with a sigh and a laugh—"Nelly, the hearts of all the men will be broken."

"Pray heaven," said my lord, "that the fragments of one, at least, be put together again."

"This is idle talk," said madam. "Mistress Elinor will despise us after the grave discourse to which, no doubt, she has been accustomed in Virginia."

"We had grave discourse," I explained, "when the Reverend Matthew Marling came to see us, twice a year.

At other times we talked about the crops, and my father's sport, and such topics."

Presently Lord Eardesley took his leave with more compliments. When he went away it seemed as if some of the sunshine of the room had gone with him. To be sure, a great deal of the colour had gone, for his coat was of scarlet silk, and he wore a crimson sash for his sword.

"Do not think, Nelly," said Jenny, in her quick way, "that lords associate every day with City merchants, or that we know more than one peer. Lord Eardesley has had money affairs with my father for many years, and the custom has grown up for him to call upon us whenever he calls at the counting-house. O Nelly! they did not tell us what to expect."

"My dear," I said, "you will make me vain. And, indeed, I am not so pretty as you."

"Oh, I? I am a City girl, little and saucy; but I know what a beautiful lady of family should be—she should be like you. You ought to be Lady——"

"Jenny," her mother interrupted, "for shame! As for Lord Eardesley, Elinor, he is an excellent young man; but he is, unfortunately, very poor, his father having gambled away all the money and most of the estates. Poor young Lord Eardesley will probably have to take service with the Austrian."

Jenny shook her head.

"He had better carry the Virginian colours," she said, with a laugh. "Come with me, Nelly. I will show you your room."

They had bestowed me in the best room on the first floor, which had a little room beside it for Alice. I was at first much awed by the magnificence of the bed, which was much finer and more richly hung than any in our Virginian home. But familiarity presently reconciles us to the most majestic things. Here I found my boxes and trunks, which had been brought ashore, and here was Alice taking everything out. Jenny looked on, naturally interested at the display of dress, and though she kindly said nothing, it was plain to me that she found my frocks of a fashion quite impossible to wear in London. Presently, however, we came to my jewel-case, wherein lay all the family treasures, which had been my mother's; and her delight was extraordinary when she had dressed herself up in all the necklaces, bracelets, rings, chains, and glittering gauds which had been worn by many successive matrons in the Carellis family. She then threw her little head back, waved her hands, and went through a hundred posturings and bowings.

"I am Mrs. Bracegirdle, at the theatre," she said. "This is how she looks and carries her fan, and makes eyes at the beaux in the pit."

However, we could not stop playing there, because madam sent word that the alderman was ready to see me.

It was now past six, and candles were lit. Madam herself led me to the back of the house, where was a covered way to the counting-house. Here the alderman himself was sitting with his clerk, Christopher March. One foot was wrapped in flannel, and laying on a cushion; a stick stood by the side of the arm-chair in which he sat, with a pillow to give him ease; bundles of papers were on the table before him.

"Come in, my dear," he said, in a cheery voice—"come in. Leave her here, wife, to talk to me. Send for her when you take your dish of tea. Now, Christopher, your day's work is done. Good-night to you, and be off."

The words were peremptory, but the tone was gentle. Christopher March bowed low to him, and lower still to madam, and departed. Meanwhile I looked to see what manner of man this guardian of mine might be. He was a man of sixty or so, and he had a monstrously red face, but his nose was redder still; his lips were thick and projecting; his wig was pushed a little off one side, which made him look, somehow, as if he were going to say something to make everybody laugh. His eyes were kind and soft, and his voice, though a little rough, was kind, too. In fact, as I afterwards found out, the alderman was well known for being the kindest man who ever sat on the bench of magistrates, or ruled a great house with many clerks and servants.

The first thing that he did, however, was not reassuring. He clutched the arm of his chair, leaned forward, and gazing upon me with intense eyes he shouted—

"Death and zounds!"

Naturally, I shrank back, frightened.

"Do not be alarmed, my dear," said his wife calmly. "It is his only relief when a pinch seizes his toe."

I thought he would have a fit, for his eyes stood out of his head, and his face became quite purple. But he recovered suddenly, and, with a sigh of relief, resumed the benevolent expression which the redness of his face and his puffed cheeks could not altogether conceal.

"Sit down, my dear," he said. "I am better now! Phew! That was a pinch. If you want to know what gout is like, take a hair-pin from your pretty head and put it in the fire till it is a white heat. Then put it to the middle joint of—your thumb will do for illustration—and hold it there tight; and if you find that any method besides swearing will relieve you, I shall be glad to know what that method is. Sit down, my dear, and let us talk."

I took a chair opposite to him, and madam left us alone. He arranged his papers, and began to talk to me about my affairs.

First, after some kind compliments on my beauty (which I may pass over), he told me of his grief on receiving intelligence of my father's death, by which unhappy event he had lost a much esteemed correspondent. He had always hoped, he said, to see my honoured father some day at his poor home, and offer him such hospitality as a London merchant, with the aid of his company—that of the Grocers —could command. He added, with much consideration, that it would have been his duty to recommend my father to the hospitality of the Lord Mayor, as a Virginian Gentleman Adventurer of the highest position; and he gave me to understand that in the important matter of turtle soup and fat capons, without speaking of venison, turkey, Christmas ducks, small fowl, haunches of mutton, and barons of beef, and without dwelling on the hypocras, loving cups, and

their vast cellars filled with such wine as even kings cannot
equal, the Worshipful Company of Grocers stood pre-eminent
among the City guilds.

"Our kitchen motto," he added, with a fine feeling of
pride, which, somehow, seemed to reflect credit upon him,
as indicating a thrifty habit as well as a large enjoyment of
good things, "is one which should be engraven on the heart
of every one who loveth the good gifts of Heaven, 'Waste
not—spare not;' so that while the reputation of the City be
maintained, we may ever remember that there are others
outside our hall not so richly favoured as ourselves. And
you may see, my dear, within a stone's throw of Grocers'
Hall itself, boys and even men who have, poor wretches, to
make a dinner off a penny dish of beef broth, with a cup of
small ale added by the charity of the cook."

After this digression, he proceeded with the main thread
of his discourse, which was to the effect that, although I
had some two years to wait before I attained my majority,
it was his duty to lay before me an account of my affairs and
of his stewardship.

And then occurred the greatest surprise of all my life. Of
course I knew without being told that the daughter of Mr.
Robert Carellis, his only child, was certain to be what in
Virginia would be called wealthy. I could not live in the
rough splendour of the plantation without looking on myself
as belonging to the ranks of those who are called rich. But
I was not prepared for the greatness of the fortune which
my guardian announced to me.

The successive owners of the Carellis estate had all trans-
mitted their tobacco every year to Medlycott & Company.
The merchants received the cargo, sold it, and after remitting
to Virginia all those things which were required, invested
the remainder of the money as advantageously as was
possible. Mine was the fourth generation of this annual
consignment; and though some years might be poor, some
cargoes might be wrecked or spoiled, yet in the space of a
hundred years the profits of the tobacco had grown up to a
vast amount of money. In a word, I was a very great

heiress. My guardian held in trust for me over one hundred thousand pounds, and my plantation in Virginia produced, even under the careless and easy rule of my father, more than a thousand pounds a year.

"You are worth," said Mr. Medlycott, looking at the figures with admiring eyes, "you are worth more than a plum." He smacked his lips over the word. "A plum, my dear. How few of us, unworthy and unprofitable servants that we are, achieve a plum! and how many things can be bought when one has a plum in one's hand to buy them with."

By a plum, I learned afterwards, he meant a hundred thousand pounds.

"But what am I to do with all this money?" I cried aghast.

"You will buy, my dear," he said, laughing, "falbalas for your frocks, quilted petticoats, gold kickshaws, china, pet negro boys——"

"Oh no," I said, laughing; "I have had quite enough of negro boys already."

"Then there is one expense saved. And as for the rest, why, my child, unless we take heed, your husband—nay, never blush—will show you how to spend it. There are gamblers enough, I warrant, among the gallants of St. James's, who would cock their hats for our Virginian heiress, and leave her in the end as ragged as any fishwife. But fear not, Cousin Elinor. Here shall we keep you under lock and ward, safe from the Mohocks."

Presently he stopped, and I, fearing to trespass longer on his patience, rose to go.

He took my hand, and was about to raise it to his lips, when another twinge of gout seized him.

"My dear ward—— Death and zounds!"

When I returned to the parlour I found Jenny waiting for me.

"Come," she said, "let us sit down and talk. We shall be alone for half an hour, and we have so many things to say that one does not know where to begin."

I noticed then that there was some appearance of preparation.

"It is our evening for cards," Jenny explained. "Most ladies in the City have one evening a week; and, indeed, my mother, who is fond of a game, generally plays four or five evenings in the week. But, for my part, I love better to sit out and talk."

Two silver candlesticks were on the mantelshelf, lighted, and four more stood, ready to be lighted, on the card-table, set out with counters and cards.

"Have we," I asked, "so much to say?"

"Why, surely, Princess Pocahontas. We are to be friends, and to tell each other everything. Now, show your friendship by telling me how you like the name—the name"—here she blushed and laughed—"of Lysander?"

"Of Lysander?"

"And Clarissa? Lysander and Clarissa. Do they go well together? I will show you his poems, and on Sunday next I will show you—himself."

I began to understand. It was a little love story that was to be confided to me.

"And does no one know anything about it?"

"Hush—sh!" She opened her eyes very wide and shook her pretty head. "No one. Christopher March receives his letters and gives them to me privately. I send mine to Wills's Coffee House. It is like the novel of 'Clarinda, or the Secrets of a Heart,' all in letters. And on Sunday mornings we sigh at each other across the pews while the people are singing the psalms."

The young man, Christopher March, then, was assisting to deceive his master by secretly receiving letters for his master's daughter. This was very remarkable in so good a young man. But I could say no more then, because the company began to arrive. They were all ladies, except Christopher March himself, who had assumed a gayer coat for the evening; and, still with the exception of that young man, they all came to play cards. A little delay, at which some waxed impatient, happened while I was introduced as the Virginian newly arrived, but presently they were all seated at the table and deep in play. Among them were one or two quite young girls, no older than Jenny or myself, and it surprised me to see them staking and losing little piles of counters, which meant, I knew, money. The ladies were very finely dressed, with patches set on artfully—some of them with more paint than I could approve—and their manners very stately. But, Lord! to see what a change the chances of the game presently wrought in my hostess's face, which had naturally so much kindness in it. For her colour came and went, her eyes brightened, and her mouth stiffened. She represented in turns, and in a most lively manner, the varied emotions of hope, terror, indignation, joy, and despair. The other ladies were like her, but they concerned me less.

"Look at my mother," whispered Jenny. "That is the way with her every night. She says there is no other joy so great as to win at cards. Let us play and sing."

She played the spinet very prettily, and presently sang with great spirit, "As down in the meadows I chanced to pass."

Christopher March applauded, and then asked me to sing. I declined, because I wished to do nothing but look on that first night. Then he began to talk to us, and paid compliments, at which Jenny laughed contemptuously—it was clear that her father's clerk was a person of small position in her eyes.

At twelve o'clock the chairs came, and the ladies presently rose to go. After what promised to be an endless shouting of bearers and link-boys, with more swearing, the chairs were got away at last.

Madam sank into a seat, and pressed her hands to her head.

"Did ever woman have such luck?" she cried, lifting her face.

"You have lost, madam?" asked Christopher, with a grave face.

She groaned.

"I shall want to see you to-morrow morning, Christopher," she said. "Girls, go to bed. Elinor, my dear, I thought you would bring me good luck."

To be sure, as the sequel proved, my arrival was the beginning of the worst luck in the world.

All night I lay awake listening to the rolling and rumbling of carts and coaches, which never seemed to stop. About three in the morning there was a lull, but the noise began again at six, and at seven it was at its height again, with shouting of men and cries of the streets.

"O nurse!" I cried, "is London always so full of noise?"

"Always," she replied. "There is never any lull from year to year. It is the labour of the world which makes this noise."

She dressed me, and I went downstairs. No one was there yet, although it was already half-past seven, and Betty, the maid, when she came to clear away the card-tables and set out the breakfast, was astonished to see me so early. I waited a little, and then took refuge with Jenny, who was lying awake, reading Lysander's last.

"It is beautiful, Nelly," she cried, with sparkling eyes. "How should you like to have a man writing to you—verses, you know, not prose—beautiful verses like this—

> Sure, Jenny hath some secret charm
>   That she doth guard, but not discovers,
> To raise the hopes and soothe th' alarm
>   Of all her sighing, anxious lovers."

It did not seem to me very real, or if the poet meant it; but it would have been unkind to say so.

"When my mother loses at cards," she told me, "she always sends for Christopher March. He gives her money without my father knowing anything about it. What she does with the money which she wins I cannot tell."

Then we went downstairs and had a dish of chocolate for breakfast. The chocolate was good, but I missed the abundant and plentiful provision of things which we had in Virginia. Not that one wanted to eat more, but in America, as I have already said, there is always on the table a prodigality of good things, as if nature was lavish with her gifts.

After breakfast I stood at the window and looked at the people. There was a company of soldiers in red coats going through drill; at the right-hand side, a little in advance, stood the fugleman, with a pike, and it seemed to me as if the men were all copying him; in front of them was a sergeant, brave with ribbons, giving the orders in a hoarse voice, and with him a drummer boy, smart and ready. The open space north of the Tower was crowded with groups of sailors waiting to be hired by the captains of trading ships, who marched gravely about among them, asking questions of one and another, and sometimes engaging one. In one place a quarrel and a fight, quickly begun and soon ended; in another a pump, whither I see a crowd haling a boy with shout and laughter, and presently pumping upon him till he is half drowned. Then they let him go, and he creeps away, wet and faint with ill-usage.

Then, when I had tired of looking out of the window, nothing would please Jenny but that I must go a-shopping in Cheapside. It was already eleven of the forenoon, and the streets were filled with people. I was so rustic and ignorant that I was for stopping at every shop and gazing stupidly at every crowd, so that people had much ado not to run against me. However, Jenny made me take the wall, and by leading me through the narrow lanes and passages which make this wonderful city like an anthill, she conveyed me safely to Cheapside, where for two hours we were shown the most wonderful things, and I laid out a great sum of money, by Jenny's advice and instigation all to make me fine. There were wadded calico wrappers; a musk-coloured velvet mantle, lined with squirrel skins; falbalas; laced shoes with high heels; roundabout aprons with pockets; hoods; satin frocks; whalebone hoops; a gold repeating watch, with a gold chain; a gold *étui* for needles and scissors; and all sorts of vanities, the like of which I had never before dreamed of; and yet they pleased me, Heaven knows, being a girl, and therefore by nature prone to love these worthless yet pretty things. Besides, as Jenny said, "You are a great heiress, my dear. It is fitting that you should dress so that no one will mistake you for a poor, penniless country maid." I wanted to present her with something to hansel friendship, but she would have nothing except an ostrich egg, set in a rim and feet of silver, which took her fancy, together with a silver-gilt box for caraway comfits, to be taken during long sermons: the lid, I remember, was beautifully enamelled with a Cupid fishing for hearts. And one little thing she bought herself. It was a ninepenny-piece, bent both ways by no less a person than the great Lilly, the fortune-teller. Jenny bought it for luck at langter-a-loo. But I never heard that it brought her any, and I fear that the man who sold it was dishonest—perhaps Lilly never saw the coin, and the dealer himself may have bent that piece. As for lip-salves, rouge, and all the things which we were asked to buy, I would have none of them; and, indeed, Jenny owned that I needed not the artifices with which some of the pale City madams are fain to heighten and set off their graces.

The next day we went to church at ten in the morning. The church of our parish was that of St. Olave, a beautiful structure, built by that great architect Sir Christopher Wren. Our own pew was square, with straw hassocks and red serge seats, high and narrow. I was astonished to see the ladies as they came in bowing to their friends in the pews. Nor did it seem to me becoming for gentlemen carrying their hats under one arm, and having their canes suspended from the button of their right sleeve, to take out little telescopes and look up and down the church, spying out their friends. Several of these tubes were directed at our pew, and I saw Jenny suddenly drop her eyes upon her prayer-book, and assume an air of devotion which I had not thought to belong to her nature.

In Virginia we had service for all alike, the household, the convicts, and the negroes, so that I was sorry to see in this church none but the well-to-do, with the respectable clerks and their wives. Surely, I thought, free-born Britons of all kinds should be brought to the ordinances of religion as much as negroes and convict slaves. The clergyman who read the prayers was a young gentleman fresh from the University of Oxford, where, I learn, they for ever run after some new thing. The language of the prayer-book was not, it seems, to his liking. He would have "pardons" instead of "pardoneth," and "absolves" for "absolveth;" but I think his taste was wrong when he chose to read "endue 'um, enrich 'um, prosper 'um," instead of "endue them," &c., as I had been accustomed to read.

When the psalms were singing, Jenny nudged me gently with her hand, and I saw her turn her head half round and look straight across the church. Then she shut her eyes, and gently raised and dropped her head, and I remembered what she told me about their sighs in church. Sure enough, on the opposite side of the church, was a young gentleman who was affected in exactly the same manner. He did not appear to me to be possessed of a very noble appearance, being small, pale, and with a turned-up nose, a feature which in men should be straight, or perhaps Roman. When we sat down, our heads being well below the top of the pew, Jenny whispered to me that it was Lysander. The lesson for the day was a chapter of Proverbs, and there were in it certain verses which seemed a special rebuke for the frivolity of us girls. "Favour is deceitful and beauty is vain; but a woman that feareth the Lord, she shall be praised."

The sermon, a very long one under five heads, was preached by the rector himself, in whose face and voice I seemed to perceive some resemblance to my guardian the alderman, for his cheeks and nose were red and puffed, and his voice was thick. He was, in fact, the chaplain of the Grocers' Company, and, as such, was present at all their feasts. At last he finished the sermon, and we all got up and came away. If the ragged boys had not come to the service, at least they were standing outside the doors, and while we thronged the porch there was a cry of pick-pocket, and one of them darted from the crowd and fled through some of the lanes, followed by two or three.

The next day, after serious talk with madam, I began to

undertake the study of those things in which I could not fail to be ignorant. The most important were that I should learn to dance, and that I should be improved in music and singing, and for these I had masters. My dancing-master, who took the first place, and considered himself an artist of the greatest distinction, was Sieur Isaac Lemire, a French gentleman of Huguenot descent, born in London. He was a man of little stature, somewhat over the middle age, with thin features and bright eyes. He was very careful about his dress, which was always in accordance with the most recent French fashion; he spoke English as well as French; and when he went out to give a lesson he was followed by a negro boy carrying the fiddle with which he accompanied his instruction.

"Mademoiselle," he said with a profound bow, on being introduced to me, "I am charmed by the prospect of lending a fresh grace to one already possessed of so fine a figure and so beautiful a face. Mistress Jenny, I am your very humble servant. You will, I trust, assist us in our task."

Jenny always stayed, partly because she loved dancing and partly because this professor talked during the whole lesson, and gave us the latest West End news, which we could not get from the "Postman" or the "Examiner."

"A young lady dancing," said the professor, tuning his fiddle and occasionally allowing one foot a preliminary flourish as if for a treat; "a young lady dancing is a brandished torch of beauty. She is then most dangerous to the heart of man; she is then most powerful." Twang-twang. "You will now, mademoiselle, have the goodness to pay attention to the carriage of Miss Jenny while she treads with me the *minuet de la cour.*" It is a beautiful dance, the minuet. My heart warmed for it at once; the stateliness of it; the respect for woman which is taught by it; the careful bearing of the body, the grace of the studied gestures, which must be in harmony with the music; all these things made me love the minuet. That was our first lesson; but the professor was not contented with the minuet only, although that dance was the most important. We had, besides, the

English country dances; we danced the Hey, with Joan Sanderson, the Scotch reel, the round, and the jig. He taught us, besides, the old-fashioned dances, such as used to be danced at Court, the saraband, which Jenny did very prettily, with the help of castanets, and coranto, and the cotillon. And then he taught us figures of his own country, such as the Auvergne *bourrée*, the basque step, and the jigs of Poitou and Picardy.

Once, when we were in the midst of our lesson, Lord Eardesley paid us a visit. Then it was delightful to practise with him as a partner, while Jenny played the spinet and the professor the violin. And his lordship and the professor, and Jenny too, all said kind things of my grace and quickness in learning.

So began my new life, with kindness, hospitality, and affection, such as I had not looked for nor expected. When the alderman grew better I found him the most delightful of companions, full of stories about the greatness of London and the vastness of her commerce. I was troubled, however, in my mind when I thought what he would say if he knew that his wife secretly took money from Christopher March, and that his daughter, by help of the same agent, was carrying on a correspondence with a secret lover.

As for nurse, she began by being heavy and dull, whereat I guessed, rightly, that she was thinking over that bad past which never left her mind. She spoke little of it, but once when we were crossing Tower Hill, and I gave a penny to a ragged brat, she began to cry gently, and told me that she had once a son who might have been like that poor boy, as friendless and neglected. "And their end, my dear, is to carry a musket for sixpence a day, and so get killed in battle, or to go a-thieving, and so get hung."

After a while, however, she cheered up and found her way to the place which most delighted her, the still-room. Here she sat among the bottles and compounds, making lavender water, ratafia water, decoction of primroses for toothache, cowslip wine, elder-flower wine, and elder-berry wine, preserving poppy-heads and camomile for fever pains, horehound for coughs, trying all the thousand recipes which a woman of her condition of life should, if she be a notable woman and take a pride in her own knowledge, understand perfectly. And madam said that she had never a still-room maid with half her handiness and knowledge.

CHAPTER III.

RIVAL SUITORS.

NATURALLY, I had to unlearn a good many of the opinions which I had learned in Virginia. For instance, I thought there that in England every one was honest except those few exceptions who, being caught, were either hanged or else branded in the hand, well flogged, and sent across the seas to us. I now learned that for one so caught there were a hundred thieves at large, and that every unknown person was considered dishonest until the contrary was proved. As for my ideas of religion, it was always difficult for me to believe that the fine ladies and gentlemen in the City churches were so devout as our poor Virginian convicts. As for our amusements, I could not learn to like cards, because it seemed to me cruel to take the money of a player who could not afford to lose it. But I liked the City shows, when we could look out from a window and see the processions, the Lord Mayor's day of state when he sat in his gilded coach, preceded by the train-bands, the City companies, and the masons, singing, " Hey! the merry masons! Ho! the merry masons," as they went, while the cannon were fired and the bells clashed. On the Fifth of November they carried Gog and Magog through the streets with more bands. Sometimes the butchers made a wedding merry-making with bones and cleavers. At Christmas the waits came at midnight—

> Sing high, sing low, sing to and fro,
> Go tell it out with speed ;

and the mummers came without being invited — Turks, sweeps, kings and queens—and frolicked among us as long as they listed. And at the New Year we had parties at which the alderman would have no cards but only the merry old games of blind man's buff, hot cockles, and country bumpkin. On Twelfth Night we looked for the bean in the cake. In the spring, when the flowers came, whenever there was a City rejoicing we had gardeners' walks made in the streets and lanes with green arches and rows of flowers—lupins, bachelors' buttons, peony roses, ribbon grass, and the like. There was, indeed, no lack of amusement for me, a girl who had seen so little.

It took me long to learn the value of money. To teach it was the alderman's share in my education. He gave me whatever I wanted, but made me enter it in a book which he kept for the purpose. I put it down on the left-hand side, and on the right I set out all that I had bought. It was a record of vanity, for the most part, and my cheeks burned while the alderman read it aloud.

"To laced gloves, two shillings; to satin for a frock, five guineas; to hoops for ditto, twelve shillings. Truly, my dear, no husband will be wanted to teach thee how money may be spent. Let us consider how it has been made. These gloves of thine stand for eight pounds of tobacco; this satin for four hundredweight—a grievous load of tobacco for your young slender shoulders. How many naked wretches have risen early and toiled all day in the sun beneath the whip to sow, plant, weed, keep clean, pick, and roll this tobacco before it could be sold or exchanged for thy satin frock? They have fared of the worst, these creatures, and toiled the hardest, all that thou mightest go in satin and hoops. Of a truth, my dear, thy lines have been cast in pleasant places."

The alderman, to be sure, had his own weaknesses. I might have asked him, for example, why he ate turtle soup and drank the strong wine of Oporto, when so many boys were running ragged and uncared for about the streets. Nevertheless, his words were timely, and made me understand what a thoughtless girl was I, who could, without reflection, thus waste and lavish the money which the labour of so many poor wretches had been given to save up. And yet, whether I spent the money or whether I saved it, made no difference to the convicts or to the negroes.

But the thing which most astonished me was the conversation of the young ladies who called upon Jenny and me, and were our friends. For, when we were all alone together, they talked about nothing but love-making and how to attract the admiration and attention of men. For my own part, I suppose that if I had ever thought about it at all, I had considered it likely that I should some day marry some one, and so dismissed the matter from my mind. The ordered course of things would come in due time. But these girls were continually thinking and talking about the lover of the present or of the future; they had their little secrets; they would show each other songs and verses addressed to their fair eyes, just as Jenny did; they discussed the beaux, their dress, their carriage, their impudence, or their wit (mostly, I believe, their wit was impudence); and they openly pitied, or derided, any of their friends who had failed to find a lover and was destined to lead apes in that place which frivolous and thoughtless persons are too ready to name lightly.

"Were you not so tall, Nelly," said Jenny, when I first remonstrated with her on this idle talk, "I would call you little Puritan. But prithee consider. If it were not for the attention and thought that men bestow upon us and we upon them, what would become of the men? It is for their own good, my dear, more than for ours, that we seek to attract their foolish eyes."

Here, indeed, was a pretty turning of the tables!

"No man, my dear," she went on laughing, "can possibly make any figure in the world until he begins to hope for our favours. Then, indeed, he pays attention to his figure and his manners, learns to talk, dresses himself in the latest mode, carries himself with a fashionable air, and becomes a pretty fellow. Then, to attract the eyes of one of us, he studies to distinguish himself, and when he cannot succeed he tries to be different from his fellows, and commits a thousand pretty follies. Such, my dear, are a few of the benefits we confer upon our lovers."

Jenny stopped and laughed again.

"What part does Lysander play?" I asked.

At that she smiled and blushed prettily. "Lysander," she said, "has offended his Clarissa. I have had enough verses, and I have written to say that if he wishes to gain my favours in reality, he must now, in person, inform me of his rank and name."

"Good heavens, child!" I cried. "Do you mean that you have been in correspondence with a man whose very name you have not learned?"

"'Tis even so," she replied, laughing. "No harm has been done, my fair Puritan princess; Clarissa has written nothing that would hurt her reputation; trust Clarissa, who is a Londoner, for taking care of herself. As Lysander prettily says, 'Clarissa doth demand an awe, would straight confound the great Bashaw.' He may be a lord, or he may be a templar; I fear he is the latter. But what a noble air he shows, particularly when he sighs during the psalms!"

I thought of his turned-up nose, and was unable to agree with Jenny, but did not tell her so.

The one thing which displeased me at this time was the constant intrusion of Christopher March into all our plans and conversation. We could go nowhere without meeting him, and then he would walk with us; if we were playing or singing he would join us without being asked; he generally took dinner with us, and on madam's evenings was always one of the company. That did not matter much but for his attentions to me, which were incessant, especially before company. It was as if he wished the world to consider me as his property. Of course, I was not so foolish but that I understood the meaning of his politeness; a week of Jenny's talk had been sufficient to remove the ignorance of my Virginian days; but, naturally, being a Carellis, I was not so mad as to think of encouraging the mere clerk of my guardian, a paid servant, to aspire to such a thing as marriage with me. My only difficulty was to know how, without being cruel and unkind, I could get rid of the man.

I supposed, and rightly too, that it was he who sent me

verses and epistles written in the same extravagant fashion as that followed by Jenny's Lysander, and signed " A Lover." I kept them all carefully and said nothing even to Jenny. But I told Nurse Alice, and bade her watch and find out by what means they were conveyed to my bedroom.

Alice presently informed me that they were placed on my table by Prudence, the housemaid. So I sent for the young woman and roundly taxed her with the fact, which she confessed with tears and promises of amendment.

" But, girl," I said, " who gave you the verses?"

At first she refused to tell me, but being pressed and threatened, she owned that it was none other than Christopher March. And here I made another discovery. Not only had this man won the alderman's complete confidence by reason of his industry and zeal, not only had he gotten a hold over madam by secretly giving her money, and over Jenny by conniving at her correspondence, but he had made the very servants afraid of him by acquiring a knowledge of their secrets, and by letting them feel that their situations and characters depended upon his pleasure. When I understood the state of the case I considered whether I ought not to let the alderman know, and to ask him whether it was proper for one of his servants to gain this footing and authority in his own house. And yet I dared not for the sake of madam, for I knew not how much money Christopher had supplied her with. I would that I had told him all, and so saved—but that I could not know—the honour and the fortune of that good old man.

Well; I sent away the girl forgiven and a little comforted —be sure I did not ask the nature of her secret—and I determined to seek out Christopher March and explain myself openly to him.

I waited till one afternoon, when Madam and Jenny had both gone out a-shopping, and I was private in the parlour. Then I sent Alice to invite my gallant to an interview.

He came straight from the counting-house, wearing his office brown coat, and looking exactly what he was, a merchant's clerk and servant. Yet he tried to assume a gallant air, and stepped with as much courtliness as he could manage.

"Christopher March," I began, "I have asked you to come here when I am alone because I have a serious discourse to hold with you."

He bowed and made no reply.

"I am an ignorant American girl," I went on, "and unused to the ways of London. But I am not so ignorant as not to know the meaning of those compliments and attentions with which you have honoured me."

"O Mistress Elinor!" he cried, sinking on his knees, "give your most humble adorer a little hope."

"Get up immediately," I said, "or I will leave the room. Get up, sir, and stand or sit, as you will, but do not presume again to address me in that way." I was now really angry. "Remember, sir, if you can, that I am a gentlewoman, and you are a clerk. Know your position."

He rose as I bade him.

"In London," he said, in a soft, slow voice, with down-dropped eyes, "young men of obscure family have a chance of rising. Many a Lord Mayor began by being an errand-boy. It is true that I have no coat-of-arms. Yet I am already well-considered. If the alderman does not make me a partner, some other merchant may. No clerk in the tobacco trade has a better reputation than I have. I could bring your ladyship a good name and an honest heart. What better things can a man have than honesty and honour?"

"Assuredly, nothing. Give them, therefore, to some young woman of your own station. Meantime, Master Christopher March, take back these foolish verses and these letters. Let me have no more nonsense. There can be no question of that kind between us; none at all."

He received the letters with dark and gloomy brow.

"You will not only cease your letters, you will entirely cease your compliments and your attentions. You understand what you have to do?"

"And if I disobey your ladyship's commands?"

"In that case I must inform the alderman. I should, at the same time, ask him to consider the nature of that 'honour and honesty' of which you make such boast, when it permits you to advance madam sums of money of which her husband knows nothing ; secretly to assist his daughter in a silly correspondence ; and secretly to threaten his servants."

"You would, then," he replied coldly, "do much more harm to the alderman's happiness than you would do to mine."

"Perhaps. But I should do all the harm to you that I wish; which is nothing but that you should continue to be the faithful servant which the alderman believes you to be, that you should not aspire beyond your station, and that you should confine yourself entirely, so far as I am concerned, to your duties. Perhaps you had better return, then, at once to the counting-house, or the alderman may be examining the books for himself, and find out where some of his money goes."

He turned suddenly white, and glared at me with eyes which had as much terror as rage in them. Then he left me without another word. But I knew that I had made of Christopher March an enemy, though being young and foolish I did not believe he could harm me. I have since learned that there is no man, however humble, who cannot at least do mischief. Some men, by their evil lives and base thoughts, may lose the power of doing good ; but the power of wickedness never leaves us. I had, however, the good sense to tell Alice what I had done. She, though this I knew not till afterwards, began to watch the movements of the man until, long before the rest of us knew anything about him, she had learned all his secrets.

"I told Jenny something of what had passed, and, to my great joy, she laughed and clapped her hands, and kissed me.

"O Nelly !" she said, "I am so glad. I have seen for a long while what was coming, and I did not dare to warn you. Besides, he threatened——"

"Jenny !" I cried. "Is it possible ? Did you allow your father's servant to threaten you ?"

"What could I do?" she replied. "He knows all about—about Lysander, you know."

"Oh! this is dreadful, Jenny. Go straight and tell your father, child, and then you can laugh at him." But this she would not do, fearing the alderman's displeasure.

The next thing I tried to do was to persuade madam to go to her husband for money to pay her debts of honour. The good lady was growing more passionately addicted to cards every day, and, whether she played ill or had continual bad luck, she seemed never to win. Then it was difficult for me, a young woman, to remonstrate freely with her, and though I spoke a little of my mind once, Jenny being out of the room, I could not persuade her to tell her husband all. So that failed. Yet had I succeeded, all the unhappiness that was to follow would have been averted. Fate, as the Turk calls it, or Providence, as we more rightly say, is too strong to be set aside by the efforts of a weak girl. We were all to be punished in a way little expected for our sins and weaknesses, and the wicked man was to work his wicked will for a little space.

"Alas!" said Jenny, sitting in my room, where we could talk freely. "He is a dangerous man, and I would he were not so much in my father's confidence. Before you came the attentions which displeased you were offered to me. He actually wanted me to marry him! Perhaps that would have been my fate but for your arrival. The chance of getting a hundred thousand pounds for a fortune with such a wife as you turned his head, and I now fear him no longer. It would, indeed, be a rise in life for a gutter-boy like him to marry you, the Virginian heiress."

"Why do you call him a gutter-child?"

"Because he was, as much as any of those ragged little wretches playing out there on Tower Hill. He would willingly hide the story if he could; but he never shall, so long as I live to tell it for him. Such as those boys are, such was he; as ragged, as dirty, as thievish, I dare say; as ready to beg for a penny to get him a dish of broth. He was found lying on the doorstep one cold wintry day in

March, barefooted, bareheaded, stupid with cold and hunger. My father had him taken to the kitchen to be warmed and fed. Then, seized with pity for a boy so forlorn, he gave him to one of his porters to be brought up at his expense. Then he sent the lad to school, where he got on, being quick and clever. Finally he took him into his own counting-house, and gave him a chance to rise in the world, as so many poor boys have already done in London. Methinks he has risen already high enough."

Let us leave Christopher March for the present, and talk of more pleasant things.

I have said that Lord Eardesley once or twice called upon us when we were with Monsieur Lemire, the dancing-master, and took part in our lesson. During the winter he came but little, to my chagrin; because, having then no thought of what was to follow, I found his manner and discourse pleasing. He brought new air to the house, and talked of things which otherwise we should not have heard of. It did us all good when his lordship came in the evening and took a dish of tea with us. Then madam forgot her cards, Jenny put on her finest airs, and the alderman, who generally despised tea, joined us and told stories. The best tea-cups were set out—those, namely, brought from Canton by one of the alderman's seafaring friends—the reserve or company candles were lit, and the tea brewed was stronger and better than that which we allowed ourselves. After tea we would go to the spinet and sing, Jenny and I in turn or together.

Those were pleasant evenings, but there were few of them. My lord was a most cheerful and agreeable man, without any of the fashionable affectations of which Jenny had told me; full of sense and understanding. He did not waste the time in paying us foolish compliments, and when he spoke of himself, he laughed at his own lamentable condition as an impoverished peer. He told us once, I remember, that he seldom dined at his friend's houses, because he could not afford the vails expected by the servants.

So the winter passed quickly away, and the spring came

upon us with those easterly winds which in England do so poison and corrupt that sweet season.

As the year advanced the attention of every one was settled upon that great bubble, the South Sea Company, whose stock advanced daily till it reached seven hundred, eight hundred, and even a thousand pounds. I knew little, indeed, and cared nothing, because I understood nothing, of the general greediness; yet we heard daily from the alderman, at dinner and supper, how the shares were fought for, and what prodigious prices they fetched. And once he took me to the Exchange, where I saw a crowd of finely-dressed ladies and gentlemen mixed with a throng of merchants and tradesmen, all struggling, fighting, and shouting together. They were buying and selling South Sea Stock. The street posts or the backs of porters served for writing-desks; he who had a bunk or a stall commanded as much rent as if it had been a great house in Eastcheap; and, in that crowd, a petty huckster of Houndsditch, if he had but a single share, was as great a man as a lord.

"See, Nelly," said the alderman; "the love of money is like the hand of death; for it strikes at all alike, both rich and poor."

The alderman, who believed that Sir Robert Walpole was the greatest and wisest of statesmen, took fright when he heard that the minister had spoken in the House vehemently against the South Sea Scheme, to which, before this, he had perhaps secretly inclined. "It was a project," said this great man, "which would lure many thousands of greedy and unwary people to their ruin; holding out promises which it never could keep, and offering dividends which no scheme ever devised could maintain."

While everybody else was mad with this dream of wealth, we in our house were full of our own thoughts, careless of the tumult which raged in every heart. As the spring advanced, Lord Eardesley came oftener, and would go with us when we drove out to take the air. London is a great city, indeed, but it is richly provided with fields, gardens, parks, and places of recreation. We could drive to the spring gardens of Knightsbridge; to the bowling green of Marylebone; to the fields beyond Islington, where we bought cakes; to those of Stepney, where there is another kind of cake; or to the walk of Chelsea, where there are buns. We could go farther afield, and visit Caen Wood and Hampstead, or to the gardens beyond Hyde Park, where they sold syllabubs. We were a gay and happy party whenever we had his lordship with us. And for one thing I am grateful, indeed, to Jenny, that though she suspected what was coming, she was so good as not to spoil the innocence of my happiness by telling me her suspicions.

One evening in April—ah! happy evening—Lord Eardesley took us to the theatre.

Suppose you were never to go to a theatre at all until you were nineteen years of age; suppose you had read of a dramatic performance, but never seen one; and suppose you had no idea whatever what it would be like. Then think of going—for the first time!

It was to Drury Lane. We drove to the doors, where we were met by my lord, in brave attire. He led us to the first row of boxes, where, for the most part, only ladies of quality are found, the wives of citizens commonly using the second row. Truly it passes my power to express the happiness of this evening and the splendour of the scene. The pit contained only gentlemen, but the boxes in which we sat were full of ladies dressed in extravagance of splendour of which I had never dreamed, nor Jenny either. But the patches spoiled all; nor could I ever, although for the sake of the mode, I wore two or three small ones, reconcile myself to the custom of sticking black spots over a pretty face. The house was brilliantly lit with many thousands of candles. I say nothing about the play, except that the players did so artfully represent the characters, that you would have thought the house, with all the audience, a dream, and only the play itself the reality. Yet I was astonished to find so many fine ladies whispering, laughing, and flirting with the fan, while the most moving scene and the most eloquent passages failed to rouse their interest.

"You know not your sex, fair Virginian," said Lord Eardesley, when I ventured to take this objection to the behaviour of the spectators. "The ladies do not come here to see, but to be seen. They are the principal spectacle of the house to the gentlemen in the pit."

And then I observed that, although I myself could see with the greatest ease whatever was done upon the stage, and the faces of the actors and actresses, a large number of gentlemen, especially those of the younger kind, were afflicted with a sort of blindness which forced them to carry to the theatre the little magnifying tubes which I had seen in church. And such was the strange callousness of these unfortunate young men to the piece performed, that many of them at the side of the pit stood with their backs to the stage, and, with their tubes held to one eye, surveyed the glittering rows of beauties on the first tier of boxes.

"Nelly," whispered Jenny, "you are the prettiest girl in the house. Half a hundred beaux are gazing upon you."

In the delight of the play I forgot the annoyance of this attention, and, perhaps, Jenny was mistaken.

When we came away, at the falling of the curtain, we found the entrance-hall lined with a double row of pretty fellows, all hat under arm and right leg thrust forward. One of them stepped audaciously forward to the front and offered to lead me to the coach.

"This young lady, sir," said my lord, "is of my party. We thank you."

The young fellow said something about pretty faces and hoods, upon which our escort stepped forward and whispered in his ear.

"I am Lord Eardesley," he said aloud. "You can find me when you please."

I did not know enough of polite customs to suspect that the altercation might possibly, although so slight, lead to a duel.

Alas! that this custom of duelling should make every young man hold his life in his hand; so that it is less dangerous to cross the Atlantic Ocean, or to travel among the Indians of Western Virginia, or to serve a campaign against the Turk, than it is to live in London for a season—I mean, for a young gentleman of birth and rank. As for plain citizens, I have never heard that the custom of the duello has been brought into the manners of the London merchant.

I thought little that night of the matter, my head being full of the wonderful play. But the next day, when I was sitting alone and feeling a little sad, as is the way with foolish girls after an evening of great happiness, Jenny burst in upon me in a half hysterical state of excitement.

"Nelly!" she cried, "have you heard the news? They have fought, and my lord has pricked his man."

"What do you mean?" I asked.

"You remember the dapper little man at the theatre last night, who insulted us by calling us pretty girls—the wretch! As if we did not know so much already. 'Twas an officer in the Guards. Lord Eardesley fought him this morning in the Park with small swords, and ran him through the left shoulder. He is as brave as he is generous."

It was quite true. Our evening's pleasure had ended in two gallant gentlemen trying to kill each other, and one being wounded. Surely the laws of honour did not need so tragic a conclusion to so simple an adventure. Nevertheless, I was proud of Lord Eardesley, and rejoiced that he was so brave a gentleman.

He came that evening. Madam was abroad, playing cards. Jenny and I were alone, and presently Jenny rose and left the room. She told me afterwards that my lord had asked her to do so.

Then he begged permission to speak seriously to me, and my heart beat, because I knew, somehow, what he was going to say.

That is, I knew what his speech would contain, but I could not guess the manner in which he would say it. He began by saying that he was the poorest man of his rank in Great Britain; that all his wealth consisted of a barren mountain, a marshy valley, and a ruined castle in Wales;

that in offering his hand to a rich heiress like myself he should be accused of fortune-hunting.

"Nay, Mistress Nelly," he went on, "I must confess that at first my thoughts ran much upon the money of which you are possessed. That was the reason why, having had the happiness of seeing you, I came here once or twice, and then ceased my visits. But," he added, "I was constrained to return. And having come, I was drawn daily by irresistible ropes to the shrine of my affection." He took my hand and held it. "Nelly, rich or poor, believe that I love you tenderly."

I made no reply. Oh! that life could be one long rapture such as that which followed when he took me in his arms and kissed my lips.

I cannot write more of that moment. It would be a sacrilege of that first baptism or sacrament of love when we promised our hands and hearts to each other.

Presently, however, Jenny came back, discreetly knocking at the door—the little witch!

"Jenny, my dear," cried my lord, "come kiss me." He laid his hands upon her shoulders, and kissed the pretty little laughing thing as gaily as if a kiss meant nothing. Heavens, what had it meant to me? "See, this Princess of Virginia, this queen of fair maidens—she has promised, my pretty Jenny, to be my wife."

"No—not a queen at all," I murmured, while Jenny flew into my arms and kissed me again and again. "Not a queen —only my lord's handmaid. It may be that I have found favour in the sight of my king——"

"Not a queen? No," he replied, kissing my hands. "No—not a queen—only my mistress sweet and fond—only Nelly, my Heart's Delight!"

CHAPTER IV.

MY LORD EARDESLEY.

WHEN my lover left me he immediately sought the alderman, in order to convey to his worship the substance of what he had said to me. My guardian heard the story patiently, and then, falling into a kind of muse, sat with his head upon his hands saying never a word.

" Why, sir," said my lord with some heat, after waiting for a reply, " surely my proposal hath no dishonour in it. I can but offer Mistress Elinor what I have to give. It is little, as you know, besides my hand and a coronet."

" Sit down, my lord," said the alderman gravely. " I have much to say."

He then proceeded in such terms, as would give the young suitor as little pain as possible, to remind him that his own estates, save for the mountain and valley in Wales, were gone altogether, and that by his father's rashness over the gaming-tables, so that had it not been for the small fortune left him by his mother, his lordship would have nothing. But, said the alderman, the lack of fortune would have been a small thing, considering the ample inheritance of his ward, were he assured that none of the late lamented peer's weaknesses had descended upon his son. Lord Eardesley must excuse him for speaking plainly, but it was rumoured, rightly or wrongly, that he himself was addicted to the same pernicious habit.

Here my lord protested strongly that the rumour was based upon no foundation whatever in fact, and that he never gambled.

" Indeed," the alderman replied gravely. " Then am I rejoiced, and I hope that these words of yours can be made good."

After this he became more serious still, and, speaking in a whisper, he reminded the young lord that there were other sins besides the grievous sin of gaming, that many—nay, most of the young gentlemen of rank—took a pleasure and pride in deriding and breaking all God's laws; that they were profane swearers, professed atheists, secret Jacobites, duellists, deceivers of maidens, and contemners of order; that the voice of rumour had been busy with his name as concerns these vices as well.

Here Lord Eardesley protested again. He would confess to none of these things. A duel he had certainly fought only a few days before, but that was in defence of two ladies—in fact, Mistress Elinor Carellis herself and Mistress Jenny, the alderman's own daughter—but, he added, he had spared the life of his adversary, and only given him a lesson. That personally he abhorred the cursed laws of so-called honour, which obliged a gentleman to risk his life or seek to take another life at any fancied insult. As for the other vices mentioned by the alderman, he declared that he was not guilty of any of them; that his life and conversation were pure, and his religion that of his forefathers.

"It may be so," said the alderman. "Nevertheless, we do well to be careful. The young lady is an orphan; she hath neither brother nor near relation to protect her, should her husband use her ill; she is a stranger in the land and ignorant of the wickedness of this great town; like all innocent maidens, she is accustomed to look on every stranger, if he be a gentleman, as a good man; she admires a gallant carriage, a noble name, a long pedigree, a handsome face—and all these, my lord, she admires in you. Then she is a great heiress; her husband will have, with her, a hundred thousand pounds in bonds, scrip, and mortgages, and none of your perilous South Sea stock, besides a great estate in Virginia. Think of all this, my lord. Consider further that she hath been placed in my charge as a most sacred trust by my far-off cousin, Robert Carellis, now deceased, out of great confidence which he was good enough to repose in me—and own that I do well to be careful. Remember that she is all virtue and innocence; and that, according to the voice of rumour, you, my lord—pardon the plain speaking —are addicted to the—the same manner of life as most young noblemen. Why, you would be a wicked man, indeed, if you thought that I should easily consent to her marriage and without due forethought."

" Take all forethought and care possible," said my lord. " I assure you the voice of rumour was never so wrong as when it assigned me the possession of those fashionable follies which, I may remind you, require the waste of a great deal of money."

" True," my guardian replied. " That is a weighty argument in your favour. Meanwhile, my lord, we thank you for the honour you have offered to confer upon this house. I am sure that his lordship Robert Carellis would have wished for no higher alliance for his daughter, were he satisfied on those points on which I have ventured to speak. I go now, my lord, or I shall go shortly, to make such inquiry into your private life as is possible. I expect that, meanwhile, you will abstain from visiting this house or from making any attempt to see my ward. The delay shall not be longer than I can help, and if the issue be what your words assure me, there shall be no further opposition on my part, but, on the contrary, rejoicing and thankfulness."

He bowed low to his lordship and conducted him to the door of the counting-house, which led to the outer office. Christopher March was there; he looked up, and seeing Lord Eardesley, he changed colour. The alderman, walking slowly back, beckoned his chief clerk.

" You told me," he said, " that Lord Eardesley fought a duel the other day."

" Yes. On account of some quarrel over cards, I heard," said Christopher.

" Where did you hear it ? "

" It was the talk at Wills's-Coffee House. It was the talk at all the coffee-houses."

" So they make free with his name, then ? "

" They make free with every name," replied Christopher. " Yes, sir, they call him gamester, like his father; duellist, like his father; profligate, like his father. Of course, I know nothing except what I learn from these rumours."

" Ay, ay," the alderman mused. " No smoke without fire. It is, indeed, a perilous thing to be born to rank and title !

We humble folk, Christopher, should thank Heaven continually that we are not tempted, in the same way as our betters, to overstep the bounds of the moral law. No dicing, no profligacy, for the sober London merchant."

I understood, presently, that I was not to see my lord until the alderman was perfectly satisfied as to his private character.

This gave me no uneasiness, as I was so assured of my lover's goodness that I felt no pain on that score, and was only anxious for the time of probation to be passed.

Now a thing happened during the time when my lord was conferring with the alderman concerning his suit, which caused in my mind a little surprise, but which I thought no more of for the moment. It was this.

Outside the house my lord's servant, holding his horse, was waiting for his master. It was midsummer, and the evening was quite light. One does not in general pay much heed to men-servants, but this fellow caught my eye as I stood at the window and wondered what my guardian would say. When the mind is greatly excited a little thing distracts the attention for the moment and gives relief. Therefore I observed that the groom was a rosy-faced fellow, not very young, but fresh of cheek, who looked as if he had come up from the country only the day before, so brown and rustic was his appearance. In his mouth there was a straw, and his hair was of a bright red, of the kind called shock. While I was idly noting these matters I saw Christopher March standing by one of the posts of the streets, looking, as men will do, at the horse. Presently the groom looked in his direction, and a sudden change came over him. For his rosy cheeks grew pale and his knees trembled.

Then Christopher started and slowly walked nearer the horse. He spoke to the man, and began stroking the animal's neck, as if he were talking about the horse. I knew, however, by some instinct, perhaps because I now suspected Christopher in everything, that he was not talking of the horse at all. But what could he have to say to a country bumpkin, the groom of Lord Eardesley? I watched more narrowly. They were having some sort of explanation.

Gradually my bumpkin seemed to recover from his apprehension, and began to laugh at something Christopher said. And when the latter left him he nodded after him with a familiarity that was odd indeed.

Nor was that all. While I was still wondering, partly how the alderman would take it, and partly who this servant could be, that he should be an old acquaintance of Christopher March, another thing happened.

Alice, who had been out on some errand or other connected with my wants, was returning home. I saw the dear old woman slowly walking along the rough stones within the posts, and transferred my thoughts easily enough to her and her fidelity. Why, I should have something that night to tell her worth the hearing! Then, all of a sudden—was I dreaming?—she, too, stopped short on sight of Thomas Marigold, which was, I learned afterwards, the fellow's name, and gazed upon him with an air of wonder and doubt. Then she, too, stepped out into the road and accosted him. Again that look of terror on his face; and again, after a few moments' talk, the look of relief.

What they said was this, as nurse told me afterwards. She touched his arm and said sharply, "What are you doing here?"

Then it was that he turned pale.

"What are you doing, Canvas Dick?"

Upon this he staggered and nearly dropped the reins.

"Who—who—are you?" he asked.

"Never mind who I am. It is enough that I remember you, and that you are Canvas Dick, and that what I know about you is enough to hang you any day."

Then his knees trembled and his jaws chattered for fear.

"It is nigh upon twenty years ago," he said, "since I heard that name. Too long for anybody to remember; and, besides, what is it you know? Perhaps, after all, you are only pretending."

"Then will this help you? A man and two boys, one of them fifteen years of age, that is yourself, and one six or seven years younger; a house in the Ratcliffe Highway; a great robbery of jewels, planned by a man and carried out by the boldness and dexterity of the two boys ; and——"

"Hush!" whispered the man. "Don't say another word. Tell me who you are."

"They call me Alice," said nurse, looking him straight in the face. "That does not help you much. If you want to know more, I am nurse to Mistress Carellis, who lives in this house."

The man stared hard at her. "No," he said; "I can't remember who you are. Do you mean mischief, or do you mean halves?"

"First, what are you doing here?"

"I'm groom to Lord Eardesley." He grinned from ear to ear. "Who would think to find me as Tummas Marigold, honest Tummas, fresh from the country, and grooming a nobleman's horse?"

"Groom to Lord Eardesley, are you? Oh!" and here a sudden light sprang into her face. "And what," she asked with a catch in her voice, "what became of the other boy?"

Honest Tummas hesitated. Then he replied, taking the straw out of his mouth and stroking the horse's neck: "Why —the other boy—the little un'—he was hanged a matter of five years ago, on account of a girl's purse which he snatched in the fields behind Sadler's Wells."

"Oh!" she groaned, with a kind of despair. "It was the end to be looked for. It is the end of you all."

"Ay," he said; "give us a long day and plenty of rope. Then we climbed the ladder gaily and kick off the shoes, game to the last."

She shook her head. "Well," she said, "now I know where to find you, I must use you for my own purposes. Come here if you can to-morrow evening at nine, and I will ask you certain questions. Be sure that you answer me truthfully."

"Then you don't mean mischief?"

"If you serve me faithfully I will not harm you. If you dare to play me false I will tell his worship, Alderman

Medlycott, who you are, and give evidence against you at Newgate."

The man still hesitated. Presently, however, he held out his hand.

"Honour," he said, "was the only thing on which poor rogues and gentlemen of the road had to depend. And as he was satisfied that the good lady meant him no harm, he would meet her the next day and take her to a quiet place in the fields were they could talk."

Here nurse laughed. "Thou art a villain indeed, Dick, but put that thought out of your mind. An old woman like me may be knocked o' the head, but suppose she writes a history of Thomas Marigold, and lays it in a place where, after her murder, it might be found!"

Thomas laughed at this, and protested that he was a most honest and harmless fellow, and that he would certainly come and answer all her questions.

That night, nurse, Jenny, and I had a long and serious talk together in my chamber; so long that when I went to bed the watchman below was bawling, "Past two o'clock and a fine night." And all our talk was about my lord.

Nurse had foreseen what was coming; so had Jenny; so had everybody except the principal person concerned. Nurse was sure that he was as good as he was brave and handsome, and only owned to some misgivings on the subject of wine, which, she said, when gentlemen exceeded their couple of bottles or so, was apt to fly to the head and make them quarrelsome. Then, because she was a very wise woman, and knew the world, she began to tell me how different my life would be when I was a peeress.

"Oh!" said Jenny, with a long sigh, "I wonder if Lysander is a peer. There is an air about him; he may be anything. Happy, happy, happy Nelly!" she cried, kissing me before she went to bed. "To marry such a man, and to gain a title and—oh! Lysander!"

She ran upstairs to her own room—and I began to undress.

"As for my lord's character," said nurse, "the alderman

may make any inquiries he pleases. But I have a surer way to find the truth."

In two or three days she told me that she had learned all. Lord Eardesley was the most quiet and steady young man in London. He was studious, and read and wrote a great deal. In the evening he might be seen at a coffee-house or at the play. He went but little into society. He neither drank nor gambled. He attended church. His friends were chiefly gentlemen older than himself. No character could have been more satisfactory. I was in the highest spirits. I did not ask nurse how she came by the information, which I trusted entirely; and I waited impatiently for the alderman to tell me that all was well, and that my lord was coming to the house as my betrothed lover.

It was bright sunny weather in early summer, I remember. The June and July of 1720 were full of splendid days, in which every stone in the White Tower stood out clear and distinct, and the river sparkled in the sunshine. They were all days of hope and joy.

Yet a week—a fortnight—passed, and the alderman made no sign. That is, he became more silent. He had an attack of gout upon him, though not a serious one. Yet it laid him up, so that he could not get about.

One day I sought him in the counting-house, and asked him, seeing that he was alone, what was the meaning of his continued silence.

"My dear," he said, "I hope you will receive with resignation the news I have to give you. I would fain have spared you yet. But you force it from me."

"Go on quickly," I said. "Is Lord Eardesley ill?"

"More than that," he replied solemnly. "He is not worthy of your hand. He must not marry you."

He laid his kindly hand on mine, to keep me quiet, while with sad eyes and sad voice he said what he had to say.

"He is a fortune-hunter, Elinor. He is a gamester; he is a wine-bibber; he is a profligate. Such as his father was, so is he; and the late Lord Eardesley was the most notorious of all the men about Court twenty years ago. Such as his grandfather was so is he; and the grandfather was the private friend and intimate of Charles the Second, Buckingham, and Rochester."

"How do you know, sir, that the son inherits the vices of the father? You speak from some envious and lying report."

"Nay, child, nay. I would I did. At first I had only my fears on account of idle reports which reached my ears; now, however, these reports are confirmed, and I know from a most certain, although a secret source, the whole private life of this young nobleman."

I was silent, bewildered.

"Consider for a moment, child, what a dreadful thing it is to be the wife of a gambler. At the beginning of an evening's play he hath a noble fortune, say, perhaps a hundred thousand pounds; at the close of the night all is gone—all gone. Think of that. The money which represents the patience of generations and the labours of hundreds of men all gone in a moment—in the twinkling of an eye, fooled away upon a chance. Why, girl, the profligate and the drunkard are better; they, at least, have some semblance of pleasure for their money; the gambler alone hath none."

"I do not believe," I said doggedly, "that my lord is a gambler at all." Then I remembered my nurse's discoveries. "Why, my dear alderman, I can prove you are wrong. I have my secret way of finding out, too, and my information is trustworthy. What do you say to that?"

"I say, Elinor," replied the alderman, "that I cannot promise the hand of the daughter of my late correspondent and honoured friend, Robert Carellis, to the young Lord Eardesley, and that I have written to tell him so. Believe me, child, it was the hardest letter that I ever had to write. Now it is written."

"In a year or so I shall be of age," I said bitterly. "Then I shall not want your consent."

"Be it so," he replied. "Let me do my duty meanwhile as it becomes an honest man. Go, child. You are sorrowful, and with reason. The day will come when you will own that I have acted rightly."

I returned sadly. Jenny and madam knew what had been done, and we sat and cried together. Presently Jenny whispered, "What if Lysander should prove a gambler!"

"All the sorrow in the world," said madam solemnly, "comes from the extreme wickedness of man. What vice is so terrible as the love of gaming?"

I thought of her own passion for cards and wondered. I know, now, that people are never so virtuously indignant as when they denounce the sins to which they are themselves most prone.

Before night a letter was brought to me. It was from my lord.

"Dearest and best of women," he said, and I seemed to feel again the touch of his hand and to hear his soft and steady voice, so that my head swam and my heart sank, "I have received a letter from the alderman, in which I learn that I possess such vices as unfit me for your hand. I know not, in very truth, what they are. Have courage, my dear, and cheer your Geoffrey with an assurance that you will trust him until he can clear away these clouds. I have promised that I will not intrude myself upon your house. My intention is to do nothing for a week or two, and then to ask if the alderman will bring before me the reasons, clearly and certainly, for his bad opinion. So now farewell, and believe that I may be unworthy of so great a blessing as your love, but that I am not insensible to it and not ungrateful."

Had any girl so sweet a letter? Be sure I answered it with such silly words as I could command, telling him that I was altogether his, and that I firmly believed in his innocence. And so, with lighter heart and with an assured hope in the future, I lay down to sleep on the first night after my lover was sent from me.

CHAPTER V.

GETTING AT THE TRUTH.

IT was hard upon us. We were at the mercy of two most hardened villains, who had no conscience, no fear, no gratitude, nor any principles at all of truth or virtue. One of them, of course, was the man who called himself Thomas Marigold; the other, as you will presently see, was Christopher March. So far, we knew no more against the alderman's factor than that he consented to receive Jenny's secret letters, advanced money to madam that she might pay her card debts, and knew all the little doings of the maids, so that he could threaten them into obedience. We were to learn before long that his power in the house, the confidence of his master, and his position, were all used for our own undoing, and that if seven devils possessed the spirit of Thomas Marigold, seventy times seven held that of Christopher March.

When the valet found that all the old woman wanted was authentic information on the private life of his master, he was greatly relieved, and swore that nothing but truth should pass his lips. And then he revealed so sweet a picture of a virtuous life, that the tears came into my eyes, and thankfulness with praise into my heart, when first I heard it from my nurse. An end, now, to those fears and anxieties which, in spite of faith in my lord, would yet sometimes darken my soul.

But one day, shortly after her first discovery of the servant, Alice found out the chief cause of the alderman's prejudice against my suitor. It was caused, indeed, by no other than Thomas Marigold himself, at the instigation or the bidding of Chistopher March.

It was in the morning, and the door of the outer office was open. Alice, who was in the fore-yard, saw the groom walk in, a letter in his hand: he handed this with a reverence to Christopher, who in his turn carried it into the inner office, to his master.   Alice waited, hidden behind some bales, looked, and listened.

Then the alderman called his clerk.

"Christopher," he said with a groan, "this will not last long.   Make up to-day his lordship's book."

"Does he want more money, sir?"

"Ay, lad—more money—every day more money.   And for what?   It grieves me sore that so well-spoken and so frank a gentleman should be so ready to protest the thing which is not.   Let me write to him."

Christopher left him and came back to the outer office, leaving the door open.

"Well, honest Thomas," he said, speaking loud, "how doth the noble lord, your master, this morning?"

"Bad, sir," said Thomas, shaking his honest shock of yellow hair.

"Speak up, you fool you," whispered Christopher.   Then, loud again: "I am sorry, Thomas, to hear it."

"Drunk again last night, sir," the man went on, in louder key, "and at the gaming-table till three this morning.   Such a life! 'twould kill an ox."

"'Tis pity," Christopher said, glancing at the door of the counting-house, where his worship was listening to the talk, pen in hand.   "Pity.   Tell me, good man, couldst thou not, respectfully, put in a word of advice?"

"Nay, sir," said Thomas; "I am but a poor servant, with my character to keep."

"But you might try.   Is his temper quick?   Louder, this time."

"As for his temper," Thomas lifted up his voice and laughed, "'tis a word, and an oath, and a blow.   One poor fellow, as honest and sober a creature as walks, his lordship disabled by breaking three ribs, so that he now goes with short breath, and is nothing but a stable help or does odd jobs, and lives on cabbage-stalks."

Christopher groaned.

"A spendthrift, a gamester, a brawler, and striker—what a character is this for a Christian man!"

Just then the alderman came out with the money in a little bag of brown sackcloth.

"Be careful, good Thomas," he said. "There is the money, and here is a note for his lordship. Be careful; rogues are abroad. But yesterday se'nnight an honest clerk carrying two hundred pounds to a goldsmith in Lombard Street was tripped up, so that he fell and dropped the bag, which, when he recovered his feet, was gone."

"I will take care, sir," said Thomas. So he made a leg and came away. But outside the house he found Nurse Alice.

"So," she said, "I shall, after all, have to make an end of thee for a blacked-hearted and lying villain."

"Why, mother, what is the matter?"

"I have overheard all that you told Christopher March but now."

Thomas changed colour, but presently laughed and whistled.

"Phew!" he said. "Why, is that all? I have told you no lies, mistress. Be sure of that."

"Then why tell lies to him, for the alderman to hear?"

"That is a little business between me and the respectable Christopher, mother."

"You and Christopher? What has Christopher got to do with you?"

Now we all knew—nurse as well as the rest of us—that Christopher had been picked up out of the street; yet it did not occur to her that there could possibly be any acquaintance between the chief factor and this professed thief, so great is the power of fine clothes.

Thomas Marigold chewed his straw for a few moments before he answered.

"Suppose he wants the alderman to believe that Lord Eardesley is a lad of spirit and a gallant player, and suppose he pays me to say so; think you I should refuse his money?"

This seemed plausible, because the fellow never pretended to any kind of honesty. He would bear false witness, just as he would cheat, lie, and rob, for money.

"He a gamester!" continued Thomas, with a laugh of superiority. "A dull and tedious gentleman, who spends his time a reading. Now, mother, I don't tell you no lies. You go on a trusting of me, and never mind what I tell the alderman to please that Christopher. Set him up!"

"But tell no more lies about Lord Eardesley. Mind, Dick, that is my last word. If I find you out again I shall act at once."

"Between the pair of you," said Thomas, scratching his head, "a man's fairly sped. Look you, mistress, for a spell I must do what he wants." He jerked his thumb over his shoulder to indicate Christopher. "Curse him! You don't think I like him. Running another man's neck into the noose, and keeping his own out." This he said in a lower voice. "Only you wait a day or two, and I do no more service for Christopher March."

"A day or two." She thought very little mischief could be done in so short a time. "What service doth he require of you besides that of lying?"

"None," he replied quickly. "Oh, don't you go to think that I would do anything dishonest, mother. Come, now, a poor man may repent and turn over a new leaf."

"Ay," said Alice, "he may. But he seldom does. And you, Dick, are, I doubt not, a rogue in grain."

Nurse told me these things, and we talked them over, but without any present understanding how best to act.

Meantime, I received daily letters from my lord. In them he assured me of his passionate love, and exhorted me to patience and constancy. As regarded himself, we knew, he said, the worst of him; that he was of a verity exceeding poor, and possessed of little beside a barren mountain, a swamp, and a ruined castle in Wales which he could not sell; that he was not versed in those arts by which men become rich; that he had no party in politics; and that he could court no man's favour for place or pension. Indeed, he spoke of himself at all times with the true modesty which ever attends virtue.

Jenny knew that I was in communication with Lord

Eardesley, and delighted in the contemplation of an amour
which possessed the first element of intrigue—namely, that
it was carried on in opposition to the will of my guardian.
This reminded her of her own affair with Lysander, which
seemed to progress slowly.

"Why," she asked once, "if the man really wants me,
cannot he see my father and tell him so?"

"Because," I said, "that would be too commonplace a
plan, and your lover would fain, being a poet, nourish his
passion in rhymes a little longer—perhaps as long as your
patience will allow. Pray, Mistress Jenny," I asked, "do
you, too, reply with a madrigal, and send him a sigh in a
sonnet?"

Jenny blushed.

"Girls," she said, pursing up her pretty lips, "must not
be asked the little secrets of their courtship. My Lysander
is satisfied with the answers which I send him."

I was not, however, and it did not please me to be, taking
a part, however small, in an affair which was kept a secret
from the good old alderman and from madam his wife, whose
only fault was her love of cards. And the sequel proved that
I had reason to be uneasy.

We resolved, after Alice had spoken with the groom, to
let matters go on as they were for the time named by the
man. We should have gone to the alderman immediately
and told him all. But we knew little of the great web of
plots with which this Christopher March had surrounded us
all. We found it quite easy to understand that the man
should wish the character of Lord Eardesley to be represented
in the blackest light; that was common revenge upon me.
We also saw clearly that the alderman could easily be brought
to believe that Christopher as well as himself had been
deceived by the servant.

Now, two days after Thomas Marigold opened himself on
the subject of Christopher March, he came voluntarily and
frightened us out of our senses. First, he said that he wanted
the young lady to hear what he had to tell. When I was
fetched, he told us that he was going to leave the service of

his lordship in a day or two; that as he could do no more for us than he had done, he wished to tell us that Christopher March was a black-hearted villain, who would stick at nothing; that he hated Lord Eardesley, and would do him an ill turn if he could; that he would never rest till his lordship was ruined, and that, in the end, he would be the ruin of every one who had benefited him.

Then Alice asked him how it was that he knew Christopher so well.

The fellow replied that perhaps he would tell her when next they met. Meantime, he said, he had warned us, and his mind was clear. "While I was with his lordship," he added, "no harm should be done to him; but after I leave his service I cannot answer for him."

Then we began to look at each other and to tremble, and I lined the man's palm with five pieces of gold for his honesty.

"I almost wish," he said, putting up the money, "that I had come to your ladyship first. Anyhow, them lies about his lordship are soon set right."

So he went away, and we began to consider what was best to be done.

"The man will tell us," said Alice, "no more than he chooses. If he goes away to-morrow from his lordship's service, I shall not see him again. That is very certain. How can we prove anything against Christopher?"

Nothing could be proved, but it would be well to set Lord Eardesley on his guard and to inform him of what had passed. We decided, at length, that we would go ourselves to his lodgings on the morrow, and lay before him the whole matter.

So far, very little mischief had been done. The character of a man of honour and virtue had been maligned, but only in the ear of the alderman, who would easily be led back to his former confidence. This is what we said to each other. Alas! we little knew all the mischief that had been done, and was, even then, on the point of discovery.

While we talked, the alderman sent me an invitation to converse with him.

He was suffering from another attack of gout—an unfortunate thing in all respects, because it prevented him from getting about and making those inquiries into the private life of my lord as he had promised. He was now, being dependent on the reports of Christopher March and the man, in great mental trouble about Lord Eardesley.

"I do not disguise from myself, my ward," he said, "that an alliance with a nobleman of his exalted rank (albeit his estates are small) would have been gratifying to your lamented father, as it would, under other circumstances, to myself. Yet the profligacy of the young man is such that no hope can be entertained of his amendment before his final ruin overtakes him."

"You know of his profligacy," I replied, "only by report and rumour. Have you asked any of his friends about him?"

"His friends, child? I am a plain London citizen, and have no acquaintance with noblemen. Besides, they would be, doubtless, all of a tale. But I have clear proof. Not only hath his man confessed to Christopher March, in my hearing, that his master gambles, but to pay his losses he sends to me sometimes daily, sometimes thrice a week, for money. Very soon, sooner than his lordship thinks, there will be an end. Doth he hope, then, to send your hundred thousand pounds after his own hundreds? My dear, should I be an honest guardian did I counsel thee to marry a gamester?"

The good old man! It was the last time that I received any admonition from him at all, almost the last time that I ever saw him; because his troubles began almost on that very day—with my own, and Jenny's, and my lord's, and even my nurse's.

I confess I was staggered at first. I must needs believe in my lover's truth and fidelity. What has a girl to trust in if she cannot trust her lover? Yet that he should send nearly every day to the alderman for money, when he had so little left, and when his lodgings were so mean and ill-proportioned to his rank—why, what did that mean?

I went to my nurse and consulted with her. She, too, began to fear that the man might have played us false, and that the information which he gave to Christopher March was true.

"You must see him at once, my dear," she said. "There must be no time lost. You must see him somehow by himself, and speak to him, and ask him what it means. Let me consider."

I could not ask him to the house, because he had promised the alderman that he would not come without his permission. It would be best, on all accounts, to seek him secretly.

Then my nurse proposed a thing which, I own, I should have been afraid by myself to undertake.

It was our evening for cards. Alice advised me to make some excuse, while madam was entertaining and receiving her visitors, to slip out of the room. I was to choose a time when the tables were laid, and the ladies were in the first height and interest of the game. Thus I should not be missed. I was to run upstairs, where she would be in waiting for me with dominoes and hoods, in which she and I would take coach and go ourselves in search of his lordship. In case of necessity, I was to take Jenny into confidence.

I confess my heart beat when I thought of this adventure. For a young girl to go out alone, or protected only by an old nurse, was a perilous thing, indeed.

Still, we were not going into the country, or as far as the fields of Knightsbridge, and we were not going to be out late at night. And then there was the necessity of seeing my lord as soon as possible. In fine, I consented to go. Glad am I now and thankful for a resolution which, if anything could have been, was an inspiration from Heaven, and served to save, out of the general wreck, at least one pair of happy lovers.

This, then, was decided. Nurse went away to buy the masks and hoods. I stayed at home and went on with my usual work.

At three we dined as usual, the alderman being laid up, as I have said, with gout.

At four we all walked into the City to Cheapside, where we bought some ribbons and stuffs, and presently returned; we two girls being both silent and depressed, but neither noticing, till later on, the trouble of the other. At six o'clock some visitors called, and we had a dish of tea. The time seemed long before our guests arrived and the cards were laid out. I excused myself from playing, and after they were all sat down, and madam's attention was entirely occupied with the game, I slipped out of the room, and found my nurse waiting for me with the masks and the hoods. I did not tell Jenny anything, and, indeed, thought nothing about her at all.

The hood was so long that it hid the whole of my dress and covered my head, while the mask, made of black silk, covered and concealed my face, except the eyes. It was impossible for any one to recognise me. Alice was attired in exactly the same fashion; and, thus disguised, we slipped down the stairs and were out of the door without any one having the least suspicion of my absence.

It was just striking half-past eight. We took a coach on Tower Hill, and ordered the driver to proceed to Bury Street, where Lord Eardesley had lodgings. We proposed driving to the very door of the house, so as to encounter as little risk as possible from fellows who think it no shame to address a lady who may be unprotected.

The streets were full, and the progress of the coach was slow. In Fleet Street the driver got down to fight a drayman who refused to make way or to go on. The battle lasted for ten minutes, while we trembled within. The drayman defeated, his horses were drawn out of the way, and we went on. It was a rainy evening, and dark, though in the middle of summer. There was a high wind, and I remember how, to the noise and fury of the combatants and their friends, was added the dreadful shrieking and groaning of the great signs which swung over our heads. Surely shopkeepers might find a more convenient method of advertising their goods than by hanging out a sign which is so heavy that it threatens to drag down the front of the house and so noisy that it keeps one awake at night, and so surrounded by the other great signs that passers-by cannot see it.

When we got through Temple Bar we made better way, and after a little further delay at Charing Cross, we finally arrived safely at Bury Street.

But his lordship was abroad, nor did the maid know with any certainty when he would return.   We sent for his servant.

When Thomas saw us, he became suddenly pale.

"Man!" cried nurse angrily.   "What ails him?   One would think he had never set eyes on us before."

He recovered, but showed such hesitation in his manner as made me sure that there was something wrong.

"You would see my lord?" he said.   "His lordship is abroad this evening."

"Where can you find him, Thomas?" I asked.   "Our business with him is urgent."

He hesitated again.

"I know where he is," he replied at last.   "He went to the Royal Chocolate House, in St. James's Street, intending to go afterwards to the Theatre in Lincoln's Inn Fields. But he met some friends, who have taken him instead to Covent Garden, to the house kept by one Dunton."

"What is the house kept for?" I asked.   "And can ladies get in?"

"It is kept for music, dancing, supper, and gambling. Ladies can go in if they have the pass-word."

"But how can we get the pass-word?   Can we not send for my lord?"

Thomas shook his head.   Then he considered, and presently said that he might be able to get us the pass-word, because the porter was a friend of his.   He also assured us that though the company was not entirely what I might wish, we need be under no apprehensions of ill-usage or insult; and that ladies, especially court ladies, often put on a hood and mask, and so disguised, went to this house, or to Cupid's Gardens, or the Folly on the Thames, for a frolic—where they could see without being seen, and watch their lovers or their husbands.

Truly, it seemed a chance. If my lord was what this creature had told his confederate, now was the time to find him out; if not, then we had proof to the contrary in our own hands.

So, with Thomas on the box beside the coachman, we drove to Covent Garden—oh! the crowded, dirty place, with its pile of cabbage-stalks!—and presently stopped at a door where there was no light. We got down and told the coachman to wait for half an hour. Then Thomas knocked gently, and the door was opened by one of the biggest and most ferocious-looking fellows I ever saw. After a little parley, he let us in, and called up the stairs, whereupon another tall bully appeared, bearing a light.

"This way, ladies," he said. "Up the stairs. Have no fear. There is goodly company here to-night."

There was, indeed, a goodly company. Many ladies were present, all of them, like ourselves, with hoods and masks; some alone, but mostly in pairs. They walked about the rooms, which were *en suite*, and all brilliantly lit with wax candles, talking incessantly to the men, some of whom they addressed by name. The men seemed to consist almost of the very rich class, so splendid were their laced ruffles and their coats; and upon their faces there was mostly that assured look which one never finds except among gentlemen whose position and rank cannot be questioned.

In the first room there was a band of music, which was playing a minuet as we entered. Four couples were dancing. I looked hurriedly to see if my lord was among them, but he was not. It was a foolish girl's jealousy. Why should he not dance, if the fancy took him? We passed on, my nurse and I, while many a curious look was turned upon us, to the next room. Here there was supper laid out, with bottles of Port, Malmsey, and Bordeaux in plenty, apparently free for all comers. But no one as yet was eating or drinking.

Then we came to the third room, where there were tables set with cards and counters, and parties were sitting at them playing ombre and quadrille, just as madam at home, at that same time, was playing with her friends. Lastly, there was the fourth room. And this was crowded. For here they were gambling indeed. At a table sat one who held the bank; he played against all; a pile of gold was before him; a man stood on either side of him raking in the money and paying it out; round the table were clustered a group of players, men and women. Several of the women had discarded their masks and thrown back their hoods; one or two were young and pretty, most of them were old or middle-aged; but all alike, men and women, had stamped upon their faces the same eager look—that of the gambler. It is anxious, it is expectant, it is hopeful, yet it is despairing, because at heart there is no gamester but knows that in the end ruin awaits him.

I looked hurriedly round the tables. Lord Eardesley was not playing at any. But I saw him presently standing beside one of the doors, in company with a gentleman, not young, whose star and ribbon, as well as his splendid apparel, spoke his high rank.

I moved nearer to him and listened. He looked handsome and noble, and there was no trace in his clear eyes and lofty brow of the profligacy, drink, and gambling with which my guardian charged him.

"Come," said his companion. "Shall we, for half an hour, try fortune?"

But Lord Eardesley shook his head.

"I think," he said, "that my House has had enough of the green table. You know that I never play."

His friend ceased to press him, and joined the throng at the table.

Lord Eardesley watched the play a little, and then, as if it had little interest for him, he began to walk through the rooms.

I would have followed him, but Alice touched my arm and pointed to another figure at the table.

Heavens! It was Christopher March. He was attired in a brave show of scarlet and silk, with a sword at his side, a wig fully equal to any other in the room, and laced ruffles very fine indeed. And he was gaming with a sort of madness. I watched him lose time after time, yet he never ceased to play; his eyes were lit with a fire of anxiety; his cheek was flushed; his hands trembled; he played on with a sort of rapture. Once he turned round suddenly and saw Lord Eardesley. Then he started and half sprang from his seat; but the voice of the banker called him back, and he turned round again, preferring play to revenge.

"What do you make of this, Alice?" I asked.

"This will be something new to tell the alderman," she said. "Do not let his lordship go before you can speak with him."

One moment I waited, because I saw another familiar face. There sat Jenny's Lysander.

He was winning. His sharp and mean little features were full of satisfaction as he raked in the money. He seemed, too, to be winning a great deal.

"Jenny," I thought, "this will be something new for you. Lysander gambles."

Then I hastened after Lord Eardesley. The black look of hatred which shot out of Christopher's eyes when they turned upon his enemy, as he, perhaps, thought him, warned me that the man Thomas had spoken the truth, and that Christopher would do him a hurt if he could. I did not want to see my Lord mixed up in a vulgar brawl at a common gambling-house, got up by a City clerk.

Alice it was who accosted him.

"My lord," she said, in a low voice, "this is not a wholesome air for you. Better leave it."

He looked surprised. He did not recognise her voice.

"Why not wholesome, fair incognita?"

"Because, first, Mistress Carellis would not like it."

"Come with me," she said, "and I will show you—what it will please your lordship to see."

I had descended the stairs, and was waiting. We went

out, all three together. I got into the carriage and took off my mask.

"Nelly!" he cried, springing into the coach after me. "My Nelly! Here!"

"It is for your sake," I said. "There is mischief brewing against you."

"What mischief?"

"First tell me—nay, my lord, leave my hands alone. This is serious. Tell me why it is that you send your servant to the alderman thrice a week for money?"

He stared at this.

"Thrice a week! Nelly, I have not asked the alderman for money these three months."

This was a pretty discovery of villany. Then, who had forged the letters and the drafts?

The man who brought them?

Alice said he could not read. We looked at each other, and I whispered, "Christopher March."

On the way back, my lord sitting beside me, I told him how we had detected his servant giving false information at the suborning of Christopher March; how the man had warned us against him; and how the alderman was grieved at paying those daily drafts.

"As for the drafts," said my lord, "there has been some grievous forgery. I will call on the alderman to-morrow. As for the factor, Christopher March, why does he seek my injury?

"Because—oh, my lord! indeed, I gave him no encouragement—because he dared to fall in love with—a person whom you have thought worthy of your own love."

The drivers cursed and swore at each other; the rain fell; the sign-boards groaned; the people crowded and pressed in the narrow ways; the link-boys ran by shouting.

I heeded not the noise or crowd; for I had taken my love away from the place where his enemy might harm him, and he was sitting beside me, and I was ready to clear his character.

We parted at the alderman's door. The adventure had

taken altogether about two hours; and, on my return to the
party, I discovered that, as I had hoped, my absence had not
been remarked.   Only two hours, and yet how much had
happened!   But who could tell that my cheek was glowing
with my lover's kiss, and my eyes were bright with the fruition of hope deferred?   The ladies were playing as eagerly
as the company I had left at Dunton's house in Covent
Garden.

I was greatly excited and out of myself, as they say, by
what had happened.   Yet I could not but observe that Jenny
had red eyes, as if she had been crying.   So I sat down
beside her and took her hand in mine.

"What is it, Jenny, my dear?" I asked.

She looked at me sorrowfully, and her eyes filled with tears
again.   Then she turned away her head and did not answer.

After our guests departed, Jenny ran away quickly, so that
her mother might not notice her eyes.   But madam was too
full of the various fortunes of the evening to heed her, and
she kept me waiting half an hour while she fought the battles
over again.

CHAPTER VI.

A DAY OF FATE.

THE morrow was the date of fate.   Could one read the
future, each day would be a day of fate, full of issues
important and eventful.   But just as we cannot foresee the
future, so we forget the lesser links in the chains of the past.
Methinks he who would prophesy must first be able to remember.

In the morning Alice began to talk about the forged drafts.
She said that considering everything, how Christopher March
was a gambler, how he hated my lord, and how he knew, or
had some power over, Thomas Marigold, she could have no
doubt that he, and none but he, was the forger.   Indeed, who
else could it be?   But the difficulty would be to bring it
home to him and prove it.

My lord was to call upon the alderman at twelve. A little before noon I went to the counting - house and found my guardian sitting, as usual, before books and papers, but with his foot still bandaged. His gout had not left him.

"My dear," he said kindly, "I am always glad to see you here. Sit down and let us talk. Nay, the papers can wait. Did you have a merry party last night?"

"Why, truly, sir," I replied, "I do not play at cards. But the ladies seemed to enjoy their game."

"Ay," he said, with a cloud over his face. "Those who won doubtless enjoyed their game. Do not play cards, girl. Never play cards. You have an example in "—I thought he was going to say, "my own wife," but he did not—"in my Lord Eardesley."

"It is of him that I would speak with you this morning, sir," I said.

"Nay, Elinor. There lacks but a little while, a twelve-month or so, of the time when you will pass out of your minority. Let us leave your spendthrift lord till then. I have said my say and cannot alter it."

"Nevertheless, sir," I said, laughing, for I could very well afford to be merry now; "nevertheless, I prophesy that you will alter your say before another half-hour is over."

"Say you so, lass? Why, then, let us wait. Where lies the wind now?"

"Lord Eardesley is coming to see you, sir, at twelve of the clock. You will not refuse to see him?"

"Not if he brings with him anything beyond his word."

"Alas! sir. Can you not trust the word of a noble-man?"

The alderman shook his head but said nothing. And just then, as the clocks began to strike twelve, and there arose the mighty clamour which betokens the dinner-hour of all the craftsmen, lightermen, dock labourers, boatmen, porters, and carters who throng about Tower Hill, Christopher March opened the door and announced the arrival of his lordship. I snatched a glance at Christopher's face; nothing that

I

would recall the eager, frantic gambler of last night; a calm, sober air, such as befits an honest factor with a conscience at ease. Yet I thought his cheek was pale and his eyes anxious.

"I hope," said my lord, "that all is well with my old friend."

"No," replied the alderman; "all is ill. I doubt if we shall ever make things well again between your lordship and myself. Yet my ward will have it that you have an important communication to make."

"Mr. Alderman," Lord Eardesley said, "I have many things to say. But first, because Mistress Elinor Carellis has told me a thing which surprised me greatly; let me know when last you honoured any draft of mine."

"Surely," said the alderman, "yesterday morning, and the day before, and twice last week, and I think three times the week before last—— "

"Stop! The last draft I sent to you for cash was more than two months ago."

"What!" cried the alderman. "Say that again."

"I repeat that the last time I drew upon you for money was more than two months ago."

"Then there has been villany. Elinor, go call Christopher March. Christopher," he cried, in quick and peremptory tones, "my lord's book, and quickly; and all his latest drafts, his drafts of the last six months. Quick, I say."

The clerk obeyed, and brought the books, standing beside his master as if ready to answer questions. But his hands trembled and his eyes were dropped.

The alderman seemed changed suddenly. He, the most gentle of men, was now rough, quick, and even rude.

"Now, my lord," he said, snatching the drafts from Christopher's hands. "We shall see. Your man brought the drafts and received the money. Where is he?"

"Gone. He went away without notice, last night."

"That is suspicious. Could he write?"

"No. He was a common country lad, out of Gloucestershire," he said.

"Well, then, here are the drafts, which we duly honoured and cashed. Look at them all, my lord."

Lord Eardesley looked them through. The earlier ones he laid aside. Those dated during the last eight weeks he put together in a separate pile.

"There," he said, "are the forged drafts."

They represented the sum of two thousand and fifty pounds, so that the moneys belonging to Lord Eardesley still in the alderman's hands now amounted to no more than three hundred pounds and some odd shillings.

"I wonder," said my lord, showing one to the alderman, "that so clumsy a cheat was not suspected."

"Why, indeed," the alderman was looking at the paper, "it is not like your lordship's writing. Christopher, you received and opened the letters. Had you no suspicion?"

"I looked at the signature, sir," replied the clerk; "and if you will look at that carefully, I think you will agree with me that it is so like his lordship's writing as to deceive any one."

"Let me look," I cried. "My lord, I have certain letters of yours by me which no one, I think, will deny to be your own." In fact there were then lying in my bosom a collection of the sweetest letters ever received by love-sick maid. I pulled them forth, and, taking one, opened it and laid it beside the draft. "There, my guardian," I said, "compare the two."

There was no comparison possible, because in the forged draft the body of the document was not in the least like Lord Eardesley's handwriting, and the signature alone had been imitated, but this so clumsily, that even the slightest acquaintance with his hand should have been enough to detect the forgery.

"Why," said the alderman, "this is palpable. This is so gross a forgery that even——Christopher March, hast thou taken leave of thy senses?"

"With submission, sir," said Christopher, speaking slowly and steadily, "am I to blame? I am imperfectly acquainted with my lord's hand; I received the letters from his servant; I opened them to save you trouble——"

"Ay, ay," said the merchant. "You did your best, Christopher, no doubt.   The house has been robbed, not you, my lord.   The house must bear this loss."

"Surely, my kind old friend," Lord Eardesley went on, "you might have asked yourself for what purpose I wanted these constant supplies, for what extravagances and follies they were required."

"Alas! I knew too well.   They were wanted, I thought, to repair your losses at the gaming-table."

Then I spoke.

"The alderman has been greatly deceived, Geoffrey, in this as in other things.   I know that your servant, Thomas Marigold, suborned by a person who was also, I believe, the forger of these drafts"—here I glanced at Christopher, and his eyes, full of a fearful curiosity, met mine for a moment before they fell again—"reported in the alderman's hearing, day after day, tales of drunkenness, gambling, and other wickednesses such as gentlemen practice who forget their Christian profession.   And these stories he invented to suit the purpose of this other man with whom he shared the proceeds of the crime."

"We seem to be surrounded by villains," said the alderman.   "Speak, Christopher: what do you know?"

"Nothing, sir.   I suspected nothing.   It is true that the man told me in your hearing the stories of his lordship's alleged profligacy."

"He did.   But those other reports.   Why, Christopher, 'twas you yourself brought them."

Lord Eardesley drew himself up, and turned towards the clerk, who was trying his utmost to preserve an appearance of composure.

"You—you spread reports about me?   Pray, Master Clerk, what business have you with me?"

"None, my lord.   Nor am I a carrier of tales.   I but answered a question of the alderman's and told him what had been said at a coffee-house."

Then my lord recollected what I had told him, that it was none other than Christopher March himself who had suborned his man, and was proposing to do himself some harm.

"Well," he said, turning it off for the time, "there will be something to be said another time between you and me, Master March."

"Mr. Alderman," I struck in, fearful that the villain should be too soon accused of the crime, "let us address ourselves to the forgery. The servant was but the tool. We want to find the instigator and principal." The papers were lying close to the hand of the clerk. I snatched them up. "We must find the man who wrote the drafts; it matters little who presented them. I venture to advise that the alderman initials every one of them, and that my lord keeps them and carries them about. It will not be difficult," I said this with an air of confidence, "to find out the man who wrote them."

"You are right, child," said the alderman. "I will not keep these papers; Lord Eardesley shall have them, with my name to each. My lord, I confess to you that my opinion was formed by the bad reports brought to me by Christopher March, and by the tales I heard your servant tell, and by the rapidity with which your fortune was wasting away."

"Nay," said Geoffrey; "surely you should have known me better, who have known me so long. Do I look like a drunkard? Hath my face the open and manifest signs, legible to all the world, which belong to the man who drinks much wine? Believe me, sir, on the honour of a peer, that I have never in my life touched cards or played with dice."

"I believe you," said the alderman, holding out his hand.

"If," interrupted Christopher, in a strange strident voice, "if Mistress Elinor thinks it easy to find the forger, she would perhaps kindly advise us which way to begin, for I confess I am at fault."

"You have to find out, Christopher March, in the first place, a man who thinks he has an object to gain in robbing or inflicting other injury on Lord Eardesley; he must, next, be one who had some previous friendship with the servant;

he must be a man in want of money for his own secret vices; he must be wicked enough to conceive and bold enough to carry out so vile a plot. Indeed, I could lay my hand on such a man."

He lifted his face, and tried to meet my gaze, but he could not.

"All this helps nothing," he said.

"Well, Christopher," said the alderman. "Go now, and think, or consult a lawyer—leave me with his lordship."

Christopher took his departure. I longed to tell the alderman what we knew, where we had seen his clerk, and what we suspected; but I refrained. I thought the next day would do as well. Besides, my lord turned the talk away.

"Let us leave the forgeries awhile," he said. "Mr Alderman, I have to speak of other things. Again I have the honour to ask your consent to marry your ward. You have seen that the worst accusations are false. Believe that the others are as unfounded and as slanderous."

"I cannot choose," said the alderman, "but believe. My lord, as the guardian of Mistress Elinor, I confide her to your care and protection."

He sat upright in his chair, and cleared his voice. We knew what was coming. On any occasion of ceremony and importance, a London citizen loves to deliver an appropriate discourse. It is a goodly custom and laudable, inasmuch as it enables every man to magnify his own office and dignity. Now, the best safeguard against vice is, methinks, respect of oneself.

"My Lord Eardesley," he began, "and Elinor Carellis, my ward. The condition of matrimony (wherein the bond of love should be, from each to either, equal and lasting; and wherein the one should be well assured of the other's virtue and goodness) hath been specially designed by Heaven for the solace and happiness of the human race. Wherefore, if——"

Here he was interrupted by an admonition in the great toe, which demanded all his attention. He stopped, turned purple and even black in the cheeks, and presently thundered forth a volley of oaths, which seemed to linger about the corners of the room, and echoed from the walls, so that it was like a very tempest. When he recovered, the thread of his discourse was lost, and he could only murmur, lying back on his pillows, exhausted with his efforts: "Take her, my lord, and make her happy." Then he whispered, with the least little nod of his head in the direction of the door: "And never let her play cards."

Thus we were betrothed.

Alas! This day, which should have been the first of many happy days, proved the beginning of our calamities.

We left the alderman, and sought madam, to whom I presented my lord as my accepted lover. The good lady, who, in all but her passion for cards, was a most kind and unselfish woman, rejoiced with us, and wished us happiness, and then, by means of a pack of cards, told us our fortunes. The most important part of it was, that after surmounting certain obstacles and checks placed in our way by a dark man, we should undertake a long voyage, and meet with great prosperity ever after.

It is, indeed, strange how the chance disposition of foolish cards enables some to read the future. The dark man could be none other than Christopher. We had, immediately after our betrothal, such checks and hindrances as fall to the lot of few; we did make a long voyage; and we have enjoyed prosperity and increase. Yet it is against the divine ordinance to inquire of any oracle, and I cannot but think the punishment of witches in New England, of which so much has been said, was necessary, albeit severe.

Then Jenny came downstairs, and we had to tell her. She was very pale, and had dark rims round her eyes, with traces of tears. She fell on my neck and kissed me, and burst out crying.

"Why, Jenny, foolish child," I said; "why do you cry?"

"O Nelly! I cry because I am glad for you and sorry for myself. Nelly, Nelly, I am a wretch."

I could not understand, but it was not the time to press her, and nothing would serve my lord but that we should all drive to his lodgings, there to dine and afterwards to get such amusements as the town at that season afforded. Jenny excused herself, saying that she had a headache, and could not go. We left her at home, therefore, and took a coach—madam, my lord, and I. On the way we stopped at a goldsmith's, where Geoffrey presented me with a beautiful emerald ring, and so to his lodgings in Bury Street.

Our entertainment was simple, the dinner being sent over from a tavern. Madam was in high spirits, and talked and laughed. I was glad of this, because my heart was too full for talk. After dinner we walked in the park, which was crowded with a collection of ladies of quality, beaux, gallants, and courtiers, with ragamuffins, pickpockets, girls selling flowers, women with curds-and-whey, soldiers, grave clergymen, solemn physicians, members of Parliament, beggars, and common thieves. Everybody looked at us as we passed along with a stream of people. I was afraid that there was something wrong with my dress, for, indeed, though I had been in London so long, I was still somewhat distrustful when we went abroad. But Geoffrey said they stared at my face and figure, not at my dress. Many other pleasant things he said that day, which I pass over. After the promenade in the park, which I should have liked better had I been alone with him, we went back to his lodgings. Here a dish of tea was waiting for us, and after tea we went to the theatre in the Haymarket. The play was—but I forget play, actors, and everything. I sat in a dream, thinking of what had happened; wondering if it were true, and fearing that I did not possess attractions enough to fix the affections of so handsome, gallant, and noble a lover as he who sat by my side.

At last it ended, and we were on our way home. The streets were crowded with people—link-boys ran up and down; the coaches rumbled along the way; we passed out of the broad Strand into narrow Fleet Street, and in a few minutes were set down in Tower Hill, at the door of the alderman's house. My lord paid the man, who drove off, and we stood at our door waiting for it to be opened. It was about half-past eleven, or a little before midnight; the sky was clear, and there was no darkness—only twilight.

At that hour Tower Hill is comparatively deserted; there was no one in the street. Yet in the darkness of a penthouse higher up the Hill I saw the forms of two men lurking, and a thought of uneasiness crossed my heart. But only for a moment.

Madam went in as the door was opened; we stood outside, and my lord took my hand and held it.

"Will my Nelly, my Princess of Virginia, always trust her love?" he whispered.

"Always and always," I replied. "Oh, who am I, I ask again and again, that you should love me so?"

"You are the dearest girl in all the world," he said, kissing my hands. "You are my own sweet Nelly."

He drew me towards him by both my hands and kissed my lips. Then he tore himself away and left me. The maid —I hoped she had not seen that lover-like farewell—held the door for me. I stepped forward; then, moved by the impulse of love, I turned my head to catch a last glimpse of my betrothed. He was striding with manly step over the stones. When he was just at the turning which led from Tower Hill, I saw the two men whose figures I had discerned beneath the penthouse rush out upon him, and I saw the gleam of steel in their hands. I rushed down the steps and along the road, crying, "Geoffrey, Geoffrey! Help, help! They will murder him!"

It was my voice, thank God for ever, which saved his life, else he had been stabbed in the back. He turned, saw his assailants, and in a moment drew his sword and was on guard. As I still ran and cried I saw his sword flashing in the moonlight, and one man fell; but his foot slipped as I reached him. I threw myself before him, and while my arms were thrown about his neck, the thrust which would have pierced him to the heart pierced me instead.

That moment will live for ever in my memory. As the cruel cold steel ran through me I saw that the wounded man, whose mask had fallen off, was Thomas Marigold; and the other, my murderer, whom I knew, although he was masked, by his figure, his dress, his voice—as he cried out on seeing me—was none other than Christopher March. He fled at once, and was lost in the dark and winding lanes of the city.

They carried me home, Geoffrey and the maid, and sent for a surgeon. The alderman and madam wept and cried over me. Alice had me carried to my own bed, and cut away my dress—that bravery of silver gauze and crimson satin and lace in which I had been so fine all day—and tried to staunch the blood, while my lord bathed my face and whispered prayers until the surgeon came and turned him out.

He was a pompous man in an immense wig. After he had probed the wound and applied some lint, and instructed the nurse in other matters, he descended and found the whole household, servants, and all, waiting to hear his judgment.

"She will live," he said, speaking like an oracle, "through the night, I doubt not. In the morning inflammation will set in and she will die."

They all burst into tears and lamentations.

"Where is Jenny?" cried madam. "Go call her, one of you. Let her come down and weep with us."

"Nay," said the alderman; "what use? Let her sleep on. As for my lord and me, we will wait with this learned gentleman. Do you all go to bed."

But no one went to bed that night.

Presently there was a knocking at the door. It was a pair of constables bringing with them a wounded man.

"He will be brought here, sir," they explained to the alderman. "We know not if your worship knows him."

"Know him!" cried Lord Eardesley, "why it is my own man Thomas. You, too, among the murderers?"

"Yes, my lord," said the man, whose face was pale with death. "I'd rather help you to die than see myself hung. There was all them forgeries in your pocket."

"Who was the forger?" asked his master.

The fellow was silent.

"Man!" said the alderman, "you are on the brink of eternity. Let it be reckoned as proof of a death-bed repentance that you give up the name of the forger."

Thomas laughed. At the point of death he laughed. But it was laughter without merriment.

"Honour among thieves," he said. "Let me see the woman, Mistress Carellis's nurse. I want to speak with her."

She would not leave my bed. But the doctor promised that if a change took place she should be called. And then she went slowly downstairs.

"Alas!" she cried, "that you should be a murderer, and that you should murder the innocent young lady."

"I did not," he said. "I tried to kill my lord, to save my own neck. And he hath killed me. So am I sped."

"And the other man! Who was he?"

"Tell me first," he said, "who you are, and how you know me for Canvas Dick?"

She bent over him and whispered—

"I was once, long ago, a woman of your gang. I was Kate Collyer!"

"Ay!" he murmured, his face feebly lighting up. "I remember you now, Kate Collyer!"

"And who was the other murderer?" she repeated.

"He was the forger, of course; he was the villain who pushed me on; he threatened to betray me; he was the man who took all the money; he spent it where he spent his master's money—in the gaming-house, and lost it there. He has boasted to me that he has ruined you all—he is——

"Christopher March?" asked my nurse.

"You've guessed it, Kate. But you needn't be too proud of it, now you do know it, although he is your own son."

"My son! Christopher March my son!"

"'Tis true, Kate. Little Jack Collyer that was; the cleverest and safest young thief that ever cracked a crib, even before you was lagged, and cleverer since. Your son, Kate. Lift up my head." His voice sank. "I've cheated Tyburn tree. Yes, I never—could—abide—the—thought —of that—that cart—and that—dance upon nothing."

His head fell back, and he was dead. Alice took no heed; her hands were clenched, and she murmured—

"The hand of God is heavy upon me. My son! my son!"

CHAPTER VII.

BETWEEN LIFE AND DEATH.

THIS, indeed, was a most dreadful discovery. Yet it was no time for poor Alice to sit and weep, or to think about her son. She had that gift, denied to men, and granted only to women, which enables them to repress and drive back for the time one grief so that it shall not hinder the discharge of the present duty. Therefore my nurse forced herself to leave the matter for the time, and, after calling to the constables to remove the dead man, she mounted the stairs and returned to the chamber where I lay unconscious and under the surgeon's hands.

The wound was right through the body from the back under the left shoulder, and when I recovered from the swoon I began to feel such tortures of pain as I did not believe were possible for the body to endure and yet to live. For the passage made by the sword was like a rod of red-hot iron.

All that night I lay and suffered, while Alice watched by the bedside, and my lord, the alderman, and madam remained below waiting for news. The news which the surgeon brought from time to time was the worst possible. "Inflammation," he said, "has set in, with violent pain. It should be followed by fever: that will produce delirium: death will follow."

At break of day, when I was a little quieter, Alice went to the still-room and came back bearing a basket full of simples. I was not yet light-headed, and I knew that she was going to take me out of the doctor's hands and nurse me herself with the herbs in which all countrywomen put their trust. She turned the contents of the basket upon the table.

"Patience, my dear, patience. Oh! patience for a little while, my pretty lamb. Here is St. John's wort and here is knapweed to lay in the open wound, and plaintains to close it up, and bloodwort if the knapweed fails: and here is self-heal, but I doubt if it is strong enough; and Comfrey, which never fails; and strong kiss-me-quick. Courage, my pretty. We have here what is better than all the 'pothecaries' shops."

Then I found that the pain was growing greater than I could bear, and I called upon my nurse to tear off the bandage and let me die. And then some good angel came to my bedside and helped me up and carried me away—far—far away—to sweet Virginia.

I was back in the old plantation. It was Sunday morning, and we were all going to church—my father, my mother, my nurse, and I, the convicts standing in a line to let his honour pass: the negroes chattering and grinning, who understood, poor souls! little enough of the service they were going to hear, but yet could sing the psalms, having sweet voices, and ears which caught the tune correctly; and in the pine-wood pulpit was our convict-chaplain, proclaiming aloud that we—meaning everybody outside his honour's pew— were all miserable sinners.

It was many days before my reason came back to me, and then I was weak and helpless indeed; though my nurse multiplied her infusions of galangale for internal strength, and tea of thyme for headache, and snakeweed to keep me safe from infection, which is fatal to poor creatures just recovering from illness. Would I could describe the joy and thankfulness which I felt when, on coming to my senses, I found my lover by my bedside, and saw by his eyes that he had been weeping for me.

No one else was in the room. He thought I was sleeping.

When he saw that my eyes were open he thought I was still in my lightheadedness, about to prattle of all things that have no sense. First of all, I did not understand things, though I knew him, and wondered where I was and how I came to be lying there, and he to be in my room. Then it all came back to me little by little, the attack upon my lover and my wound.

"Geoffrey," I whispered, "are you watching over me?"

He was like one who knows not what to say when he found that I was indeed in my right mind. But he had sense to command himself, and bade me, while he tenderly kissed my lips, keep silence and be quiet. Then he thanked God solemnly, for my lord was never one of those men who think they honour themselves and gain credit among their fellows by dishonouring their Creator. And then he left me, and in a moment my nurse came back, and seeing that I was in my senses again, and that the fever had left me—hands and brow being cool and moist—she, too, burst into a cry for thankfulness, and fell to kissing my hands and cheeks. Oh, poor woman! Because, now that my trouble was over, her own was to begin. I slept well that night, and next morning was stronger and able to take broth and other things which my nurse got for me. Presently I remembered Jenny, and asked that she might be brought to see me.

Then Alice changed colour and pretended not to hear; and when I repeated my question she said—

"Oh! Mistress Jenny is not at home. She has gone abroad on a visit."

With that I was fain to be content, although I saw that something had happened, and besides being still weak and faint, was glad to forego further questions and go to sleep again.

Next day, I asked after madam, and again my nurse seemed confused, and put me off.

This set me wondering. It was strange, indeed, that neither Jenny nor her mother came to see me, and no message from the alderman. Yet a week passed and it was not till I was quite well enough to hear any kind of news however bad, that my lord entreated my permission for him to tell me things which, he said, gravely and grievously, affected both himself and me.

He was, indeed, very grave, and told me the story little by little, fearful lest too many dreadful events at the same time might bring back my illness. Nor was it till many days afterwards that I was able to put everything together, and to understand it all.

When the alderman, one of the most benevolent and charitable citizens of London, received the boy whom he found starving with hunger and cold (as seemed from his pretending) on his doorstep, he prepared for himself, even by this most Christian act, his own absolute and hopeless ruin. The boy, as I have said, rapidly received instruction, and proved himself a lad of astonishing quick parts, with great industry, sober habits, and respectful, obedient behaviour. The alderman, who made haste to put the boy into his counting-house, thought he had never before been blessed with a servant more honest, more willing, and more capable; therefore, he advanced him rapidly; and when his own confidential clerk and chief factor died, he put the young man, then about twenty-five years of age, into his place.

Christopher March had all the keys, knew of all the securities, bills, drafts, mortgages, ventures, debts, and profit of the house; he opened the letters, received the customers, and carried on the correspondence. So blind, in short, did the alderman become, that he ceased, for the most part, to carry on his business himself, and was generally content with receiving his clerk's report.

The house held the private fortunes of many gentlemen of Virginia, besides that of my late father; it also held in trust the fortune of the Lord Eardesley, as we have seen, and of many widows, orphans, and poor pensioners, who had nothing to depend upon but the integrity of the alderman. Of that, indeed, there was never any doubt. The business of the house, again, was large, and the income of the alderman substantial. I know not what was the amount of his savings, but I have been well assured that there were few merchants even in the great and prosperous city of London who surpassed him in fortune. His condition would have been more splendid, but for the thousand charitable actions which he continually practised. However, there was a capital stock in the alderman's hands, including that accumulated by his own thrift, the principal employed in his business, and the moneys entrusted to him, amounting to near a quarter of a million of money.

There was one thing that Christopher March could not do. He might persuade his master to ventures; he might deceive him with false reports; but he could never persuade him to have aught to do with South Sea Stock, nor could he make him consent to sign papers without first learning and approving their contents. Therefore, as Geoffrey told me, every one of the receipts, agreements, and papers of advance, with regard to South Sea Stock, in the counting - house were forgeries. Nor could there be any reasonable doubt as to the forgeries in the sale and transfer of mortgages and securities.

When the books of the house were placed in the hands of accountants skilled in examining and detecting frauds, it was discovered that, not only were these robberies of many years' standing, with the falsifying of accounts, and the forgery of authority given under the alderman's own hand, but that during the excitement of the late few months, Christopher March under cover of his forgeries had been trading, day after day, in South Sea Stock, in bubble companies, and in any kind of reckless speculation. He had lent money for short terms of a week or a fortnight on South Sea Stock; he had bought the stock on account of his master; he held shares in a dozen schemes, each of which pretended to be able by itself to make the fortune of the smallest shareholder; there was no project so wild and visionary but that he must invest in it. Now, I do not believe that Christopher March was so foolish as to believe that his shares were going to make his fortune. Not at all; he was impelled into the struggle for shares by the desire to prey upon his fellow-creatures. They were like silly sheep; he was the wolf. He would sell his shares again when the price went up.

There were no methods of deception which were not tried by this wicked man. He received moneys and kept no account; he pretended to pay money and put it in his pocket; the liabilities of the house remained unpaid, while the poor alderman was cheated by the books, which told a lying tale;

ships which brought rich cargoes were omitted in the books; great sales were not entered; and because Christopher March was the only man who in the later days approached the master, no one knew, no one suspected, what was being done; and those who thought there was something wrong in the house, once so respectable and of such tried integrity, attributed it to the speculation and madness of the hour, and hoped that Benjamin Medlycott would come well out of it.

None to speak to the old man; not one to warn him; none to remonstrate on the madness of his supposed investments—truly it was pitiful. And he, and all of us, living in a fool's paradise, having no suspicion, not the least. We girls occupied with our little love affairs, madam with her cards, and the whole house rushing headlong to ruin.

The trouble began with my wound. Next day, when the alderman called his household together for morning prayers, Jenny did not appear with the rest. Her mother sent to call her for a lazy lie-abed. The maid came running downstairs, scared and pale—Mistress Jenny had not slept in her bed all night. A note was found lying on the pillow. "Dear parents," said poor silly Jenny, "I hope you will forgive me, for I have gone off with my Lysander. Your affectionate daughter."

There were no prayers, and no breakfast either, that morning. The alderman said nothing, but went to his counting-house, without even asking who Lysander was, and then sat down in great unhappiness. · And truly it was a cruel thing of Jenny thus to abuse the love and confidence of a father who had ever treated her with so much indulgence and affection.

"My ward," he said presently to Christopher March, "is lying at the point of death, being murdered by a villain. My daughter has left me. What is the news with you, man, that you look so pale?"

"Am I pale, sir?" asked Christopher. "It is perhaps the sudden shock of your news. Mistress Jenny gone, sir? With whom?"

K

"I know not. That is her concern. Ask me no questions, Christopher. Let us to business. We build our estates and pile up our gold, and we know not who shall spend it."

Alas! poor man. His own gold had been already spent.

"Well,"—he tried to speak as if he were no longer concerned about his daughter—"and what about the great madness?"

"The stock is falling, sir," said Christopher. "There is a run upon it. It was yesterday morning at six hundred, and is now at two hundred and ninety. Yet I cannot but think it will recover."

"Recover!" echoed the alderman. "Can a burst bladder recover its shape? Can a felon recover his honour? Go to, Christopher. Let us thank Heaven that we have been spared this infectious plague, and have continued sober citizens—to make our money by thrift, and save it for our——," children, he was going to say, but he refrained, and groaned, "O Jenny, Jenny!"

Then there came into his counting-house two friends of his —grave and quiet merchants, well known on 'Change and of his own company.

Christopher March bowed to them with humility, and immediately retired.

"How goes it, brother alderman?" asked one.

"Badly," replied my guardian. "It goes very badly."

"Why," said the other, "we guessed it, to our sorrow, and so we have come to render any help we can."

"It is neighbourly," said the alderman, "but the case is not one for friends. None can help me in such a plight. What is gone, is gone."

"Ah! That is true. Let us hope it is not so much as people have spread about."

"As much, man?" My guardian stared. "Why, what mean you?—as much as people say?"

"There are various rumours, Alderman Medlycott," the younger man interposed. "Some say that a hundred thousand would not clear you. Others think you may stand the loss of fifty thousand.   Your creditors, of whom I am one, as you know——"

"Nay—nay," said the alderman, putting his hand on a great book. "Not so, friend Paterson. We have your quittance here. But what does this mean? Have I not trouble enough, but there must be rumours to touch my credit?"

The visitors stared at one another.

"Truly, alderman," said the first, "we do not understand you.   Tell us first what is this trouble that you lament."

"It is that my daughter hath left me, to fly with I know not whom; and that my ward hath been foully wounded—I think to death; and that I have been cheated out of two thousand pounds by forgeries.   Call ye that trouble?"

They sat down, like the friends of Job, and were silent for a space.

"I would not," said the elder, "add to thy grief, my old friend.   But it is right to bid you be up and doing, because your name is very freely handled this morning."

"But why—why?"

"Why—why?" His visitor spoke angrily. "This is childishness, alderman.   Know you not of the fall in South Sea Stock?"

"Ah; what has that to do with me?"

Was the man mad?   Did he understand nothing since his daughter had left him?

"Alderman," said the younger, "think.   Your reason is tottering under the blows of Providence.   Try to speak calmly.   That quittance of mine you spoke of—where is it?"

"Surely, here," said the alderman, opening the book which contained receipts and quittances.   "See—here it is—here —with your signature and date."

The merchant looked surprised; then he took the book in his hands, carried it to the window for better light, and looked at the signature.

"Here is villainy," he said; "that receipt is a forgery, alderman.   I have not received the money from you."

"Forgery?—more forgeries?" murmured the alderman. "Call Christopher March.   He is without."

He was not, however, without.   He had gone away, leaving no message.

"Christopher March told me he had paid it himself," said my guardian.   "But go on.   Tell me more, if there is more. What is this about my credit?   What is South Sea Stock to me?"

"My friend," said the elder man, laying his hand on the alderman, "this is no time for trifling.   We may all be ruined at any moment.   Why—why—did this madness seize you?"

"I think," replied the alderman, "since you came here. What madness?"

"Doth not all the world know by this time, although you kept the secret so well, that of all the adventurers in this new stock and these new projects, no one has been more venturous than yourself?"

The alderman looked from one to the other.

"Where is Christopher March?" he asked.   "I cannot be going mad."

"Christopher March," replied his friend, "is the man who negotiated all your transactions for you."

"My transactions?   Man, I have had no transactions.   I have neither bought nor sold South Sea Stock.   I have never meddled with the accursed thing."

While they were all thus gazing upon each other there burst upon them a third man.   His wig was disordered, his ruffles were loose.

"Mr. Alderman," he cried, "I crave your indulgence for a day or two; or for a week, perhaps, when, doubtless, I shall be able to repay the money."

"The money, friend?   I know not you, and I know not your money.   Tell me more."

"The ten thousand pounds you lent me on security—of my South Sea Stock."   He whispered this eagerly, looking with suspicion upon the other men.

The alderman gazed at him with a wonder full of affright.

"I lent you nothing," he said.

"Oh, pardon, sir. Believe me, I would defraud no one. You have my securities; they were bonds worth nine hundred apiece when I borrowed the money. Now, alas! they are worth but a poor hundred and thirty. But I will defraud no one."

And while he yet spake, there came another, a creditor.

"I come," he said, "Mr. Alderman, from Mr. Ephraim Fouracre, your wife's draper, about your bill of five thousand pounds fourteen shillings and threepence, money lent on security of South Sea Stock."

"Good heavens!" cried the first visitor. "Did he both borrow and lend on the stock?"

That it appeared was the case, for the very securities on which one man had borrowed ten thousand of Christopher March, had been pledged to this honest woollen-draper for five thousand.

"My friends," said the alderman, trying to assume a calm which he did not feel, "help me in this trouble. Is there witchcraft in it, think you?"

"Nay," replied the elder merchant. "But such villainy as the world, thank Heaven! seldom sees. Where is this man, this Christopher March, that we may bring him to the gallows?"

He never came back. The game was up, he felt, when the stock, which was at one thousand on August 1, steadily went down and never recovered, day by day, its figure of the day before. Then despair seized him. Nothing now could save him. And on the morning after his desperate assault upon my lord, he vanished on the first appearance of visitors to his master.

I hardly know why he tried to murder Lord Eardesley. My fortune was gone; my lord's was gone; the moneys entrusted to the alderman were all stolen and wasted. As regards the forgeries, they were but a small trifle in comparison with the rest—the countless pile of frauds, forgeries and deceits, by which he had carried on his wicked course, and lulled his master into confidence. Why, then, did he try to murder my lord? Perhaps, because this crime was the first discovered, and if followed up would lead to the discovery of all the rest. But one never knows the secret springs of action in the career of any man, even a good man. Let it suffice that Christopher March was a murderer if ever there was one, though his victim escaped him.

Now all that day the alderman sat, steady as a rock, in the counting-house. Little by little the whole truth was got at. One man after the other called; one after the other revealed a fresh tale of treachery. It is true that most of the frauds had been committed quite recently, and evidently with a'view to meet the most pressing claims rising out of old ones, so as to put off the evil day as long as possible. By nightfall the poor old man knew all. He had lost not only his own fortune, but his good name. Hardly a merchant of credit but had been cheated by him—that is, in his name; those who had entrusted their money to him—the poor widows and orphans—had lost it: the Gentlemen Adventurers of Virginia who had made him their banker had lost all their savings; men like Lord Eardesley who had deposited with him their few thousands found their little fortunes stolen. I, the great Virginian heiress, who had inherited the thrift and accumulations of three generations of prosperity, had lost every farthing. Of all my hundred thousand pounds, my much envied "plum," not one penny was left.

This, all this, did the poor alderman have to learn and to endure. It took many days to get at the whole, to discover the extent of the ruin. Yet his creditors—the poor women whose daily bread was gone, the tradesman who saw no way left except bankruptcy and perhaps a lifelong prison —were kind to him. He had been so honest, he had been so benevolent, so religious, so charitable, that none upbraided him. There were no reproachful eyes upon him when, the accountants having laid everything bare, nothing more remaining to be learned, he called his creditors together. told them all, which indeed they knew already, and spoke his farewell speech.

"My friends," he said, "I am old, and have been young; yet never have I seen the righteous man beg his bread. I have been righteous, according to my lights. God knoweth when we do amiss. As for this trouble that hath fallen upon you all, I pray you to remember that man is prone to err. I have been over-confident, and I have been deceived and robbed. In this cursed South Sea Stock, remember, I pray you, that I had neither part nor lot. Forgeries, forgeries all around me—with forgeries have I been undone."

His lips trembled as he tottered slowly to the door. Lord Eardesley, who was there, supported him from the counting-house to his own parlour. There sat his wife, sad and terrified.

They brought him wine, but he refused to drink it, sitting mute and sorrowful. His wife knelt before him, crying and sobbing, and imploring pardon for all her follies. He meekly bade her rise, saying that she had been a good wife to him, albeit fond of cards, and that during the years which were left to him and to her, there would be little fear of cards interfering between them. Then he turned to Lord Eardesley, and very piteously lamented the loss of his fortune and that of his betrothed, myself.

"Nevertheless," he said, just and righteous to the last, "I lament not so much for you, my lord, and my dear ward Elinor, as for those poor women—those widows—whose honourable bread is gone. For who will help them? who will feed them, unless it is He who fed the prophet? And chiefly let us pray for that wretched boy, Christopher March, who hath brought this terrible trouble upon us, that he may be led to repent."

Neither his wife nor Lord Eardesley spoke. I think that at the moment they would rather have joined in prayer that he might speedily meet with the rope that was to hang him.

"Wife," he said, trying to rise, "let me to bed. I have much to think of."

They led him to his room, and presently left him.

All night long his wife sat beside him watching. His

eyes were closed, but he was not sleeping, and from time to time he spoke.   Yet at last he dropped asleep.

Early in the morning he sat up, looked about him and asked in his usual voice if all was well.   Being assured that all was well, he fell back, and slept like a child.

They awakened him at ten in the forenoon.   His face was rather pale, but smiling and happy.   And—oh! wonderful interposition of Providential benevolence!—he knew nothing, simply nothing, of what had happened.   My poor old guardian had gone mad.

Afterwards, when I was recovered, Lord Eardesley took me to a place where they kept him.   His friends, the company over which he had presided, and the Court of Aldermen, could not bear to think that the good old man, reduced to the utmost penury, should suffer in his lunacy. They placed him in the house of a physician, where but a few madmen were received—not the great awful Hospital of St. Bethlehem—and provided for him a room to himself, with such creature comforts as were judged best for him. Hither came, every day to sit with him, soothe him, and please him, his faithful wife.   Was it possible that this good, devoted, and honourable creature could have been the woman who once found all her happiness in cards, and all her hope in a good hand?   It was but once that I saw him. We passed through a hall whose horrors were enough to drive faith in the goodness of Heaven away for ever from the breast, where poor creatures were chained by short lengths to the wall like wild beasts, and wandered round and round like them, crying and howling with rage and fury and despair.   When we reached my poor old guardian's room, we found him playing a game of backgammon with his wife.   He did that all day long; he never tired of it; she played with him, without a murmur.   And when he won, he would laugh and crow.

He did not know us.   He only invited us to sit down and watch the game.

The only sign of any recollection of the past that he gave

was once or twice a week, when he used to laugh feebly, rub
his hands, and say—

"Wife, I always said that South Sea Stock was no better
than any bubble."

CHAPTER VIII.

HOME AGAIN.

IT was in August that I was stricken; it was late in
September that the fever left me; it was in October
that I learned all—the wreck of our fortunes, the ruin and
madness of my poor guardian, the elopement of Jenny.

"My Nelly," said Geoffrey, "we have nothing; neither
you nor I. The very daily expenses of this house are
maintained by money borrowed from a friend, who lends
it, I know, willingly enough. Will you come with me to
my poor barren acres in Wales, where we may live, somehow
like rustics, on pig, cow, sheep, garden, and orchard? The
acres are broad enough, I know, but they are overgrown
with wood and corrupted with marsh. No one will take
my farms; there is not a tenant in the place. Yet what
else can I offer you?"

To me it seemed like a haven of bliss. Anything to get
away from London, from this dreadful place of corruption
whence, like the Valley of Hinnom, the stench and flame
went up to the high heavens. Anything to change the
current of my thoughts. Wales! The broad barren acres!
Why the place would be like Virginia. I should see, once
more, forests and hills.

I hesitated not; I would marry my lord where and when
he pleased. We were married at the parish church, at St.
Olave's, by the good old clergyman, whose manner of reading
the service reminded me so much of the alderman. He was
proud to marry a nobleman, and as there was no wedding
feast he made us a little speech in the vestry-room. He
reminded us that adversity, like good fortune, was a jade
which came and went, according to the behests of high

Heaven; that we must not look forward to a continuation of those buffets by which our worldly effects had been suddenly and violently bereft from us; but rather must cast around for means to use that rank, to which it had pleased God to call my husband, as a stepping-stone to fortune. Above all, we might bear in mind that the world is for the young, that success is for the brave, and that where there is no ambition there is no struggle, and where no struggle there no glory. He meant well, the good old man, and when I took him aside and asked him if he knew aught of my poor Jenny, the tears ran down his cheeks and into the corners of his great fat lips. But he knew nothing.

So we were married. There was no ringing of bells; there was no wedding feast; there were no rejoicings; my old nurse was present, crying, my only friend; the clerk gave me away : no one was in the church; outside the carts and waggons drove up and down the narrow street; the drivers swore; the porters set down their loads and fought; the signs hanging over the shop windows creaked and groaned in the autumn breeze; and no one took any notice of it.

After the ceremony I bade farewell for a while to my nurse, who returned for the present to the desolate house on Tower Hill, and we took coach to my lord's lodgings in Bury Street.

Here we remained for a fortnight or three weeks. He had but few friends—where should a poor nobleman find friends?—but these came to see me and invited us to their great houses, and were as civil as if we were rich instead of being paupers.

In those days we talked a great deal about our future. We were young, and laughed at the disaster of losing all our money—at least, I did. We were to go, he said, to Wales; we would repair a corner of the ruined castle, and farm such of the land as was not too barren; we would live away from the world, forgotten, and cultivate the simple mode of life praised by philosophers. That was our dream. I thought so much of Wales that I forgot Virginia. But one day a sudden thought came into my head.

"My dear," I said, "the man Christopher March could not have gambled away my estate in Virginia."

He started. "Surely not," he said, "unless your title-deeds were in his hands."

"I believe we have no title-deeds," I replied. "I should wonder, however, if any would dare to dispute the right of a Carellis. Geoffrey, look into it. Oh! my dear, we are not poor but rich. There is no estate like it in Virginia. It produces more than a thousand pounds by the year, and might produce two in careful hands. Geoffrey," I added, laying my hand on his arm and looking into his noble face, "shall we go to Virginia, you and I, and grow rich on our own lands?"

Well; he was strangely moved at the proposal, and went away to consult a lawyer. By this time all the poor alderman's papers were in the hands of attorneys. It was discovered that he had never possessed my title-deeds, which were still in Virginia. Here was good news, indeed; and now my whole thought was how to get away from this London, this city of villainy and rogues, and find myself back in my own country, where, if we lived among thieves, which was true, they were in bondage and enduring hardness.

My husband reasoned with me soberly about it. He was at first averse to leaving England. He thought that if we had a thousand pounds a year we might live on his estate in Wales, build a house, and, though we could not hope to make a figure, yet we might maintain a household in some degree worthy of our rank. I replied that I was as careful as he could be to keep up the dignity of a peer: but that we must remember how the plantation was governed by servants, who, though they might be now men of integrity, might also become through temptation men like Christopher March himself, and rob us of all we had. This was so true that it turned the scale, and my husband consented to embark for Virginia, there to become a planter of tobacco.

Now, after my marriage—though this I did not learn till long after—my nurse, free at last to remember her own private troubles, set to work to find her son. She rightly guessed that he would, while the hue-and-cry was hot after him, take refuge in those dens and dark holes of London known to none but the professional rogue. She knew these places, and had lived in them in the days of her degradation. Now she began to seek them out afresh. She put on an old and ragged dress, carried a basket, assumed the manner of a decrepit woman, and ventured boldly into the dark dens where an honest person's life was not worth the chance of a fourpenny-piece.

Here she asked for her son by his old name. Some knew nothing of him; some remembered the name; some told, with pride, how he had become a great gentleman, and was robbing on the grand scale. This was no new thing among them; for although it was, perhaps, the first time that a pickpocket and common thief had become a City merchant, yet it was quite common for one of them, when he had gotten a gallant suit of clothes and a sword, to become a gamester and adventurer of the dice, and so ruffle it among the best while fortune lasted.

At first, however, she could learn nothing about him. But after patience for three or four days, she was rewarded. It was a woman, quite a young woman, who answered her whispered inquiries with a fierce question, and the usual profane oath, what she wanted to know about him for.

"Because," said Alice boldly, "because I am his mother."

"You're not," replied the girl. "His mother was hanged."

My nurse shook her head.

"I was not hanged," she said, showing her hand, which was branded by the executioner. "I was reprieved and sent to Virginia. My name is Kate Collyer, and I want to find my son. You know that the hue-and-cry is out for him, and the reward is proclaimed. They will hang him if they catch him. The mob will tear him to pieces if they can."

"How am I to know, if you are his mother?"

"Because I say so. But that, I doubt, is not enough. See, then, tell him this." She whispered in her ear. "Ask him who could know that except his mother. Then take me to him."

She sat down in the doorway and waited. The girl, with a look of suspicion and distrust, walked swiftly down the narrow and filthy street they call Houndsditch, and disappeared.

Alice waited for about an hour. She knew the kind of people. If she got up and went away, she would be suspected; if she remained where she was, suspicion might be lulled. Presently the girl returned.

"You may come with me," she said; "but if you have deceived me or betrayed him, I will kill you—remember that."

I know not where the girl took Alice. They passed from one lane full of rogues and thieves to another; everywhere wickedness, profanity, and drinking. At last the girl stopped at a house, and, opening the door, led Alice to a small room at the back, dark and dirty, where Christopher March was sitting alone. His fine cloth coat and waistcoat were exchanged for a suit of common workman's clothes; a red cotton handkerchief tied up his neck; he had discarded his wig and grown his own hair; he looked in his new disguise what he was, the thief and burglar of twenty years before—grown up, but not reformed.

When he saw Alice, he sprang to his feet with an oath.

"You?" he cried. "She said it was my mother. You? The nurse?"

"Yes; it is I, my son."

Alice sat down upon the bed and sighed heavily.

"I only knew, on the night when you tried to murder Lord Eardesley, that you were my son."

"Dick told you, did he? Then he knew, too, and kept it from me. Yet I thought I saw him killed."

"Such as he take time to die. They are allowed to live a little, so that they may tell something of their wickedness before they die. He told me—he—that you were the boy whom, in an evil hour, I brought into the world."

"Well," said Christopher, "if you come to that, we were

all brought into the world at an evil hour. We live and thieve, and then we get hanged. Fool that I was, when I might have lived honestly and died in my bed."

"He told me that when the gang was broken up——"

"It lasted two years after you were lagged at Bristol. We thought you were hanged."

"They respited me at the last moment. I have been in Virginia."

"I know—go on."

"That when the gang was broken up in consequence of the cry after the great diamond robbery——"

"My doing!" said Christopher, laughing. All the years of his education and work in an honest office had not destroyed that pride in a successful villainy which was taught him in his infancy, and by the poor woman who stood before him repentant and shamed.

"You were sent, to get out of the way, into the very heart of the enemy's camp, to the house of Alderman Medlycott himself; you were educated by him; taken into the house by him; paid well by him; and, in return, you robbed him."

"Why, mother," cried the son in great surprise, "you are not come here to preach—you!"

It was part of her punishment. Her very son, who had been for fifteen years and more under godly tutors, could not even yet understand that a wicked woman could ever turn away from her wickedness.

She shook her head.

"No, no," she said, "I shall not preach. For you I can only pray. But this is foolish talk. Let us rather consider how you may best escape."

"Why," he replied, "I think I am safest here. Bess, here—but you don't know Bess—will look after me."

"You are never safe where there are so many who know you. Why, there is a hundred guineas reward offered for your apprehension. Once caught, they will have no mercy on you, be sure of that."

"I am sure," he said; "I knew it all along. Why, what

odds a little danger? I am not caught yet, and perhaps there is many a jolly day between this and the journey to Tyburn; isn't there, Bess?"

The girl laughed uneasily. She was one of those who can never contemplate without a shudder the certainty of her doom, and the uncertainty of its appointed time.

"Confess, mother," the hardened villain went on, "I have done well. A dozen years of good behaviour, with church on Wednesday and Friday evenings, as well as Sunday; ten years of slavery and hard work, and then the reward came —a rich and unexpected reward: the confidence of the most confiding merchant in London; a double set of books: the handling of vast sums of money; all day long robbing the alderman; all night long gaming and drinking, and living like a lord. A fine time, Bess, wasn't it?"

"Yes, it was," she said; "pity it is over."

"I would have made it last longer, but my luck became so bad. I believe it was your girl Elinor Carellis who brought me bad luck. Little she knew that every evening some of her fortune was being melted away in Covent Garden."

"Why did you dare to make love to her?"

"He make love to her!" cried the girl, springing to her feet like a mad thing. "He make love to her?"

"Easy, Bess, easy—sit down." Christopher took her by the waist, and sat her on his knee. "You don't understand. Why, girl, I wanted her money to put back the rest—Lord Eardesley's and the alderman's and the others. Then we should have started fair again; he would have made me a partner, and all would have gone merrily."

She was not satisfied, and her colour came and went, while her breath was quick and her eyes bright.

"I should like to kill her," she murmured between her teeth. .

"You need not be jealous," said Alice; "she is married and gone away."

"Ho! ho!" laughed Christopher, "without a penny-piece. That's revenge worth having, isn't it, mother?"

Then his mother grew sick at heart, and weary, and rose to go.

"I cannot see you any more. I cannot bear to look upon you, or to hear you talk. But I would aid you to escape before it is yet too late. Perhaps, if you escape now, your heart may be softened in after years. But I warn you. Among all the rogues and thieves who surround you, there must be many—try to think how many—who know where you are hiding, and who will be tempted by the reward. A hundred guineas! It is a great sum of money. Leave London; go where no one knows you. Go where you may find some honest means of livelihood. See, I have brought you all my savings." She drew out a little bag, and poured some money into her lap. Christopher and the girl bent eagerly over it with greedy eyes. "There are ten guineas and some silver pieces. Take them, and fly for your life out of the City of Destruction."

There was no hesitation about taking the money ; not the least. Nor about promising whatever the man's mother wished.

"I will go," he said. "I will go this very evening. We will try the north. This will keep us for a while, and then we shall see. Yes, mother"—he thrust his tongue in his cheek for the amusement of the girl—"honesty is the only thing. You are right. Henceforth I am a respectable tradesman, ruined by the wicked directors of the South Sea Scheme."

She left him without taking his hand, or saying more words. And she lived to learn that he had broken his word, was still lurking in London, and had been captured.

All this she told me later, when we were far away from land on the blue ocean.

Then we began our preparations for Virginia. We wanted little, because everything was already on the plantation. My lord's interest procured us a passage on board the *Gloucester*, one of His Majesty's ships, under orders for James Town, and we were to set sail at Portsmouth.

A week before we started a letter was brought to me by

a meanly-dressed, poor little creature of a servant-maid. It was addressed to Mistress Elinor Carellis, care of Lord Eardesley.

O Heaven! it was from my dear, flighty, foolish Jenny.

"Dearest Nelly," she began. "I know not if I dare to address you as I used. Forgive me and pity me. I am very unhappy. I know about my father's bankrupt condition and his madness. Pray Heaven it be not caused partly by my undutiful conduct. Come quickly to me, for I have much to tell you. My mother will not forgive me, and my husband is such a wretch that you will pity me when you know. But, oh! that such a man as Christopher March should have been allowed to live! Your affectionate Jenny."

The letter was dated from a street near High Holborn, called Fetter Lane, where I supposed she had found lodgings. My husband, who would not let me go alone, accompanied me, and we carried with us the little half-starved girl in a coach.

Alas! the street was narrow and noisy, full of shops, and crowded with rough people. Jenny's lodging was in a court leading off the street. Who, then, was her Lysander? Could he have deceived her for the sake of the money which it might be reasonably supposed she would have?

The girl led us into a mean house with narrow passages and dirty stairs. In a room at the back, ill-furnished, squalid, and unwashed, I found the poor girl. She was in dishabille, her hair hanging about her shoulders, her feet in slippers. Before her stood, cowering, the man who had carried her off. But was this Lysander? Why, all the bravery had gone out of the man; the ruffle and smirk; the square carriage of his elbows; the toss of his head; all were gone. His clothes were shabby and common; his wig lay on the table, and a handkerchief tied up his head. I think they had been quarrelling, for when Jenny heard our footsteps and turned to me, her face was flushed and her lips were quivering.

"Nelly!" she said, throwing herself into my arms. "O

Nelly, Nelly! what a wretch—what a foolish wretch I have been!"

Then she tore herself from me passionately, and placed me in a chair, while she pointed the finger of scorn at her husband.

"Sit there. You shall hear, you and my lord, what I have suffered from this man."

Lysander looked as if he fain would escape, but knew not how. I do not think he was a brave man, because his knees shook while his wronged wife poured out her tale.

"You know how he used to write me poems, Nelly? The poems were copied. You remember his letters? They were stolen from a book. The wretch hath no knowledge of writing, save of copying for a shop cashbook. He told me a tale of himself: he said he was the son of a country squire—O lying villain!—that his father wished him to marry a lady of title; that his only chance was a secret marriage, after which his father would certainly relent; that he would never be able to persuade the alderman to any secret course; and that if I would elope with him all would go well afterwards.

"Nelly! you know what a fool I have always been, loving to read about men and love-making—all this went to my heart. It seemed so noble in a gentleman to fall in love with the daughter of a citizen: it was grand to be carried away. No secret marriage in London would do with my fine gentleman; no Fleet marriage, if you please; nothing but a coach and four, and Scotland.

"So I went. Oh! the long, long journey on the road; and the shaking over the roads; but who so grand as this great gentleman, if you please? His hand was ready with a guinea for the post boy and a crown for boots; while at the sound of horses on the road none so brave as he, with his sword ready loosened in the scabbard, and his pistols before him in the coach. 'If we are caught,' he said, 'if we have to fight, I will die rather than surrender my Clarissa.' I felt proud of being about to have a husband who, if he was little in stature, had yet so high a spirit.

"We got safely to Scotland, after many days, and there we were married.

"Then we came home again, but without the grandeur with which we went. This time we travelled to York by posting, and then all the way to London by the coach.

"When I got to town I learned all that had happened; your wound; my father's ruin and illness; the villainy of Christopher March. I thought my heart would break, to think of all the troubles that had fallen upon us. Yet there was some comfort; I should not be a burden upon my friends, poor and in misery. I should, perhaps, be able to help them."

She stopped, and the miserable man, now that the climax was approaching, trembled not only in his knees, but all over, while a cold moisture broke out on his forehead.

"One more misfortune was to fall upon me—one more trouble. I deserved it. I must not repine; but it was harder to bear than all the rest. O Nelly! See him now. Does he look at all like the son of a country esquire? Hath he any air of gentle blood and noble birth? Does he look like a man who would marry a lady of rank? I found out at length, but not until his money was come to an end. I found out, I say, from his own confession, who he is and what. Nelly, he made the money for our wedding journey by gambling. He was lucky, and won enough to pay for all in a single night. And he is not a gentleman at all. He is but just out of his apprenticeship. He is a hosier by trade. His name is Joshua Crump. I am plain Mistress Crump, wife of the hosier's apprentice, who was once Jenny Medlycott, and daughter of an alderman who had passed the chair! Oh! oh! oh!"

She paused. Then, fired to fury with the thought of her wrongs, she cried again, with a passion of tears, "O villain!" and gave her husband, one with each hand, two such mighty boxes on the ear that I expected, little as she was, some dreadful injury would be done to him. I pulled her from him; for, indeed, she was now quite mad with passion, and no longer mistress of herself.

Joshua Crump, all this time, said nothing, only he gazed with appealing eyes to me, as if for protection.

My husband stepped forward while I was soothing Jenny.

"Tell me," he asked the man, "have you any money?"

"No, my lord, none, except a single guinea."

"And when that is done, what will you do next?"

"I know not, my lord, indeed."

"Are you not a pretty villain, thus to carry away a young lady deceived by these lies?"

"I am, my lord. Yet I thought her father was rich, and would forgive us."

"Come outside, and speak with me."

They went outside, and I heard my husband speaking gravely. They talked for a quarter of an hour. Then my lord returned alone.

"Come, Nelly," he said; "the coach waits. Jenny, child, will you come with us and share our lot? Your husband will let you go, and it shall be as if you had never been married."

I dressed her hair, and tied on her hat, and led her crying and sobbing down the stairs.

She never saw her husband again.

So, on a fine morning in late autumn, we left London for good; and rode, stopping at Guildford for the night, all together—my husband, myself, Jenny, and Nurse Alice, with my husband's new man. And so we journeyed to Portsmouth, where we embarked on board His Majesty's man-of-war *Gloucester*, seventy-five guns, then lying off Spithead, and presently were standing gallantly across the open sea, all sails set, making for my dear Virginia.

My story is finished. It only remains for me to say a few words more.

First, I have been a happy wife in the affection of a great and noble husband. We lived on our plantation, without once wishing to leave it, for five and twenty years. At the end of that time, our affairs having prospered beyond our expectation, my husband was seized with a longing to go

home and live the rest of his life upon his own estate in
Wales, where, he thought, he might build a house, and
cultivate the ground, and, perhaps, help the advancement of
our eldest son. The second son we left in Virginia. He
hath taken the surname of Carellis, and I hope that there
may never fail a Carellis in the colony to illustrate by his
own virtues and worth those of the English race. So we
returned, and, in the autumn of our lives, before old age
dims my memory or impairs my faculties, I have written
this story of my sorrows and my joys, and have called it,
fondly, after the name by which my dear husband, who hath
ever been my lover, still delights to call his wife.

About a year after we landed my husband had a letter
from London, in which an unknown correspondent informed
him that he would be interested in learning the death of
Master Joshua Crump, formerly a hosier's apprentice. I
showed the letter to Jenny, who first looked grave, as was
becoming, and then became joyful.

"After all," she said, "it was the only thing he could do to
prove his repentance. I think better of him for dying, and
perhaps I may forgive him altogether in time. But now I
can think of nothing but that I am free."

She was; and a few weeks later she married a young
gentleman of great promise and a considerable estate upon
the Potomac River. She has brought up a large family of
handsome children, and no one but myself and my husband
ever knew the story of her elopement. Alice knew, of course,
but Alice never talked. And here I may relate that when
(after many years) we returned to London, the first time I
walked again in Cheapside I espied a monstrous great sign
of a golden glove hanging over my head, and read the name
written below of J. Crump. I remembered Lysander, and,
moved with curiosity, I entered the shop. Why, there
behind the counter, stood Lysander himself. He was little
changed, except for a certain smugness of aspect peculiar to
the thriving London hosier. He bowed, and asked me what
I might be pleased to lack.

I leaned across the counter and whispered—

"Hath Lysander quite forgotten his Clarissa ? "

He trembled and turned pale, and his yard wand dropped from his hands.

"Madam," he whispered, "I know your ladyship now. You are Lady Eardesley. For Heaven's sake! I am married and the father of ten—— "

" Fear not, Lysander," I replied, "your secret is safe with me. After the death of her first husband Clarissa found consolation in the arms of a second."

So I left him abashed and confounded.

We had been in Virginia five years or so when our overseer came to me one morning, my husband being then shooting in the forest, with a tale about a certain convict servant whom he had bought at James Town, and conveyed, with others, to the estate. He was a man about thirty-three or four, who had been found guilty and sentenced to be hanged, but, by the clemency of the judge, was branded and sent to the plantations. The offence was shop-lifting. This gloomy story was too common to move my pity. But the overseer added, when the man heard that Lord Eardesley had bought him, he fell upon his knees, and begged that he might never be seen by his lordship.

A dreadful suspicion seized me. I bade the overseer lead me to the man. He was sitting in chains, waiting to be told off for a field gang. I never went near our wretched people on their first arrival, or when they were at work in the fields, for the sound of the lash, even though one knew that it was part of the punishment, or felt that if it was a negro receiving chastisement it was part of his education in religion and civilisation, never failed to bring the tears to my eyes.

The overseer called him, and he lifted his head. At sight of me he fell grovelling and crying at my feet. For it was Christopher March.

I said nothing to him, good or bad, but being assured that it was the wicked wretch himself, thus placed by Providence in our hands, I left him and went home. When my husband returned I told him all.

It would be too long a story to relate how my lord sent for this rogue, whose sins had found him out, and discoursed with him upon his miraculous escape and the occasion mercifully laid open to him for repentance, and how the man with plentiful tears declared that he was already deeply penitent. We kept from Alice the knowledge that her son was on the estate until such time as the overseers reported favourably of the man's good behaviour and willingness. We then granted to nurse, for her own use, a strip of ground at the far north of our plantation, which had a cottage on it; and we assigned her own son to her as servant, so that no one on the estate should know of the relationship.

When she died, a year or two later, it was in the thankful confidence that her son was as deeply and sincerely penitent as she was herself.

I never greatly believed in the repentance of one whose sins showed so hard a heart, but I was glad that his hanging did not take place until after the death of his mother. He was executed at James Town, and hung in chains, for a high-way robbery, quite unnecessary and wanton, because at the time he was in easy circumstances.

As I write these last lines, the setting sun is shining on the Welsh hills; in the gardens are playing my grand-children; sitting about me are my three daughters, happy matrons all; walking up the broad valley I see my husband, and, with him, two gallant sons. My heart is full.

OVER THE SEA WITH A SAILOR

OVER THE SEA WITH A SAILOR

CHAPTER I.

IN THE PORT OF BOSCASTLE.

ON a certain evening in early summer a couple of young men were lying on the brow of a cliff between Boscastle and Tintagel on the Cornish coast. Before them was the broad Atlantic, with no land between them and the coast of Labrador except a little bit of Newfoundland—no mankind all the way, an exhilarating thought; below them on one side was the little harbour and old-world town of Boscastle, and on the other, two or three miles to the south, Trevenna and King Arthur's Stronghold. Everybody knows that there are two ways of lying on a sea-board cliff. You may lie as if you were where you most wished to be, in perfect repose, lazily looking out at the blue stretch of water, idly following the course of a sea-gull, and marking on the horizon a sail or the smoke of a steamer, while the sun gently warms you all over till you feel " done through," like a conscientious steak on the gridiron, while sweet breezes play on your cheek, and you feel as if you would hardly exchange these zephyrs for the breath of your mistress, and as if you intended to remain until that great king and despot, who, as Rabelais teaches, commands everything, causes the invention of every-thing, is Lord of all, and must be obeyed, namely, Hunger, orders you to get up and walk in the direction of provant. The other is the restless and uneasy manner, as if your heart was not in idleness and your mind not in harmony with the seeming repose of legs and spinal column. Both methods were apparent in the attitude and appearance of the two companions. They illustrated in their friendship a very old maxim of philosophy. It is not in Solomon's Proverbs nor is it in Plato, but I am sure it is old, because it is too profound for myself, or any other modern philosopher, to have invented. " It is best," said the anonymous sage—very likely he was a Chinaman—" in choosing a friend to choose one who will wear. Therefore he must not follow the same calling as yourself. In true friendship there must be no professional jealousy, no rivalry." Now one of these young men—he who sat and rested with such perfect joy—was a poet ; and the other—the restless person—was a painter. The poet, by an unlucky stroke of fate, did not look poetical ; he was short in stature, wore a beard and spectacles, and his legs were not so straight as those of more favoured brethren—in fact, they formed that interesting conic section, an elongated ellipse. This curve, applied to human legs, is said to be bad for stopping pigs. As for his name, as it has got nothing to do with the story, and as it was an ugly name, and as the poet always committed the sin of cursing his ancestors for having such a name whenever he thought about it, and as his friends always called him Poet, Maker, Bard, or Inspired One, there is no need to mention it at all. He wrote his immortal verses under an assumed name, and used to grind his teeth when admiring maidens (of ravishing beauty) wrote him rapturous letters, and he was fain to remember straight hair, curly legs, and unromantic name.

The artist, on the other hand, who could not write verses, had curly brown hair, the brightest eyes possible, a manly complexion composed of brown, red, and white, laid on in artful gradations by nature, and features as straight and handsome as those which made the pride of Paris's mother. For young maidens to look upon those features was a sovereign specific for headache, ennui, languor, despondency, listlessness, vapours, and lowness of spirits, for they straightway began to sit upright, grow cheerful, take a bright

view of life, pity the sad condition of nuns, and think
how thankful they themselves ought to be to Heaven
for making them so beautiful. For comeliness in man,
they thought, not knowing that even ugly men have
their feelings, is attracted magnetically towards beauty in
woman.

His name was much better than the poet's, being Davenant,
and his Christian name was something of the romantic and
reverent kind greatly favoured by tender mothers in the days
when Miss Sewell's novels prepared the way for a generation
of Cyrils, Guys, and Cyprians, few of whom have proved
themselves fathers of the Church, though many have become
her prodigal sons. But, by reason of a certain quality in
the youth which one cannot explain, he was always called
by his friends Jack. This being so, it is useless to give his
real name in full. The curious may refer to his baptismal
register.

He it was, as I have said, who looked restless. Something
was on his mind, else he would have felt the repose of the
hour and enjoyed the splendour of the setting sun.

The poet spoke slowly and critically—

"I agree with you, Jack. She is pretty—she is very
pretty, indeed. I like the dark blue eyes best, I think, of
all eyes that be. Wordsworth might have written a sonnet
on the Dark Blue Eye." He took out his pocket-book and
made a note. "I am sure that Wordsworth would have
written a sonnet, had he thought of it, on the Dark Blue
Eye—dark and true and tender—beautiful collocation!—
pity I am too late with it. Her features are straight.
In this day of snub noses and little round faces it
is refreshing to come across the classical type. Her
figure——"

"I declare," Jack cried, "that you poets are the least
imaginative of mortals. To be sure it must be destructive
to the imagination to be for ever thinking what ought to
be said about a thing. You 'agree with me!' Hang it,
man, you talk as if you were discussing the merits of a
poem. I say that her beauty is a beauty that takes

possession of a man—unless he be a poet—and fills his brain, and makes him go mad with longing and delight."

"Take care, Jack."

"What am I to take care of? Think of her hair, man of sluggish blood! how it ripples like silk threads in the sunshine; Dorothea by the brook had not such long and lovely locks; and then think of her figure, the tall graciousness of her presence. Helen of Troy was not more queenly than this village girl. Think of her voice, so musical and clear; it is the voice of Juliet. With such tones that maiden ravished the heart of Romeo. Think of her smile, when one is happy enough to make her smile; did ever man dream of a woman's smile more sweet? Venus must never laugh, but she should smile often. Think of her eyes when she looks at you, Poet! They are the eyes of the Goddess of Love herself, the Queen of Heaven and of Earth."

"Take care, Jack," repeated his friend again.

"Why should I take care?" he asked for the second time.

"Granted that she is about a tenth part as beautiful as you say and think; granted that you fancy yourself in love with her; granted, again, that she is as good as a woman can be——"

"This methodical and cold-blooded person calls himself," said Jack, "a poet!"

"How would it do to transplant her to London? For a cottage by the sea, a house and a studio in the Abbey Road; for the companionship of fishermen, that of your friends; for a boat in the harbour, a walk in Regent's Park."

"Poor child!" said Jack the Lover; "but we would come to Cornwall as often as we could. I should paint nothing but the cliffs of Boscastle."

"How would she like the ladies who would call upon her? How would the ladies like her? Jack, give it up."

"I shall not give it up. I can never forget her face.

Why, I think of her all day long, and when I think of her I tremble."

"Poor old boy! Do you think she is worth it?"

"I am sure she is worth all the worship and respect a man can give her. Every woman is for that matter."

"Humph!" said the poet. "Go on, Jack."

"It is by the special mercy of Heaven," continued the painter, "that such women are sent into the world: else the standard of things beautiful would be lowered, and so our endeavours slacken, and all mankind sink back into the mud."

"I will take a note of that idea, Jack." The poet made his note. "If you take no thought yourself how things should be said, permit me to do so. Thank you, I am now listening again."

"No," replied Jack, "I have done. My mind is made up. I shall ask Avis to marry me. If she will not take me—and I don't know—" he added this ruefully, as if unaware of his good looks, pleasant ways and gallant bearing—"I don't know why she should, being what she is compared with what I am, why then we will go away, and the sooner the better."

"I think, Jack," said the poet, "that Miss Avis will say Yes. Who would have thought that out of a simple journey to the · Cornish coast such dreadful things could follow?"

Jack laughed.

"Was it for this," continued his friend, "that I who hate walking and love London, and especially the Temple, in June, was persuaded to assume the disguise of a muscular Christian —" he pointed to his knickerbockers — "and to put on a knapsack, whereby my shoulders are bruised into a horrible black and blue, instead of remaining a pearly white? We were to travel all the summer, to make sketches, collect legends, examine pools by the seaside, grow learned over anemones. What have we done? Sat down in a village and fallen in love with a country girl."

"I can't help it," Jack groaned. Then he said stoutly : "I wouldn't help it, if I could. It would be too great happiness for me to win Avis." His voice sank as he pronounced the sacred name of the girl he loved.

"How shall I go back to the club and tell them that their Jack is lost to them—their Jack of trumps—because he is engaged to marry a young lady of surprising beauty, niece to a seafaring party—I think party is the right word—who has certainly been a mariner, who has certainly been a pilot, and is also suspected of having been a pirate ? "

"Pirates are scarce," said Jack. "I shall swear he has been a pirate. I will paint his portrait in character."

" True, there is distinction in being a pirate."

"As for those little awkward things," Jack continued, harking back to a previous point, "the conveniences of society, the tone of the world, I would as soon that Avis never changed at all : I want no change in her, Heaven knows. The man or woman either—only women are so confoundedly jealous of each other—who can't see with half an eye that here is a gracious and blessed damoisel fresh from heaven, to whom the world can add no charm of manner or of style——"

"Spare me, Jack."

"Why, that man or that woman," I say, " may go to the devil."

" A very lame and commonplace conclusion to a sentence begun with commendable originality. Well, what am I to do? Shall I up, take off these confounded knickerbockers, and go back to town ? "

" No," said Jack; " you are going to stay here and see me through it."

"I will, Jack, I will, if I have to wear knickerbockers for a twelvemonth; only let us send to Exeter or somewhere for some decent 'bacca, and, as I am not in love, and like a glass of respectable claret, let us order some to be brought as quickly as may be. And one thing I am quite certain of: the girl, whether it is the village beauty or anybody else, who marries Jack Davenant, will get as good a husband as she deserves, and I hope she will behave according."

They had been together enjoying the girl's society, yet one had fallen in love with her and the other had not. To be sure the lover was an Artist. Now people whose thoughts are occupied a great deal with form and colour are naturally susceptible; and when one of them really meets with a woman whose form is a dream of beautiful curves, and whose colouring drives a painter to despair, so delicate is it, yet so firm, so beautifully shaded, and so full of light, he is at once ready to believe that here must be the long sought for perfect woman. Poets experience greater difficulty in losing their hearts; it is not, as Jack irreverently said, that they are of slow imagination, but that the ideal woman, the dream of a poet, is so hard to find; mere grace will not do, nor exquisite colour. They would have her at once lovely as Phryne, sweet as Laura, sympathetic as Cordelia, quick as Rosalind, queenly as Cleopatra, loving as Juliet, and wise as Heloise. Now, Nature makes few such women; there are more poets than mistresses for them, therefore they fall in love less readily than men of coarser mould. So that when Jack saw in that simple Cornish maiden the one girl in all the world whom he would care to marry, when he raved of her beauty and her grace, when he contrasted her with the girls of society —poor girls of society! how rough is their treatment in love stories, yet how well they do marry as a rule!—when he prated (I have omitted most of his prating) of artificial ways and the falsities of London life, the poet only saw a tall and pretty girl, whose beauty he could have wished to express by magic art in immortal verse; whom always in poetry, he would have decked with most of the virtues. He might, too, have fallen in love, not with the sweet girl of flesh and blood, but with the phantom of his own creation, as in the leading case of Pygmalion, or as a certain noble Roman fell in love—bigamously—with the pictures of Atalanta and Helen, and another—but this story

M

I take to be an allegory—who conceived a violent passion
for an Effigies of Fortune.

It was in the year 1863. You who can remember seventeen years may pass over the next page or two; you who
cannot, being yet in the bloom and blossom of youth, on
which happy circumstance I congratulate you, and wish
you every kind of enjoyment while it lasts, must not,
on any account, omit to learn something of that older
generation which seems to you already far advanced in
fogeydom.

There were a great many more places, in that year, to
begin with, where the traveller could find quiet nooks,
pleasant abiding-places, sea-side villages, unknown to the
general autumn outpouring, than there are now. He would
put up at a simple inn, and sit in the evening, pipe in mouth
among the rustics on a shiny settle; or he would find a bed
over the shop of the universal provider of the place, which
smelt of everything all at once, but mostly of tallow, soap,
and bacon. When he went home he made his friends
envious with reminiscences of the beauty of that place.
Gradually the bruit and renown of it spread abroad, people
flocked, a hotel was built, and its principal charm was
gone.

The man who did most mischief in causing these discoveries and developments was Charles Kingsley, for he not
only taught people how to look at beautiful places, what to find
at the seashore, and how to talk about a seaboard village, but
he also inspired them with a craving to search for new
places. Also by the might and magic of his pen he peopled
the coasts of North Devon and Cornwall with fiction-folk
far more real than any creatures of real blood, so that at
Clovelly one always thinks of Sebastian Yeo, just as on
Exmoor one thinks of Lorna Doone—which proves how good
and great and desirable a thing it is to be a novelist, and what
a benefactor he is who can so touch the hearts of kindly
folk. Again, by his own enthusiasm and its contagion, he
stimulated the sluggish brains of men and women, who, but
for him, would have gone to the end of their days contented

with the Parade of Brighton, or even the jetty of Margate, and sent them abroad, all athirst for rock and valley, cliff and rolling wave. The love of things beautiful is not, if you please, born with us—it must be taught; the child of nature stands unmoved looking upon the curves of the valley which broadens as it slopes towards the sea, whether the rains slant upon its hanging woods, or the sunshine lies on every leaf; whether the ocean lies beyond, far and far away, a sheet of burnished gold in the evening sunset, or the sea-fog rolls up the comb with the morning, and clings to every meadow like a bridal veil. Therefore children of nature, as well as inn-keepers, lodging-house keepers, and owners of seaside property, ought to be very grateful to Charles Kingsley, Mr. Blackmore, and all who teach them what to see and what to love, and their statues should be erected in every town and village on the north coast of Devon or wherever they have led the people to wander and admire.

Another thing, which was a curious feature of this seventeen years' old time, was his doing: he gave the people a taste for what, in those unscientific days, was called science. After he had written "Westward Ho" and "Two Years Ago," tourists of the "higher culture" used to carry hammers, and solemnly knock off bits of rock, never weary of collecting specimens, which they afterwards mixed; or they would, with much gravity, drag home ropes of gruesome seaweed; or they would peer into the pools left by the sea, as once, they remembered, had peered that great and good and crafty Tom Thurnal, whom you, young friends, have clean forgotten. Yet, Tom was once a person of considerable influence.

They did not learn a great deal of science, I think, for all their chippings, collections, and pool-gazings. Geology and natural history remained very much where they were. As for the young men and maidens, it made them feel like having an improving time when they looked about for anemones, unrolled the seaweed, found Latin names, and reflected how much superior they were to their grandparents (who had stayed at home and minded the shop and made the money). And there was another thing. When it came to gazing in the pools by the rocks, it not unfrequently happened that the agile shrimp, the crafty water beetle, the crab with his sidelong glance, the limpet, the cockle, the anemone, and the green slime, were all neglected when, in the untroubled mirror of the surface, eye met eye and gazed each upon either with more intentness and meaning than had been bestowed upon the wonders of the deep. This led to the study of another kind of knowledge, namely, how one person can lay himself out to the best advantage in order to please another person. This is a very delightful and interesting study at a certain time of life, and, indirectly, proves beneficial to trade—notably, in stimulating the industry of the plain gold ring, the mystery of the artificial orange blossom, and the craft of wedding-cakes, which shows that everybody can set a ball a rolling, but no one knows where it will stop.

Other visitors, such as the middle-aged, who had already studied this branch of philosophy, but were now fired by the new love of science, went about with bottles and nets, caught a triton, and put him into an aquarium, where they watched his kicks and his customs, and dreamed ambitiously of writing a monagram upon him which should for ever place them on a pinnacle of fame. Alas! the worship of this nameless " science " is over; the triton lives unregarded in his pool, the sea-anemone attracts but little attention, and middle-aged men have ceased to net grubs and water-lizards in stagnant pools.

As for the amusements of that remote period, young folks played croquet and archery; they danced, but their waltzing was of the kind called *deux temps*, which, for most of the dancers, meant a rush and a scramble; athletics were in their infancy, and unfortunate girls had to wear crinoline. A whole generation, a seven years' generation, of girls wore hideous hoops—the recollection of them brings tears to the eyes and rage to the heart, so ugly, so misshapen, so inartistic, so abominable and horrible was the fashion.

I think that it was somewhere about the year 1860 that
the Evil One put it into the heads of women that the best
way to set themselves off to advantage was to put on hoops.
They did so; they put them on; they allowed them to
grow greater and greater, until those girls who were pretty
—an enthusiastic Frenchman once said that no young
woman can possibly be called plain—looked like rose-buds
growing out of summer cabbages, and those who were not
pretty looked like a continuation or upper blossom of the
cabbage. The pity of it!

For the rest, there are a good many things nowadays
which were not then even thought of. I am afraid the
new inventions, however, are chiefly intended to make
life more uncomfortable. They got on without telephones,
dynamite, electric bells, electric lights, or torpedoes, though
these were just getting invented. The whole of England
was looking on the great Civil War of America, and most
of our people—though we are rather ashamed of it now,
and wish we hadn't—were taking the wrong side, which
meant the defence of the Peculiar Institution. We are,
indeed, a strange and a wonderful people: a problem for all
foreign countries to gaze upon in wonder. Why we sym-
pathised with the South, why we, as a body, were ready
to believe the worst of the North, and failed to understand
the passionate resolution to keep together their splendid
country, and to destroy the traffic in human flesh, is a
thing which passeth all understanding. Therefore I cannot stop here to expound at length my great theory that
at times there falls upon the nations of the earth a plague
or pestilence of stupidity, wrong-headedness, or madness,
whereby evil appears good. No remedy has been found
for this disease, and the only medicine yet tried—that
of continual talk, stump oratory, and leading articles—
has only, as yet, made the mischief worse.

A few weeks before the conversation above recorded,
there was gathered together in the bar parlour of the
Wellington Arms, in the village of Boscastle, a certain
club, consisting of the better sort, who met nightly to talk,

smoke a pipe, and discuss the affairs of the parish, the country, and the world. It was the intellectual centre of Boscastle — its only solace, distraction, and amusement. What would life be in an English country town, to the people who never leave it, without the inn where they can sit of an evening and talk?

On this evening there were two strangers present—gentlemen from London, that day arrived, having walked over from Bude carrying their knapsacks. It was early in the season for tourists, but those who visit Cornwall in May are wiser in their times of walking than those who go in August. For the inns are not yet full, and the air is that sweet air of early summer which in this far east of London we so seldom breathe. While the season is young the tourist meets with a warmer welcome, the people are not yet weary of the perpetual coming and going of the curious stranger; they have forgotten the questions asked last season ; they are ready to advance a visitor's knowledge as to local matters; they even try to guess at the distances of neighbouring places for him; his presence is a change in the perennial parliament, which after the long winter has become a little dull and wants a fillip. Yet the presence of a stranger brings with it some restraint ; the customary jokes are not understood by him, and have to be explained; allusions to personal peculiarities, historiettes of the past, the small change of conversation which passes current, as a rule, and serves to keep the talk from awkward pauses, seems out of place before strangers; and without these counters of conversation the men feel strange.

The club this evening, among whom were Joel Heard the blacksmith, William Hellyer the sexton, Isaac Jago the shipwright, and others of lesser note, sat mostly silent, every man with his pipe in his hand, while the two strangers, whom we already know, tried to get up the talk.

Jack asked if there were many wrecks upon the coast. It appeared that there were many, but no one volunteered any further information about wrecks. The Poet inquired if there was any smuggling going on. It appeared that there had once been a creditably large trade in smuggling, but that was in the good old war times, when things were taxed, and brandy was worth any price. But, even then, their smuggling was nothing compared to that on the south coast.

An attempt to draw the men on the subject of local traditions and legends broke down completely, as no one knew any legends; no one had ever heard King Arthur's name; nor been told of pixy or fairy; nor whispered to each other ghostly stories round a winter fire—feared no ghosts, in fact; and were altogether as practical a folk as could be expected anywhere. But then, the way to get to the superstitions of a man is not to ask him what they are; that only makes him declare loudly that he has got none, just as a demand for money inclines the mean of spirit to button up their pockets. To extract the jewel of folk-lore another and a better way must be adopted.

"You gentlemen want stories," said the Sexton. "There's some can tell a story, and some can't. I'm one of them as can't. First you gets the storm: then a ship she comes drivin' down upon the rocks, and gets wrecked into lucifer matches; then the sailors they gets drownded and cast ashore; then they gets buried by the sexton and the parson. I don't see much of a story in that. But Stephen Cobbledick, he would spin you a yarn about that, or any other wreck, would keep you gentlemen listening all a winter evening. Pilot, he was, in America, where they are fighting."

"Ay!" murmured another; "Stephen Cobbledick, who has been in foreign parts and sailed the world around and round again, and fought with pirates and sharks, he can tell a tale or two. Stephen hath gifts."

At that moment the door opened, and the great man himself walked in.

The visitors observed that a place had been kept for him, which he immediately occupied with the air of one who steps into his own seat. It was the most comfortable seat in the room, that in the corner nearest the fire-place, with an arm for one elbow, the fender for a footstool, and the table within reaching distance.

He was a man of about sixty years of age, or perhaps more. He had white hair, curling about his head as thickly as when he was a young man; his eyes were hazel and bright; his nose was broad and rather flat; his expression, which was naturally good-natured and somewhat weak, conveyed the idea that he wished to seem stern and fierce; he was not above the middle height, and he wore a suit of blue, as becomes a seafaring man.

The maid of the inn followed him.

He sat down, looked at her with great severity for some moments, and then said—

"I will take, Mary, a glass of rum and water—hot, with a slice of lemon."

The girl instantly set it before him, because, knowing his tastes, she had brought it into the room with her.

"Hope you are well, gentlemen," he began affably. "The wind is freshening, and if it blows up you'll have a chance of seeing a bit of a sea on to-morrow. You can't say you have seen our coast till yon've seen it in a nor'-wester. Lord! I've seen it in every wind that blows, ay in such a gale that we had to be lashed to the masts."

"Never a gale that would wreck you?" said one of the company.

Mr. Cobbledick made no reply to this compliment.

"I know this coast, gentlemen, as well as I know any, except, perhaps, the coast of the Carolinas, where I was pilot. I know this coast, and this coast knows me."

"Queer if it didn't," said the Blacksmith.

"I have been, gentlemen," the Pilot had a little American drawl, due doubtless to his long residence in Carolina, "north, south, east, and west; and there are not many ports on this earth into which I could not find my way. Nor is there many charts which I have not larned, till I knowed them as well as I knowed how to box the compass, and could give the soundings; ay, even among the West

Injy Cays. The world is a big place to landlubbers, but we seafarin' men take the measure of it between us."

"A hard life," murmured one of the young men.

"No, sir, not a hard life. Regular work, regular food, regular pay. What more does a man want? There's no women aboard to fall in love with; you can't get married if you keep where you be; whereas, ashore, the difficulty is to keep single. Pitfalls everywhere."

"I have not felt any difficulty yet," said the Poet, "in keeping single."

"Any fool can get married," the Pilot went on, "but it takes a strong man to keep single. For why? The single man grows unmindful of his blessings; he waxes fat and kicks, like Jeshurun; he goes to sleep on watch, whereby he falls a victim to the first as dares to tackle him."

A murmur of assent.

"I grant you," continued the Pilot, "that there's dangers even in the single life: he drinks too much rum, maybe; he smokes too much baccy; he keeps himself too much to his own craft, whereby his wisdom is lost to his fellow man, and his remarks and maxums are throwed away upon the boy."

"There seems a great deal in what you say," observed one of the strangers.

"We all know," said the Sexton, "that Stephen is a rover, with a rover's eye."

"Gentlemen, a man who remains unmarried, especially a seaman, generally does have something good to say. Do not think that my maxums, which may be next best to Solomon's Proverbs (though he was a married man), growed of their own accord. They come of long reflection and observation, from a putting of two and two together, and a separating of two and two into one."

"But if you are not married, Stephen," said the Sexton, "you can show the experience of them as is husbands. For you have had your niece in the house for three months and more."

"A niece isn't a wife," said the Pilot. "When I feel to

want a cruise, I can up sail and away. Could I h'ist the blue-peter with a wife in the house ? "

"I saw her to-day," said the Shipwright; "she grows tall and comely, Stephen."

"She does, Isaac Jago. She grows to favour the Cobbledicks. She's got the Cobbledick chin which means determination; and the Cobbledick eyes. About those eyes, gentlemen, they do tell the story that my father, who was a bo's'n in the Royal Navy, and greatly resembled me, had eyes of such a fierceness, with eyebrows so like bolsters for shagginess, that when they boarded he was always reckoned as three—one for his cutlass and two for his eyes. When it came to the prize money, they cheated him out of two shares, and only counted him as one; which shows how the best men in this world have been treated. Else Stephen Cobbledick would this day be sitting among you all a rich man, and gladly would he stand the drinks around. As for her nose, it is the exact picture of mine "—the young men stared straight at the feature named, but forebore to laugh; the Pilot's nose, indeed, besides being broader than a nose should be, was rosy red, and possessed more flesh than becomes a maiden's nose—" and her figure is just my own to a T." Here the young men smiled. "As for her voice "—his was a rich and husky organ—"I shouldn't wonder, come to hear her sing, that you'd say she even beat her poor old uncle. The toast," he sang in a hoarse and rusty bass, "For 'twas Saturday night, was the wind that blows, and the ship that goes, and the lass that loves a sailor."

"This is truly wonderful," whispered the Poet.

"And one day you'll have to be marryin' of the young maid, Stephen," said the Sexton. "What will you say then to the chap as marries her? Will you up and tell him and her what a fool he be ? "

"I never said," replied the Pilot, "that 'twasn't good for women to be married, did I? It is their nature to, as dogs delight to bark and bite. Else they would go off their chumps with chatter and clack."

"Delicately and feelingly put," said Jack.

"A sentiment, sir," said the Poet, "which I have heard before, but never in language more befitting its truth and beauty. Truth is always beautiful, however conveyed— whether it be handed up in a shovel with rags, broken bottles, and dust, or brought on a silver salver."

"You mean well, gentlemen, no doubt," said the Pilot, "but you are a talkin' just a bit too high for me. When my niece marries I shall find a jolly sailor for her—an honest Cornishman, or even an American maybe, for the Americans, come to plain swearing, will take the wind out of any Englishman's sails. Or a Devonshire lad, at least. None of your finikin' fine gentlemen for me. There was one down here last week, high connected, being a draper's assistant at Camelford. Well, I sent him to the rightabout before he got ever a chance to speak to the gell."

"No doubt, sir," said the Poet, "you are quite right; and your reasons for preferring an American do you credit. It would be an enviable distinction indeed to boast in one's family the possession of a really hard swearer. I should lead him to the Thames bank, on a Sunday afternoon, just to take the conceit out of the riverside men. I suppose, sir, you would, to a certain extent, consult the young lady's feelings."

"I should, sir," replied the Pilot with dignity; "my niece's feelings, as a good young woman's, would go the same way as her uncle's. I pass the word: she feels accordin'. Mary, another glass of rum and water."

With his fourth glass of rum, the worthy Pilot became more personal, and communicated to the young men—the rest of the company having already gone—many valuable and useful facts connected with his own life. He was, it appeared, one of those who put their light in a lamp, and then hold it up on high.

"I have been, gentlemen," he said, "upon blue water since I was a boy that high." He held his hand about nine inches from the ground, to show the very early age at which he first embarked. "I could handle the ropes, take a rope's endin' without so much as a wink, play the fife while they raised the anchor, make a sea-pie, pour down a glass o' rum, dance a hornpipe—ay! and even make love to the gells— before most boys left their nurses' laps. That's Stephen Cobbledick, gentlemen."

The Poet said that this information warmed his own heart, because he had himself been also such a boy.

"Since then, gentlemen," said Stephen, swallowing the rest of his glass, "where haven't I been?"

"I suppose," said the Poet, "that Ulysses was nothing to it?"

"I don't know them seas," Stephen replied, catching the last syllable; "but I've been in all other seas as roll—roll they high or roll they low—while the stormy winds do blow, and the land-lubbers lyin' down below. I've fought with pirates, sharks, whales, and sea-sarpents; I've been blowed about with monsoons, tornadoes, cyclones, and hurricanes; I've been wrecked on most every shore——"

"Have another glass," said Jack.

"Sir," his voice began to thicken a little, "you're a gentle- man. Now there's a singular thing about me—nothing never hurt me yet. I'm one o' them as nothing never can hurt. Not fevers, nor choleras, nor even a mangrove swamp on the New Guinea coast. Not crimps, nor gam- bling saloons, nor drinkin' shops, nor sing-songs, nor dignity balls, where the drink is free and knives is handy. Not alligators, nor rattles, nor cobras, nor hippopotamosses, nor bears, nor panthers. Not arrows, nor stinkpots, nor creases, nor assegais, nor six-shooters, nor spears. It can't be done, gentlemen."

He then proceeded to narrate circumstantially a few diabolical things connected with natives, in which he had been concerned with one Captain Ramsay, an officer whose gallantry, spirit, and freedom from the restraints of the Ten Commandments he esteemed as of the highest value and most proper for universal admiration. He retired about eleven o'clock, having had as much as it was safe even for so seasoned a vessel to carry, and started for home, the night being fine with but little wind, and that from a quarter favourable to one so heavily laden, bound in his direction.

"Jack," said the Poet, "I should like to see Miss Cobbledick."

"So should I," replied Jack. "Such a young lady, with her uncle's nose, his voice, his eyes—those eyes which were like gimlets, and made a Cobbledick when going a boarding count for three, one for his cutlass and two for his eyes—his figure, which is a truly beautiful figure for any girl to own—such a girl, my boy, will be a pleasing subject for me to paint and for you to sing."

"Of such stuff as the Pilot," said the Poet reflectively, "are novelists made. He is a Captain Marryat spoiled. Did you observe the broad square brow, and the sharp observant eye? The lips, too, are mobile, which shows imagination."

"No," said Jack, "his is the mobility caused by rum. I think he has been a pirate."

"A novelist wasted. No, not wasted. He amuses his neighbours. Did you remark how his old comrade, Captain Ramsay, has seized upon his imagination? Unless, indeed, Captain Ramsay is a delicate creation of the fancy. And did you further remark how Captain Ramsay is a most desperate rogue, who ought to be hanged from the yardarm? It is pleasant to look upon an old man, and reflect that, with better opportunities, he might have become even a poet."

CHAPTER II.

STEPHEN COBBLEDICK, PILOT.

I DO not know, for reasons I will presently explain, who my parents were, nor where I was born, nor how old I am, nor when I was christened (if indeed that ceremony was ever performed upon me), nor my Christian name, nor my surname. So that I start at a great disadvantage compared with other people. For a long time I thought my Christian name was Avis and my surname Cobbledick. But now I am not at all sure.

When I began to remember anything I answered to the name of Avis, and was the charge of an old granny who was very good to me and never tired of looking after me. When I was old enough to feel the want of a surname I asked her what mine was. She replied that she did not know, but that as my uncle's name was Cobbledick she supposed that might be mine also. Therefore I remained Cobbledick. She taught me, while I was with her, a good many useful and solid things: to behave nicely and to repeat the Catechism; to tell the truth and to say grace before meat: to sew a hem and read my book; to make a bed or a pudding; fold a blanket, toss up pastry, and sing hymns. I am sure that when you come to think of it, that means a good deal of teaching. Much more she did not teach me, because that was all she knew. My uncle it was who committed me to her charge, and his lawyer or the person who had charge of his money paid the bills. My uncle was a pilot in America. When I was (to guess) eleven years of age and a great girl, I was sent by this man of business to school. It was at Launceston, and because my poor granny presently died I remained at school; the school bills continuing to be paid by my uncle's order, as was supposed, for six or seven years.

It was disagreeable at first to have the deficiencies of my condition thrown in one's teeth by the other girls, but gradually they grew to like me, and then it became a really romantic distinction to be uncertain in those points where all the rest were certain. I suppose a girl with two heads might in the same way come to be envied. And, to be sure, if there is nothing enviable, there is nothing disgraceful in the accident of knowing nothing about yourself. A foundling is in exactly the same situation. And for myself, I had a most respectable uncle, pilot in America, who, when I came to know him, would, of course, be able to explain all doubtful points to my entire satisfaction.

As a guardian he was not what one could wish, because he never sent me any letters, messages, or tokens of affection of any kind. It was not until I was already past seventeen, as near as could be guessed, that he wrote to me. It was not at all a pleasant letter. It was badly written, and badly spelt; evidently the letter of an illiterate person. He grumbled about the expenses of school, said that he had come home for good, and ordered me to join him at Boscastle.

"My dear," said my schoolmistress, when with a sinking heart I showed her the note, "we must judge people by their actions. Your uncle has evidently never studied the art of expressing ideas in kindly words. But you must remember that for many years he has cheerfully borne the charges of your maintenance and education. Therefore, child, go to him with hopefulness."

This was suitable advice, and I resolved to be of good courage and to hope for the best.

"Now," I said on the last evening at school, "I am going to find a father and a mother: perhaps, who knows, a sister and a brother; I shall find a birthday, a christening, one godfather and two godmothers, a Christian name, a surname" —because I never believed that a really nice girl could have such a surname as Cobbledick—"and an age. Fancy! I may be twenty, or thirty, or forty. Oh! my dears, suppose I turn out to be forty."

In the school at Launceston we were a quiet collection of girls, mostly daughters of professional men, retired officers, and so forth; they looked forward to a quiet life, whose mornings should be spent in household matters, and evenings over needlework, music, and books. Somebody would come some day to marry them, then they would lead the lives which their mothers had led before them, wrestling with servants, watchful of children, anxious to make both ends meet. And they envied me the romance of my position.

I came away from the school with hundreds of good wishes, little presents, and prophecies of happiness. Alas! I little knew that I was taking a blindfold leap to that lower level, beneath the "respectable" stratum, out of which a woman finds it so difficult to climb. To be sure, my schoolfellows were not distinguished for birth and family, but they were the daughters of men who could call themselves gentlemen and expect Esquire after their names, although they did not belong to the gentry and bore no coats of arms. As for me — but you shall learn. It is painful to tell the truth about one who had done so much for me; but if I write my part of the narrative at all, I must set down exactly what occurred, and how my guardian behaved to me, and what he did for me, after I came home to him. I will exaggerate nothing, and I will try to write without anger or bitterness. But, indeed, I have long since forgiven.

Boscastle, when I got there after a long journey of sixteen miles up and down the Cornish hills, seemed to me the very queerest place one would wish to see. I left my boxes at the inn where I was set down, and without asking for my uncle, set off to find him somewhere in the town.

The houses of Boscastle stand for the most part on the slope of the hill above the little landlocked harbour. There are not many houses, because there are not many people living there. I looked from one to the other, wondering which was my uncle's. Standing apart from the small cottages, which made up most of the village, were two or three pretty villas. I at first made up my mind that he must be living in one of these; it had always formed part of my ideal life to live in such a villa, with such wide and ample gardens as these houses possessed. But I thought of my letter and trembled. The rude spelling, the blunt expressions, the roughness of the letter, would not allow me to associate the writer with houses so pretty, trim, and well kept. I thought I would first try the humbler cottages.

One of these attracted my attention by the fact of its having a mast — with ropes, rigging, and yard-arm complete—run up in the front; also a flag was flying. Such an ornamental structure is like a sign-post: it shows that a nautical man lives in the house to which it belongs. I believe they are generally used to decorate the back garden, but at Boscastle the cottages have no back garden. Therefore it was put up in the front, where a few broken palings served to form a small enclosure adorned by a tub and a heap of oyster-shells, broken bottles, and other things which in well-ordered houses are generally taken away to their own place.

The house was a small stone-built cottage, with a window on each side of the door, an upper storey with a similar pair of windows, a slated roof, and a very large porch, also built of stone and with its own slated roof. The porch was out of all proportion to the size of the house, being about as big as a church porch, with a window in it. It was set up sideways so as to face the east and to keep its back to the sea, whence blow the south-west gales. It formed, in fact, except in such cold weather as seldom falls upon King Arthur's Land, another room to the house. In it was an arm-chair, and upon the arm-chair I saw an old man. His feet were crossed, his hands were folded, his head was on one side, his eyes were closed; he was at peace with all the world, for he was sound asleep.

Any one who saw that old man sleeping would have fallen in love with him on the spot; he should have been painted for the everlasting admiration of the world; his hair was curly, and of a beautiful silvery whiteness; his features were strong and rugged as if carved by a skilful

N

sculptor who knew exactly what lines to put in and where
to put them, and did not spoil his subject by anything
which would interfere with his original conception; his
cheek was browned by sun and rain and wind; his hands
were not only browned by the weather but they bore
also marks of tar; he wore white ducks in the construction
of which great liberality had been bestowed in the matter
of stuff, a blue flannel shirt, a black ribbon tied loosely
under the collar, a blue cloth jacket, and at his feet lay a
"shiny" hat.

"This man," I thought, "is a sailor; he is clearly above
the rank of common sailor; he lives in a house which
is better, but not much better, than the neighbouring
cottages; he is well enough off to be able to spend his
afternoons asleep; he seems by his face to be a good old
man; I believe he must be my uncle and guardian, himself."

My footsteps, as I lifted the latch and walked into the
garden, awakened the sleeper; he opened his eyes, rubbed
them, yawned, stretched his legs, yawned again, and finally
stood upon his feet and stared at his visitor.

A very curious thing happened then. It takes a sleeper
a few moments to recover consciousness; during those few
moments I observed a remarkable change come over the face
of this benevolent-looking old sailor. He was not, in fact,
so benevolent-looking awake as he was asleep. His face
now showed a lower level of virtue; the lines changed,
the features broadened, the mouth widened; it became a
common face, that of a man, you could easily see, who
was self-indulgent: his eyes were fiery, the veins in his
forehead swelled up and became blue; one became aware
of tobacco and rum without seeing any. And I began
to hope that this person, at least, might not be my uncle.
Alas! he was.

"Who are you?" he growled, still half asleep.

"I am in search of Mr. Stephen Cobbledick," I said.

"Oh! you are, are you? Then," here he yawned, "you
couldn't have come, my pretty, to no more likely a man to

give you such information as you can trust about that man and gallant officer. Cause no man on this airth knows him better and loves him more nor me." He spoke with a slight American accent, which strengthened my suspicions.

"Pray, sir, are you yourself Mr. Cobbledick!" It is so unusual a thing in this jealous and censorious world for one man to speak well of another, that I now felt almost sure of my conjecture.

"Why not?" he replied, giving question for question, after the Scotch manner. "Why not? And what might you be wanting?"

"I want," I said—"I want a few words of conversation with him."

"And that, my dear," he replied airily, being now fully awake, "you shall have. Lord bless my soul! a few minutes? you shall have a few hours. Hang me if I wouldn't like to make it a few years. Step inside, my beauty, and sit down. If you are not too proud—as many of your sect, within my recollection, and not so very long ago, didn't used to be too proud—there's rum in the locker."

"I would rather," I replied, "shirking the reference to rum, "talk outside for the present."

"Outside, my dear, if you please. Though if you ask them as once run after Steve Cobbledick, his communications was straightfor'ard and his walk upright. Nothin' mean about Stephen, old or young. On the deck you might find him, the broad, the wide, the ever free, visible for all eyes to see. Therefore, pretty, whether in the open or below, up steam and forge ahead, trustful. I am a listening. You comes here first, and you axes, sayin', 'Where is that pride and boast of the Cornish coast?' says you. Full speed it is."

I was perfectly overwhelmed by this burst, and could not for the moment think of a suitable reply.

"Ah! Time was," he went on, without waiting for one, "not so long ago, when they came to Stephen in swarms they did; not more than others he deserved, but more he got. Sought out he was, and loved by high and low. Sought for by short and tall, black hair and brown, curls and plain. Now he's grown old, they mostly ranges alongside of the curate. With his crowkett and his crickett, and his boat upon the bay. And it's hymns they do sing and sweetly they do play. Go on, my dear. Your cheeks is a thought paler than the cheeks in Plymouth Port, but you've a figger of your own as makes amends. You comes here, you says, for old Steve Cobbledick. 'Tis hard, they say at Boscastle, to find a properer man."

"I want to see him, certainly, and, as I make out, you are yourself—— But I think I should like to talk to Mrs. Cobbledick first, if I could."

A look of the most profound amazement greeted this proposal.

"Mrs. Cobbledick? Mrs. Cob——" he cried. "Now, pretty, look at me straight in the face. Do I look like the sort to have a missus? Missus Cobbledick! My pretty, Stephen may have his tender points. Find them out first, and lead him with a hairpin ever after; he may have his weaknesses: them as knew him best loved him better therefore. You and your Missus Cobbledickery! Like Lord Nelson he has his faults. But to take and make a Missus Cob—— Come, young woman, say you didn't mean it. Young folks is skittish and will have their jokes."

"It was not a joke at all," I said, feeling rather frightened. "I am your niece, Avis, and I thought I would like to——"

"You my niece? You Avis? Ay, that's the name. Avis?" His face showed a variety of conflicting expressions, in which I vainly endeavoured to find one indicative of affection. Mostly, I read disappointment and disgust.

"You wrote me a letter——" I began, trembling.

"I did," he said. "D'rectly I found out what had been agoin' on. That's the way us poor fellows of the sea gets robbed."

"What do you mean?" I asked. For it really seemed as if he meant that I had been robbing him.

"I leave this girl," he replied, addressing the world at large and the high heavens, "in charge of a old woman to be brought up accordin'. I give over all my money to my man of business when I ships for North Carolina shore, and I tells him about that little girl. I keeps sendin' him over the money as fast as it comes in; never thinkin' nothing in the world about her; and when I comes home after close upon twenty years of work, I find they've been spendin' a matter of sixty pounds a year—nigh upon seventy pounds a year—in bringin' of her up ontoe pride, luxury, kid gloves, high livin', and piannerforty. That's the way they treated my money!"

"Then do you mean," I said, "that you did not intend to educate me?"

"I tell you," he replied, "that I clean forgot all about you. I gave the old woman a pocketful of money, and I said: 'There's the little one, take care of her.' And then I came away and clean forgot it."

"Then you are not glad to see me?"

"Not at all," he replied. "I'm tarnation sorry, and that's a fact."

"Then you would have allowed your niece to starve?"

"I dare say somebody would have taken you," he replied sulkily. "As for starvin'—well, there, I was in America. It wasn't no business of mine. I suppose there's the parish."

I stood considering what to do or to say. What I might have told him, with justice, was that he was a wicked and selfish old man, and that I owed him nothing, since it was by an accident that I had been so well and carefully brought up. What I did say was this—being a good deal shaken by so surprising a reception, and feeling inclined to sit down and cry—

"Will you let me have shelter and food here while I look round and think what to do? I will pay you back, later on."

"I suppose I must," he replied; "you can come for a little while."

It was beginning to rain, and I was glad to avail myself of the permission. I followed my uncle into a small sitting-room, intolerably close, and reeking with the smell of grog and tobacco, I threw open the window.

"What are you doin' that for?" he asked.

"Fresh air. This room is stifling."

"Fresh air!" he growled. "If a sailor wants fresh air, he goes on deck for it; there's the porch for you. Now, then, sit down; let us hear if you have been taught anything useful to earn your grub. Seventy pounds a year! There's a outlay! How is that to be got back?"

"I am afraid," I said, "that I could never pay back all that money."

"No; that's gone, that is. Clean chucked away." He plunged his hands into his pockets, and looked surprisingly unlike the old man I had found asleep.

"I might be a governess," I suggested meekly, thinking how truly horrid it must be to go out as a governess. "I could teach what I have learned myself."

He nodded his head grimly.

"Some gells," he said, "go into service; there's house-maids, ladies'-maids, and kitchen-maids; some go dress-making, which is more genteel. There's always a openin' down Plymouth way, for a gell as is good-lookin', in the barmaid line. The sailors, both officers and men, like 'em pretty, and it's a cheerful life, especially for them as can take a joke, and box a fellow's ears when he gets sassy."

I shuddered.

"I think I could not very well take that kind of place. But I am too much taken by surprise—I did not expect—I will try to do something and keep myself."

"Spoken like a honest gell," he said. "That's what I like. Give me a independent sperrit. As for hangin' around in idleness, I never could abide it in man or woman specially woman. And for why? Because, the more work they do, the less mischief they make."

I thought this a favourable opportunity for asking a few questions about myself.

"Will you tell me," I said, "who and what my father was?"

"Let me see,"—he looked at me thoughtfully—"you're my niece, ain't you? And Avis is your name? Likewise your nature." I think he meant nothing at all by this last remark, except to gain time while he reflected. "You are the daughter of my brother Ben, now gone to Davy's locker, where he lays all his days in the Bay of Biscay oh."

"What was he by profession?"

"A Bible Christian, he was."

"I mean what was his trade?"

"Why don't you say what you mean, then? Look here, my gell; if you and me is to continue friends, don't ask too many questions, and let them questions be straight. He was third officer, he was, aboard a East Indiaman."

"Oh! and how did he die?"

"A shark took him off Rangoon. When the shark had done a-bitin' of him he was dead."

"How long ago is that?"

"Nigh upon thirty years ago, that was. I was aboard at the time, and see it with my own eyes."

"It cannot be so long, because I am sure that I am not more than eighteen."

"Then it was about eighteen years ago, I dare say. I can't be particular to a year."

"And my mother?"

"Here's more questions! Here's curiosity! What do you want to know about your mother for?"

"Is she living?"

He shook his head. "No, she's dead, too."

"What did she die of?"

"Yellow Jack. We buried her at Kingston in Jamaica."

"What was she doing in Jamaica?"

"How can I tell you what she was doing."

"Did she leave nothing for me? Were there no books, no mementoes of any kind, not even a portrait?"

"She hadn't got no books, because she couldn't read; and nobody hadn't taken her picture."

"Who was she by birth?"

"She was——" He reflected for a few moments. "She was a Knobbling at Devonport. It was a most respectable family. You may be proud of your connections, both sides. Her father carved ships' figureheads in his backyard, and her brother was transported for twenty years for forging the admiral's name—nothing short of the admiral, if you please, which shows a soarin' spirit — for five hundred pounds. She was known in port as Lively Bess, and her lines were gen'ally considered as clean cut, though built more for show than for speed, as any woman's on the coast."

I began to hope that the rest of the family had remained in obscurity. If this is the end of the romance, I thought, it must be better to be commonplace, and know from the beginning who one's parents actually were.

"Now," he continued. "Have you any more questions to put?"

"One or two, if you please. Had I any brothers or sisters?"

"No; you were a lone orphan, by yourself."

"Do my mother's relations know of my existence?"

"No; they do not. And if you go to Plymouth you won't find them, cause they've gone, and it's no use expectin' nothing from them." He said this very quickly, as if afraid of my making demands upon them.

"I wonder how my mother came to be in Jamaica, when I was in England?"

"I told you I don't know."

"Yet you were with her, you say, when she died. And with my father, when he died. It is very strange. Where was I born?"

"I never axed and I never heard."

"Where was I christened?"

"I can't say. Now you know all about yourself, and we'll change the subject. As for slingin' your hammock and stayin' here a bit, now."

It was evident that he would not answer any more questions. I therefore refrained from asking any, and waited for him to explain his views. This he did at length, and we presently proceeded to draw up certain articles which were to govern the household.

He started with the maxim that in marriage, or any other condition of life in which a woman is concerned, the only way to ensure happiness is to live as much apart from that woman as the dimensions of the roof will permit. He therefore placed at my disposal the room in which we were then sitting, and one of the bedrooms upstairs. I was to have the right to open the windows in them as much as I pleased; he wouldn't interfere with me in any way.

He, for his part, was to have the kitchen, the porch, and the other bedroom. And I was not to interfere with him. As regards the cost of my maintenance, that was .to be defrayed by him, with such other small money as might be necessary to keep me neat; it being understood that these charges were to be considered as a loan, to be repaid afterwards, when I began to earn money by going a governessing, or being called to the bar, or by any other method which I should choose to adopt; the said cost of maintenance being set down at thirty shillings a week. When one comes to think of it, the bargain was not disadvantageous to him.

"And that, my gell," he continued, "is what I will do for you. Don't hurry yourself. Look round a bit. Stay a month or so. You can easily pay me back. Though as to that outlay, that seventy pounds a year, I reckon I shan't get that back in a hurry. Unless," he added reflectively, "that was to turn up which once I fondly hoped and still will fondly pray."

I did not understand what he meant, but was afraid to ask.

"Some British uncles," he said, with a rolling of his head which meant great pride and satisfaction with himself, "even among seafarin' men, would ha' said: 'Take and go and get your own livin'; you and your seventy pounds a year!' Stephen Cobbledick is not one of that sort. He is resigned; he says sweetly, 'Heaven's will be done!' He offers his prodigal niece forgiveness, and open his arms with a uncular blessin' and a bedroom all to herself."

He did open his arms, but I did not fall into them. I would gladly have kissed that nobly benevolent old man whom I found asleep in a chair. But the other old man —so full of words, so selfish, so inflated with self-satisfaction—I could not kiss, even to receive an "uncular" blessing.

The convention agreed to on both sides, my uncle, whom I purpose to call for the future, partly because everybody called him so, and partly for other reasons which will presently appear, Stephen Cobbledick, went in quest of my luggage, and the new life began.

Thus was I enriched with relations; at last I had learned who my father was; it was now apparent that I belonged to the lower class of the Queen's subjects; it was also clear that the fewer inquiries I made into the history of my connections, the better it would be for my pride. This was the end of my dreams. Instead of an affectionate uncle, I found a rough sailor, who had been made to pay for me without knowing it and by mistake; instead of a welcome, I received a plain notice that I must expect nothing more; instead of the pleasant ways of ladyhood, I was to look for a life of poverty, hard work, and dependence. It was with a heavy heart that I sought my room that night and tried to face my fortune with courage.

Well, never mind the tears of disappointment at this sudden blow to my hopes. One may cry, but the inevitable had to be faced, and my new life began.

Its manner was simple. We lived, as Stephen wished, almost entirely apart. I "messed in the cabin," and he in the kitchen. After breakfast he took his pipe to the port, and sat upon the quay among the great hawsers, watching and criticising any little operation which might be in hand, such as the repairing of a ship, or unlading her cargo, or warping her out of port. This occupied the morning. Dinner was served at one. This meal was regarded by Stephen as a mere taking in of coal and water. You need not sit down to it, or wash your hands for it, or put on your coat for it, or pull down your sleeves for it, or brush your hair for it, or lay a cloth for it. Nothing of the kind ever entered into his head. He preferred to conduct his own cooking on principles well known to the retired British sailor: a piece of pork should be boiled for so long; the flavour of a cabbage is enhanced by companionship with the pork in a pot; potatoes may be made ready in twenty minutes; onions may be fixed in less time; anybody can put a chop or steak on a "griddle;" victuals, when cooked, can be turned out into any dish that is handy, and then, messmates, fall to and eat, standing or sitting, as seems you best; for knives, what better than the great clasp-knife which does duty for everything? For grace, what better than a preliminary sharpening of the blade?

Dinner over, a single glass of grog with a pipe prepared him for his afternoon nap in the porch; another critical visit to the port completed the labours of the day, and brought nearer the evening, which he spent at the Wellington Arms. On Saturday evening he was always carried or led home by his friends; and he sang songs as he tumbled up the stairs to his bed. At first I was frightened, because a girl who has been naturally taught to regard drunkenness as a most horrible thing, cannot suddenly be got to regard it without loathing. But one becomes used to most dreadful habits. On Sunday morning (being none the worse for his Saturday evening's excess) Stephen went to chapel. He had "found religion," he said, while in America.

This made him conform outwardly to the Bible Christians. I never observed that his religion produced the least effect upon his life, his manners, his thoughts, or his conversation.

I must confess that, next to the shame of having to take a lower level than I had fondly hoped, I was chiefly concerned with the necessity for earning my daily bread. I do not think there could have been anything more dreadful for me than thus suddenly to discover that there was absolutely nothing for me to fall back upon—no friends, no relations, no helping hands. I was waiting there, like one of Nero's Christians in his prison, before being thrown to the lions who lived in the outer world. All I knew of that outer world was what I had gathered from the talk of girls in a little town and from certain novels. Women who have to work, I knew, are mostly horribly cheated and imposed upon; they are paid wretched wages; they have long hours; they cannot make money; they are scolded if they are not cheerful, and bullied if they are not brisk. And then there is so tremendous a gulf fixed between the women who work and those who do not. Alas! the latter, who should be kinder, make the difference felt. Perhaps in those days we thought woman's work more unlovely than we do now, when our sex are better paid, better taught, better able to hold their own. Yet I think that whatever improvements are made, it will always be the happier lot to sit at home and enjoy the fruits of others' labour. The novels of the time were full of the woes of governesses, their doleful lives, the wickedness of men and the cruelty of women who engaged them. Even the more cheerful novels never held out a better prospect than that of marrying the curate. For my own part I always disliked that prospect, and hoped to marry a man of some more hopeful profession.

At the beginning Stephen left me altogether alone; by degrees he seemed to tolerate my presence; he even offered me the indulgence of a chair in his own porch; and, when he found out that I could listen, he gave way to a natural garrulity and began to tell me stories about himself. I learned from them that he had been a sailor for many years before the mast; that he rose somehow to the rank of chief officer; that he had made money in certain ventures the nature of which he did not communicate; that he had the good sense to bring the money home and give it to a trustworthy person to keep for him; and that, for reasons unexplained, he left the open sea and became a pilot in the port of Wilmington, North Carolina. When the war broke out he retired, having saved more money, and returned to England, resolved to roam no more.

I found that he was a very great boaster; all his talk turned upon his own extraordinary ferocity, smartness, and insight. Certainly no sailor ever had so many adventures, or passed through them with such immunity from accidents.

Now in most of his perils he seemed to have been accompanied by a certain Captain Ramsay, who seemed to my uncle a sort of demi-god or hero. To me this model of a gallant and chivalrous sailor seemed a filibuster certainly, a pirate probably, and a murderer if he were a pirate. But my uncle was dominated by Captain Ramsay; he seemed to lose sight of morality, honour, and religion in contemplating the career of this man. What in other men he might have loathed, in Captain Ramsay seemed additional proof of the man's heroic character. And although he professed, as I have said, to have " found religion," and was by profession a Bible Christian, he certainly lost sight of what he had found when he talked of his former chief. His admiration was perhaps heightened by the fact that the object was twenty years younger than himself.

Presently I made a very interesting discovery. It was Stephen's custom to vary his stories every time he told them, changing the place, the surroundings, and the circumstances which he always gave in great detail, and the actors, whom he always described at length, giving, so far as he knew it, the family history of each in all its branches.

Thus, if he began a story say at four in the afternoon, after his nap, he would make it last until seven or eight o'clock, when it was time to go to the tavern. It was startling at first, until I became accustomed to it, to note the discrepancies in his statements about them. Once or twice I turned his attention to my father or my mother. At different times I learned that my father had been an officer on board an Indiaman, a ship's carpenter, the purser, and the quartermaster. Also that he was bitten in two by a shark; that he died of cholera; that he was wrecked off Hallygoey Bay; and that he was knocked on the head at a dignity ball. As regards my mother, she was by birth a Knobling, a Chick, and a Tamplin; she was a native of Looe, St. Austell, and Plymouth; her father followed the callings of figure-head carver, dealer in marine stores, market gardener, pay agent, and ropemaker. She died at Kingston, Jamaica (my uncle being present), of Yellow Jack; and at Halifax, Nova Scotia (expiring in his arms), of frost-bite; at Falmouth (my uncle buried her) of dropsy; and at Wilmington (my uncle engaged in vain the first doctors) of earache. Why she was travelling about was never explained; and, indeed, these statements were extremely hard to reconcile. In plain terms I found that Stephen was a most untruthful person; that he was, so to speak, niggardly of truth, avaricious of expending facts, and of most brilliant imagination.

Again, there was an old woman who came every day to "do" for us. Stephen proposed at first that I should do her work, so as to save the money, but I refused. She has nothing whatever to do with this story except for one thing. In conversation with her one day, I learned that she, being at that time nigh upon a hundred years of age, yet fresh and vigorous, with all her faculties about her, had known her master from childhood. And she told me, which was a very great surprise, that he had neither brother nor sister.

So that I could not be his niece.

I forebore to bring this discovery before Stephen, because I knew very well that he would at once invent some

new story to account for and explain those which had gone
before.

So far, therefore, from finding father and mother and the
rest of it, I remained in as great an uncertainty as ever,
and was only quite convinced upon one point, that not
one word Stephen said could be believed.

I am ashamed, now, to think how poor-spirited and
feeble a creature I must have been. Some girls would
have strained every nerve to get some situation by which
they could be relieved of such a dependence as mine. I
only wrote to my school-mistress and asked her help. She
promised to " let me know if she heard "—the usual phrase.
Then I sat down and waited. I suppose she heard of
nothing, because nothing offered. And I was too ignorant
to know how to help myself.

Then I began to fall into bad ways. I had no companions. There were no girls at Boscastle with whom I
could associate, being—save the mark!—a young lady,
whose mother was a Knobling born in three different
towns and buried in three more towns, and whose father
followed at least four professions at once and died in four
different ways, all painful, and whose uncle had had neither
brother nor sister. With that distinguished connection I
could not foregather with the honest rosy-faced lasses of
the village. Stephen, again, was a Bible Christian, like
most Cornish men. Now I could not bear the chapel,
and yet I could not walk to Forrabury by myself, and
feel that the people were saying that this girl was she
who went by the name of Stephen Cobbledick's niece,
whereas it was well known that Stephen was an only
child. It was a foolish feeling, of course, but I was young
and shy. Therefore I left off going to church, which was
wrong. Presently I left off going out for walks, except
in the evenings, for much the same reason. I fancied
that people turned and looked at me, and thought they
were sneering at me for not being like any other sailor's
daughters, red-armed, bareheaded, and dressed in a flannel
frock. What business had I, indeed, to go about in the

disguise of a young lady? Also another terror, suppose any of my old schoolfellows should come to Boscastle and meet me! With what face should I return their greetings? With what shame should I explain my fall from the levels of Launceston respectability and tea-parties?

That dreadful debt, the thirty shillings a week, went on growing. Stephen kept a book in which I was to enter the weekly bill. I did so faithfully, and used to look at the amount with a kind of terror. For it quickly grew from shillings to pounds—five pounds—ten pounds—fifteen pounds. I had nothing to pay it with; I knew no way to make money; I had no spirit to inquire or to try, being dejected with the trouble of my position and too much solitude. Yet the time must come when I should have to pay up in full. And the bill became a horrible nightmare.

It was in February that I went to Boscastle. It was four months afterwards, in June, that the time of my deliverance began, and kind Heaven took pity on a helpless girl, yet after such strange adventures as fall to the lot of few.

One thing alone redeemed the life. Stephen had a boat, which he called the *Carolina*. It was his custom, when the weather permitted, to go a sailing in her outside the harbour along the grand and terrible coast of Cornwall. It was not often in the stormy and windy spring of that year that he would venture in his little craft outside the quay. One day, however, he asked me if I would go with him. I acceded listlessly. Now whether it was that he had experienced my powers of listening, or whether he found me good, as he said, at holding the lines and obeying orders, he asked me again, and so we took to sailing together every day that weather permitted, and while he talked I looked at the cliffs, and, although on shore I continually brooded over my unhappy position, the grandeur of the rocks and headlands grew upon me, and while the *Carolina* flew over the water I forgot my troubles.

Yet I never received from my guardian one word of affection or even friendship. I was with him on sufferance : I ought not to have lived. The loss of all that money was a thing he could not forgive.

CHAPTER III.

JACK BEARS A HAND.

"BOSCASTLE in the morning," said the young man who answered to the name of Jack, "is, if anything, finer than Boscastle in the evening." It was seven o'clock, and a sunny morning, and they were coming out of the inn, bearing towels, with intent to have a swim. "Poet, look about you, and think what rhymes to harbour, sunshine, landlocked water, green water, boats at anchor, and overhanging rocks; because your poem on Boscastle will have to contain all those things."

They were, in fact, at the most curious place in all England. Here the sea has pushed a winding creek through rocks which rise steep on either hand; where this "arm of the sea," as geographers call it, which is really only a finger, a baby's little finger, comes to an end, they have made a toy port by running out a pier, which leaves room at the end for a craft of reasonable smallness to be towed and warped in and out; great hawsers as thick as any used to tow the hull of the fighting Téméraire lie about on the pier in readiness. There is generally one ship in the harbour and a dozen boats lying within the pier; the water is so green and transparent that you can see the crabs, big and little, taking their walks abroad on the stony bottom; on either side of the little harbour stand workshops, where pigmy things in the shipwright way are done to the craft which trade to Boscastle. Standing upon the hill and looking seawards, you may mark how the little inlet winds between its guardian rocks; if the stormy winds do blow, especially from the south-west, you may see the waves madly rolling and rushing with white foam into this narrow prison from the broad Atlantic. It is bad, then, for ships to be off this ruthless coast. Or. you may see it when the sun is setting upon a cloudless day, when the sky and ocean have no parting line, and a splendid glow of colour lies upon the rocks and is reflected in the motionless waters below. Whether you see it in storm or in calm, you gaze upon a place as wild, as strange, as picturesque as any on the coast of England.

The two young men bathed, sat on the rocks, looked at Willapark Headland and Meachard Island, where there is a great souffleur in windy weather, and presently made their way back with a view to breakfast. On their way they saw Stephen Cobbledick, the hero of last night's talk.

"See," said Jack, while the gallant tar was yet afar off, "there is the man whose niece has a figure exactly like his own. Remarkable, yet happy maiden! We must make the acquaintance of that niece. I must draw her. She should be better known. Such a figure in one so young is a distinction I have never before met with. Good-morning, my captain," he shouted.

"Mornin', gentlemen," replied Stephen; "fine mornin'. Are you for a sail this mornin'? I am going to get my boat ready while the rasher is a fryin' and the water is a boilin'. Soft tommy and cocoa, that's what we come to in our old age."

"No doubt," said the Poet, "when you were young it was curried peppercorns and boiling brandy. You've been a devil of a fellow, Mr. Cobbledick. Plenty to repent of in your old age—eh?"

"You may well say that, gentlemen. Repentance is a solid job with an old salt like me. Lord! Lord! Well"— he heaved a deep sigh—"I dessay it'll be got through with after a bit. Though there's work ahead. It's a lovely breeze to-day. Come with me, and I'll show you as good a bit o' coast in a small way as you're likely to see. Not the Andes, nor the coast of Peru. I can't promise you that, but a tidy show of cliff."

They accepted the invitation and went on their way.

"The retired Pilot," said Jack, at breakfast, "seems inclined to be friendly. Give me another sole—I like them with the bread-crumbs—and pour me out more tea. I think this place is good for us. Let us roam no more, Poet. Let us fix the camp at Boscastle, go out sailing with our friend, sketch the cliffs—that's a splendid fellow with the ragged edges opposite Willapark—bathe in the morning, watch the sun set in the evening—Nature is good at scene-painting—and hear all the Pilot's yarns. What a splendid old liar it is! No doubt you'll get some verses soon." Jack thought that verses came to poets like trout to anglers. And I dare say they do.

They found the old fellow, presently, on the pier waiting for them. There was lying in the harbour, besides a couple of schooners engaged in the potato trade, a little half-decked yacht twenty feet long moored beside the steps.

This was the Pilot's boat.

"Look at her, gentlemen," he said. "There's a beauty! She was built at Falmouth, on lines laid down by me." This, like most of his statements, was a fabrication, to which he presently gave the lie by asserting that the boat had been built first for the Prince of Wales. "I rigged her; I carved her figurehead; I christened her; I painted her. Nobody's hands but mine and the shipwright's touched that craft, and she's the fastest boat of her size that you'll find outside the Solent. I called her the *Carolina* in remembrance of the country where I made that proud and glorious name as a pilot which you've read of in the papers. And here comes my niece with the tiller and the lines."

The young men turned their heads quickly to see the niece who in figure, voice, and features was reported to resemble so marvellously her uncle. They looked and saw; their eyes caught each other's and fell with a kind of shame.

For they saw a tall and beautiful girl of eighteen or nineteen, of graceful carriage, stepping delicately over the rough stones. She was dressed simply, with a straw hat, white cotton gloves, and some sort of plain stuff dress.

They took off their hats and saluted this delectable nymph.

"Jump in, Avis," said her uncle. "Gentlemen, this is my niece. She ships as cox'un. I'm captain and crew, and you're the passengers. Now, then, all aboord."

Avis took her place in the stern, saying nothing. The young men sat on each side of her. If they caught each other's eyes they were abashed, thinking of the blasphemy against beauty of which they had been guilty in talking lightly of the pilot's niece; and they tried not to be caught looking at her face, but this was difficult.

There is fashion in faces and figures, as there is fashion in dress. Now in the year eighteen hundred and sixty-three faces were round, noses were tip-tilted, figures were short, tall girls were rare. Later fashions have caused the growth of tall and slender maidens with classical features. Girls are, I am told, instructed while at school how to conduct their growing according to the requirements of fashion. It is not an extra, and is taught to all alike; but, of course, all are not equally successful. The prizes are obvious. Avis was one of the unsuccessful girls; that is, she had grown beyond the fashionable stature, and her features were of the Grecian type. She wore her hair—unconsciously, for she thought little of the fashion in those sad days—in a simple knot, which went straight to the hearts of both painter and poet. The latter, after the wont of his tribe, began to think by what collection of words, phrases, and rhymes he could best illustrate this beauteous image. Poets and book-people are unhappy in this respect, that they must needs perpetually be the slaves of words. Jack, on the other hand, who was not concerned with description, immediately felt his heart leap up in contemplating the most perfect and wonderful work of creation, the last and best, a lovely girl. Stephen Cobbledick put out his sculls and rowed the boat along the narrow and winding creek to the mouth. Then he put up his sail, and the little vessel caught the breeze and glided out to sea.

They ran along the shore to the east, under headlands and cliffs of dark slate, mined by the sea into deep caverns, where seals resort, and fishermen go at night to knock them on their silly heads; past broad bays and narrow coves and gloomy chasms in the rocks, which look like prison houses for criminal tritons. The breeze was fresh; the sea was crisped with little waves, and heaving with the mighty roll of the Atlantic.

"Think," said the Poet softly, addressing no one in particular, but looking at the face of the coxswain, "how the waves would dash and the spray fly over these cliffs, in stormy weather."

The girl lifted her eyes, but made no reply.

"Ay," said the Pilot, "think of having this coast on your lee at such a time! I was once—thirty years ago and more—sailing the *Merry Maid* of Penzance, two hundred ton barque, bound from Falmouth to Bristol Port." He proceeded at full length to tell how by extraordinary craft of seamanship he had succeeded, when such a storm fell upon them, and all thought they were doomed to certain destruction, in steering that vessel straight into Boscastle Harbour, and bringing her up taut and safe, not a spar carried away, nor a rope lost.

While he related this story his hearers were silent, looking about them. It was a dull story, told with an immense number of details, with the names of the sailors who could be called upon to testify to the truth of his statement, if required; a story which called for no listening.

"That is a most interesting yarn, Mr. Cobbledick," said the Poet. "I am sure you have another to tell us. We would much rather listen than talk."

They listened while the garrulous old man told them

another, and then a third, and a fourth, while still the little craft discovered headland after headland, and still the black inhospitable rocks rose steep and high, a fortification of Nature's own design.

Jack said not a word; the presence of the girl, so silent, so beautiful, so mysterious, weighed down his soul. How could such a girl belong to such a man? She had not spoken. Perhaps her beauty was one of these accidents whereby out of a rustic and common stock sometimes a beautiful flower is produced; the village beauty is often the daughter of a hind no whit distinguished above his fellows; her grace, her bearing, her face, come to her as a gift of the gods; such a girl should be called Theodora. But generally when she speaks the charm is broken; for out of that maiden's mouth there drop no pearls, but quite the contrary; and the beauty of the village belle is too often of the kind which we are taught to associate with the devil; it looks better upon the stage, whither it is generally brought, than in the drawing-room, where it is seldom allowed to appear. This girl possessed such a profile, such delicate drawing, such graceful lines, as might belong to the descendant of a hundred queens of beauty. Where did she get it from? Was Cobbledick of aristocratic descent? Have noble families intermarried with the Cobbledicks? Are they connected by half a dozen descents with royalty? All the morning long they sailed—all the morning long the old Pilot gasconaded with story after story of his own extraordinary courage—in situations where a lesser creature must have been crushed. Captain Ramsay was generally with him. He went on, the young men observed, without seeming to care whether any one listened or not; he took no notice whatever of his niece. The girl remained perfectly silent; once or twice, when the Poet addressed her by name, she replied with a "yes" or "no," without adding a word. Still Jack lay and looked, listened and wondered.

Presently their captain put the ship about and they made for home, beating up against the wind. Then there were fewer stories, because frequent tacks cause the thread of a narrative to be broken, and it is difficult when one is interrupted in the full flight of imagination, and has to descend to earth, to renew with fidelity, truthfulness, and consistency. Now, Stephen was always consistent in his details while the story lasted. He only altered the story when he told it on another occasion.

The voyage homeward, therefore, was more silent. The girl still preserved the same reserve; the Poet ceased his endeavours to make her talk. Jack still wondered. Presently the boat entered the creek of Boscastle: Stephen lowered sail, and in a few minutes they were standing on the quay. The girl, with a slight inclination of her head, walked quickly away.

"Poet," said Jack, when a few minutes later they were standing on the rocks above—"Poet, this is some of your handiwork. I have dreamed a dream. I thought we were in a boat out at sea; there were cruel cliffs along the shore, with sharp teeth ready to grind and destroy any ship that should be driven upon them; there were black caves; there were long, hungry-looking reefs running out to sea; there were rocks of strange shapes standing by themselves in the water; there was a bright sunshine and a dancing sea; there was an old sailor whose talk was like the sound of the brook which ceases not, as the splash of the water from the roof on a rainy day; and there was a maiden—such a maiden, so dainty, so sweet. Give me back my dream."

"Do you remember," Jack presently asked, "what the old fellow was saying?"

"Not a word," replied the Poet. "I was thinking how such a girl could be his niece. Why, his wife, and his daughters, his female cousins, and their daughters, his female connections by marriage, and their daughters, must be, or have been, or are about to be, dumpy, blowsy, full-blown, broad-nosed. Call that girl his niece?"

"I was thinking about her, too," said Jack; "I was

thinking how she came there. Do you think she is really a person named Cobbledick? Beauty should have a graceful name. Every girl who turns out well ought to be allowed to change her name for something appropriate, just as the actresses do. Avis is pretty. How did she get that name, I wonder? Did you notice how sad she seemed? What is the matter with her, I wonder? She would not speak; she did not smile; her face is too pale; her eyes are weighed down with some grief. Good heavens! Does that old villain ill-treat her?" Jack clenched his fists as the thought came into his mind.

For two days they had no chance of seeing her again, because she did not leave the cottage. Yet the weather was fine. Was she ill? Did she never come out?

"I must and will see her," said Jack, on the third day.

His mind was made up; he would attack the citadel itself. He boldly went to the cottage; no one was in the porch; the door stood open; he stepped in; before him was another door; he knocked gently, receiving the customary invitation; he opened it and found within the girl he desired to speak to. She was sitting at the table; before her was a book, but it was shut; she was leaning her head upon her hand, in a weary listless way.

"Do you want my uncle?" she asked. "You will find him at the harbour."

"No," said Jack, turning very red. "I wanted to speak to you."

"To me?" She looked up wondering. "To me?"

"Yes." Jack blushed more violently. "I am guilty of great presumption in daring to call here; but," here he stammered, "the truth is, you are unhappy, and I want to know if I, if we, my friend and I, can help?"

"What makes you think that I am unhappy?" she asked coldly.

"Because you are pale, and you eyes are heavy; because you stay indoors all day, when you ought to be in the sunshine; because you never once smiled during the whole time when we were in the boat. Do not think that I alone remarked these things; my companion saw them too. I know you are unhappy."

"You cannot help," she said sadly. "No one can help."

"Let me try," he replied. "Believe me, I am not forcing myself upon you through any idle curiosity. I know the world better than you—better, perhaps, than your uncle—— "

She shuddered slightly, as if the name pained her. Was it, then, a fact that this old villain ill-treated her? "Let us advise—— "

"Oh!" she replied; "you are very good, but you cannot help. If you could do me any good, I think I would take your help. You look as if you were a gentleman, and true."

"I do my best to be a gentleman, and true," said Jack humbly. "Try me."

She shook her head again. He saw that the tears stood in her eyes.

"Come," said Jack. "Will you do one thing which will help ?"

"What is that ?"

"Put on your hat and come with me for a walk upon the cliffs. That will do you good."

She hesitated. It was not through the fear that to walk with a young man would be improper, because she had never learned by experience or example that certain most innocent things may be regarded as improper. Not only was the girl innocent herself, but she was also ignorant of conventionalities. How should she learn them, brought up in a school where no men were present or talked about ?

"Come," said the tempter. "The day is bright and warm ; it is a pleasure even to breathe on such a day as this. Come with me."

She looked at him again. He was tall and handsome. Perhaps comeliness does produce some effect upon the minds of girls, though they certainly manage to fall in love with the most remarkably ugly men. The face was bright, too, and the eyes were "straight." She looked and yielded.

Ten minutes later the port and town of Boscastle were lying at their feet, far below them. They were climbing the headland of Willapark. The girl was a good walker, though she had taken to bad ways of late, and stayed indoors.

When they reached the top, her pale face was flushed, and her eyes were bright; the set look had left her lips, and on her mouth was a smile.

Jack was almost afraid to look at her; she seemed to him, still, a kind of dream.

"Let us talk," he said.

They sat down, side by side, as if they had known each other since infancy.

The first day they talked about the place: the second day Jack felt his way to more personal and confidential talk: the third day he astonished himself by his boldness and success.

"Let me be your brother," he began, this artful deceiver, who would have refused the offer of becoming the young lady's brother if it had been made in earnest. "My name is Davenant, and they always call me Jack; that is, my name is not John, you know; but if you will call me Jack, it would make things simpler."

"But I hardly know you at all," she replied, with a little laugh. "It is so odd to see a man for the third time or so, and then to call him by his Christian name!"

"Not if that man calls you by your Christian name. Let us try. Now then: Avis—what a pretty name!"

"Jack!"—she blushed a rosy red—"what a good name—for a man!"

"Avis," he repeated, "now then that we are brother and sister, let us take hands upon it"—he held out his right hand and folded hers with his strong grasp—"tell me why you are unhappy?"

"That would be to tell you all my poor little history."

"Then tell it me."

She told him, as we know it. He was a youth of quick sympathies, and guessed more than what she told him. How could he help?

"Avis," he said, "this kind of life cannot go on. You must leave your guardian as soon as possible. Strange! I wonder if he told the truth when he said you were his niece?"

"I do not know. The old woman who waits upon us says that he had neither brother nor sister."

"I do not believe that you are his niece at all," said Jack stoutly; "but that does not matter. By his own showing, your education was an accident; you owe him nothing for that; he makes no pretence at affection; he even charges you an exorbitant sum every week for your simple maintenance; you are left wholly alone and neglected; you know no one in this place; you must leave it quickly."

"But I can hear of nothing to do. My schoolmistress can find me no place as governess, and, indeed, I fear I am not clever enough to teach; and I am haunted, day and night, with the thought that he will force me to take any place that I can get—even—even—to stand behind a bar and serve sailors with rum."

"By heaven!" cried Jack, "that would be too much. But, Avis, there are other people in the world besides your schoolmistress. There are, for instance, the Poet and myself."

"Now I have told you," she said simply, "I feel as if hope was coming back to me. Jack,"—she blushed again very prettily as she called him a second time by his name —"you will not think I am ashamed to work, and would rather live on with him in the little cottage. To be sure, it is not pleasant for a girl to be told that she is not, which she always thought she was, a lady, but only a common sailor's daughter, or a ship-carpenter's daughter, or whatever profession my uncle's fancy chooses to give my father; and it is dreadful to think of leaving the very pretence and outward show of being a lady, and of descending to the lower levels; and then there is the terrible debt.   However can that money be paid?   I owe him now for fifteen weeks, at thirty shillings a week."

"I know a way of paying that debt," said Jack.

"I cannot take money from you, Mr. Davenant," she replied, with a sudden change in her manner.

"You shall not, Avis.   Here is my plan.   I am a painter, an artist.   What I paint best are heads.   My pictures are worth—well, not too much, but something. I will paint your head, and I will offer you for the permission to make that painting the sum of thirty guineas. Then you can pay your debt."

"But that is taking money from you," she said.

"Not at all.   It is earning money by work.   You will have to sit to me a dozen times while I am painting it. That is your part of the work, and very tedious work it is. When the picture is finished, it will be sent to the Royal Academy, and, if it is sold, will fetch a hundred guineas, at least."

"But if it is not sold?"

"Then it will be worth to me," said Jack, "a great deal more than a hundred guineas."

But she refused to take his money, though she promised to let him paint her.   Two days afterwards she was astonished by a most unexpected burst of generosity on the part of Stephen Cobbledick, who informed her, with effusion, that she was to consider the debt due to him on account of board and lodging as wiped off the books.

"Stephen Cobbledick," he said, "was always a generous man.   None of his enemies ever accused him of meanness. Therefore, when his niece came to stay with him, he was content to share and share so long as there remained a shot in the locker."   So that, in fine, the past was to count as nothing, and the thirty shillings a week was to begin from that day only.

He did not think it necessary to inform the girl that
in an interview with Mr. Davenant, that young gentleman
had used strong expressions as to the vices of greed and
graspingness; that Mr. Davenant had further informed
him that he was not fit to have a girl at all in his charge;
that it was his, Mr. Davenant's, intention to find a more
fitting asylum for her; and that, meantime, he would
pay her generous benefactor for what he had already
spent upon her since her arrival, at the rate of a pound a
week.

Stephen was not one of those thin-skinned people who
shrink into their shell on the administration of rebuke;
not at all. It was customary on board ship both to give
and to take admonition, with or without kicks, rope's-
ending, cudgelling, or knocking down, and no offence on
either side, or subsequent malice, grumpiness, or thought
of revenge. He therefore took the money; acknowledged
by his salute Jack's rank as a superior officer, and made
no difference in his cheerful manner when he met him that
evening at the Wellington Arms. He liked Jack, in fact, all
the better for it.

Mr. Davenant, he said, was born to tread the quarter-deck
and to give his orders through a trumpet. He should have
been sent to sea, by rights, where he would have turned out
an admiral, or a pilot, at the very least.

As for the Poet, Mr. Cobbledick regarded him with aver-
sion. He was always sneering, he said; he turned up his
nose at the finest yarn, and asked searching questions as
if they were not true.

He was not such a fool as not to see that the girl was
pretty, and that Jack had eyes, and that the best way
to get rid of his niece, and at the same time to secure
a firm hold upon her financially, was to facilitate, as well
as his inexperience would allow, the growth of a tender
feeling towards the girl, as well as the interest she had
already aroused in the heart of the young fellow from
London.

He wanted ardently to get rid of her. She was in his

way; he could not live as he liked while she was there; he wanted, as most people do, to revert as much as possible to the ways of the Primitive Man; he would have gnawed his bones, cracked them with his teeth to extract the marrow; he would not have been unwilling to clothe himself in skins, if there were any to be got; and he would have made his cottage like the cave of the flint weapon period. It is painful to reflect that mankind have not only to be dragged against their will to the chilly heights of culture, but that they must be kept there forcibly, else they will relapse and wallow once more in the mire. Poor Pat, who loves the society of his pig in his cabin, is a type of what we should all become but for the tyranny of people who are not only clean but also powerful.

Next to getting rid of her, he wanted to recover the money which had been, against his knowledge, spent upon the girl. Seventy pounds a year! This dreadful prodigality for ten years at least, besides what he had spent before; and when he complained to his man of business with whom he had left his money, that unfeeling person called him names. He reckoned it up. Seventy pounds a year for ten years: that made seven hundred, with which he could have bought half-a-dozen cottages, the only form of investment which he knew. Then there was the interest —three pounds a year, at least; thirty pounds more gone. Now, if a gentleman — Stephen thought that all gentlemen were rich—were to fall in love with Avis, it would be hard if he could not extract from him, either before or after marriage, the return of that sum, with a little more. "I should make it," he said, with glistening eyes: "I should make it—ay—a round thousand, or fifteen hundred pounds. Hang me, if for such a girl as Avis a man ought not to pay two thousand down. And that would make me very comfortable; very comfortable indeed, it would. Ah! if you do keep a goin' on a castin' of your bread upon the waters, how it does come back, some day, to be sure! If I'd forty nieces, blowed if I wouldn't treat 'em all the same way — make 'em ladies, with silk stockings and white hands, and take two thousand pound apiece for 'em all round when their chaps came to marry them. It's beautiful! It's what the lawyers call, I suppose, a marriage settlement. I only wish I'd had forty—ay, or fifty nieces —or a hundred, at the same rate."

With this blissful dream of a numerous and penniless family all dependent on himself, all girls, and all bringing him large dots, he indulged his waking hours.

"I must take you back to town, Jack," said the Poet.

"Not yet. I must paint her face. I have promised that."

"Do not promise too much," the Poet added, with a meaning in his words. It was at this period that the conversation was held which I have already recorded. "Do not promise too much."

Jack turned from his friend with impatience, because at this time he was ready to promise anything.

She was changed in those few days since first he saw her; no longer silent and depressed. She was bright, smiling, and ready to talk and ask questions. Life had begun to look cheerful again; hope was in her heart, but not yet love. She was humble; the knowledge of her birth had made her more humble than before. She was ignorant of the world, but she knew enough to be sure a gentleman ought not to marry beneath him; not to marry at all seemed a light affliction to her, and she was resolute that, since no gentleman could marry her, she would marry no one at all. Had she been brought up among girls of Stephen Cobbledick's class, she would, on the other hand, have dreamed continually of some gentleman falling in love with her. That is, indeed, the dream of the London dressmaker, and, I dare say, of the humblest girl that lives. The king and the beggar-maid; the Prince and Cinderella; how many stories have been written, how many dreams dreamed, upon this theme? Because poor Avis had been taught to believe, as all gentlewomen try to believe, that a gentleman cannot fall in love below his station, she concluded that she was never to marry at all. A sad thing to have no lover, no husband, and no joy of little children; a grievous thing, yet a light thing in comparison with that threatened descent into the rough world, from which her new friend promised somehow to rescue her. She had no thought of love. Jack, the kind and generous-hearted Jack, pitied her loneliness; he would find something for her, some place somewhere; she asked not what or when; she left it trustfully to him.

The portrait, too, was begun. While she sat Jack could gaze upon her without reproach.

As he looked and transferred her features to the canvas, he fell more and more in love. Yet he said no word of love; nor did he by any of those outward signs, common among lovers, betray his passion. For as yet he was uncertain what to do; he thought of her happiness, or tried to think of that, first; but while he set himself to work to reason out the thing calmly, the recollection of her voice, which was cheerful and sweet—not low, which is so common an affectation among women—came upon him, and his heart leaped up; or he thought of her eyes so limpid and so deep; or the outline of her face, which he drew perpetually upon every margin; or her tall and lissom figure; and he could not reason because he felt.

At first he argued with himself that a girl living in such a manner could not but be coarse in her ideas; yet she had so lived, he remembered, but three short months, and it was pain and misery to her. There are minds which can never be coarse and common, just as there are some which can never be pure and sweet.

It had not entered into his scheme of life to marry early. He was one of the men who preach the doctrine that it is best to make your way first, your name, if that is possible, and your income, before you commit yourself to the chances of matrimony. Now, his name was not yet made, but was already in the making, so to speak; and his fortune was all to be made. As for any feeling that he would marry beneath him, that was far from being in his thoughts at all. Who marries Avis, he said, cannot possibly marry beneath him.

It was so pleasant, this time of roaming about with the girl, talking, sitting together, walking on the cliffs, or sailing in the boat, that he was loth to disturb it. The days went on, and every day he saw more of her; the honest fishermen of Boscastle took it for granted that they were courting. Avis had no shame to run and meet him when he was afar off; she had no shame in telling him all she thought and hoped; she showed him her very soul unconsciously in perfect trust. Together they made journeys to see the places of which the girl had heard so many weird legends in her childhood. The Castle of Tintagel, St. Nighton's Keive, and Minster Church, where Jack made sketches, always with Avis in the foreground; and they went to Forrabury Church together, Avis haunted no more by the foolish fear of meeting any of her schoolfellows.

"I told the girls," she said, "that I was going into the world to find a father and a mother, and, perhaps, a sister and a brother. But, Jack, I never thought that I should find so kind a brother as you."

Remarks such as these are difficult to receive under similar circumstances. Yet Jack, through some fear of the result, or some scruple about himself, would not say the words which would sever that fraternal bond.

CHAPTER IV.

RAMSAY, ALIAS ANGEL.

NOW, while these two were rapidly passing through all those nicely graduated emotions of admiration, wonder, respect, longing, and ardent desire for each other's society, which make up and lead to the delightful passion of love (which, unless a man feel it at least once in his life, he had better never have been born), an event happened which was destined to trouble everything. Always that detestable hitch in human affairs which interrupts and hinders! The American poet observes on this point, that the course of true love may fitly be compared with the flow of the Mississippi; for it is a full and mighty stream; and it is irresistible; and it has snags; and there are in certain of its latitudes alligators in its waters, and rattles on its shores, besides fevers. The snags, also, are not found in the early reaches of the river, which further assists that poet's metaphor.

The event was this.

Stephen Cobbledick was one morning seated on a hawser on the harbour quay. His short pipe was in his mouth, his legs were stretched out, and he was contemplating, with an air of great satisfaction, the wreaths of tobacco smoke, for they contained a delicious castle of Spain connected with the "marriage settlement" of his niece. It had occurred to the wicked old man that, while he was about it, eighty or even ninety pounds a year might as easily be set down as the cost of Avis's maintenance as seventy, and the same sum might be charged for every year of her existence. Now, as she was eighteen years of age, that meant a total of sixteen hundred and twenty pounds, as he chalked it up on a neighbouring stone.

"She owes me," he said, "sixteen hundred and twenty pounds; or, countin' the interest out of which I have been choused, seventeen hundred pounds in all. There's a sum! She shall go for it, though. I shall charge nothing—nothing at all—for loss of her services and agonies at parting from my dearly beloved niece. What a uncle I am!"

He was, indeed, as he was about to prove, the most remarkable of all uncles recorded in history, except perhaps Richard the Third, the guardian of the Babes in the Wood, and the Barber Fiend.

So rapt was he in the vision of his own goodness, that he paid no attention to the operation conducted just below him, of inserting a new plank in the side of a coaster, nor did he hear the footsteps of a man who was walking leisurely towards him. He was a thin, slenderly-built man, about the average height, dressed in a black frock coat, buttoned up, black trousers, and a tall hat. He might have been a dissenting minister, or a traveller for a religious publication, or a temperance lecturer, or a promoter of public companies, so much did his appearance betoken ostentatious respectability. His age might have been anything, but was certainly over forty, as was manifested by the crows'-feet round his eyes. His features were good and certainly handsome, though too long and sharp; his eyes were keen and small; his lips were thin, with a nervous twitch in them, and they were flexible; his hands and feet were small and delicate.

He stood awhile looking at the good visionary, who sat gazing into space as he counted up his gains, and heard him not. The stranger smiled. "What mischief is the old man thinking of now?" he murmured. "He looks aged, but there's work in Stephen yet."

He stepped over the ropes which lay about the quay, and laid his hand on Stephen's shoulder, not heavily, but with a quick, hard grip, as if he had caught his victim at last.

"Shipmate," he said, "how goes it?"

Stephen started, looked up in his face, jumped to his feet, dropping his pipe, which was smashed on the stones, and forgetting his vision of marriage settlements. Never was man more astonished. His jaw dropped, his eyes opened, he spread out his hands in helpless astonishment.

"Cap'en Ramsay!" he cried at length. "It is hisself."

"Shake hands, old salt," said the other. "It is myself, I guess. No other hoss has got into this skin. Why there; it's cheerful lookin' at your old face again. Kind o' brings back the old days; doesn't it?"

"It does; it does," responded Stephen. "But come, Cap'en, this demands a drink."

" Hold hard ; you come in my tow so long as I'm here," said Captain Ramsay.   " Let us go to the bar."

They went there, and drank each other's health at the Captain's expense.

" And where," asked the stranger, " can we have a place where we can sit and talk by ourselves, with nobody prickin' up their ears to listen ? "

Stephen led the way to his own cottage where, appropriating Avis's room for the occasion, they sat and talked.

" To think," cried Stephen, " that I should live to see you a settin' down in my own house."

" Here I am, you see.   I was at Liverpool, when I remembered that you had given up the piloting, and were come home.   And by reason of your sometimes answering to the name of Boscastle Steve, I concluded to run down here, and prospect around till I found you."

" In my own house," replied the other with iteration ; " the same house as I bought with half a dozen others when I come home eighteen years ago, after that little job of ours, where we done so well."

" What little job ? "

" You know, the black job, when we shipped—Ho ! ho ! —that crew of darkies in Boston, pretendin'—Ho ! ho ! ho ! —that we were bound for Liverpool, and run 'em down to New Orleans and sold 'em every man jack."

" I remember," Captain Ramsay replied ; " and divided the plunder.   It was risky but creditable.   It wouldn't quite do to have shown up in Boston for a while after that, would it ? "

" And what have you been a doin' of since, Cap'en ?   Have you sot down to enjoy the proceeds of honest industry, or have you fooled away your pile ? "

" I've fooled away that pile, and I've made more piles, and I've fooled them away."

" Euchre ? " asked the pilot.

" And monty, and any other darned thing going.   Guess if the Prodigal Son had gone to New Orleans he would have dropped the old man's dollars in a way to reflect credit on that city."

"Ay, ay. When I set eyes last upon you, Cap'en, you was a Salem man, and a Quaker by profession when in shore-going togs, and religion was useful. And you'd changed your name from Ramsay to Angel. Ho! ho! Angel!"

"Your memory is so good, old mate, that I must ask you to remember nothing about me 'cept what I tell you. And what I tell you now is this: I am Ramsay again, Jefferson Ramsay, Commodore in the Navy of the Confederate States. I was born and reared in Norfolk. I am Secesh to the backbone. Bully for the blue flag! I hail from the South, the land of chivalry, where no abolitionist skunk shall be permitted to dwell, and all the whites air gentlemen born, most of them of the ancient aristocracy of Great Britain. We air fightin', sir, for liberty and our constitution. The Peculiar Institution has been forced upon us by our ancestors. We shall consider it when we have established our freedom from the North. Abolition we abhor, because we love our niggers too well to give them the liberty they would convert into licence. No, sir, the South at this moment is the proud champion of constitutional right, and the defender of morality and religion."

He delivered this harangue with a slowness which greatly added to the effect.

Stephen Cobbledick was affected almost to tears. "He ought," he exclaimed, "to have been a bishop!"

"So I ought," said Captain Ramsay, "if everybody had what was best for him. I should like to be a bishop—in England."

Stephen then began to narrate his own experiences. The Commodore of the Confederate Navy sat in the attitude of listening, which was polite, because the Pilot was prolix. After a quarter of an hour or so of patient pretence, he pulled up the narrator short.

"Say," he began, "what do you mean to do next?"

"Nothing," replied Stephen.

"What? Stay in this forsaken hole? Sit here and rot like an old hulk in harbour?"

"Ay. Sit here is the word, Cap'en. Time's come when I'm bound to lay up. I've got religion. I've got a dozen cottages; I collect the rents of a Saturday; I'm sixty-five years of age; there's no pilotin' to do; and as for black jobs, why I doubt whether that trade will ever again be worth what it used to be. Lord! sometimes, when the minister is a boomin' away in the chapel, I sit and think of the droves of 'em, bought for a song, as one may say, sometimes took for nothing, drivers and all, hurried over the Atlantic in a clipper that could show her heels to any British frigate afloat, and put up at New Orleans or Havannah for——" Here he stopped and sighed. "It's comfortin' to think of those times. It brings out the flavour of the hymns. You should get religion, Cap'en."

"Some day, maybe, Stephen. 'Spose there was piloting to do?"

"Ay, ay?" The old fellow sat upright and listened intently.

"'Spose I was to say to myself, 'I've got a job that wants a light hand, a quick eye, and a knowledge of the coast?'"

"What coast?" asked Stephen.

"The coast of North Car'lina and the port of Wilmington."

"He means blockade runnin'!" cried Stephen with enthusiasm. "Where there's danger, there's Cap'en Ramsay! Where there's money to be made, there's the gallant Cap'en! Where there's fightin' and runnin' away, and a shootin' of six-shooters, there he is in the middle of it, whether it's filibusterin', or slavin', or the South Sea trade, or runnin' the blockade! What a man! What a Nero!"

"You've guessed the job, old shipmate. Some men would ha' let me beat about the bush for an hour. But you've got a head upon your shoulders, Stephen, screwed on tight, right end up, and eyes in that head as can see straight. You've guessed it!"

"Go on, Cap; go on." This sagacious flattery increased the good old man's desire to hear more. Blockade-running was next to piracy; therefore dear to his heart. For he was one of those perverse brethren who ever love the thing that is illegal because it is illegal.

"I've been blockade-running since that little game began, and I haven't been caught yet. And I don't mean to be, though they've put on the coast some new and fast cruisers. For I've got, at Liverpool, loading for me, a craft, Stephen, as would make your eyes water. Yes, I reckon you would weep for joy that you had lived to see such a craft."

"Ah!"

"Such lines; such gracefulness; such lightness; such speed."

"Oh!"

"You shall see her, Stephen. Whether you fall in with my proposal or not, you shall see her and judge for yourself. Now, listen. In my last trip we did well; got in and out without a brush or a shot. Some of the boys aboard were pretty rough—that's a fact—and just before we sighted Nassau there was a little difficulty between the pilot and the chief officer. The chief officer didn't matter, because his sort, though he was a plucky one, air plentiful, and Nassau swarms with young English chaps mad for a run; but when the pilot had to send in his checks too, and we heaved both overboard at once, it was a real loss, and rough upon us, as was generally felt. For pilots air like angels—they air skarse."

"Young men," said Stephen, "will be young men. I've drawed a bowie myself before now, and let daylight into the other chap. But for both to go at once! That seems a most extravagant waste."

"So, being at Liverpool, I remembered you, Stephen. I said: 'This is a chance which does not often happen. If Stephen Cobbledick gets it, he is a made man.'"

"I'm too old," said Stephen.

"Nonsense. You're as young as you feel. Your hand is

firm, and your eye is straight; and what's more, you know every inch of the coast."

"I do.   No man better."

"Why, then, we're half agreed already.   And now, old pal, you shall see what a thing it is I am goin' to give you a share of."   He pulled some papers and the stump of a pencil out of his pocket.   "First, you shall have, for the double trip, seven—hundred—and—fifty pounds—nigh upon four thousand dollars."

"What?" Stephen jumped out of his chair. "How much?"

"Seven—hundred—and—fifty pounds sterling.   Half paid down on the day you go aboard; the other half when we get back to Nassau.   Stop a minute, I haven't done yet. Every man is allowed space for his own ventures.   You shall have room for a dozen cases if you like.   More than that, I've bought them for you, and they are shipped ready for you.   I give them to you!"

"If I could!" cried Stephen.

"Why not?   What's to prevent?"

"There's that gell o' mine; my niece.   Hanged if I don't think they kep' her alive a purpose to worry an' interfere."

"Leave her behind."

"I might do that."

"A dozen cases, all your own.   They're full of the things that sell in Richmond and the other places.   There's· women's stays, kid gloves, tooth-brushes, Cockle's pills, lucifer matches—man! whatever you take will sell, 'less it's raw cotton."

"Ay."

"This good uncle was meditating a scheme for the happiness of his niece.

"As for danger, there's none.   Not that you are the man to show a white feather.   There's plenty at Liverpool could do it, but I want you. 'Steve Cobbledick,' I said, 'would enjoy the business.   Steve Cobbledick, as I've known these twenty years and more, since I was little bigger than a boy.'"

"You were on'y next door to a boy," said Stephen, "when you came aboard as third mate. 'Twas at Havannah. You were then, you said, the son of an English gentleman, and you'd run away. You shipped in the name of Peregrine Pickle, which afterwards I saw in a printed book. That was the first "—he looked round him with admiration—"of his names and his descriptions. Never any man had so many parents. And wicked? How a lad so young could pick up so much wickedness the Lord knows. Yet there he was. And drink? Like a mermaid. And swear? Don't name it. And fight? Like Great Alexander; for the walloping of a nig, to get the work out of him, I don't suppose there was ever a lad, Spaniard, Mexican, or Yankee, could come within a mile of him. And the sweetest temper with it; not proud, not puffed up with vain conceits; easy and affable with all alike. And at a dignity ball, the cock of the walk, though Mexican yellow noses, which are well known to be more jealous than a alligator, were waitin' outside with knives sharpened on the door-step to have his blood."

"Then you will go with me?" said the hero of this praise, unmoved. "You will be my pilot? I'm part owner of the ship and cargo, as well as skipper."

"When do you want to sail?"

"In a fortnight."

"Give me three days. I think I can go, Cap'en. It's only that cussed gell. She's lost me a thousand pounds a'ready, and I want to get that back. I think the job is as good as done. Three days, my noble Cap'en."

In the evening Stephen produced an electrical effect in the smoking-room of the Wellington Arms by the introduction of his friend Captain Ramsay, who was, he added, Commodore in the Confederate Navy.

Now Cap'en Ramsay was, as has been explained, a familiar name with every man who was privileged to hear the conversation of Mr. Stephen Cobbledick. For whenever he had to tell of a deed of peculiar atrocity, an act of more than common treachery, a deed which made the flesh to creep and

murderer, Captain Ramsay. Avis, once more, can you love me? Will you send me away empty, after all our talks and walks and happy times, Avis? You called me your brother once; I will not be your brother any more. I must be your lover, Avis, or nothing."

She shyly put out her hand.

"I cannot give up my friend," she said, smiling through her tears; "and if he means what he says, and his hand-maid has found favour in his sight, and he will take her for his sweetheart, who loves him——"

The noblest man in the world to marry the noblest woman! This is a dream which has always presented itself to me in the form of a nightmare. One can imagine the loneliness, the terrible isolation of a household so perfect as to be a standing and perpetual reproach to all the world; one may feel how husband and wife, after many months of keeping up an exhibition of the noblest virtues to each other as well as to all the world, would at last fly apart with execrations, and descend to a lower level and—separate. I have, besides, never met any whom I could call either the noblest man or the noblest woman. I have always found in the former certain failings due to vanity, jealousy, love of adulation, or even a passion for port; and in the other I have sometimes noted a tendency to positiveness, smallness, and inability to recognise in the world anything but what she sees. I am sure that Avis was neither the noblest nor the best of women. To begin with, she was not one of the best educated, had few accomplishments, knew nothing of society at all, was imperfectly instructed in the fashions, and had little to recommend her except her beauty and — an old-fashioned quality, but uncommon in these days—her virtue and goodness. But, for an average pair of imperfect mortals, with a good average share of virtues, and a general leaning to what is good rather than to what is evil, and a power of unselfishness, and a belief in each other as well as in goodness as an abstract quality, I declare that Jack and Avis promised to be as well mated as Adam and Eve, who, as we know were imperfect.

"Poet," said Jack, later on, with a strange light in his eyes and a little shaking in his voice, "I have asked Avis to marry me. She is good enough to take me."

"I congratulate you," replied the man of song. "My belief is that you have done the best thing you possibly could for yourself. Now that you are engaged, take her away as fast as ever you can ; the sooner the better."

"We shall be married," said Jack—he repeated the word, as if it gave him gratification—"some time in the autumn. I've got to find a house and furnish it."

"Don't wait for the autumn. Take her away out of this, as soon as you can."

"What do you mean ?"

"I mean that the atmosphere is dangerous."

"If you will explain——"

"Well, then, what I mean is that I have eyes in my head, even although I wear spectacles ; that I have been using them ; that I have been watching the piratical scoundrel who calls himself Commodore Ramsay—no more an officer of the Confederate States than of the British Navy. He is a tiger and a man-eater."

"Go on—go on."

"And I think he has cast eyes of affection on—on your *fiancée*."

Jack clenched his fist and swore a great oath.

"They are unholy eyes, Jack ; take her away at once."

"He cannot run away with her under my very eyes," said Jack presently. "If he dares to say one word to her, by Heaven——" Here he choked.

In these days it is extremely difficult for an Englishman to threaten an enemy. He cannot make daylight through him with a revolver, as a Texan might or a gentleman of Colorado. He cannot call him out, with a choice of pistols or swords. He cannot even promise to punch his head, because it is undignified. He can do nothing. The law is to do everything. Yet, even in the most law-abiding country in the world, there is always that possible return to the habits of the pre-historic man, who carried a stick, sharpened its point in the fire, and carved his flint axes mainly for the purpose of enjoying himself upon his enemy should he get the chance.

One thing Jack could do—which he did, and with surprising results. He would see old Cobbledick and tell him what he was going to do. Accordingly, he sought the worthy Pilot, and, without thinking it necessary to ask the permission of Avis's guardian, which is a formality observed by most suitors, he informed him that he was about to marry her.

"Since," he said, "she is good enough to think me worthy of being a husband, we shall be married as quickly as possible. So you will be free of your charge, and happy again. You will be able to live as you like, never open the windows, never clean the place, spread your dinner on the floor, and get as drunk as you please."

This, to be sure, was exactly what Stephen most wanted; but he was not going to let the girl go without getting what he could for himself. And when Jack used the word "worthy" in his humility, Stephen thought of the other meaning attached to the word "worth." Therefore, he replied—

"Easy a bit, young gentleman; soft and easy is the word. Now, before we go a bit further into this business, we must have the marriage settlements laid down and agreed upon."

"The marriage settlements?"

"Just so, Mr. Davenant"—the old man looked unspeakably cunning—"just so, sir; the marriage settlements. Of course you don't expect that I am going to let Avis go with nothing."

Jack was rather surprised at this. Still, as a guardian, Stephen was perhaps justified in expecting something to be settled on Avis.

"I am not a rich man," he said; "and I cannot settle

money upon my wife which I have not got. But I will insure my life for her benefit, for any reasonable amount. That ought to satisfy you."

"Insure your life for her benefit!" Stephen was astonished at the young man's stupidity. "Well, I don't mind; that's just as you like. I was talking of marriage settlements, not insuring of lives for her benefit. Who's a-talkin' of her benefit?"

"And I was saying that I will secure her from want by means of an insurance in place of a marriage settlement. That is quite a usual thing to do, believe me."

"Lord! Lord!" cried Stephen. "Why can't a man speak up plain and direct? When I said marriage settlement, I meant marriage settlement! If you want me to go and beat about—this tack and that tack—like a lawyer, say so; if not, answer me plain and straight. How much am I to have?"

"You to have? You?"

"Me, Mr. Davenant. Do you suppose that I've paid for that gell's education, as fine as if she'd been a duchess, sixty pounds—I mean ninety pounds a year, money out of pocket for eighteen years, for nothing. No, sir; I calculate not."

He added the last words for the sake of emphasis, and with due American intonation.

"Good Heaven!" cried Jack.

"I think if you tot up that sum, Mr. Davenant, you will find it come to nigh upon one thousand and eight hundred pound. Then there's the interest, which would be—ah, I dessay a hundred pound more. That makes, altogether, pretty near two thousand pound. Now, the man who marries that gell has got to make a marriage settlement upon me of all that money as I have laid out upon her to make her what she is. She can play the pianner, I am told; she can sing, when she isn't sulky, like a angel; she can patter French, they tell me, in a way as would astonish you; she can dress up to make her husband proud; she can talk pretty, when she isn't in a temper; and she can go along, holdin' of her petticuts in her hand, like a lady. That's what she is, a real lady to look at; besides belongin' to a most respectable family. It was for this that I laid out the money. 'Do not grudge it, Stephen,' I says to myself; 'it is a-castin' upon the waters, it will be brought back ontoe you, like a runaway nig.' And I make no charge for the love, nor for the affection, nor for the grief—which might settle on the chest, and be the death of a man, or turn to lumbago—at losin' of her; and as for——"

"Stop!" cried Jack, "you infernal old humbug and impostor."

"Mr. Davenant!" Alarmed at this response, Stephen began to wish he had put his figures a little lower.

"I know what you have done. How you went away and forgot all about the child; how the man who held your money went on paying for the girl and placed her in a respectable school; how you welcomed her back with reproaches and grumbling. Why, she owes you nothing, not even thanks. Now listen, and then shut up. I shall give you not one farthing; do you hear?"

"Not one farthin'. Do you mean, Mr. Davenant, that you will not pay me back even the money I spent on her?"

"Not one farthing. That is my answer. You will do what you please; but beware of any harsh word or act to Avis."

Jack withdrew, leaving Stephen in a state of such disgust and disappointment as he had never before experienced. For the hope of getting back his money had grown in his mind during the progress of Jack's brief courtship, until he almost saw it within his grasp. It was because he felt so certain that he had allowed himself to multiply the amount by about three. It may be owned that if Stephen had been acquainted with the nature of geometrical progression, and its relation to compound interest, his claims would certainly have been far higher than they were. But to get nothing, absolutely nothing at all! Was that possible? Was it, this good man asked, just and Christian so to act? And how, if not by means of Jack, was this casting of the bread upon the waters to be returned to him?

As for Avis's marriage, that was the very thing he wanted. Nothing could possibly suit him better. She would be off his hands, and out of his house; he need not trouble about her when he was away. But the cruel disappointment, and when he had made quite certain that Mr. Davenant was a real gentleman, who would be only too pleased to pay for his fancy.

The conversation took place in the porch, while Avis herself was sitting on the cliff thinking over the wonderful happiness which had befallen her. So disturbed in mind was her uncle, by Jack's ungentlemanlike and mean response to his proposal that he was fain to have a tumbler of rum and water at once, and to load another pipe. The grog despatched, he sat gloomily in his arm-chair growling menaces, interjections, and expressions of discontent, as one who has believed too much in humanity, and now, like David, is inclined to say, in his haste, unkind things about all conditions of men.

While in this mood, he was joined by Captain Ramsay, who, without speaking, took a chair and tilted it against the wall so that he could sit back comfortably. As usual, he was provided with an immense cigar, which he smoked continuously.

After a while the Commodore spoke.

" Well, mate, got an answer ready ? "

" I'll go," said Stephen.

" What about the gal ? "

" She may go—where she darn please," replied the Pilot. " She may go to the devil. I wish I had never seen her. I wish I'd never spent a farthing upon her. Gratitude? Not a bit; whistle for it. She may marry who she likes. I don't care who she marries; she may——"

" Dry up, man," said Captain Ramsay. " There's more to be said. Let us understand one another. You will come with me ? "

"There's my hand on it," said Stephen. "When I came home with my little pile I said I'd have nothing more to do with niggers. Besides, I've got religion. And I never did love the blacks; not to feel kind o' hearty toewards their shiny skins; not even when I was shippin' of 'em across the pond for the Cuban market. Some skippers loved 'em like their own brothers and cowhided 'em like their own sons. Put their hearts, they did, into the cat-'o-nine-tails. I never did."

"As for your religion," said the Commodore, "and as for your virtue—there." He made a gesture which implied that he believed Stephen's late-born virtue to be like other flowers of autumn, a pale and scentless weed. "Well that's settled. Half the money shall be paid to you before we ship, the other half when we get back to Nassau; the cases of notions I promised you shall be yours. Did I ever treat an old shipmate unfair, Steve?"

"Never, Cap."

"Very well, then. If we're caught—but that's unlikely—we shall have a taste of a Northern prison; if not, we'll have another merry run, and another at the back of that. And long may the war last, and happy may we be!"

Stephen sprang to his feet and waved his hat with a cheer.

"Now, Steve"—the Captain was more than affable, he was affectionate to-day—"there's another thing. That gal of yours is as fine a gal as one would wish to see. I don't remember nowhere any gal as come nigh her for good looks and a straight back; and I conclude that she hasn't got any call to make that fine figure of hers look finer by stuffin' and things."

"No call whatsoever," said her uncle; "she is a Cobbledick, which accounts for her figure—where she takes after me—as well as her face. But if you come to gratitude——"

"Now, shipmate"—the Commodore was still lying back in the chair, with his feet upon the back of another chair, and he spoke without taking the trouble to remove the cigar from his lips—"I've took a fancy to that gal o' yourn, and I tell you what I'll do for her—I will marry her."

"Yon, Cap'en? Marry my gell?" Here, indeed, was condescension! The greatest man then living in the world, the most perfect hero, the man who had set at defiance more laws than any other man, proposed to marry into Stephen's family! He forgot that he had only an hour before received Jack's announcement without opposition; he was dazzled by the brilliancy of the prospect before him. The simple honour of the proposal took away his breath. So surprised and delighted was he that he even forgot his projected marriage settlements, and never once thought of even suggesting the subject to his revered chief. Probably he knew beforehand that the demand was not likely to be well received. Gentlemen like Captain Ramsay, with a wide experience of humanity, do not as a rule receive statements which accompany claims with a leaning in the direction of credulity.

"Look at me, Steve," said the Commodore.

"Yes, Cap; I am a-lookin' my level best," Stephen replied, gazing hard.

"I am forty years of age; I am hard as nails; I feel as young as a ship just out of dock; there are dollars in the locker and more coming in as long as this providential and religious war goes on. And that gal has fetched me as I never thought to be fetched again; she is the kind of woman a man would not get tired of. Neat-handed, quick, as proud as Lucifer, and as beautiful as a picture. I'm willin' to marry that gell; we'll take her over to Nassau and marry her there, if you like; or we'll have the marriage here, if you like; or anywhere."

"Have you spoke the gell?" For Stephen recollected suddenly that Jack had "spoke" the girl, and he felt that there might be breakers ahead.

"No; you can tell her what she's got to do," said the Captain. "When she knows, it will be time for me to come along with soft sawder."

Then Stephen remembered another thing.

"When I saw Liberty Wicks last," he said, "and it was at Norfolk port, two years ago, he told me that you were married. He'd seen you somewheres North with your wife. Said she was a sweet and beautiful young thing—black hair and eyes—answered to the name of Olive. You can't marry two wives, Cap; not even you can't do that, 'less you keep 'em to different sides of the sea."

The Captain's face darkened. Stephen knew the expression; it meant mischief for some one.

"Liberty Wicks," he said softly, "was quite right; I was married. But now I'm free."

Here his choler rose, and he swore vehemently against some unknown person of the opposite sex, whom Stephen supposed to be his late wife.

"Did she die, Cap? Did you—now—chuck her overboard?"

He made this abominable suggestion as if it were a most probable and even praiseworthy thing to have been done.

"No; I wish I had. I found what seemed a more artful plan. I took her to the state of Indiana, and I di-vorced her."

"Oh, you di-vorced her. And how did she take that? Did she take it quiet?"

"No: like wild cats. She followed me around; last thing, she came over to Liverpool, and found me out. There she is now."

"Ah," Stephen sighed; "women never know what's good for them. When we act for the best, accordin' to our lights, they screeches for the worst. You was too kind to her, Cap'en, I doubt."

The words which fell from the chief's lips proved that if he had ever been too kind, he was now repentant, and would do so no more.

"It might be awkward, mightn't it," asked Stephen, "if that young woman was to turn up at Nassau just when you'd got the hammocks slung comfortable, and the cabbages

planted in the back garden, and the scarlet-runners climbing pretty over the wall ? "

The Captain remarked curtly that if a scene of rural
felicity, such as that described by the Pilot, was to be so
interrupted, chucking overboard or something equivalent,
short, direct, and efficacious, would certainly follow.

"Then," said Stephen, "here comes Avis, and if you'll
leave her to me, Cap, I'll speak to her now, at once. She
is a good girl, and her feelings jumps with her uncle's
and runs along the same lines. A gay and a gallant sailor
I've always promised her; but such a honour as this was
beyond her hopes and her prayers. For which may we
be truly thankful ! "

CHAPTER VI.

NOTHING BUT A COMMON PICK-ME-UP.

LIFE had become suddenly delightful to Avis. Wonderful
it is to note the difference made by a little sunshine
in the heart. Deliverance had come to her in the shape
considered by maidens the most desirable, namely, a lover.
What were past anxieties now ? No more worth considering
than the earache she might have had when a child. She
felt kindly disposed, and even affectionate, towards her
uncle—the more so, of course, because she was going to
leave him. Odd, that parting should produce much the
same effect on the mind towards the people you love and
those you do not. Therefore, when her uncle invited her
to converse with him for a few moments, she blushed a rosy
red, and her eyes lit up, and her lips parted with the
sweetest smile ever seen, for she thought that Jack must
have been with her uncle. So he had, but the pride and
splendour of the second offer had, for the moment, completely
driven the first out of the old man's head.

"That is right, my dear," Stephen began kindly; "sit
down and be comfortable. Because I've got a thing to tell

you that'll make you jest jump clean out of your shoes for joy ; never had a girl such a fine chance."

"What is it?" she asked, thinking, little hypocrite, that she knew very well what it was.

"I've always said to myself, Avis," he began with solemnity, having just thought of a lie quite new and appropriate to the occasion, "when I was considerin' out in Carolina about my little maid here in Cornwall, that the time would come when a husband would have to be found for her; and I was glad that she was bein' taught to play the pianner, because I was wishful that she should have a husband out of the common. Therefore you were brought up to full blow-outs of duff, lie in your bunk as long as you please, never ordered before the mast, run about as you like, and all."

"That is quite true," said Avis humbly. "I fear I have not been grateful enough."

"This is not the time," said Stephen with pride, "to talk about gratitude; I have found a husband for you."

"Then he has spoken to you," Avis said with brightening eye. "He said he should tell you as soon as he could."

The Captain, thought Stephen, forgetting Jack for the moment, must have had a word or two first. To deny it showed a lack of candour ; still, it made his own task easier.

"He certainly has spoken," Stephen replied, "else how should I be a tellin' of it to you? So he spoke to you first, did he? Well, he certainly always was a masterful man, with a way of gettin' over 'em most surprisin'."

"Why," asked Avis, surprised, and not quite understanding what was meant, "how do you know that?"

"How do I know that?" This in great contempt. "Have I got eyes? Have I got ears? Can I remember? Well now, Avis, tell me just exactly what he said."

"I can't," she replied: "I can never tell any one what he said. But I can never forget what he said."

"I don't want the soft sawder," said her uncle, leaning back in his chair. "Tell me now "—he looked very cunning —"did he ask you anything about the money ? "

"No; what money?"

"My money, stupid! Did he ask how much I had, and where it was stowed, and if it was easy to get at, and could you find your way to the place where it was kept? No? Well, that shows the story about the little pile at Nassau may be true." It might also be taken to show how deep is the trust reposed in each other by gentlemen of the Pilot's school of honour. "Did he say anything about going away?"

"We were to go to London," he said.

"London, eh? Ah! he told me Nassau. But that doesn't matter; and perhaps he forgot you was a sailor's gell, not to be frightened with a little blue water. London, did he say! Well, of all the artfullest——Did he promise you anything?"

"Only—only that he would make me happy always——"

"I know—I know; they always say that. Did he promise to give up his gambling?"

"Gambling? Why Jack does not gamble."

"'Jack,' too," the Pilot repeated with admiration. "What a man! He'll be Timothy to one, and Jack to another, and Julius Cæsar to a third. Not gamble, my dear? Why there isn't—not even in Mexico nor Rooshia—a man who will begin earlier nor leave off later. Gamble? While a red cent is left behind. As for betting, he'll bet on anything; if he was making a party up to go out and be hanged, he'd lay his money on a bet to kick longer than any of 'em. Not a gambler? Well, my dear, gamblin', in a way, is a nice, quiet amusement; it keeps a man out of mischief; he can't be shootin' around, that's certain, nor drinkin' cocktails in a saloon, when he's quiet and comfortable over a pack of cards or a pair of dice. No woman of sense need be jealous of her husband so long as he's usefully occupied that way with his friends. But, if I was you, Avis"—here Mr. Cobbledick bent his head and whispered—"If I was you, and going to marry him, I'd begin by getting all the money—every dollar—in my own hands first. Have that handed over before the parson brings aboard the weddin' tackle. Let him gamble with the next stroke o' good luck if he likes."

"I cannot understand it," she said. "Oh! I am sure you are mistaken."

"I am never mistaken. How should I be mistaken in such a simple matter? As for drink, I suppose it's no good askin' him to make promises. They always promise, and they never keep their word."

"But Jack does not drink."

"Doesn't he?" The Pilot laughed. "That's what he has been telling you, I suppose. Not drink? I've seen him drink a three-decker full o' Bourbon, and then ask for more. No," he continued reflectively, "I think about the drink you'd better let him alone. I'm trying to advise you for the best, Avis, my gell, because you are but a young thing, and you know nothing of the world, though you've been brought up in virtue and the maxums of your uncle. I think you'd best let the whisky alone. Only, I should say, when he is on the burst, and pretty certain to come home at night ragin' around and dangerous in a peaceful house, I would contrive to let him have the cabin all to himself, even if you had to sleep on the bare boards."

"Good heavens!" cried Avis; "what does this mean?"

"As for jealousy, now, you must remember, he's not a common man. They run after him wherever he goes. Wherefore you keep your eyes shut and your tongue quiet, whatever you may say or hear. And then, my dear, you'll have a peaceful and a loving life, with such a husband as all the world might envy. But let him be. Else—well —theer."

Avis shook her head in sheer bewilderment.

"I never thought," the Pilot continued, "that so great a honour would be done you. To me you owe it all. Some honest sailor lad, I thought, skipper, maybe, of a coaster, or officer in charge of a gentleman's yacht; but such a MAN"—he put the word into capitals—"such an out-and-out, straight up and down man as you're going to have, never occurred to me. Why, girl, if you was going to marry a duke, I couldn't be better pleased. Dukes haven't been in command of clipper-ships, dukes haven't been chased night and day for a fortnight, dukes haven't been chased day and night by British cruisers, and yet landed their cargo safe, and never a man or woman lost all the way from the Gold Coast to Cuba; dukes can't run a blockade. Why, he's been put in the papers, he has; they know all about him in New York and Liverpool; they point him out when he lands, and when he drops into a saloon they crowd around to stand him drinks."

Avis clasped her hands to her head.   Was this a dream?

"Pray," she said, "will you tell me of whom you are speaking?"

"Why, of Cap'en Ramsay, to be sure; who else should I be speaking of?"

"I am speaking of Mr. Davenant. It is he, not Captain Ramsay, who has asked me to marry him. Has he not spoken to you about it?"

"I haven't set eyes on him," said the mendacious one. "This is a pretty thing to be told, this is; with Cap'en Ramsay—actually Cap'en Ramsay—holdin' out his hand!"

"He said he would speak to you at once," replied Avis.

"If he had a-come to me, I should ha' turned him out of the house.   Who's Mr. Davenant?"

"I have told him I would marry him."

There was no mistake about the determination with which the girl spoke.

Mr. Cobbledick replied in the manner customary to the British sailor. Then the girl repeated that she had given Mr. Davenant her word.   Then he tried persuasion.

"But you won't, Avis, you won't," he said in a voice which seemed calm, but had in it that little tremor which sometimes betokens a coming storm. "You won't, my gell, will ye?"

"O uncle!" she replied, "I have promised him.   And, besides, he is the only man I could ever love."

"I don't know nothing about love," said Stephen.   "Look here, lass; my old shipmate, Captain Ramsay, as gallant a sailor as floats, has asked me to let him marry my niece. Now, I haven't got two nieces, but only one; consequently, if I don't give you to him, there's nobody to give. Therefore, as my word is passed, you must marry him. What's your word compared to mine?"

"But I cannot," said the girl.

"But you must, and you shall," said her uncle, "or I'll know the reason why. So don't let us have no more words about it. This is a very pretty state of things, when a gell thinks she's agoing to marry who she pleases."

The girl did not burst into tears, nor did she faint, nor did she turn deathly pale, nor did her hands tremble, as they used in novels. Not at all; she only repeated, firmly standing before her uncle—

"I cannot, and I will not."

"Then," said Mr. Cobbledick, "I'll lock you in your room till you do."

"No, you will not," she said; "because if you are rough and violent, I shall call out of the window to the first who passes to fetch Mr. Davenant."

The enraged guardian swore that a dozen Mr. Davenants should not prevent him from doing what he liked with his own. Was she not his niece? Did she not owe him obedience? Had he not brought her up with his own hands almost? What sort of a return was this for all he had done for her? Where was gratitude? Where filial piety? Where the reverence due to parents and guardians? As for Mr. Davenant, he should learn the strength of a British sailor's arm, with a club at the end of it. He should remember the name of Cobbledick all his life; he should be sent back to his own place with broken neck, broken ribs, broken arms, and broken legs. Did Avis think he would let a whipper-snapper, a counter-jumper, a measly fine gentleman, a painted peacock, with no money even, such as Mr. Davenant, stand between himself or Avis, and a man who was a man!

Avis let him run on without interruption. Then she repeated that she had given her word, and she would keep it.

"By your own showing," she said, "you would have

me marry a man who is a gambler and a drunkard, who breaks laws and lives a violent life. Instead of him I have taken a gentleman, who is, I am sure, a good and true man. And he says that he loves me." The girl's eyes softened. Then at the sight of this old man in undignified and foolish rage they hardened again. "Have you not often complained of the expense I have been to you? Have you not told me to look about for work to do? Have you not threatened to make me a barmaid? Have you ever shown me the slightest affection, that I should consult your wishes?"

"That's the way with 'em." Stephen sat down, ready to weep over the ingratitude of womankind. "First you stint and spare for 'em, then you give 'em all they wants, pamper 'em, dress 'em up fine, and they turn upon you. Gratitude? Not a ounce. Respect? Devil a bit. Do what is best for 'em, lie awake and think how to make 'em happy, and this is the end of it. Best way after all"—he shook his head as if this conviction was forced upon him— "to wallop 'em till they follow to heel obedient, like them black Australian gins, the only women in the world truly and religiously reared."

"You will be reasonable," Avis went on, disregarding this attack upon her sex. "You will reflect that I am not bound to consider your wishes at all, as you are chiefly anxious to get rid of me; and that I have seen a great deal of Mr. Davenant, while I know nothing of Captain Ramsay except what you have told me about him, which is quite enough to make me refuse outright to marry him——"

"I know him," interrupted Stephen with rising wrath. "Isn't that enough? Now I will have no more talking. Will you marry the Cap'en?"

"No, I will not."

"Then pack—put up your things, and pack. Go, I say. Leave the house. Pack."

Avis hesitated a moment.

"Go to your lover; let him take care of you."

This was bringing things to a crisis, indeed.

The plain speech of which the honest sailor prided himself had never been so plain before. Avis had seen him grumpy, greedy, lying, and drunk; she knew that her uncle based his conduct of life on maxims disliked in certain circles. and that he admired things which many moralists condemn. She had never before, however, seen in him the ungovernable rage which now possessed him. He stood, shaking both fists in her face; he spluttered and swore, and then could find no words but more curses to express his meaning. His face was purple with wrath.

It was, perhaps, fortunate for Avis—because things looked much as if the Pilot would begin to act upon his newly-discovered principle for the training of girls, and wallop her there and then—that the discussion was here interrupted by the arrival on the scene of Captain Ramsay himself.

"Be off, I say. Out of the house with you."

More spluttering. Then he saw, through the tears of his righteous indignation, the very man who was the innocent cause of it all.

"Cap'en," he cried, hoarse with passion, "look at this here. Say, did ever man see the like! I've brought up this gell, since she was a baby, in the laps and legs of luxury; never asked her to do nothing for me but once—that was to-day—and she won't do it."

"What was it he wanted you to do, if I may ask?" said the Commodore gravely.

"He asked me to marry you," said Avis.

"And will you not?" He spoke softly and solemnly, as if he had thought out the matter with gravity and de-liberation. "Can you not? I am, it is true, older than you, and I may seem an unfit companion for a girl so young and so pretty. But I am not too old, child; I am as steady as ever, and as strong."

"Always as strong," murmured Stephen. "Nothing makes no difference with him. Not years, nor Bourbon whisky, nor Jamaica rum, nor six-shooters in a difficulty, nor English cruisers, nor Yankee blockaders. Here's a MAN for you."

"Can you not regard me with kindness, Avis?" the hero went on.

"I am engaged to another man," she replied simply.

His manner was beautiful; it was at once respectful to himself and to the young lady; his voice was gentle, and his eyes were soft; he looked almost good.

"I am very unfortunate," he said; "we sailors spend our lives apart from the refinement of women; we are apt to get rough and coarse—I know that; and when I saw you first, Miss Avis, you looked so sweet and good that I said to myself, 'Here is a girl who could lead a man to heaven even against his will.' And you are really engaged?"

"I cannot break it," she said; "I would not, if I could."

"No need then to say what I hoped to say; that all my dollars and my estates are yours if you will take me." Stephen began to wonder what estates were these. "There are gardens and palaces, flowers, fruits, horses and carriages, and a faithful servant to command—myself."

He smiled sadly as he spoke.

Avis shook her head.

"It is impossible," she said.

Then Stephen broke out again.

"Come," he cried, "don't let us waste time; get out, and let me see your face no more. Come, Cap'en, don't take on; there's lots of better girls than her. Let her go. I give you five minutes." He braced himself up as if for a tremendous effort. "And now you've drove me to it, I've more to tell you——"

"Easy, Stephen," said the Captain.

"Lucky for her," the old man growled, "that you came in. But she shall hear it. I thought to die with the secret. Nobody shouldn't know nothing about it, only me. Fine airs you've gave yourself all along. Pride that was —pride in being a Cobbledick. That's what made her stick out her chin and hold up her petticuts, wasn't it? Gar! And all for nought; for now I'll tell you, madam, that you're no more a Cobbledick than the Cap'en here—

not a touch of the Cobbledick about you, as might be known by your conducks. For, whereas a true-born Cobbledick ever loves a sailor, and would never marry, could she see her way out of it, any but sich, here we see you, to the shame and disgrace of Boscastle port, which is proud of the Cobbledicks, little though it be—refusing a Nero, and takin' up with a mere landlubber and counter-skipper."

"If I am not of your family," asked the girl, as soon as she could get in a word, "who am I?"

"You are nothing but a Common Pick-me-up." Stephen pronounced these words with peculiar emphasis, so as to bring out the full measure of the contempt involved. "A Common Pick-me-up, you were."

"What is that?"

"You was found (by me) on a raft in the Bay of Bengal; picked up (by me) off of that raft. You was in the arms of a dead Indian ayah. There was three sailors on that raft who was also dead. You was wropped up in four silk bandanners when we carried you off to the ship, a baby of a year old or thereabouts, and gave you to a negress to nurse. You a Cobbledick? With an ayah. Wropped in bandanners. On a raft. In the middle of the starved sailors. Nursed by a negress. A Common Pick-me-up!"

The Pilot spoke as if the recovery of babies in this manner was so common as to entail disgrace upon all so found.

"Did you find nothing more about me?"

"No. The men searched the pockets of the dead sailors for their money. Then they chucked them overboard and broke up the raft, because such things is dangerous. You're nobody's daughter, you are."

"At all events," said Avis quietly, for even a worm will turn, "it is some kind of relief to know that I am not yours, nor the daughter of anybody connected with you."

"As for your names," he went on, "I gave you the

name of Avis because it was my mother's, and Cobbledick because it was my own. Give me them names back. Avis "—here he made a gesture as of one who takes a thing from another and dashes it on the ground—"Avis, now you've got no Christian name to your back. Cobbledick " — here he made a similar gesture — "Cobbledick, now you've got no surname to your back; and now, my Lady No Name, you may pack. You and your Mr. Davenant."

The Captain stepped forward.

"Pardon me, Miss Avis, are you engaged to Mr. Davenant, the young gentleman at the hotel? I am sorry indeed that my unfortunate aspiration "—he smiled sadly—"should have led to these disagreeable consequences. Had I been aware of your engagement, I should have been the last——"

"Oh yes, yes!" said Avis; "but I am nearly driven mad by this man's talk and violence. Let me go."

"Yes, let her go; a Common Pick-me-up!"

Mr. Cobbledick waved his arms and shook his head, with that well-known gesture of contempt, chiefly practised by ladies of the lower rank, which consists in tightly pressing your mouth and closing your eyes, while you shake your head.

"Stay, Stephen." The Captain pushed him gently back into his chair. "We must not manage things in this way. If Miss Avis cannot see her way—being already promised to a happier man—she must not be abused or ill-treated. Though, no doubt, you mean it for the best."

"Any way," said Stephen, "she knows the truth now. And she can go."

"No, Stephen, she cannot go "—Captain Ramsay stood between them like the guardian angel, or the representative genius, of benevolence—"things must not be managed in that way. Miss Avis will remember that, niece or not, she has enjoyed your protection for eighteen years. You, my old comrade "—it was remarkable how the gallant Commodore seemed to drop the American accent altogether —"you will remember how she has become a credit to your liberality, and stands before you a perfect as well as a beautiful lady. And, for such a lady, give me England."

"I have heard you say, Cap'en, that New York or Baltimore beats all creation."

"When I was there, old friend. But when one is in England, one is bound to confess that English beauty bears the palm. Come now, Stephen, you were disappointed. You hoped that Avis would take the offer of an old friend and comrade of your own. Well, she can't. Perhaps if she had not been engaged, there would have been a chance. But we are too late. Very good, then. I withdraw, with an apology. Since you cannot think of me, Avis, let me only say, that I shall never marry, or think of another woman again."

"O Lord!" cried Stephen.

"Because your image will never be obliterated from my heart." This was very noble and grand. It seemed to do good to all alike. "I had hoped," the Commodore went on, "to have settled down, after this run, to that beautiful life led by the Southern planters, cheered by the affection of an English wife and the devotion of my faithful blacks."

"With a rattan and a cow-hide," Stephen interposed, by way of illustrating the depth of negro affection, and its deeply-rooted nature.

"Since that is not to be, I must give up the thought of it. Meantime, my dear young lady, this has been a painful scene for all concerned. I am sure you will agree with me that it is best forgotten. And if our friend here, whose heart is cast in the truest mould of friendship, has forgotten, in his zeal for me, what is due to a delicately brought up woman, you will, I am sure, forgive him." Stephen stared and gasped. What could be the meaning of this? "You have a perfect right," continued the Captain, "to marry whom you please. It will be better, however, for you to have your guardian's consent; and if Mr. Davenant, as I doubt not he will, proves to be a moral sort of man, of sound principles, no opposition will be made, and all shall be as you wish."

"Lord!" murmured Stephen, not knowing what to make of this. Never had he seen the Captain so silky, so polite, so considerate.

"My dear," the Captain went on, taking Avis's hand in his, and pressing it in paternal fashion, "I am sure we shall all part friends. Stephen, you used hard words to your ward."

"I did," said Stephen, perceiving that the admission was expected of him.

"Tell her you are sorry"

"I am sorry," said Stephen, obedient to command.

"And that you did not mean them."

"Never meant 'em," he repeated.

"Is it true," asked Avis, "about the raft?"

"That," said Stephen, "is Gospel of St. Matthew truth. Wropped up you were in four red silk bandanners. Latitude about twenty south, and, as for longitude, why, it might have been anywheres north-east of Ceylon. Pity we were in such a hurry, because else we should have searched for papers and letters. Well, I'm sorry I told you, that's a fact."

"And all the stories about my mother being a Knobling——"

"Go on, let me have it," said Stephen.

"And her dying at Jamaica; and my father and the shark; and the cousin who was transported——"

"All lies, my gell; lies and base deceptions, invented to put you off your guard, and not to suspect them bandanners."

"What am I to call myself, then?"

"Well," said Stephen, "since things are smoothed over, I don't greatly mind if you go on bein' Avis Cobbledick. No one needn't know; so you can go on a stickin' out your chin with the same pride in your family as you always have a stuck it out."

The face of her guardian was restored to its usual expression of joviality mingled with cunning; the Captain, seated in a chair, was nursing his chin in his hand, thoughtfully and sadly.

"I will go now, I think," she said. "Mr. Cobbledick, I thank you for your care of me. As I am not your niece at all, I will—I will ask Jack if we cannot somehow pay something of that heavy debt which I owe you. Captain Ramsay, I am deeply grateful for your forbearance."

She held out her hand. He stooped and kissed it.

"Indeed," he said, "I have done nothing. I hope, however, that I may win your trust and, perhaps, your friendship."

As Avis walked slowly away she tried, but in vain, to reconcile the picture drawn by Mr. Cobbledick of his hero, the drunkard and gambler, with the man himself, so mild, so gentle, and so beautifully spoken.

"Cap'en," whispered Stephen hoarsely, "what the blazes does this mean ?"

"It means," replied Captain Ramsay, "that there are more ways than one for a man to get what he wants. If it suits me to sing small and pretty—hymn-books is the word."

Stephen shook his head; this was beyond him.

"About this raft business, Steve ?"

"All true, Cap. Every word true."

"You are such an almighty liar, as a general rule——"

"Ask anybody in this port of Boscastle, where I was born, whether I had e'er a brother or a sister. A gell can't be a man's niece when that man is a only child. Likewise a orphan."

"She might be your daughter."

"I've not got no daughters. Picked her off of a raft, I did—just as I told her—wropped in four bandanners, with five-and-twenty dead niggers around. In the China seas."

"Then, what in thunder made you bring up the child ?"

"I put it this way, Cap'en. I said to myself: ' Here's a child of respectable people, 'cos she's got a nurse all to herself; and the bandanners was the very best. They'll think she's drowned. Wait a bit. When she's four years old, or risin' five, a age when children are pretty, I'll advertise for her parents, and I will take the reward.'"

This, the Captain assured him, was a prudent and far-seeing design.   But why had he not carried it out?

"Because," Stephen explained, "I forgot the child. When I was away to North Carolina, in the piloting line, I forgot her altogether; and there she was eatin' her head off, and my money meltin' away without my knowledge. Such wickedness as no one never dreamed of, with the workus not far off; which was meant by heaven, and built by religious people, for Pick-me-ups, and such as are widowless and in affliction, and dependent on their uncles."

This seemed like a faint reminiscence of the Litany, but the allusion was lost on Captain Ramsay, who had not yet "found religion."

"Then why did you call her your niece when you came home?"

"I couldn't let on about the raft, bless you. Why, she might ha' claimed the reward herself."

The reward was a fixed idea with him, just as the marriage settlement had become, only the former was the growth of years.

"As it is," he murmured, "I've done wrong in tellin' her. But the temptation was great to take down her pride. There, perhaps she won't think of it, and I can advertise and get the reward all the same."

"Steve," said the Captain, clapping him on the shoulder, "you've got a head after all. The reward is not unlikely to come off.   But we must move carefully."

"We?"

"Yes, we. I shall be entitled to all the reward if there is any. But I'm not going to play it low on an old ship-mate, and you shall have a fourth of whatever comes."

"What on airth ha' you got to do with it, Cap'en?"

"Only this; that I am going to be the lady's husband, and as such, you see, Steve—— Ah! you shouldn't let out little secrets. That was always your great fault."

CHAPTER VII.

THE CLEVERNESS OF THE COMMODORE.

"IF that is what you mean," said Stephen blankly, "hang me if I know how you are goin' to do it. First, you tells the girl you are very sorry and you wish you hadn't spoke. Next, you sends your love to her spark. After tellin' her, straight, that you don't want her no more, and you're sorry you spoke, you tell me—— Hang me if I know what you mean."

"I did not think you would. Listen now, while I give the sailing orders. You get them in your head tight, and you go on obeying them orders and no others, and then you shall see."

He then proceeded in brief but intelligible terms to dictate those orders. The Pilot nodded his head as they fell one by one from his superior officer's lips. They were easy to learn and to execute, but harder to understand. As his captain proceeded, however, the good old man's face lit up with surprise, admiration, and delight. For a simpler plan of diabolical villainy was never before unfolded. It was almost too simple. Stephen slapped his leg as the plan unfolded itself, till the echoes were awakened among the rocks and resounded from cliff to cliff like a volley of musketry. These gestures he naturally accompanied with a pæan of congratulation and joy, consisting entirely of these interjections which are not found in grammars, yet are generally sought after by persons who aim at straightforward clearness rather than elegance of language.

"I always said it!" he cried, when the orders had been fully laid down. "I always said it!" He looked at the captain with the most profound admiration. "Never a man in all the world his equal for devilment and craft! Who'd ha' thought of that, now?"

"Not you, Steve, certainly. Is this better than turning the gal out of doors, and driving her into the arms of her chap? I guess, Steve, you don't quite know my sort of stuff yet."

"Better!—ah!" Stephen drew a long breath. "And now, considerin' the high honour to which Avis is going to be raised, I'm only sorry I told her anything at all about the raft. She'll only be frettin', when it's all over, that she isn't a Cobbledick after all, just to give her a position more equal to her future rank."

"You think the scheme worth trying then?"

"It will reel off, Cap'en, like a heavin' of the log. No vi'lence; no quarrellin'; no cryin' and forcin'; and the end of the story most beautiful. I always did like a story to end well. So they lived happy ever afterwards, and had ten sweet children, nine of 'em twins."

The Pilot spent the rest of his day in a kind of exaltation; he felt light of heart; his soul was merry within him. And when Jack Davenant, whom Avis had without delay informed of this new revelation respecting the raft, came for more information, he was received with hilarity and joyousness which made him suspect strong waters. For once he was wrong. Stephen was perfectly sober and unfeignedly glad and happy.

"You are always welcome, Mr. Davenant," he exclaimed. "Come in and sit down. Never mind the marriage settlements. The Cobbledicks, sir (Avis's mother having been a Knobling, also a most respectable family), can afford to be generous."

"How about the raft story, then?"

"Oh yes!" He was not in the least disconcerted. "The raft, Mr. Davenant, is the truth. But I've always been accustomed to consider that dear gell as my niece, so that the family, as it were, growed. I shall be sorry to lose the Knoblings, too, for they're a good stock to know and to talk about."

"Then she is not your niece at all?"

"Not at all, which brings my generous conduct out in a more beautiful light."

"Well, I'm glad of that anyhow. Now tell me the story of the raft over again."

"We picked up the raft in the Gulf of Mexico about two days' run to the west of Cuba, whither we were bound." Jack remarked that this statement contradicted the previous one as to the position of the raft. "No one was aboard that raft except the dead ayah and the child." Here again another alteration. "We took the child aboard without waiting to search for proofs of who she might be, and we sailed away." Another, but a trifling variation in the story.

"Ah! what was your cargo? Could it not wait while you had the common curiosity to find out, if possible, who the child might be?"

"My cargoes, in those days, young gentleman, was the kind that spile a good deal by keepin', particularly if there's any part of it gone off a bit, so to say, when it comes aboard. Some o' mine, that trip, had already begun to spile."

"Oranges, fruit, lemons?"

"No, sir, not fruit. A kind of cargo it was which certain piratical cruisers pretendin' to be British were fond of scoopin' up for theirselves. Lord! the losses I've seen in that kind of cargo; a whole shipload I've seen tossed overboard before now to save the skipper and his ship. And the sharks as busy as snappin' turtles round that ship."

"Do you mean——" Jack stopped, because he was afraid, in a sense, to say the word.

"I mean niggers. Three hundred niggers I had aboard that ship, spilin' fast for want of breathin' room, fresh air, fresh water and fresh provisions. Three hundred and sixty-five, as many as the days in the year, I landed on the hospitable shore of Cuba. But the number that spiled on the way you would hardly believe, sir. Well, the little maid was very soon aboard, and a comfortable negress had her in a jiffy, and there we were."

"I wonder if this man can tell the truth," said Jack.

"Where she came from, who she was, I don't know no more than you. As for her name, I give it to her, like I give her everything she owns, with a noble education and no expense. Whereas, for marriage settlements——"

"Your nobility is well known and acknowledged, Mr. Cobbledick. Also your command of temper when Avis does not act as you would wish."

"She's been complainin', has she? Well, Mr. Davenant, there's no call for you to find fault. Wait till you're married and found her out. As for that too—" He remembered the sailing orders, and stopped himself after one broad grin, which indeed he could not repress. "As for that, I own I did quietly whisper, as it were, when she told me about your offer, that my wishes lay other ways and I'd rather see her take up with a sailor. I pointed out her dooty to her kind, and clear, and plain. If she won't do that dooty, I can't help it, can I?"

"But you point out duty with too many—well, too strongly."

"Sailors must be swore to; what's good afloat is good ashore. No sailors in the world so smart as our'n. The reason why is that they're properly swore to both young and old. That done Avis no harm. As for you, Mr. Davenant, why, if she will have you, and you're still for your fancy, we must make the best of a bad bargain."

Jack laughed.

"Not such a very bad bargain, I hope," he said. "Well, Mr. Cobbledick, I shall do my best to make Avis as happy as she deserves."

"I did my best, too," grumbled her guardian. "And what's come of it? She won't even take the man I want her to marry. If I'd asked her for any big thing now, it would have been different—I'm too old to expect much gratitude; but for such a trifle as that — just to tell her other young man that she cannot keep company with him no longer because a better feller has put into port—theer! it's enough to make a British sailor never do a honourable and generous thing no more. Better, a'most, have left her on the raft."

Jack laughed again.

"Why, surely you can't blame a girl for taking the man of her own heart?"

"Gells must do as they're told. They've got no business to have no heart."

"Well, she is not your niece, by your own showing, so I suppose she can do as she likes. Now I want to marry her as soon as I possibly can. Meantime you will, I suppose, allow her to remain here; of course I will pay for her board."

Here the Pilot began a series of winks, nods, and pantomimic gestures indicative of caution; he looked out of the window and closed it carefully; he opened the door, and looked about to see if there were any listeners. Finally, he sat down again, and whispered hoarsely—

"You'll have to take her soon, young gentleman. The sooner the better. The Commodore, who's not a man to loose his time, has come here to—— What do you think he's here for?"

"I don't know."

"To ship me as one of his officers. Nothing less. For he's got a ship and we're off in a fortnight. Says the Cap'en, 'Give me old Steve. He's sixty, but he's tough. Give me Steve at any price.'"

"Where are you going?" Jack knew very well, but it seemed polite to ask.

"Where we air a-going is a secret. Likewise the ship and all. It's a state secret, and they would stop her in port if they guessed that a Secesh officer was her captain."

"Is she another *Alabama*, then?"

"Maybe; maybe." Stephen wagged his head mysteriously. "Never mind that. Keep the secret, young man, or I'm hanged if you shall get the girl after all. The question for you is: Can you take her just as she is, in a fortnight's time?"

"I can take her to-day, if you like."

"Very good. Next question. When you've got her, I suppose you are able to keep her?"

"I am a painter. I hope to be able to keep her."

"A painter!" Stephen took him for something superior in the house painting line, and spoke with the greatest contempt. "A painter! To think that gell has throwed away a sailor, and such a sailor as the Commodore, for a painter."

"Yet even a painter may make money," said the unfortunate artist.

"Well, well. And where does your trade lie? Where is your shop? Air you a journeyman or air you a master?"

"I work in London, where my shop is, and, as I am paid by the job, I suppose I am only a journeyman."

"Here's a downfall!" Stephen spread his hands in dismay. "Yesterday the gell was a Cobbledick, her mother was a Knobling, and she might ha' married Captain Ramsay, himself. To-day she is a Common Pick-me-up, with never a name to her back, and she's goin' to marry a journeyman painter, paid by the job. Ah! pride, pride, which cometh before a squall."

"A fortnight," Jack reflected. "To-day is Monday. If I go to town to-morrow, I can manage something. We can go into lodgings for a while. I could get back on Saturday, and we might be married on Monday. That will do. You may give away the bride if you like."

"As there's no marriage settlements," said Stephen, shaking his head, and thinking that he could not sell her as he had proposed, "I s'pose I must give her away. But she ought to fetch a thousand pounds at least. Make it five hundred, Mr. Davenant, and pay up before you start," here he could not repress another smile, which broadened to a grin, "and we will call it square."

"Old Stephen, dear Avis," said Jack, presently recounting his interview, "is not, I suppose, your uncle, though I confess to doubts about the raft story. When a man cannot give the details twice in the same afternoon without varying them in every particular, I should say that the story would not be taken as evidence."

"I must be some one's daughter, Jack."

"You probably came straight down from heaven, my darling."

I always set down on paper as few of the raptures of lovers

as is consistent with conveying a clear impression that there were raptures. It will be seen from this specimen what nonsense Jack was capable of talking, and how very much he was in love.

"First," said Avis, "I used to be ashamed of having no relations except an unknown uncle in America. Next, I began to think it a distinction. The other girls had fathers and mothers; one's father was a doctor, and another a farmer, and another a lawyer, and so on; they had received their stations in the nursery. Mine was all to come. Perhaps, I thought, it might never come. I was to be a princess; the long-lost heiress of a great estate; I was to be a heroine of romance. They were all silly about me, and I suppose I was silly about myself. Then there did come as it seemed the telling of the riddle. It was a lame ending, and I was a poor weak creature to make myself unhappy over my fate. Yet it seemed dreadful to be told to go and work: to be a lady's-maid or a barmaid. And, though he had been generous to me, I could not feel that Stephen was quite what one would look for in a guardian and a father's brother."

"The Knobling connection was certainly one to be forgotten," said Jack. "Poor Avis! her mother's brother—a most distinguished man—was transported for twenty years for forging the port admiral's signature. Mr. Cobbledick has got great powers, my dear."

"But now, although it is a relief—yes, Jack, a great relief —to know that this unpleasant old man is not my uncle, remember that I have no name. Cobbledick is not pretty, but one gets used to it."

"I thought it very pretty till this afternoon," said Jack; "now I know what an ugly name it is. You shall change it, my darling, for Davenant this day week."

"O Jack! not so soon; give me time."

"Not a day longer, my dear. I feel as if I had been too long without you, years too long; we ought to have been together ever since you were born."

Then they planned their future lives. Other married

couples have troubles; this pair resolved upon having none; their path stretched before them bathed in sunshine, here and there shaded by rows of the most beautiful trees; all the road was strewn with flowers; there seemed no end of sunny days and warmth and happiness and love. It is also a part of Solomon's wondrous way of man and a maid that this dream of the perfect life should come once and for ever be remembered. The clouds hide the sun, and the pathway grows painful as the years run on. Well if the love remain, because the dream of youth has become at the end to be the recollection of a life.

Be sure that Avis told her lover of the surprising and extraordinary behaviour of Captain Ramsay, who had shown a chivalrous .courtesy worthy of the chivalrous South. She also told, and it was ascribed to the vivid imagination of the old man, how Stephen had painted this true-bred gentleman in the blackest colours. Jack, for his part, made severe animadversions on the blindness of people who practise the trade of poet. "He called him a tiger," said Jack indignantly.

That evening he sought an opportunity of speaking to Captain Ramsay in the usual place of resort.

'I have to thank you, sir," he said, "for your great courtesy and forbearance in the matter of a certain young lady."

"Say no more, Mr. Davenant," said the Captain. "A man must be a mean skunk to force himself on a young lady when she's already promised. I beg your pardon, sir, most sincerely, for intruding to the extent I did. Had I known earlier, I should not have done so. Shake hands, sir, and take a whisky cocktail made in Baltimore style. I've taught them how to do it."

Friendly relations thus established, Captain Ramsay, still speaking in a slow gentle way, and with thought, as if he was carefully looking for the right word and no other, to express his opinion, went on to assure Jack that he lamented very profoundly his late arrival on the field: that he was one of those who believe in the goodness of woman and the perfectibility of human nature by the shining example of that goodness; that he was certain from observation and experience of good women, among whom, he said, his lot when ashore had been chiefly cast, that Avis was as good as she was beautiful. These and many other beautiful and comforting things he said. And then, when the heart of Jack was really warming to him, as to a man who had seen many men and their manners, and yet preserved a certain virginal purity of thought which made him blush for himself, the Captain called for another cocktail.

It was irritating to observe the scowl with which the Poet, who was present, sat on his side of the settle and listened to this conversation.

From sentiments, the Captain passed to the narration of deeds. These had no bearing, it is true, on the ennobling nature of love, but they brought out his character in vivid light as a practiser of a code which, though not English, yet seemed in some respects justifiable.

"And really," Jack subsequently confessed, "it was not till afterwards that I found out that he had been simply confessing himself a murderer."

"In the Southern States," he said, "men become brothers. If you will be brothers with me, Mr. Davenant, I guess it may be good, some day, for one of us. For when two men air brothers, they air bound to fight for each other, to spring a bowie or a six-shooter for each other at a moment's notice; not to desert each other. I had a brother once down in Texas. Now, he was murdered. Wal, gentlemen, every time I land in Galveston, which happens once in two years, or thereabouts, I go for those murderers with a rifle, a knife and a pair of revolvers. I do not say that I land one at every visit, for there were ten; but now, as near as I can count, there are only three, and one is skeered and gone up country, where I doubt I shall never find him. The other two air fightin' the battles of the Lord in Dixie's Land: wherefore, for the present, they know that they air safe. Once the war is over and the Yank (as he will be) chawed up so that his own mother won't know him again, I shall make for those murderers again, even if they haven't got a leg nor an arm left. Because I am bound to remember my brother. And so, Mr. Davenant, if you please, we will be brothers. I envy you your wife, that's a fact. And I shall go in mourning for being too late for that beautiful young thing all the days of my life. But you've won her. Wherefore, here is my hand, fair and honest, and brothers we shall be."

Who could resist such an appeal to the deeper feelings of the heart? Not Jack, who mutely held out his hand and grasped the hand of the American. As he did so he thought he heard the Poet murmuring softly—

" He is a tiger—a man-eater ! "

" Steve Cobbledick tells me," the Captain went on, " that you are going to London to-morrow ? "

" Yes, for a few days only. I have," said Jack, with an expressive blush, " a few preparations to make."

" Nat'rally. And you come back—when ? "

" On Saturday. To be married on Monday."

Just then a telegram was brought to the Captain. He opened it, read it, threw the paper into the fire, and stroked his chin thoughtfully.

" You come back on Saturday. Good. Do not be later, because we, Steve Cobbledick and I, have very important business to look after about then. It would be a pity if you were to come after we were gone."

" Yes," said Jack; " I should like to see you off."

" A great pity it would be," said Captain Ramsay. " Ah ! Mr. Davenant, if you were not going to be married, what a time you might have with us! What a time ! "

" Are you not satisfied with one *Alabama* ? "

" No ; nor with a hundred, provided we drive the Yanks off the seas; and provided, if there be a row, that England pays. You would enjoy yourself very much with us, Mr. Davenant, I assure you, particularly "—he added this with a frank, winning smile—" if you knew who was going to be aboard with us. You'll remember the words, won't you, now ? I say you'd be uncommon happy with us, particularly if you knew, beforehand, who was going to be a passenger aboard."

Jack laughed. "I will remember," he said.

"A tiger," murmured the Poet, irreconcilable.

In the morning, with fond farewells, Jack took leave of his *fiancée*.

"It is only for a week," he said, while she clung to him and wept. "Only for a week, my Avis. I go to make my darling a nest."

"I cannot bear to let you go, Jack, Oh! it is all like a dream to me. I came here in a dream of hope. It changed to a dream of gloom and despair; then came another dream —of you, my lover; and I have lost my name and the people whom I thought to have found. Now you are going away. How do I know that I shall not to-morrow awake and find that you, too, are a dream?"

He took off his ring, a simple seal, his watch and his chain. "Keep them," he said, "for me. Wear the watch and chain. Hang the ring upon the chain, and when you look at them, think I am no ghost or phantom of a troubled brain, because no ghost who ever walked was able to carry a watch and chain."

"Yet," she said—"yet, I cannot bear to let you go. A week; a whole week. And what may happen, mean-time?"

"What should happen, dearest? You are surrounded by friends. The Poet stays here to keep watch over you. Captain Ramsay will suffer no wrong or harm to be done you. Courage, dear."

"I am foolish," she said. "Yet it is so hard to let you go, even for a week. I am not afraid of Stephen, nor of anything that I can tell you. Yet, Jack, I am afraid."

He kissed her again and again; he assured her that there was nothing in the world to fear; he promised to write every day; he pictured his speedy return—why, if he came back on Saturday, it would only be for a five days' absence; he made her blush by bidding her think of the next Monday—Saint Monday—day ever to be blessed and held most holy—when he should stand beside her at the altar. And so, at last, because time must be obeyed, he caught her in his arms and kissed a last farewell.

Alas! that kiss was the last of Jack that the girl would have to remember for many a weary day.

It was on Tuesday, then, that Jack Davenant left Boscastle, driving to Launceston to catch the train. He begged the Poet, before he went away, to keep Avis under his special charge while he was away: to amuse her, guard her, and see that no harm happened to her; a charge which the Poet accepted with great zeal and friendliness. There was then nothing to fear: Captain Ramsay was entirely to be trusted—a little rough in his expressions, but a man of greatly noble mind; Stephen, who certainly had been violent before, would not venture to break out again : everything was settled and comfortable. Yet, in spite of assurances, repeated again and again to himself, he departed for London unaccountably anxious. Perhaps Avis's terrors infected him. He felt the sudden chill which comes before a storm. The power of prophecy, for some wonderful reason, means the power of predicting the approach of unpleasantness. Cassandra, Jeremiah, and Mr. Grey utter their prophecies, but they are never of cheerful nature. Ascalon is to be made desolate; Troy is to be destroyed; Tyre is to be a rock for the spreading of nets; England is to be levelled with Holland, and so on. Never anything to make us contemplate the future with satisfaction. Not only Ahab and his grandsons, but also all mankind, have found the prophets profoundly melancholy. Why have there been no joyous foretellers, jovial seers, cheerful upraisers of man's heart by painting a future in which there shall be no injustice, no hard times, and peace, prosperity, and contentment for all alike? There must be some good times coming. Sad as the history of man has been, there has certainly been a considerable improvement in cheerfulness, which we hope may continue And when I go into the prophetic line, it will be to proclaim, in the immediate future, the most delightful time imaginable, to prepare for which we shall hang or imprison all kings, commanders of armies, inventors of arms, troublers of the peace, promoters of discontent, professional agitators, and disagreeable people. The present days, indeed, have become so eminently uncomfortable that it is almost time to begin making this announcement.

The Poet mounted guard with zeal. He was suspicious of the old man, whose sudden change of front was inexplicable; he was suspicious of the gentleness assumed by the American; such suavity was unnatural in a person of his calling and his self-confessed antecedents. Yet what harm could they do?

It seemed on the first day of Jack's absence as if Captain Ramsay, in his zeal for his "brother," was also mounting guard for the protection of the girl against unknown dangers. For he followed her about, and left the Poet few opportunities of talking to her alone. Now he so thoroughly disliked the American that he could not bear even his presence. On the second day, however, he got her to walk with him on the cliffs, and of course they talked of Jack all the time.

"Stephen," she said, "seems to have forgotten his disappointment. I suppose it is because Captain Ramsay has behaved with so much consideration. I hope, at least, that you have repented of your bad opinion of him?"

"Not at all. I have a worse opinion of him than ever."

"But that is surely prejudice. Remember how generous he has been."

"I know. That is, I know what you mean. What I cannot understand is—why he puts on this new air of virtue; I don't understand."

"But you may be wrong."

"Yes," said the Poet. "I thought when I saw him first that he looked and talked like a tiger. All the same, he may be a lamb."

"To-day is Wednesday," Avis went on, "and Jack will be with us again on Saturday. I had a letter to-day. It is the second letter, only the second letter that I have ever had in all my life. The first was a dreadful letter from my—from Stephen, telling me to leave school and go to him. But the second—oh! how do men learn to say such beautiful things?"

"Because they feel them, perhaps."

"Let us sit down," said Avis, sighing, "and you shall tell me all about Jack, and what he was like when he was a boy. I am sure you will have nothing but what is good to tell me."

This was on the Wednesday morning. The reason why Avis was left to the Poet by Captain Ramsay was that he was having a serious conversation with Stephen. The *Maryland*, he told him, had already left Liverpool; she would arrive off Boscastle Port about noon the next day. Therefore it behoved Stephen to make such arrangements as might be necessary for immediate departure. Ramsay gave him, in fulfilment of the agreement, the sum of three hundred and seventy-five pounds in Bank of England notes, half his pay as pilot from Nassau to Wilmington and back, with a written agreement for the other half on the completion of the round trip; and then they laid their heads together and whispered, though no one was within earshot, for a good half hour. When two men whisper together it is generally safe to consider that they mean mischief to some person or persons. When these two men are old slavers, filibusters, blockade-runners, and the like, it is quite safe to consider that they mean mischief.

"Then, I think," said the Captain at last, "that we have made all square and right. There can't be any difficulty. The weather looks as if it will be fine. Mate, this little job shall be pulled off in a way to do us credit. As for me, I shall give all the credit to you. Stephen, I shall say, devised the plan. Stephen carried it through. Stephen did it all."

The old man grinned with pleasure and pride. Then he thought of some disagreeable side of the business, and he became serious and even troubled.

"She'll take on awful, she will," he said.

"Let her take on. That won't matter."

"She's a plucky one, too. Cap'en, I don't half like it."

"Steve, old man, you don't feel like going back upon your word, do you? Don't say that."

Stephen Cobbledick took courage.

"My word is passed," he replied stoutly, "and shall be kep'. A sailor mustn't go back upon his word. Though, when you come to turn it over in your mind, so as to look at it all round, it does seem kind of unnat'ral for a man to kidnap his own niece."

"If she's your own niece, how about the raft?"

"Why, that's true. Seeing, then, that she isn't my niece at all——"

"And that we air old shipmates and pals——"

"And that you're goin' to behave honourable, and treat her kind——"

"And marry her in the first port, and settle down afterwards where there's no chance of nasty inquiries——"

"And keep her out of the way of that other one—Olive?"

"Ay! She shall never hear of Olive at all."

"And to pro—vide the gell with all she wants——"

"And stick on to her faithful and true——"

"Why," answered Stephen, "I'm doin' the best I can, and everybody will own it, for the gell; and I'll do it with a thankful heart."

"Spoke like a man!" cried the Captain. "Spoke like what I expected from old Steve!"

Stephen had business that afternoon which took him to Camelford. His business was to arrange for the collection of his rents and the safety of his money while he was away. As for his kit, which was not extensive, he carried it in a waterproof bag and stowed it in the locker of his boat. A busy and eventful day it was for him. In fact it was more full of fate than he at all anticipated.

While he was thus occupied Captain Ramsay spent his time with Avis.

"I come to tell you," he began, "that I have received a telegram." He handed it to her.

"The *Maryland* went out of dock this morning. She will lie-to off Boscastle Port about noon to-morrow. If the weather is bad she will put in at Falmouth."

"The weather," he said, "promises fine. It is a pity that she does not go to Falmouth, or you might have run down with Stephen and me and gone aboard her."

"I have never seen a ship," Avis said. "Except the coasters which put in here."

"Poor child!" said the Captain, with feeling. "She has never seen a ship!"

"And Stephen, does he sail with you to-morrow?"

"No; he joins us later on; we are going for a trial cruise first." The lies dropped out of this mariner's mouth as easily as out of Stephen's. "He comes aboard later on; three weeks or a month."

"I hope, Captain Ramsay," said Avis, "that you are not going to run into any terrible danger."

"You feel as if you would be sorry if I was knocked on the head with a Yankee cutlass."

"I should be very sorry, for, indeed, Captain Ramsay, I cannot tell you how grateful I am to you for your consideration."

"If I had known," he said, "that your affections were already bestowed, I should not have presumed to step in. As for Stephen's bad temper, that was all the fault of my confounded bungling. In the States a man speaks first to the gal, or she sometimes to him; which is, I guess, whether it's he first or she first, the right and natural way. I thought, being a stranger here, that a man was bound to go to a gal's parents and guardian first, and, if they didn't seem to yearn for him, hitch off and try with another batch of parents."

"If I knew how to thank you——" Avis began.

"Then," he replied, with a gush of good feeling, "do not thank me at all. As to that story about the raft——"

"Do you really think it is true? You know how Stephen exaggerates."

"I know. A beautiful liar he is. But I think the raft

story is true. Pity it was so long ago. I wonder if there was any name or mark on your clothes, or those silk handkerchiefs with which you were wrapped up?"

"I do not know, indeed. I know only what my—what Stephen told me."

"If there was any thing, and that thing was kept, I suppose it would be in the house and in Stephen's own room?"

"I suppose so," said Avis.

"It would be kind of romantic, wouldn't it," he asked, "if we were to find your parents after all? There must be somewhere in the world some folk who had a little baby lost aboard a ship coming from India eighteen years ago or so."

"I think," said Avis, "that I do not want to find any more relations. The first discovery was not encouraging. I am content to remain what Stephen feelingly called me, a Common Pick-me-up. Besides, I shall have Jack."

Notwithstanding, the Captain took an opportunity of examining Stephen again upon the point. But there was nothing to go upon. The bandannas were gone, expended in service, and there was nothing else, not even the bit of coral which the lost heiress always keeps treasured up, tied by a ribbon round her neck, and hidden in her bosom, where it must scratch horribly and be about as comfortable as a hair-shirt. Also, when Stephen was required to relate the whole story afresh, he told it with an entirely new set of circumstances, and placed the raft a thousand miles or so south of the Cape, nearly in the regions of perpetual ice. Charged with this variation, he admitted that he had been careless as to details, but swore stoutly that the child had been veritably picked up at sea, the last survivor.

With Avis, however, the Captain changed the conversation and began to narrate his adventures and perils by sea and land, especially those which brought into strong light his own generosity and many other noble gifts. And presently he told the girl of a certain enchanted castle, grange, or palace, which he had built for the solace of his soul in sunny Florida.

"I guess that when this war is over, which will be before many months, I shall return to that sweet location and stay there till the time comes for sending in the checks. There's forests of palms and tree ferns, eighty feet high, round the house; there's miles of orange trees; the pigs and the niggers are fed on nothing else but oranges; the alligators come ashore after them; they sit under the trees, and get their manners and their hides softened by eating that yaller civiliser. It never freezes there and never blows; it is never too hot; there's banks of flowers, most all of them magnolias, with creepers climbing everywhere; there's pretty parrots and little humming birds; there's plenty of niggers; you can lie in a silk hammock under the verandah, with one nigger told off for the fan, another to swing you, another to peel the oranges, another to bring cooling drinks, another to roll your cigarette, and another to light them. Avis, it's a life that you poor people livin' in a blessed island where there's mostly rain, and when it doesn't rain, it blows east wind, wouldn't understand at first. You'd say, 'Lemme be. Gimme more iced cocktail. I don't want no better heaven; this is a small bit of the happy land chopped off and put down in the Gulf of Mexico, just to let an unbelievin' world know what they may expect if they play the game right through honourable.' Some day, perhaps," he continued, "you will cross over the water and see my little plantation You and your husband, I mean."

With such discussion the crafty Captain strengthened and increased the girl's confidence in him, so that she thought she had a friend indeed in this rough yet gentle-spoken sailor. And while the Poet watched with a disquiet which he could not explain, the Captain and Avis sat all the afternoon together. When he left her he held out his hand.

"We shall say good-bye to-morrow," he said. "This is for you to say that you trust me now."

"Why," said Avis, laughing, "of course I trust you. And so does Jack."

"The other fellow doesn't," said the Captain, "but never mind him. As for Jack he ought to have been a sailor."

Avis laughed again. "All good men cannot be sailors."

"Jack ought to have been one," he repeated. "Ours is the trade for truth and honour; also for fair and open play."

Now about eleven o'clock in the forenoon of Thursday, the Poet was sitting on the rocks facing the sea. Avis was for the moment forgotten; his note-book was in one hand and a pencil in the other. He was quite happy, because after many days' wrestling he was finding freedom of expression. He had just made up his mind as to the metre fittest for his subject, which dealt with a seaside maiden and her lover; and was suggested, in fact, by Avis herself. He had already planned the story. It had a tragic conclusion, for he was young; when one gets on in life, one has seen so many tragedies, so many disappointments, so many crushed hopes, so many early deaths, that one feels it to be really sinful to add another drop to this ocean of tears. Poetry, like fiction, should be glad. But the Poet's story was a sad one: the seaside maiden was to be torn away from her lover by wicked pirates; he was to wander from land to land in search of her. He was to find her at last, but only to find her dying. The situation was so affecting that he was already beginning to shed tears over it.

Now while he pondered and made notes, he became aware of a steamer standing in, apparently, for Boscastle, whither no steamers ever came. She hove to, however, a few hundred yards from the rocks, the sea being nearly calm and the day being fair, and presently her whistle sounded sharp and clear. It was a signal.

She was so close that everything on board was easy to be made out. A small craft, but long and narrow, like a cigar, she lay low as if she was well loaded, her hull showing only about nine feet above the water; she was painted a dull grey colour; she carried no other rigging than a pair of pole masts without any yards; she was probably a boat of about five hundred tons burden. She looked from the height, where the Poet was sitting, like a toy steamer, too fragile and delicate to stand the great waves of the rolling forties.

Then a very singular thing happened. Just below the Poet's feet was the mouth of the little harbour; there came out, sailing slowly in the light breeze, Stephen Cobbledick's boat. He himself sat midships, handy for the sail; Avis held the rudder-lines; beside her sat Captain Ramsay. It was obvious that the steamer was in some way connected with the American; then the Poet saw that the sailors on board the steamer were running about, and presently a tackle was lowered. It must be Captain Ramsay's ship. Then he was going away; that was a good thing; Avis and Stephen were taking him off; that was a friendly thing to do. The little boat ran alongside the steamer; Stephen hauled in sail, while the Captain made the painter fast to the ladder. Then he assisted Avis to climb the steep and narrow ladder, and sprang up himself. Arrived on deck, the girl walk for'ard, looking about her with curiosity and interest. She was invited to see the ship, that was plain. What on earth, then, did old Stephen mean? Here, indeed, his behaviour became inexplicable. For, with so much deliberation as to show premeditation and intention, he carefully cast loose the painter, stepped out upon the ladder, and climbed up; as for the boat, she drifted slowly astern. Then the steamer, without more delay, suddenly and swiftly forged ahead; the boat was in a moment far away. The Poet saw, as the ship glided over the smooth water, Avis rushing to the side and the captain clutching at her arm. He sprang to his feet and shouted and waved his arms. Avis saw him, and he saw her struggling, while Ramsay and Stephen held her back, as if she would spring overboard in a mad attempt to escape. Then he saw her free herself from her captors and sink, despairing, on the deck. But the ship went on her course; the figures became more difficult to see; soon there was but a black hull; then but a line of smoke; then that vanished; all was out of sight.

Avis was gone! She was enticed on board the ship by the crafty American and the villain Stephen: it was no accident; she was treacherously and foully deceived; the thing was deliberately done: he had seen with his own eyes the old pilot untie the painter and set his boat adrift; she was in the power of as black a villain as ever walked. " I always said," cried the Poet, "that he was a tiger !"

. In the worst misfortune it is always a consolation to know that you have been right in your prognostications. In fact, some of your friends have always prophesied it. I have said above that no man is a prophet of joy, so that on the rare occasions when joyful things do come, the happiness they cause is never diminished by the voice of one who says he always told you so.

"I knew," repeated the poet, " that he was a man-eater, a tiger !"

He hastened down the rocks and told the sailors and people about the port what he had seen. They could not help; they knew nothing; that Stephen should go aboard with his friend was natural; that he should cast his boat adrift was incredible. It must have been an accident. They manned a boat and put off, expecting to meet the steamer coming back. The Poet went with them; outside, they picked up the little yacht, a derelict; but the steamer did not return, and presently they came back wondering. And in the " Wellington Arms " that night, when the little club met and realised the vacancy caused by Stephen's absence, they began slowly to perceive that a great crime had been committed.

All that night—the nights in June are light—the Poet wandered about the rocks on the chance that Avis might yet somehow be brought back. He had betrayed his charge, he said to himself. He ought, never to have left her while that man was in the place. He ought—— And what would Jack say—poor Jack, who had lost his bride? With what face would the Poet meet him and greet him with the dreadful news?

CHAPTER VIII.

THE WRECK OF THE "MARYLAND."

I HAVE now to tell a story of the most wicked treachery and deceit that was ever practised upon any girl. There never, surely, could have been a greater villain than Captain Ramsay, or a more ready accomplice than Stephen Cobbledick.

They lulled me, between them, into so great a confidence, that I believed the man Ramsay to be my firm and most trustworthy friend. He said Jack and he were sworn brothers; that to be brothers among the people with whom he had mostly lived meant to stand by and defend each other, to make each ready to die, if necessary, for the other. With such an affection did he pretend to regard Jack ; such mutual vows, he said, had they interchanged. He was full of protestations about honour, loyalty—playing a fair and open game. All this time the plot was laid, and the plan resolved upon, although it was not until the last moment, and then only by a pretence at a sudden thought, that I was enticed on board his ship.

It was on the Thursday—Jack having been gone two days—and early in the forenoon, that the man Ramsay came, walking slowly, to the cottage, where I was writing a letter to Jack. He had stuck one of his big cigars between his lips, and in his hand, I remember, was a wild rose, which gave him somehow the look of a man of peace. But he had put off his black clothes, and wore a smart, seaman-like dress, with a gold band round his peaked cap.

"The craft is off the mouth of the port, Miss Avis," he said sadly and gently. "I hope you will run down and give me a farewell wave of your handkerchief from the point when I am on board. Where is Stephen?"

"Here I am, Cap'en," said the old man, coming out of the kitchen. Now there was nothing, not the least sign, to show that he, too, was on the point of sailing. He was dressed as usual. He had made, so far as I could see, no preparations. To be sure, I was not suspecting any. "Is the gig sent ashore?"

"No, Stephen. You shall take me off yourself in your own boat."

I thought that friendly of him.

"I will, Cap'en; I will," replied Stephen cheerily. "It's the last thing I can do before I jine next month."

He said those words, I suppose, to put me off any suspicion. But, indeed, I had none.

"Then, Miss Avis"—the Captain held out his hand—"I will say farewell here. You will promise to stand on the point and see the last of me?"

"Why should she go to the point at all?" Stephen suggested. "Why can't she come off in the boat as usual?"

"Why not?" asked the Captain, his kind thoughtful face lighting up with a smile. "A happy thought, old friend! Will you do me so much honour as to steer me on board my own ship?"

I was pleased to be of a little service, and we all walked away to the quay, where the boat was lying ready for the trip.

When we reached the ship, Captain Ramsay asked me if, as I was there, I would like just to run up the companion and see what an ocean steamer was like.

"Let us make the painter fast first," he said.

He gave me his hand up the steps, Stephen remaining behind.

I began to look about me curiously, when suddenly I heard the engines begin to work, and felt the screw revolve. The ship was moving.

"O Captain!" I said, laughing, "you must stop her quick, for me to get out."

"Ay, ay," he replied, but said no more, and still the screw went on.

"Captain!" I cried. Then I ran to the side. There was our boat drifting away far astern, and beside me stood Stephen himself, a waterproof bag in his hand, looking so guiltily ashamed that I guessed at once the truth. The boat had been sent adrift on purpose. I was a prisoner on board the ship.

If Stephen looked ashamed, not so the Captain. He drew himself straight, with a glitter in his eye, and a smile upon his lips. It was a cruel glitter and a hard smile.

The man's face had changed; the thoughtfully sad expression was gone.

"This little plan, Miss Avis," he said quietly, "was arranged between me and Stephen. We were anxious that it should come off without any hitch, which was the reason why you were not in the secret. You are our passenger."

"O villain!" It was not to the Captain, but to Stephen, that I spoke.

He made no reply. He hung his head, and looked at the Captain, as if for help. He spoke up roughly and readily.

"You did it for the best, Steve. No kind o' use to be skeered because the girl's riled. She's nat'rally riled; anybody would be, first go off. What you've got to think is, that you done it for the best. Why, at this very moment, come to listen, you'll hear your conscience singin' hymns in your bosom with grateful joy."

"All for your own good, Avis," said Stephen, with an effort.

"That is so. Meantime, Miss Avis, if you feel like letting on, why, let yourself rip; we don't mind."

"Not a bit," said Stephen hoarsely. "I never heered a woman let on out at sea before."

I suppose I was still silent, for presently the Captain went on—

"I told you that I was in love with you. I am a man, and not a maid; so that when I set my fancy on a thing, that thing I must have. I set my fancy on you, and no other. I am powerful in love with you. I am so much in love that, rather'n lose you, I'd sink this craft with all her cargo, and the crew, and you too. I would, by——"

He strengthened the assurance with so great an oath, that it ought alone to have sunk the ship by the violence of its wickedness.

"Let's have no sinkin' of crafts," said Stephen uneasily. " Avis will come round bime-by. Give her rope."

"As for your lover," the Captain went on, "he counts for nothing. You'll forget him in a week. Make up your mind to forget him at once, for you've got to marry me. That's settled. I stand no sulks from any gell. They've got to look cheerful, and to do what they're told to do. Then things go well, and they find me a good sort."

He spoke as if he had a dozen wives.

Now, I know not what I answered, because, indeed, my mind was confused. I think I prayed them of their mercy to set me ashore. I think I recalled to the Captain's memory the many things he had said in truth and honour: that I threatened them and set them at defiance. All I remember quite clearly is that Stephen stood stupidly staring as if afraid and ashamed, that the Captain quietly stood before me, making no answer to speak of, and that when I appealed to the man at the helm, he kept one eye on the wheel and the other on the compass, and made no response whatever. I wonder how far his immobility would extend. I believe, however, that if they had thrown me overboard he would have taken no notice either by word or gesture. He was a Norfolk man (the American Norfolk)— a long-boned weedy man—who afterwards was of great service to me. His face was as red as exposure to the weather could make it, and his expression meant duty. His name was Liberty Wicks.

When I was worn out with appealing to consciences as hard as the nether millstone, I fell to tears and weeping. There was not one among all the crew who could be moved by the tears of a woman. Yet they all knew what their Captain had done.

"There is not," said the Captain, "one single man aboard this ship who will help you. Therefore you may spare your cries. And now, if you please, as there's the ship to navigate and the work to be done, p'raps you'll let me show you your cabin."

"Don't frighten her, Cap'en," said Stephen, looking uneasy again. "Tell her what you've promised: else you may find another pilot."

"Your cabin is your own," Captain Ramsay explained. "It is your private room. No one will disturb you there except your steward. I am sorry there is no stewardess. When you please, come on deck. There we shall all be your servants, and I am sure," he added, with a return to the old manner, "that we shall, in a day or two, see you happier on board the *Maryland* than you could ever have been in any other land."

He led the way, and I followed without a word. Stephen came after, still crestfallen, though by the wagging of his head and the clearing of his throat, it was apparent that he was making up his mind to listen to those hymns which, according to the Captain, his conscience was singing. The efforts made by a man who is thoroughly ashamed of himself to recover self-respect and seem at ease are very sad to witness.

The steamer had a pretty little saloon aft with a sleeping cabin on either side.

"These," said Captain Ramsay, still in the same conciliatory but determined manner, "are your quarters. I give you up the Captain's cabin. Here you will be quite private and undisturbed. You need have no fears. If any one aboard this ship were to offer an insult to my future wife, that man's remains should be thrown overboard shortly afterwards. Therefore, be under no apprehension; you shall mess by yourself."

I sat down without a word. O Jack! Jack! Who would tell you?

"The Captain means kind," said Stephen hoarsely. "Come, Avis, be comfortable. A run across the herrin' pond, and a husband on the other side of it. Such a husband too! Why it's honour and glory, not cryin' and takin' on!"

"Let her be," said the Captain. "She is riled. Give her time. Just now, Miss Avis, you think it is mean. Why all's fair in love. And after a few days, when you've picked up a bit, we shall be friends again. I am only sorry there's never a stewardess on board."

Here one of the cabin doors opened, and a woman stepped out.

"There is a stewardess, Captain Ramsay."

At sight of her the Captain stepped back with an oath.

"Olive! By all the powers!"

"O Lord!" cried Stephen, starting. "Here's his wife!"

"What do you—how did you," stammered the Captain. It was not pretty to look upon his face, on which was expressed a vehement desire to break the sixth commandment.

She was a tall and handsome woman of five-and-twenty or so, with a profusion of black hair, and black eyes. She was plainly dressed; on her finger I noticed a wedding-ring.

"I am a stowaway," she said. "You did not expect me here. Yet I told you at Liverpool that I would never leave you, and I never will!"

"She never will," murmured Stephen, in a kind of admiring stupor. "She looks as if she never would."

"I will murder you! Do you hear?" The Captain snatched at his waistcoat, as if to draw the revolver which he generally carried there. "I will murder you. You shall be thrown overboard! I say, I will kill you!"

"Do not be afraid, child," she said to me, apparently paying no attention to his angry gestures. "He will not murder me. He would, if he dared, but even the sailors of this ship, rough as they are, would not screen him if he did. And he does not desire to be hanged."

She was quite quiet; her face was very pale; her lips were set. I learned, afterwards, to love her. But at first I was afraid of her.

"This," said Stephen, "is the very deuce an' all. What's to be done now?"

"Who are you?" I asked. "Oh! tell me if you, too, are in a plot with these wretched men!"

"I am the wife of the man who calls himself Captain Ramsay," she replied. "There stands my husband."

"It's a lie!" shouted the Captain, emphasising his words in manner common among men of his kind. "It's a LIE! She has been divorced by the law of the country. I have no wife."

"I wear your wedding-ring still." She showed it on her finger. "I refuse your divorce. I will not acknowledge the law which allows a man to put away a wife without a reason. I am still your wife. I shall follow you wherever you go. I came across the Atlantic, to Liverpool, after you. I came on board this ship after you. I shall make the voyage with you."

The captain laughed.

"You shall," he said. "Hang me if you shall leave the ship till I let you. You shall follow me—whether you like it or not—to Dixie's Land."

"Even there," she said, though she shivered, "I will venture. I know what is in your wicked brain. Yet I am not afraid. I am here to protect this innocent girl. As for you," she turned to the unfortunate pilot, "I have heard of you. You are still, old man, as you always have been, the stupid tool of this man. At his bidding, and for no use or help to yourself, you are ready to throw away your immortal soul. Go out of our sight! Go, I say!"

Stephen straightened his back with an effort, and cleared his throat. He looked at me, who was now clinging to Olive, and then at his chief, who stood biting his lip, with an angry flush upon his cheek, and a look that meant revenge if he could get it.

"Come, Cap," said Stephen, "we can do no good here. Come on deck." He led the way, and mounted the companion with alacrity. "Phew!" he whistled on deck. "Trouble a brewin' now. What shall we do next?"

"If I could——" the Captain began, but stopped short.

"You can't, Captain," said Stephen. "The men would see it; Avis would see it. Put it out of your thoughts. Now mind. When I said I'd help bring the gell aboard, I never bargained for Olive as well. What about Nassau?"

"Now," said Olive kindly, when we were alone, "tell me who you are, and what has happened."

T

"Oh! he has stolen me! He asked me to come on board;
he pretended to be my friend; and he has stolen me. And
Jack is coming back on Saturday to marry me!"

"My poor child!"—her tears fell with mine—"this is
terrible, indeed. But, courage, I am here. We are on his
ship, and cannot choose but go with him. Yet—yet—I do
not think he will dare to harm either of us. My dear, he is
afraid of me."

"Are you indeed his wife?"

"It is my unhappy lot," she replied, "to be the wife of
the worst man, I believe, in all the world. Yet needs must
that I follow him, whatever be the end."

I waited to hear more.

"I was married to him," she went on, "six years ago.
He tired of me in a month. Then he deserted me, and sent
me letters from places where he never went, or else he sent
no letters at all. I found him out. Again he deserted me,
and again I found him out. He took me to the State of
Indiana, where he got something that he called a divorce.
I know not on what pretence, and do not care. He left me
there without money and without friends. But I found both,
and followed him again, tracing him from port to port, for
such as he seldom go inland. Then I learned that he had
gone to Liverpool, and I followed him, and found him
again. It was the old story. He began by cursing, and
ended by lying. He was going to London; he would send
me money. He would let things go on as if he had not got
his divorce. I did not believe him. And presently I discovered that he was at the docks every day, loading a vessel
which he was to command. I guessed pretty well where the
cargo of that ship was destined for. There are dangers in
that voyage which no woman should face, and dangers for
me that you cannot think of. Yet it seemed as if I had no
choice but to go. I learned when the ship would sail, and I
came aboard and hid myself. I ought to leave him to his
fate," she went on, sitting with clasped hands. "I have
been beaten by him like a disobedient dog; I have been
cursed and abused; I have been robbed and starved; I have

been neglected and deserted. But I cannot abandon him. I am driven to follow him wherever he may lead. It may be I shall yet—— But I do not know. His conscience is dead within him: he is no longer a man. From the first week I knew him to be a gambler, drunkard, and man-slayer; a defier of God's law; one of those who work evil with greediness; yet I cannot choose but go after him, even if my choice land me again on the shore of North Carolina."

"And why do you fear to go there?"

"Child, you do not know the Southern States." She laughed bitterly. "They are the home, in your English papers and your New York correspondents, of the chivalry and nobility of America. They are also the home of the slave. There are black slaves, brown slaves, olive-coloured slaves, and white slaves. I was a white slave. I am one of those unfortunates for whom they are fighting. I am a darkey—a Nigger."

"You?"

"Yes; I. You would not think, to look at me, perhaps. that I have been a slave. Yet it is true. The young ladies with whom I was brought up had not whiter skin than mine. Yet my great-great-grandmother was a black woman. So I was a slave. You are not an American, and so you do not shrink back with loathing. I was a slave, and one day, being then seventeen years of age, and unwilling to be the mother of more slaves, I started on a long journey by the Underground Railway, and got safe to Canada."

"Is it possible?" cried Avis, forgetting for a moment her own troubles.

"Yes; it is true. I went to Montreal, where I hoped to find employment and friends. There I met Captain Valentine Angel—as he then called himself—who was so good as to fall in love with me, and I with him. We were married. And now you know my story."

"And if you go back again to North Carolina?"

"In the old days, if a runaway slave was caught, they flogged him. Now, when the Northern soldiers are gathering round them, and their cause is hopeless; now, when they tremble lest fresh stories of cruelties to blacks should be invented or found out, I think they would hardly dare to flog a white woman. Yet one knows not. The feeling is very strong, and the women are cruel—more cruel than the men."

"But they will not know you. They cannot find you out. They will have ceased to search for you."

"My dear, there are depths of wickedness possible which you cannot suspect. My husband knows my story, because I could hide nothing from him. I have seen, in his eyes, what he thinks of doing. But courage, my child; there are many accidents. We shall put in at Nassau for coal. There we may find a chance; or we may be captured; or we may run away when we get to. Wilmington. Woman's wit against man's, my dear. They can plan their clumsy plots, but they cannot always carry them through. And he is afraid of me. That is always in our favour."

We then began to consider how we could best protect ourselves on the voyage. Olive advised that we should go on deck as much as possible, so that all the sailors should know that we were aboard, and grow accustomed to see us; that we should never for a moment leave each other; that we should share the same cabin; that we should refuse to listen to, or speak with, either the Captain or his accomplice.

"Lastly, my dear," said Olive, "among wild beasts it is well to have other means of defence than a woman's shrieks. I have—for the protection of us both—this."

She produced a revolver.

"A pretty toy," she said, "but it is loaded, and it shall be used, if need be, for the defence of you as well as myself."

Thus began this miserable voyage, wherein my heart was torn by anxieties and fears. What would be the end?

Presently we went on deck. The land was nearly out of sight; we were on the broad Atlantic. The ship rolled in the long swell; the day was bright; the breeze fresh. Beside the helm stood the Captain, who scowled, but said not a word.

The crew were lying about the deck, except one or two on

watch in the bows. As the ship carried neither yards nor sails, there was little or nothing to do, and they mostly sat sleeping or telling yarns all the voyage. Olive led me for'ard. Stephen, although the pilot, and therefore a person of great importance, was among the common sailors, sitting in the sun, his pipe in his mouth, with two or three listeners, foremost among the spinners of yarns. He sat there—whether of free choice, or because he wished to avoid me—all the voyage. Nor did he once speak to me; on the contrary, if he saw us amidships, he dived below, and if he was aft, when we came up from the saloon, he went for'ard. I think he was ashamed and anxious, for he had not reckoned on the appearance of Olive. She, for her part, knew some of the men, and addressed them by name. She had sailed with them before the war, when her husband was in some more legitimate trade. She called them by their names, one after the other. They were such names as sailors give each other, such as Liberty Wicks, who was quartermaster; Soldier Jack, so called because he was reported to have been a deserter from an English regiment in Canada; Old Nipper, the meaning of whose name I do not know; Long Tom, a lanky thin man of six feet six, with a stoop in his shoulders caused by stooping continually 'tween decks; Pegleg Smith, who went halt; and the Doctor, as they called the cook. They grinned, made a leg, and touched their foreheads; they knew that Olive was the Captain's wife; they knew that she was a stowaway, and had come after her husband; they knew that I had been entrapped aboard. That was what Olive wanted.

"For, my dear," she said, " suppose my husband was to catch me by the heels some dark night and tip me overboard, which he would very much like to do, these men would miss me, and by degrees the thing would become known."

"That would not restore you to life."

" No, my dear; but it might make things safer for you."

The Captain seemed to have no objection to our talking with the sailors. It was not his plan to show us the least unkindness on the voyage: we were to be perfectly free.

We found them a rough, reckless set of men, of the kind who would follow a leader anywhere, provided he gave them plenty to eat, drink, and smoke. Such must have been the men who went about with the pirate captains, and hoisted the black flag: they loved plunder and were not afraid of battle. Such must have been the buccaneers who would have no peace on the Spanish Main; such were the followers of Pizarro and of Cortes. They were also traders. Every man had his private venture on board—his case of "notions" —out of which he would make a hundred per cent. profit. They believed in the luck of their captain, and in his daring. Most of them knew Stephen of old, and trusted in his skill. They laughed at the risk of Yankee steel, Yankee steamers, and Yankee shot; they boasted of the runs they had had in a vessel not so fast as the *Maryland*, which could show a clean pair of heels to any cruiser Uncle Jonathan could set afloat. In a few days they would be under the fort at Wilmington, their cargo landed and sold, their private ventures converted into dollars, and their craft taking in cotton for the homeward run.

These honest fellows concerned themselves not at all about the causes and the merits of the war: that was a merry time which made them rich : that cause was righteous in which they could earn fifty pounds a man for the double trip, and frolic ashore like Nelson's bull-dogs after they were paid their prize-money. So far from wishing that the war would speedily end, they devoutly hoped that it would go on, and with the view of forwarding this object, they would encourage, if they had any voice in the matter, every Southerner who could carry a rifle or lie behind a gabion to go to the front. They were more patriotic even than the Confederates themselves; they were more sanguine of success even than the English sympathisers; and though most of them, including the Captain, were Northerners by birth, ·they vied with each other in protesting hatred undying to the Yankees and their cause.

"One thing," said Olive, "my husband might have done. He dare not do it, though, because he would lose the respect of all Americans. He might tell them that he has married a coloured girl. You would witness, then, for yourself, something of the loathing which the presence of the negro blood rouses among Americans."

I have mentioned the bo's'n and quartermaster, Liberty Wicks, who was often at the wheel. Now, one day, soon after the voyage began, a very singular thing happened.

The captain was on the bridge, Stephen was for'ard, no one was aft except Olive and myself and the quartermaster, who, as usual, was making his two eyes do double duty. We were sitting in silence, when we became aware of a hoarse whisper.

"There's friends aboard." It was Liberty Wicks. "Friends. Don't fear nothing. Wait till you get to North Car'lina. Don't look at me. Don't answer."

After this we were comforted, on every possible opportunity, with the assurance that there were friends aboard.

Then, day after day, the ship held her course, and we two women remained unmolested, walking on deck, or sitting in the little saloon, unnoticed. We talked little, having too much to think about. The Captain raised his cap to us in the morning, but he avoided the eyes of his wife. Stephen, as I have said, skulked and remained for'ard. We were supplied with what we wanted, as if we had been in a hotel. Always we had the same bright and beautiful sunshine, with fresh breezes; always the long rolling waves and billows, the broad streak of white foam which lay like a roadway where the ship had been.

When I think of that voyage, it seems to me like a bad and dreadful dream—that kind of dream in which one is wafted gently onward by some unknown agency towards a horrible, dreadful, unknown end; the dream out of which one awakens with shuddering, and a fearful sense of its reality. The days which followed slowly seemed all alike from hour to hour: that, too, was dream-like: there was no occupation, which was dream-like; the sight of the slight spare man, with the smooth cheeks and the glittering eyes, was like a dream: the mysterious protection of this woman, resolute and brave, who said she had been a slave, but whose skin was white like my own, was dream-like. What had become of the old quiet time? Was there any Boscastle? Was there any Jack at all, or was he, too, a part and parcel of this dreadful dream?

We sailed into warmer latitudes. It was pleasant to sit on deck at daybreak and watch the red sun rise fiery from the waves; or at evening, when he sank out of sight before our bows, so that we seemed as if we were steering straight into some land of enchantment, where clouds and land and sea alike were bathed in gorgeous colours and lapped in perpetual warmth; at noontide, when it was too hot to sit on deck, we lay on the sofas of the saloon, silent, or in whispers asking each other what would be the end. We had no books; we had no paper, pens, or ink; we had no dresses to make or mend, nor anything to make or mend with; there was nothing to do except to sit and wait. The silence grew awful; we ceased to feel the regular beat of the screw; it became noiseless, like a pulse which is neither heard nor felt; the Captain gave no orders; the very crew became silent; the roll of the ship was like the throbbing of her engines, monotonous and unnoticed.

So that, in the silence, our senses seemed to quicken, and one night, sitting in the saloon after nightfall, we heard voices above us on the deck.

One of the speakers was Stephen.

"It's a bad business, Cap'en," he said. "Look at it any way, no way I like it. What are we to do next?"

"I don't know, Steve; that is a fact. Your girl and me won't run easy in harness so long as the other one is about; they must be separated before we can do anything else."

Olive caught my hand. We listened for more.

"Land 'em both at Nassau, and be shot of the whole job," counselled Stephen. "No good ever come of a voyage with a passel o' women aboard. Might as well have a bishop, or Jonas himself."

"I might put Olive ashore," said the Captain; "and we could carry the other on to Wilmington. Olive would scream a bit, but then, she'd have to go. As for Nassau, we are not going to New Providence at all. Don't you think, Stephen, after it's cost me all the money to ship my crew, half paid down and all, that they're a-goin' to have the chance of gettin' ashore and stayin' there. Why, once ashore, it might be a fortnight before I could get them all back again. No; the coal's lying on Stony Cay, where we'll take it on board and so off again. We might land her on the cay, to be sure, but there's no rations and no water."

"You can't land the woman there, Cap'en. The men wouldn't stand it."

"I can't, because I've got a white-livered lot aboard who'd make a fuss. I could if I had the crew with me that I had twenty years ago when we made that famous run. You hadn't gone soft, then."

"I was younger then," said Stephen. "When a man gets twenty years older, he thinks twice before he chucks his niggers overboard or lands people on desert islands. Not that I ever approved of them ways."

"You looked on a powerful lot while such things were being carried on, at any rate. No, I think the first plan I thought of will be the best."

"What is the first plan ? "

"Never mind, Stephen. Perhaps the plan is a rough way, of which you would not approve."

"Courage, Avis," whispered Olive; "courage, child; we are not separated yet; there is always hope. Even a shot between wind and water, and a sinking of the ship with all her wicked crew, would be better than such a fate as the man intends for you. But that fate will not be yours. Some women, my dear, are prophetesses ; I think I am one; and I see, but I know not how, a happy ending out of this for you—but not for me."

There is an islet among the Bahamas lying just at the entrance of Providence Channel, some sixty miles north-east of Nassau. The small maps do not notice so insignificant a rock, but on the charts it is called Stony Cay. It is, in fact, nothing but a rock, on which nothing lives in ordinary times; but it was used in those days by blockade-runners as a small station where they could take in coal without the risk of losing men by desertion, and with little fear of observation. It is as barren as Ascension, and as stony as Aden; nothing grows upon it, and the only water is that which in the cold season lies in pools among the rocks. Two or three men were there in charge of the stores, and, as a warning to American cruisers, the Union Jack was kept flying from a mast. Thither we steered, and here the men made their final preparations.

The coaling, with these preparations, occupied three days; for they began by taking on board as much coal as they could carry, and then set to work to telescope the funnel: that is, to lay it flat upon the deck, so that instead of the long tail of smoke which shows a steamer so far off, the smoke should be discharged over the surface of the water where it would not be seen; their coal, too, was anthracite, which burns with little smoke; then they overhauled what little rigging they had, and fitted a lookout at the mast-head; they lowered the boats level with the gunwales, and the chief engineer reported on his engines.

All this time it seemed as if no watch were set upon the two prisoners; the crew came and went about their business; the Captain stood about and looked on; Stephen Cobbledick sat for'ard doing nothing, as becomes a pilot; the boats kept coming and going all day long, heavy barges full of coal; nothing seemed easier than to get ashore. But what then? The island had no inhabitants; there were no signs of water; there was no chance of any ship putting in there except for the same purpose as the *Maryland*. What could we do if we were to land?

"Patience, Avis," said Olive. "Three days more will bring us to the end of this chapter."

The steward told us what we pretty well knew before, that they were going to run the blockade into Wilmington, on the coast of North Carolina; that the place was about seven hundred miles distance from the Bahamas, and that the real danger was about to begin. Hitherto there had been none, except the chance of bad weather, for the *Maryland*, built for nothing but speed, and just heavy enough to stand the waves of an ordinary stiff breeze, would infallibly have gone down in a gale.

"The danger may mean deliverance, my dear," Olive said for my consolation. "The cruisers may take us. In that case, you are safe; you have only to seek out the British Consul, and tell him who you are, and why you were on board the ship. As for me——"

"As for you, Olive?" I asked.

"I must follow my husband," she replied. "If we are taken, he will go to a New York prison; and I must go, too, to look after him."

When the sun went down on the third day, the engines got up steam; by midnight the *Maryland* was out of the narrow waters and rolling among the great waves of the Gulf Stream. The night was exactly the kind of night which blockade-runners, buccaneers, privateers, and pirates always most delight in; a dark night with a new moon; cloudy, too. The steamer carried no lights. By the wheel stood the Captain, and old Stephen ready to take his place as pilot. As for us, we were too anxious to stay below, and were on deck looking and waiting.

At this time, when the war had been carried on for a couple of years, and there seemed little hope of a speedy conclusion, the spirit of the North was fairly roused. While the volunteers were pouring into the camp by thousands, they were sending new and fast cruisers to the Southern shores as quickly as they could be built. Every day increased the risk of a successful run; every day, however, the value of the cargo was increased.

"Stephen," we heard the Captain say, "I have got a note from Nassau. The Yanks expect me; they don't know I've arrived and started; but there's a notion among the cruisers that I'm to be met with somewhere about this time. I know what their ships are, and where they're stationed. Twenty-five steamers are lying off Wilmington this night as close as they can lie—out of the range of Fort Fisher.

Half-a-dozen more are cruising about these waters. I make no count of them. Now, Stephen, the only thing to decide is whether it's best to dash through the line or to creep along the coast."

"The coast," said Stephen, "is a awkward coast. There's nothing to steer by; there's sands, and there's never a light."

"We can show a light from the inshore side. They will answer it; they are on the look-out all night."

"I would rather," said Stephen, "make a dash for it. Once inside their line, they will find it hard to stop us."

"Can you find the mouth of the river in the night?"

"I can find the mouth of that river blindfold; never fear that; what I think of is the shifting sands along the coast, if we have to creep in."

"Pray Heaven!" whispered Olive, "that one of those half-dozen cruisers catch us."

We passed a sleepless night. Half-a-dozen times, at least, the engines were stopped on an alarm being given from the watch in the foretop, and we expected to hear a cannon-shot crash into the vessel, or an order, at least, to lay to.

Presently the engines would go on, and the ship proceed on her way, though perhaps on another course. We showed no light; our coal gave out little smoke, and that little, as I have said, was discharged from the stern, the funnel lying flat along the deck.

At daybreak we rose and went on deck again. None of the men seemed to have gone below. Stephen and the Captain stood together by the wheel; all hands were on the watch, though as yet it was too dark to see far; and the men, if they spoke at all, spoke in whispers. As the sun rose behind us, we found ourselves alone upon the ocean, not a sail was in sight.

"No cruiser yet," I whispered to Olive. "Shall we reach Wilmington to-night?"

"A steamer," cried the man in the look-out, "off the starboard bow!"

I could see nothing; the broad face of the ocean glowed in the bright sunshine.

"He sees," said Olive, "a faint wreath of smoke."

I suppose we altered our course, because we saw no more of that steamer. We ran till noon without further adventure; then another and another, and another alarm were given in quick succession, and the wheel went round and the vessel changed her course. There was no waiting to make out the distant ship; every stranger was a supposed enemy.

Before long we, too, whose interest it was that the ship should be taken, shared in the general excitement, and stood on deck watching the horizon, which lay clear and well defined, with neither mist nor fog to hide it.

No bells were rung that day. At noon the chief officer made his observations and reported to the Captain, who mechanically ordered him to "make it so," but he made it in silence. There were no meals served; any man who felt hungry went into the cook's galley and got something; the cook himself was in the bows; the steward, who brought us some tea, hurried back to be on the watch with the rest. Now and then one, tired, lay down on deck in the sun and fell asleep for an hour or two. Darkness fell; but the ship pushed on, all hands as before remaining on deck all night. We remained on deck till midnight, when we reluctantly went below.

"I almost hope," said Olive, "that we shall get through them."

In the morning, which was cloudy with a little fog, though there was a steady breeze from the north-west, we made our first escape. It was just before daybreak; we, who could not sleep, were on deck again. All night there had been frequent alarms, but happily (or unhappily) we passed the danger. This time, however, things looked as if our run had come to an end.

The mist had thickened; the day was slowing breaking; we held our course but at half speed; suddenly there seemed to spring out of the water a cruiser three times our size, under steam and sail. We were almost under her bows; they shouted to us; their men sprang into the rigging to furl the sails; we saw them hastily run out the guns.

"Avis!" cried Olive, "you are saved!"

Not yet. Captain Ramsay gave an order in his quiet voice, the wheel flew round, and the next moment we were astern of the vessel, at full speed steaming in the teeth of the wind. With such way as was on the cruiser, she was out of sight in the mist almost before we had time to look. There was a great popping of guns, and one cannon shot, but no damage done; and when the mist presently cleared, and the sun rose, we could indeed see her smoke away on the north horizon, but we were invisible to her.

That night we were to run the blockade.

The blockading fleet was chiefly concentrated round the port of Wilmington. There were, as the Captain said, twenty-five vessels lying or cruising, in a sort of semicircle, ten miles round the mouth of the river, on one bank of which was Fort Fisher. It was prudent to keep outside the range of that fortress's guns. And without the circle were some half-dozen fast-steaming cruisers always on the look-out. That evening the Captain called the men aft.

"My lads," he said, "I had intended to make a dash for it, as I have often done before. You are not the men to be afraid of a shot or two; but this unfortunate falling in with one of their ships makes it seem best to try creeping along shore, for the alarm will be given. Therefore every man to his post, and not a word spoken; and, with good luck, we will be inside Fort Fisher before daybreak."

The men retired. Then night fell, and we could hear the beating of our hearts.

Stephen now took the wheel himself, and the Captain became a sort of chief officer. At the helm, proud of his skill and new employment, Stephen looked something like that beautiful old man whom I had found sleeping. The cunning sensual look was gone from him; he stood steady as a lion, yet eager and keen, with every sense awake. Presently he ordered half-speed; then we sounded; then we forged ahead a bit; sounded again; then before us I saw, low and black in the night, the coast of America.

Stephen kept her on her way slowly and cautiously; the screw never ceased, but we crept slowly along, hugging the shore as near as he dared.

"A few more yards nearer, pilot?" asked the Captain.

"No, sir. I daren't do it. We are as near—— What's that? See now."

A long, grating sound as the bottom just touched the sand. The ship cleared the shallow, and continued her slow, silent crawling along the shore.

How long was that night! How slowly the hours crept on; how patiently the men watched and worked.

I suppose it must have been about two o'clock in the morning, or rather later, the ship still cautiously hugging the dark line of coast, that the end came.

We were moving so slowly that the motion of the screw could hardly be felt; the night was very still and dark; the sea a dead calm. We were as close to the shore as the pilot could possibly take her; the men in the bows were sounding perpetually, and sending the depth aft in whispers. We had shown a light on the inshore side; this was answered by two lights, so faint as to be invisible farther out; they were the lights to guide the pilot into the harbour. Success was already in the Captain's hand; a few minutes more and the last few yards of the long voyage would be run in safety.

Then there was a snapping of wood in the bows, a cry of alarm; and the next moment a rocket shot high in the air, On our starboard, not a hundred yards from us, was lying one of the cruisers, and the rocket had gone up from a rowing barge, sent out to signalise a chance blockade-runner, which boat we had nearly run down.

It would have been better for Captain Ramsay had we run her down altogether.

"Put on all steam," shouted the Captain, as the rocket was answered by a gun, and then another. "Let them blaze away. Now then. Five minutes' run, lads, and we'll be out of danger. Steady, pilot, steady!"

"Steady it is, sir," answered Stephen, as another cannon shot struck the water close to our stern, sending the spray flying.

"If there is to be fighting," said Olive, "we had better be below, where, at least, we shall be a little safer."

We went below; but we could not escape the horrible banging of the cannon, which seemed to be firing all around us, nor the rattling of the rifles. They fired at random, because they could not see us.

The men lay on the deck, thinking to get shelter from the bullets if any should come their way; but the Captain stood by the Pilot.

"Plenty of water, Pilot?" he asked.

"Deep water, sir. Only keep her head straight. As for them lubbers with their guns, why——" Here he stopped, and fell heavily to the deck with a groan. The wheel flew round; the little steamer swung round with it; and before the Captain could put up the helm, she ran bows on heavily into a sandbank and stopped.

"We are ashore," said Olive quietly. "I think, my dear, that we are saved."

On deck we heard a great trampling. The crew ran aft and jumped to ease her off; the engines were reversed, but the ship was hard and fast.

No one took any notice of the unfortunate pilot, the only man struck by the shot. He lay motionless.

"Cap'en," said the quartermaster and bo's'n, Liberty Wicks by name, of whom I have already spoken, "this is a bad job."

Captain Ramsay replied by a volley of oaths.

"They're putting off a boat from the Yankee, sir. Shall we lower boats?"

The Captain made no reply.

"A New York prison or a run in the Southern States, it is, Cap'en."

Still his captain made no reply.

Then the chief officer came up.

"There is no time to lose, sir. The men are lowering the boats. Shall we put in the women first?"

The Captain, still silent, went down the companion, followed by the first officer and the boatswain.

Olive had lit our lamp by this time.

"Courage, Avis," she whispered. "Now is the moment of your deliverance!"

"Come," he said roughly. "The ship is aground. Avis, and you other, come on deck and get into the boats."

"No," said Olive, "we shall remain here."

"I tell you, come!"

Olive stood before me.

"She shall not come!"

"Stand aside!" He added words of loathing and hatred which I will not write down. "Stand aside, or by the Lord I will murder you."

"She shall not go with you. O villain! she shall not go with you!"

"Cap'en, there's no time," growled the quartermaster.

The Captain drew his revolver; the chief officer knocked up his hand.

"No murder, Captain Ramsay," he said, "unless you murder me and the bo's'n too."

"The Yanks are on us!" cried the man. They seized the Captain, one by each arm, and dragged him up the companion. We heard a trampling on deck, a shouting, a pistol shot, and a sound of oars in the water.

"They are chasing the blockade-runners," said Olive. "They will be back presently to scuttle the ship and destroy the cargo. Let us go on deck."

It was too dark to see much. We heard in the distance the regular fall of the oars; we saw a flash from time to time. Then there was silence for awhile, and then we heard the oars again.

"The cruiser's men are coming back," said Olive.

In ten minutes they came alongside, and we saw them climbing on deck. There were twenty of them, armed with cutlasses and pistols, headed by a young Federal officer.

He was greatly surprised to find two ladies on board.

But he was civil, asked us who we were, and what we were doing on board a blockade-runner.

Olive told him that I was an English lady who had been brought away against her will, that her own business was my protection.

"We have no business in the South," she said, "and we have no papers."

"What can I do with you?" he asked, evidently not believing the statement. "If I take you aboard, we shall not know whether to treat you as prisoners or not. If I land you, you would be worse off than before. What is the name of this ship?"

"The *Maryland*, of Liverpool," said Olive. "This is her first run."

"And her captain?"

"Captain Ramsay."

The officer whistled.

"I wish I had known," he said. "Well, ladies, the best thing I can do, as you have come all the way to the coast of North Carolina, is to put you ashore on it. No doubt that is what you want; and I wish you joy of Dixie's Land."

"We would rather," said Olive, "that you took us to New York, even as prisoners."

He shook his head and laughed.

Here a deep moan interrupted us, and we became aware for the first time that poor old Stephen was lying wounded at the helm, where he had fallen.

"Water," he groaned.

I fetched him water. Olive raised his head.

"Which of them is this?" asked the Federal.

"He is the pilot," I replied, thinking no harm in telling the truth.

"The pilot, is he? Well, if he recovers, he will find out what the inside of a prison is; because you see, ladies, a pilot must know the shore, and a pilot must therefore be a Reb."

He felt Stephen's pulse.

"It is very low. I doubt he is dying."

I gave him the water, and he opened his eyes.

"Is that you, Avis? Keep clear of the Captain," he whispered slowly; "he's well-nigh desperate."

"Tell me," I said, "was that story true about the raft?"

"You was," he said, "a Pick-me-up, off a raft in Torres' Straits, wropped in bandanners; and your mother was a Knobling. Your father, he was admiral to the Sultan of Zanzibar." Here he fainted again.

"Come," cried the officer, "we have no time. Bo's'n."

"Sir."

"Put these ladies into the boat and land them as quickly as you can. Have you anything you wish to take with you?"

"Nothing," said Olive.

"Then——" He raised his cap, and we followed the boatswain.

We were closer to the shore than I thought. In ten minutes the sailors stood up to help us to land. Then they put off again.

The voyage was over: the ship was ashore; the cargo was lost; the blockade-runners were disappointed; and we were standing, friendless and helpless, on the shores of the New World.

CHAPTER IX.

ALL THE WAY BY THE UNDERGROUND.

"O OLIVE!" I cried, "what shall we do now?"

"I know the country," she replied; "that is a great thing to begin with. They were trying to run the blockade from Long Bay to Smith's Island; we are, therefore, I suppose, not far from the mouth of Cape Fear River. Wilmington is twenty miles to the north, and more. He must go to Wilmington first. What will he do afterwards? No one saw us landed," she said after consideration; "he will think we are taken prisoners by the Federals. He will make for New York in hopes of finding you there."

"Then, if he goes to New York," I said, "we need have no fear for ourselves."

"Nay, my dear," she replied. "Consider, we are in a country torn by civil war; we have no means of showing that we are not spies: I myself may be arrested as a fugitive slave; we have five hundred miles and more to go before we reach a place where I may be free from that danger; we have no money; we have no friends; what will become of you if I am carried off to the State gaol?"

To that I had nothing in reply. What, indeed, would become of me—what would become of her if she were arrested?

She read my thought.

"My dear," she said, "do not be anxious about me. I have no dread of the prison for myself. At the most it will be a short captivity, because sooner or later—and I think very soon—the South must collapse. Then abolition will set us all free. No fear now of any compromise. At first, indeed, when it seemed as if they were fighting for a point of law in which the South had the best of it, I trembled lest a peace might be patched up, and the cause of the slave abandoned; now, things have gone too far. The negroes must be emancipated, and with them all the poor mulattoes, octoroons, and whites who have the taint of negro blood, the most wretched victims of this most wicked system. Come," she continued, after a pause, "we must not linger on the shore. Follow me; I think I can take you to a place where, for a day or two if necessary, we shall contrive a hiding-place."

It was time to decide on something, because figures were to be seen running backwards and forwards on the sands; a bright light shot up from the ill-fated *Maryland,* and boats were seen putting off from shore.

"The Federals have set fire to the ship," said Olive; "those boats are put off by the negroes, anxious to secure something from the wreck. The light of the fire will be useful to us."

She hesitated a little.

"Close by," she said, "but whether to the right or to the

left, is a little village called Smithville; five or six miles west of Smithville is the village of Shallotte; due north of us lies the Great Green Swamp. There I am sure to find a place where no one will look for us, and where we can rest, though the accommodation will be rather rough for you. Are you tired?"

"I must be tired indeed," I said, "if I could not find strength to escape from that man."

It was still dark night. The flames of the burning ship mounted high and shed a lurid light, which was of some use to us, if not much. Olive led the way, which was over sand hills and across sandy ground, fatiguing to walk over. After half an hour's walking we came to ground which was wet and marshy.

"This," said Olive, "is the beginning of the swamp. Great swamps lie all along the coast; they were designed by Providence, I believe, for the hiding-places of runaways. Some years ago, when I made up my mind there was nothing before me but disgrace and wretchedness unless I ran away, I betook myself to this swamp. Here I lived among friendly blacks, until a way was opened for me to escape. I want to go back to my old friends and escape, with you, once more by the old route—the Underground Railway."

She went on to inform me that stations had been established by Northern sympathisers, where runaways were received, entertained, and forwarded on their way with money and provisions. Those who acted the part of hosts did so at the risk of death; because, whatever mercy might be shown them by the law, none would be shown by the mob. She did not suppose, she said, that these stations were altogether broken up by the outbreak of civil war; rather, because the abolitionists had always many friends in the South, they would be multiplied and hedged round by greater precautions.

"If we had money," she said, "I would travel openly by way of Columbia, in South Carolina, to Tennessee and Kentucky. The Hue and Cry would scarcely reach so far. Besides, we might disguise ourselves as boys if it were necessary. But without money what can we do but incur suspicion? Therefore, for the second time I will try the Underground."

We walked slowly along, I, for one, being faint from hunger. The path—if it was a path—was soft and yielding, yet Olive went on in full assurance. We had left the shore and the burning ship far behind us. Presently the day broke, and I found we were in a kind of forest, the like of which I had never seen. The soil was sometimes of silvery sand, in which grew tall pine-trees; a never-ending expanse of pine-trees; sometimes a green swamp, in which cypresses, with great trunks and roots sticking up like boulders, took their place. Among them were also the sycamore and the beech, with trees whose names I did not know. There was also a beautiful underwood of trailing vines and creepers, which climbed to the very tops of the trees and hung down in net-work. When the sun rose there rose with him flocks of great buzzards, sailing slowly over the tree-tops, and the air became musical with the notes of smaller birds. But no road or path, no cultivation, no huts, no rising smoke, no sign of human habitation.

"Before the war," said Olive, "there would have been danger from turpentine factories scattered about on the edge of the swamp. Now their owners have gone to the front, and the factories are stopped. So much the better for us."

"O Olive!" I cried, feeling as if flight were useless and it were better to drop down and let what might-be come, "is there much farther to walk?"

"Not much before we make our first halt," she replied; "but I know not what to expect for food."

I suppose a mile or so is not much; to a strong girl it means twenty minutes' walk; to me it seemed as if we should never come to an end.

"I am looking," said Olive, "for Daddy Galoon's hut. It is six years and more since last I came here; but the woods were blazed, and I have followed their guidance. And I think, Avis, I think that—— Here it is."

Within a little clump of pines standing on a knoll was a

hut, at the door of which sat an old negro. He was dressed in nothing, apparently, but a pair of cotton trousers and a cotton shirt. He was old and bowed, yet his eye was bright and keen. He rose slowly, as Olive pushed her way between the trunks, and stared at her curiously, but not as if he were frightened.

"Don't you remember me, Daddy?" she asked.

"I guess," he replied, "I tink for suah, you'm Missey Olive, from Squire Cassily's over dah way yander. What you'm doin' back again? Wan' anuder journey by dat Undergroun'? Ho!"

"I am back again, Daddy, because I couldn't help it. First, give this young lady some breakfast."

He peered into my face and took hold of my hand.

"Dis young lady not a yaller gal; guess she is from de Norf."

"No, Daddy; she is from England. She has enemies, and she has no money; she will travel with me."

He gave me some simple food—cold boiled pork, with meal and honey—which I devoured greedily; and then, overcome with fatigue, I lay down in a corner, the old man covering me with a blanket, and fell fast asleep.

It was evening when I awoke. Olive was sitting beside me, patient, watching, just as she had sat beside me on board the *Maryland*. Nothing changed her face; it was always sad; always the face of one who has suffered; always the face of one who expects more suffering, always patient.

We made our supper as we had made our breakfast, off pork and meal and honey. Then Olive told me something of her plans.

This old negro, who by some accident, or for something he had done, had long since received his freedom, came to Green Swamp thirty years before, and settled in the hut which he built there. How he lived it was difficult to say; he grew nothing; he had neither pigs nor cattle nor fowls; he did, apparently, no work; yet he had money, and bought things at the nearest village where there was a store. In fact, the old man occupied a terminus station on the great many branched Underground Railway. All the slaves in North Carolina knew that; but, at a time when to be found guilty of such a crime was enough to make the neighbourhood rise and burn the man alive, when any reward would have been offered for conviction, not a negro or a mulatto in the State ever gave information. If a "boy" wanted to run away, he would go naturally and without being told to Daddy Galoon's, who would pass him on to the next station.

The station of Green Swamp was safe too, because the place was intersected by so many streams that the hounds used in hunting fugitives were easily put off the scent. Therefore, for twenty years old Daddy had been passing them along. No one knew of his existence, except his own people: no one knew of his hut except those to whom the secret blazing of the trees had been confided.

"It is much easier than it was," said Olive. "All the men who used to live by hunting us are gone to the war; their packs of hounds are destroyed; the mean whites who loafed around, too proud to work, and only too happy to join in a nigger hunt, have all been drafted to the armies in the field; people are too busy to look much after us; I do not think we shall have much trouble, unless my—the Captain—has had me already proclaimed. The chief fear is that, as we cannot account for ourselves, we may be taken for spies. If only we had some money!"

She then told me that Daddy had gone to Wilmington to ascertain if anything had been done.

He came back next day with news which made my blood boil.

Captain Ramsay had learned that we had been put ashore; some "beach combers," some of the men who prowled about to pick up what they could from the wreck of a blockade-runner, had seen us landed by the Federal boat. His first idea was to go in search of us, but he was ignorant of the country; he next proposed to organise a hunting party in the ancient fashion, with hounds; this fell through because he could get no one to join him; the old pastime of the nigger chase was forgotten in those days of fiercer excitement; besides, there were too many English and others in Wilmington just then, for it was a time when all parties in the South were anxious to stand well with England, and not get bad reports spread about the cruelty of the Institution. Finally, he advertised us. And the old man brought us a copy of his infamous placard:

"ONE THOUSAND DOLLARS REWARD.—Run away. The girl Olive, the property of Squire Cassily, Cumberland County. Mulatto, will pass for white. Black hair, black eyes, twenty-five years of age. Also the girl Avis, eighteen years of age, mulatto, brown hair, and blue eyes. Tries to pass for an Englishwoman. Property of Jefferson Ramsay, master mariner.

"Were last seen together on the shore near Smithville. Will endeavour to escape to the North. The above reward will be given to any who will bring these girls together to the advertiser, Captain Ramsay aforesaid."

Would any one believe that a man could be so villainous? One of these women, his wife, put away by some idle form of law, and the other the girl to whom he had offered love, and the protection of a husband. He would hunt down both by slave dealers; he would hand over one to the tender mercies of her former master, and the other—what would he do with the other?

"We need not ask that question, Avis," said Olive, "because you shall not fall into his hands."

"What shall we do, Daddy?" she asked the old negro.

"Missy bes' stay here day or two. Nobody gwine come here. Dey won' hunt in the swamp. By'm-by, forget about it; den missy start right away."

This seemed good advice, and we resolved to adopt it.

After three weary days in the hut, it was determined that we should make a start. I was rested, and felt strong again in the bracing sharp air of this strange new country. We had twelve miles to make that day, with Daddy as our guide, through the wild untrodden forest land.

This stage was easily done. We halted for dinner at noon in one of the clumps of cypress of which I have spoken. and reached our night quarters—another hut, provided with little except two or three blankets and a cache of preserved soup, which he dug up from where he had put it, and of which we made our dinner.

The next day's stage was the same. All this time the country did not change. Always the swamp and the sand; always the pines and the cypresses; always overhead the buzzards; and only sometimes, to vary the monotony, a flock of wild turkeys or a herd of deer.

On the third day we were to leave the swamp and take to the roads and villages, when our danger would begin.

"Olive," I said, "if they take us prisoners, what will they do next?"

"They would be obliged, I suppose, to take us to Wilmington in order to get the reward."

"Would they—would they be cruel?"

"Well, my dear," she replied calmly, "slave-catchers are not the most kindly of men. But I doubt their daring to inflict any cruelty upon us."

I conjured up a dreadful vision of manacles, chains, and men brandishing heavy whips, which remained with me until our escape was accomplished. I was, I confess, horribly frightened. The name of slave to an English girl has something truly terrible in it; that I should be actually advertised for as a runaway slave was a thing most appalling to me. Olive, to whom it had happened before, naturally took things more quietly.

The house which was to receive us on the third day was on the confines of a little town. It belonged to a Baptist minister, who, a Northerner by birth, had long since journeyed South with the sole object of helping runaways to escape. It was courageous and noble of him; how he reconciled it with his conscience as a Christian to carry on the deception of being a violent partisan of the South and admirer of the Institution, I do not know. Daddy Galoon timed the march this day so as to bring us to the house after dark. It was a wooden house, like all the rest, standing within a small fence. The old man removed a bar and we stepped over. He led the way to a back door, at which he gave four knocks, which evidently belonged to the secrets of his trade. The door was instantly opened, and a lady invited us to step in.

We found ourselves in a room which seemed to serve as kitchen and dining-room.

Daddy stood in the doorway. He came no farther with his pilgrims. Here he took off his hat, and said solemnly, "De Lord bress de runaways!" Then he shut the door and disappeared, to return to his solitary hut in the Green Swamp and wait for more.

"Good Heaven, girls!" cried the lady; "who are you?"

I now became aware, though horribly tired and oppressed with a dreadful anxiety about my boots, the soles of which were dropping off, that we were addressed by a most delightful old lady, comely, motherly, and kind. To be sure, it was uncommon in her experience to be asked shelter by two white girls, the elder of whom was only five-and-twenty, and the younger had not one single feature of the ordinary mulatto appearance.

Olive, as usual, told the story. She told it calmly, effectively, in a few words; and so clearly that it carried with it the internal evidence of truth. Our protector was indignant. She had never, she said, heard so dreadful a case. Negroes and mulattoes in hundreds had used her house—note that the house would have been burned over their heads had one of the fugitives for hope of reward or fear of punishment informed upon them—they were running away from the lash, from separation, from slavery; but never before had she heard of a man trying to drive his wife back into slavery, and putting an English girl into the Hue and Cry as an escaped servant, so that he might force her into a form of marriage.

Long before she had concluded her indignant invective against our persecutor I was sound asleep.

We rested here for two days, and were provided by our kind hostess—her husband having gone North in charge of a runaway mulatto family—with changes of dress, of which we were greatly in want. Remember that I was "shipped" with nothing but what I stood in; while my companion, who could help me a little, had only what she could bring on board in a bag when she became a stowaway. And we were landed with nothing at all, and had marched forty miles and more over bog and rough country, and had slept three nights in log huts. We were, however, in the hands of a true Samaritan, if ever there was one. She gave us a complete new outfit, and provided us with money, which we promised to repay, in case any difficulty should arise in which the almighty dollar might exhibit to advantage.

She was of opinion that the advertisement of us in the Wilmington papers would be copied by others, so that we could not rely upon being out of danger until we were finally out of the Southern States. Virginia, she said, was the most dangerous country for us, and she counselled us to travel by night, if we could, or at all events in the evening, by short stages, and by a route laid down by her, on which we should meet with plenty of friends and sympathisers, because it was the regular way of her "Railway." She also gave us minute directions as to our next resting-place, where we should be entertained and treated in like manner by her friends and fellow-conspirators.

Thus rested and set up, we continued on the third day our long and anxious journey.

Our conductor was a young negro, who informed me, thinking that I was, in spite of blue eyes and fair hair, one of his own people, that he was really free, and had volunteered this dangerous Underground Railway business, pretending to be the minister's slave-boy.

He chose cross roads, the badness of which I could not have thought possible, to our first stage. This, like the preceding, was the first, or last, house in a little village or township, and here we were entertained in like manner, and next day went on. The indignation of our hosts, excited everywhere as we told our story, encouraged them to take every possible precaution with us. Yet once we were in great danger, and escaped only by an accident which I dare not call otherwise than providential.

The roads in North Carolina were then, whatever they are now, everywhere bad. Roads, indeed, many of them do not deserve to be called; they are mere openings through the forest of the long-leaved pine, or, as they call them, the "piny woods." There are frequent forks, so that it is more easy to lose one's way than to keep it. There are brooks to cross, and fallen trunks to get over. Every now and then we came to a clearing where maize had been planted, and a small log cottage built. In all of them we saw children, and listless, despondent white women, mostly with pipes in their mouths. All these houses were exactly alike; the furniture was rough and rude; they were dirty; they looked what they were, the houses of ignorant vagabonds, too proud to work in the fields, too lazy for any industry, too stupid for any improvement.

"It is the curse," said Olive, "which slavery brings with it. The land is accursed for the sins of its owners. Nothing prospers. There are no roads; there are no farms; there are no manufactures, because labour is considered the duty of the blacks."

There were no white men, because they were—unless they were too old—one and all away with the armies of the South. But the women of the cabins asked us no questions, and seemed indifferent whether their cause was winning or losing. They had no papers, no books. I believe most of them could not write. What a dreadful life must theirs be; shut up in the silent woods, with no knowledge of the world beyond, no thought of how life can be made beautiful! "It is the curse of slavery," said Olive.

I do not remember the names of the places we stopped at; they all seemed to me exactly alike. The roads were alike; the country seemed the same day after day. Nor do I remember how many days we had travelled—but it could not have been many—when we fell into our great danger.

It arose from our guide losing his way on the road.

Somehow or other we took the wrong fork, and presently, instead of arriving at one of the little places where we were to stay, we drove straight into the very town we wished most to avoid, Fayetteville, which is not only the principal place in North Carolina next to Raleigh, but is also connected by a railway with Wilmington. It was, indeed, a most dangerous place.

Olive instructed our guide to say that we were two ladies on our way to Richmond, and that he was our boy. We then drove to the hotel, and entered boldly. It was then just after dark. It was easy to stay in our room that evening, and a couple of dimes induced one of the servants to bring some supper to us. But the morning would bring its dangers.

We stayed in our room till breakfast-time, when, not being able to make any excuse, we descended slowly to the saloon. There the tables were crowded with guests, who all appeared too much occupied in the business of eating to pay any attention to us. Only one of the company—a sallow, evil-looking man—seemed to me to look at us more curiously than I liked. In fact, his gaze became so earnest that I became faint with terror, and was glad indeed when we could rise and leave the table.

The boy was waiting for us with the trap in which he had driven us from the last station. We brought down our luggage, paid our bill, and were ready to depart, when the man who had caused me so much terror stepped up to me and touched me on the shoulder with his forefinger.

"Guess," he said roughly, "that you've got to hev a word with me before you go."

"Olive!" I cried, catching her by the arm; "O Olive!" It was the worst thing I could have said. He laughed aloud.

"All right," he said. "Gentlemen, these are two runaway yaller gals advertised for in the *Wilmington Herald*. A thousand dollars reward."

I stood trembling. For a moment Olive lost her head. She made as if she would tear me away and fly. Only for a moment.

"Gentlemen," she said, instantly recovering herself, "bear witness, all of you, that I am the wife of an American citizen, and this young lady is an Englishwoman."

There was a movement among the little crowd which gathered round us, and murmurs.

The man replied by reading the advertisement, pointing out as he read the exactness of the description.

Olive whispered me.

"I claim," I cried, "the protection of the British Consul!"

There was no British Consul in the place.

"Is there no one here," I asked, "who will defend two helpless women against a villain?"

"Ef you air runaways," said one man in the crowd,—"ef you air yaller——" And at that fatal word all sympathies were dried up.

It seemed there was no help but we must go.

"Na—ow," said our captor, "guess you'd better go quiet, or there's handcuffs and other things."

Just then, however, a rescuer appeared, a veritable St. George, a Perseus, though in the lank shape and forbidding features of Liberty Wicks, bo's'n and quartermaster of the *Maryland*. It seemed to me a forlorn hope, but Olive cried to him by name, and he turned, and seeing us, burst through the crowd.

"Darn my scuppers! What's this? Beg your pardon, ladies," taking off his hat; "but what's this little difficulty?"

"Bo's'n," said Olive, quietly and with dignity, "when I sailed with you from New York to Havannah, four years ago, what was my name? Perhaps you will tell these gentlemen."

"You was Mistress Angel, the Captain's wife."

"You hear, gentlemen. The captain's wife. The wife of Captain Angel, of the ship *Providence*, in the Havannah trade. Is it likely that Captain Angel's wife should be a runaway? Now, will you tell these gentlemen, bo's'n, where you took on board this young lady?"

"Off the port o' Boscastle, on the coast of Cornwall, in England," he replied. "Brought aboard, she was, by the captain and the pilot."

"Now, gentlemen," said Olive, "are you satisfied?   Or shall I ask my friend here to protect us against a man, probably a mean Yankee "—she threw infinite contempt into those words—"who would pretend that we are runaway slaves?"

Liberty Wicks stepped to the front, and stood before us.

"Ef," he said resolutely, "any man here lays hands on these two ladies, he lays hands on me."   He drew a revolver from his breast, and looked round, with his finger on the trigger.   "I allow," he said, "two minutes for that onfort'nate cuss to order his coffin."

He had so resolute an air, and looked so terrible, this lanky man with the hard features and the weather-beaten cheeks, that they all drew back.

He then called our boy.

"Where, boy, was you goin' to take these ladies?" he asked.

"They was gwine," said the boy readily, "by the nearest way to Raleigh, on their way to Richmond, in Virginny, where they was to stay with their friends."

"That looks like runnin' away, that does," said Liberty, looking round with triumph.   "Goin' to Richmond.   Goin' to head-quarters.   Now, stand aside, lubbers all, and let the ladies pass.   By your leave, ma'am," he touched his hat again, "I will go part of the way with you.   Lord love us!   Here's a sweet English rosebud for you."   He addressed the crowd, but he meant me.   "A sweet and pretty blushin' young thing, and you play it that mean on her as to call her a cussed yaller gell.   Yah!   I'm ashamed o' North Car'lina. That's a fact."

We were in the carriage now.   He hitched himself on to the footboard, and we drove away as rapidly as our boy dared, the honest bo's'n hurling derision behind him in language which our would-be captor no doubt understood.   To me it was a foreign tongue.   When we were outside the town, and again in the "piny woods," he changed his tone.

"Boy," he said, "steer quick out of this road.   Take the first fork ; never mind where it takes you to.   I know that slave-hunting coon. He came down here a purpus on the hunt for the reward. Them mean whites 'ud live on rewards if they could. Thought you'd make for the nearest town, and be landed like a salmon in a net. And he won't give in 'thout another run for't. I see that in his yaller eye. He's gone to git a warrant, an' he'll make tracks after us as fast as he can lay fut to yerth. Therefore cross country is the word, unless we are all to go to the State gaol together, where you, brother Snowball, will taste the Confederate cat, and I shall grow fat on the Confederate bacon."

The boy grinned, and turned the trap off the main road into one of the little forest tracks.

"Ladies," he went on, "I know all about it, and you kin trust me, for though I was born down to Norfolk, my father was a honest Yank, and as for slavery, why, I just hate ut; there, I hate ut. As for you, marm," he addressed himself to Olive, "it may be true what that murderin' villain said, and it may not be true. All I know for sartain is that you shipped aboard with us twice; wanst you was the Cap'en's wife, and the second time, when the skipper had changed his name, you was a stowaway. And as for you, young lady, you was kidnapped. Now we're comfortable and understand each other; and so, ladies, ef you'll tell me your plans, you may trust me."

It was risky, but we were completely at his mercy, and besides, we remembered his whispers on board the ship.

Olive told him all. She confessed that she had been formerly a slave in this same State, though in appearance as white as any European; that she had escaped by the Underground Railway; that she had told Captain Jefferson Ramsay, *alias* Valentine Angel, everything before their marriage; that we now designed to effect our escape by the same way in which she had before succeeded; and that it was only by the accident of losing our way that we found ourselves at Fayetteville at all.

He approved our design, and told us, which was a great comfort for us, that Tennessee was most likely, by this time, in the hands of the North, so that once over the Alleghany Mountains we were safe.

He then went on to speak of the Captain.

"At first," he said, "he was mad at losing his ship, his cargo, and—the young lady." Then he begged Olive's pardon.

"You need not," she said. "I know my husband as well as you."

"There is nothing," he told us, "nothing on this yerth that he would not do to gain his ends. Robbery, murder, shootin' and slaughterin', conspirin' and plottin', misrepresentin' and lyin', bullyin' and threatenin': all this comes in the day's work. As for revenge, it is the Cap'en's nature to remember the bad deeds and forget the good. I'm his old shipmet. Well, what then? As fur what I've done in takin' you out o' the hands o' the 'Malakites, if he had me aboard knifin' would be too good for me. Reckon ef we meet, there'll be a hole made in the man who draws the slowest. Bad job fur that man, it'll be. Shipmets we mustn't never be no more. Pity, too, for the Cap'en's got a lucky hand, and blockade-runnin' is sweet and lovely biz for them as likes large profits. Wal, mad at first he waz, and went around like—like a eel in a ash-pit; nobody, not even the chief officer, didn't venture to go a-nigh him fur a spell. Then he heard that you ladies was seen put ashore; and then he put out them advertisements. I knowed the Cap'en for nigh twenty year, and sailed with him on many a cruise, and seen a deal o' wild and bloody work, but I never see nor hearn a more desperate wickedness than to call his own wife and the young lady whom he'd kidnapped runaway yaller gells. 'Pears most as if I should be feared of sailin' in the same craft with such a man. Talk o' Jonas! What he did wasn't nowhere near it!"

So we changed the route which had been laid down for us by our kind friends of that secret institution which had befriended so many poor creatures, and drove across the strange forest-covered country by the cross-tracks which we chose by compass, not knowing whither they would lead us, so only that we should not come out upon any town. Towns, indeed, in North Carolina, were scarce.

It was a wonderful journey, the recollection of which lives always in my mind, and will never leave me. There was the sense of being hunted, which made me wake up in the dead of night, and clutch at Olive's wrist and cry aloud for help; there was the silent deserted forest; the cottages where the poor creatures lived whose husbands were with the rebel armies, and whose children ran about as wild and as untaught as their mothers. There was the midday camp for dinner, and sometimes the night camp, when in the warm summer nights it was no great harm to sleep in the open. There were the bad corduroy roads, over which our hickory-built carriage, tough and yielding as steel, bumped and jumped us from the seat. There were the places where he had to get out and ford a stream; there were days when we could get no food, and days when we fared sumptuously. Our negro boy was always good-natured, laughing, happy, and careless; he had no fear nor any anxiety. Our protector was always grim of aspect, yet kind of speech; rough in his manner, yet a very Don Quixote for chivalry towards women. To walk beside him was to feel that one had a protector indeed as true and faithful as even my poor Jack would have been.

At last we came to the Alleghany Mountains. If I had not seen those hills, I should have thought the whole of America was one vast plain covered with pine forests; having seen them, when I think of places beautiful, my thoughts go back to the Alleghany Mountains.

Once on the other side we were soon in Tennessee.

To our great joy, the Federals held Nashville; and here, the very day we got there, we saw a great and splendid thing.

It was in the evening; a mighty crowd, almost entirely composed of negroes and coloured people, were gathered together in a square before a great building, which was, I suppose, the town hall or government house. Presently there came forth to them a man of insignificant presence, like Paul, and, like him, the bearer of good tidings.

"In the name of this great Republic," he said in a solemn voice, "I proclaim you FREE."

Olive burst out crying and sobbing. It was the beginning of the end. Slavery was doomed.

The man was Andrew Johnson. Two years later, when the murder of Abraham Lincoln put him in the President's place, and papers derided the self-made man, I thought of the great deed he had done in Tennessee, and how he had, on his own responsibility, given liberty to the thousands who, before his act, were like the cattle of the field, to be bought and sold.

We made no stay at Nashville, though there was nothing to fear, but took train, no longer in hiding or afraid, for the North; for we longed to be once more on British soil, out of the dreadful war, out of the never-ending controversy, out of the tears of women, out of the anxiety of men, out of the sights which showed us how terrible is war, and how strong of purpose were the men who would never lay down the sword till the cause was won.

When, at last, we crossed the bridge at Niagara, we had been six weeks upon our journey from the moment when we started from the flat and sandy shore to plunge into the depths of the Great Green Swamp.

Often, at night, I dream of that time. In my dream I am stumbling, tired, footsore, and hungry, over the sand among the piny woods, or across the yielding grass of the quicksands; beside me walks, patient, uncomplaining, always with a smile for me and a word of hope—always with the hopeless sadness for herself, poor Olive. It seems as if to the forest and the pines there shall never be any end. Or I am among the green slopes and wooded heights of the Alleghany Mountains. The air, here, is bright and clear; one feels stronger upon the hill-sides; we walk with elastic tread; with us is the tall, ungainly sailor, who hitches up one shoulder first, and then the other, who screws up his right eye tight, who chews tobacco as he goes; who talks with such a drawl; who inspires us with so much trust that I, for one, could laugh and sing. Or I am standing at the outer edge of that great throng of blacks, while the man of insignificant presence proclaims the freedom of the slaves, and Olive's tears are a hymn of thanks and praise.

CHAPTER THE LAST.

THE WHIRLPOOL OF NIAGARA.

AT last we were on British soil. Truly there had been no danger to us since Andrew Johnson's proclamation at Nashville; but, as I have said, the country was wild with war excitement, and one longed to be away from the dreadful anxieties depicted on every face.

The train landed us at last on the American side of the Falls; we crossed over and found on the English side a small hotel, where we thought of resting for a few days before we began to consider our plans. Olive, especially, wanted rest; she was pale and anxious; she had lost hope; she felt, she said, the approach of some fresh calamity; she knew that her husband, wherever he was, would bring her new sorrow and himself new disgrace. That dreadful punishment in which the dead were tied to the living was hers; for she was joined with a man dead to all goodness.

Here our protector left us, with thanks which were heartfelt, if any ever were. He had saved us from a most dreadful danger; he had literally torn us from the hands of our enemies; he had carried us across a rough and dangerous country, a country in which he who helped a runaway would have had a short shrift and a long rope; he had brought us to a place of safety. In addition, rude and rough sailor as he was, he had never intruded himself upon us, maintained the most perfect respect towards us; had paid all our expenses for us; and now, with a courtesy and consideration beyond all praise, he advanced us a sum of money to provide for our passage to England.

I have repaid that money long ago; but the faithful, loyal

service I can never repay. And though I know not where my protector may be, I pray for him daily.

He left us, then, to make his way to Liverpool first, and, if that failed, to Nassau, in order to find another berth in a blockade-runner, nothing daunted by the ill-success of the last. He attributed the disaster, indeed, just as poor old Stephen did, to the presence of women aboard the ship. Some sailors, except on passenger ships where their admission is necessary, believe in the superstition that my sex brings misfortune to a ship. He promised faithfully to keep out of Captain Ramsay's way; and so we parted, and I have never seen him since.

The place, on the English side, was full of Southern ladies; they did not come to gaze upon the Falls, but to watch and wait. Alas for them! Their words were full of boast and promise; but the colour was fading from their cheeks and the light from their eyes in the days when day after day passed and the armies of the South made no headway. Their brothers were with those armies; their sisters were starving in the lonely homesteads; their slaves were scattered, their fields untilled; and they believed—oh! how those poor creatures believed!—in the justice of a cause most unjust, and prayed—as only believers and faithful women can pray—for the success of arms which should never have been taken up.

I had written, every day since we left Nashville, letters to my dear Jack, telling him what we were doing and how we fared. These letters I sent to London, but he did not get them till long afterwards, for a very good reason, as you shall hear. For, when the Poet told him what had happened, with tears in his eyes, taking shame and blame to himself, who was not to blame at all, but rather the reverse, as having clearly discerned the character of the villain Ramsay from the beginning, Jack, with no more delay than was necessary to turn everything he possessed into money—it was not much, poor fellow!—took train for Liverpool. He would cross over to America and search the States through till he found me. With him came his friend, the Poet. They landed at New York; here they heard of the wreck and burning of the *Maryland* off Cape Fear, the news of which was received with great joy, because her captain's name was well known as that of a most successful runner; and this was a new and very fast steamer. They read in the papers further, how two ladies had been taken prisoners but set ashore, because it was no use carrying Southern women to a Northern gaol. Then Jack breathed with relief, for he knew who one of the ladies was, and he hoped that I was among people who would protect me from the man Ramsay. The Americans make short work of men who insult women. Presently they heard, having by this time discovered where to learn news from the South—and, indeed, partly from the newspapers, partly from private letters, and partly from the information of spies, nothing was done in North Carolina, Virginia, or any other of the Confederate States, that was not immediately known in New York—the horrible news that the villain Ramsay had taken advantage of the Southern prejudices in the matter of colour to get a Hue and Cry sent through the country after us. The man who told Jack this was one of the sailors of the *Maryland*, who knew, as all the crew knew, that Olive was the Captain's wife, and had followed her husband on board as a stowaway. Horrible! his own wife, though he had tried to put her away on a lying pretext, the woman whom he had sworn to love and protect, he had declared to be a runaway slave. As for me—Jack ground his teeth, but he could find no words fitting for his wrath and indignation. There are acts whose guilt is greater than any tongue can express; such was this act of the man who had betrayed me to cross the ocean on his ship. But then, to their joy and comfort, they heard how we had escaped, and were reported to be coming along by slow stages, and the help of the Underground Railway. If all went well, we might be expected in New York or Philadelphia in a fortnight or three weeks at latest.

As you know, our route was changed, and we came on with the help of another protector.

When we did not appear, and they learned that we had

been carried away after the danger at Fayetteville by a sailor, their anxiety was very great. It was impossible to guess with any certainty whither the man had carried us, or whether he would be loyal; or whether, after all, he was not (having been a sailor under Captain Ramsay) a mere creature and servant of his, anxious, perhaps, to show his zeal to his chief by bringing back the runaways for no reward at all. Granted that he would be true to us, whither in so troubled a time would he take us? Not through Virginia; perhaps South by way of South Carolina, and so to New Orleans, though that was a long and perilous journey; perhaps even through the worst and most dangerous part of the country, where we should be least expected to venture.   .

Then, because news of us, not being of public interest, came slowly, they went north to Toronto, on the chance of hearing more about us there from the people interested in runaways. But no one there had heard anything of our story. Then they went back to New York, and from there to Philadelphia, where they learned the latest news from Wilmington. The latest news was to the effect that Captain Ramsay was still at Wilmington waiting for his two "runaways;" but they had not been heard of, and it was thought that they had succeeded in making their escape; any way, the country was much too disturbed to allow of the old-fashioned hot chase. Captain Ramsay had learned the part played by his bo's'n in our escape, and went about stating his intentions (which were closely copied from the old modes of torture) with regard to that knight-errant.

Then, because publicity would now be a great thing for us, Jack wrote an account of the story so far as he knew it —be sure he made the most of Ramsay's marriage, and his treatment of his wife, though he knew nothing of the Indiana divorce—and sent it to one of the New York papers, which immediately published it. All the other papers copied it with comments. This, then, was the kind of thing which was possible in the South! A man marries a runaway mulatto, brings her back to North Carolina, and advertises her as a fugitive slave, while he advertises for an English girl, whom he has kidnapped, on the same pretext. Did ever an indignant world hear the like? Was there ever an institution like that called by its supporters the Peculiar and the Domestic? When the story had gone the round of the Northern journals, some treating it as a hoax, it was actually copied by a Richmond paper, in order to show the kind of rubbish with which Yankee abolitionists entertained their readers. The facts were, of course, indignantly denied; not only were they denied, but people with common sense were asked if it were even possible that they could be true. A Southerner, they said, could never, to begin with, marry a mulatto runaway; if he did, it was incredible that he should bring her back to her master—the lowest of humanity would revolt at such a wickedness; and then we were asked to believe that a man, whose name was mentioned, and who was at the very time among his friends at Wilmington, had still further kidnapped an English girl, and was trying to get her back when she had escaped, under the pretence that she, too, was a slave. Why, the story was monstrous!

Everybody at Wilmington knew the truth, because you cannot silence men's mouths, and the crew talked; yet so vigorously did Captain Ramsay adhere to his own statement, and so calmly resolute were his announced intentions of letting daylight into any who ventured to make assertions to the contrary, that public opinion only showed itself in a general desire to avoid his presence. This method, adopted at first by the more peaceful of the citizens, was gradually followed by the very rowdiest among the sailors and wild creatures who haunted the Wilmington saloons. If the Captain showed at a bar, there would be silence; presently the visitors at that bar dropped away one after the other, having immediate and important business elsewhere. This was galling to Captain Ramsay; he could not shoot a whole townful of men for the crime of having business elsewhere when he entered a saloon; and as nobody offered him any pretext, there was no shooting to be done. Presently, as Jack heard, there were murmurs abroad, the citizens met and talked things over, the Hue and Cry was torn down from the walls,

and the name of Lynch was freely mentioned.   At this junc-
ture, Captain Ramsay disappeared.

"I know that he will run the inland blockade," said Olive,
talking over things at Niagara.   "He will cross the lines
and make for New York.   Then he will come North.   I
shall wait for him here."

"Will you forgive him?" I asked.

"Forgive?   Oh, my dear, it is not a question of forgiveness.   What have I not forgiven?   What have I not en-
dured?   I must be with him to save him from worse things
if I may.   And——What is it, child?"

For below us, walking in the road, on the shady side,
were no other than Jack and the Poet, and I was running and
crying to fly into the arms of my lover.   How he greeted
me—with what words of affection and rejoicing—I cannot
set down.   When he let me go for a moment, I shook
hands with the Poet, who hung his head guiltily.

"It was all my fault, Miss Avis," he said; "I ought to
have followed you day and night.   I knew he was a man-
eater.   I saw that from the very beginning."

"He would come with me, Avis," said Jack.   "He has
never left me day or night.   See what it is to have a
faithful Poet!"

He spoke in his old light, airy way, but his voice shook,
and the tears stood in his eyes as he held my hands in his.

"You have suffered much, Avis.   My poor girl; I would
I could have suffered for you."

"I think you have suffered for me too, Jack."

And then I told him of Olive, who had left us together,
and of what she had done, and of Liberty Wicks, the
quartermaster.   Nothing would do now for Jack but we
must be married at once, to prevent any further chance, he
said, of the man Ramsay, or Angel, or whatever he called
himself, running away with me.   Why, indeed, he said,
should we wait?   Such protection and guardianship as had
been grudingly afforded me by Stephen Cobbledick was
now withdrawn, because the old man was killed (so far as

we then knew). I had no friends to consult, and we loved
each other. That consideration, indeed, was all that we
wanted. Could I refuse my boy what he so ardently desired
—the right to call me his own? We went, therefore, two
days afterwards to the little Episcopal Chapel of Cliftonville,
where we were married, the Poet giving me away. He gave
me also, I remember, the most beautiful bracelet to be got
at Niagara—it had been the property of a poor Southern
lady, who sold it to pay her hotel bill—and a collection of
feather fans bought at the little shops beside the Falls.
And when we came to England, he gave me his book of
poetry, which I shall always read with pleasure, though I
prefer Tennyson and Longfellow, out of gratitude to my
Jack's best friend.

One morning, a week after our marriage, Olive came and
told me, with tears, how she had just heard from some
quarter whence she got secret information, that a warrant
had been issued against Valentine Angel, *alias* Jefferson
Ramsay, *alias* a great many other names, including his
first, Peregrine Pickle, for piracy on the high seas. It was
one of those great and gallant deeds remembered and lauded
by Stephen Cobbledick, committed some years before. They
had other charges against him, but this would be taken first.
The little matter of kidnapping a whole crew of free blacks
at Boston and selling them at New Orleans would also be
brought up again. Meantime there was reason to believe
that he was making for British territory; that he would
cross the frontier at Niagara; and, unless he were captured
before, would be taken on the bridge.

Olive spent that day on the other side, watching and
waiting, if haply she might give her husband warning.

The next day and the next she sat or walked. All night,
too, she had no sleep; she never left her watch; he might
come at any moment.

On the fourth day he came.

He was in some kind of disguise, but she knew him. It
was already growing dark; he walked in the shadows of the

great square hotels, away from the lights in the shop windows. She touched his arm. He turned, and recognised her with an oath.

"Do not cross the bridge to-night!" she said. "They are on the watch for you everywhere; lie in hiding; you will be arrested."

He pushed her roughly from him with another oath, walked quickly to the toll-gate, paid his toll, and hurried over the bridge. What sign had been sent across I do not know, nor how they knew their man; but as he neared the English side, three men stepped from the gate-house.

They were armed to the teeth with rifles and pistols, for they were going to catch a wild beast.

"Stand," cried one; "we arrest you, Angel, *alias* Ramsay, for piracy on the high seas."

He looked back; armed men were at the other end of the bridge. He drew his revolver, fired twice and missed, and, with a bound, leaped to the railings of the bridge, and dived headlong into the river, a hundred and fifty feet below.

Here the stream is narrow, and the deep water, between perpendicular rocks, rushes black, vehement, terrible even on the sunniest days, as if anxious to get away from the horror of the awful leap it has taken over the Fall behind. He would be a good swimmer who would keep his head above the water in such a stream; he would be a strong swimmer who could think of holding his own even with the current, in such a rush and roar of headlong waves until he could come to a place where the cliffs sink down and a landing-place might be found. Ramsay disappeared in the stream. A moment afterwards his head appeared upon the surface; he had not, then, been killed by the leap; he was alive and he was swimming. Crack! crack! crack! Three rifles were fired. His head disappeared again and was no more seen. Olive's husband had met his fate.

Three miles or so below the Falls there is a place which visitors are always taken to see. The force of the water has hollowed out a round basin in the rocks, and a bank has been formed at the bottom of earth and crumbled rock, where grow the wild vine, the maple, and the hemlock of the Canadian woods, with a thousand flowers, bushes, and climbing things which make this place a dream of loveliness. You may clamber round this bank, among this growth, and watch at your feet the great round whirlpool, which the river forms. The season changes; men come and go; but the boiling, roaring water never ceases to rush round and round as if mad to devour something, and for ever in a fierce insatiable hunger and rage. Strange things sometimes come down from the Falls and are carried round upon its surface until, by some accident, they drift out of the whirling circle, and are either carried away down stream or thrown up on this bank; no stranger or more awful thing ever came into this whirlpool, and was carried round and round, than that which was seen the day after Captain Ramsay's desperate leap. It was the body of a man. The waters hurried him ceaselessly round the sweeping circle; in his hand he held a revolver; hand and pistol were above the water, the rest of the body, black in the gloomy pool, only visible when the current bore it near the bank. And by the water's edge sat a woman with pale face and sunken eyes and clasped hands. She was waiting for the river to give up its dead.

For three days that awful hand, its fingers closed upon the pistol, was hurried round; in the night of the third day the body of Captain Ramsay floated ashore, and was laid by the river itself as if moved to pity at so much patience and so much grief, at the very feet of his widow.

They buried him in the churchyard at Cliftonville. At his head Olive placed a marble cross, with his initials and the date of his death, and beneath she wrote the words, "Thy mercy, Jesu!"

When all was over we took her away.

She came with us as far as Quebec, where we were to embark for England. Here she parted from us.

"My life," she said, "has gone from me; there is but one thing left to do—to pray for a dead man; there is only one

Church which permits me so to pray. I shall enter a convent and pray for him night and day."

She kissed and wept over me; she prayed for my happiness; she thanked God that she had been of service to me; and then the doors of the convent closed upon her, and Olive became, too, as one dead.

I am glad to be able to add that Stephen was not killed; they carried him aboard the cruiser, where, for a spell, he had a pretty bad time; then he pulled round and presently found himself in a New York gaol, where he lay cooling his heels and reflecting for a good space, because, as I have said, they were hard on pilots. In the fulness of time, however, he returned to Boscastle, where, his rents having been collected for him in his absence, he settled down again to the comfortable old life.

He accounted for his departure by swearing that the notorious pirate, Captain Ramsay, had kidnapped him together with his niece; that in the rescue of that dear girl, at the end of their run—he could not avoid narrating the brilliant way in which he almost navigated the ship right into Wilmington on the darkest night ever known—he had received wounds innumerable, which he did not regret. Sometimes his friends would pull him up to ask how, seeing he had no brothers or sisters, the young lady could be called his niece. Then he reverted to the story of the raft, into which my husband and I never inquired further. The locality and the minor details always varied according to the geographical fancy of the moment; but he adhered to the leading situations of the story.

"I picked her up, gentlemen, lyin', with a hundred and fifty-three poor fellows—sailors—all starved to death upon a raft. She was wropped in four bandanners. It was in latitude twenty-two and a half, where its pretty hot, off the coast of Chili. Wherefore I took her aboard, fed her myself night and mornin' with a spoon and bottle, and giv' her for her benefit the name of Cobbledick. Also, to make her feel properly proud of her family, I said her mother was a Knobling. This made her grow up haughty. I sought for her, gentlemen; I thought for her; I fought for her. I crossed the sea with her. I rescued her from the pirate, and I chucked him over the bridge into Niagara Rapids. Yet she remembered, in the long run, that she was but a Common Pick-me-up, after all, and married, in spite of her family connections, a journeyman painter who hadn't the money to pay for his Marriage Settlements."

THE END.

PRINTED BY BALLANTYNE HANSON AND CO.
EDINBURGH AND LONDON

A LIST OF BOOKS

PUBLISHED BY

CHATTO & WINDUS,

214, PICCADILLY, LONDON, W.

Sold by all Booksellers, or sent post free for the published price by the Publishers:

About.—The Fellah: An Egyptian Novel. By EDMOND ABOUT. Translated by Sir RANDAL ROBERTS. Post 8vo, illustrated boards, 2s. ; cloth limp, 2s. 6d.

Adams (W. Davenport), Works by:
A Dictionary of the Drama. Being a comprehensive Guide to the Plays, Playwrights, Players, and Playhouses of the United Kingdom and America, from the Earliest to the Present Times. Crown 8vo, halfbound, 12s. 6d. [*Preparing.*
Quips and Quiddities. Selected by W. DAVENPORT ADAMS. Post 8vo, cloth limp, 2s. 6d.

Advertising, A History of, from the Earliest Times. Illustrated by Anecdotes, Curious Specimens, and Notices of Successful Advertisers. By HENRY SAMPSON. Crown 8vo, with Coloured Frontispiece and Illustrations, cloth gilt, 7s. 6d.

Agony Column (The) of "The Times," from 1800 to 1870. Edited, with an Introduction, by ALICE CLAY. Post 8vo, cloth limp, 2s. 6d.

Aïdé (Hamilton), Works by:
Post 8vo, illustrated boards, 2s. each.
Carr of Carrlyon. | Confidences.

Alexander (Mrs.), Novels by:
Post 8vo, illustrated boards, 2s. each.
Maid, Wife, or Widow?
Valerie's Fate.

Allen (Grant), Works by:
Crown 8vo, cloth extra, 6s. each.
The Evolutionist at Large. Second Edition, revised.
Vignettes from Nature.
Colin Clout's Calendar.

ALLEN (GRANT), *continued*—
Strange Stories. With Frontispiece by GEORGE DU MAURIER. Cr. 8vo, cl. ex., 6s. ; post 8vo, illust. bds., 2s.
Philistia: A Novel. Crown 8vo, cloth extra, 3s. 6d.; post 8vo, illust. bds., 2s.
Babylon: A Novel. Post 8vo, illust. boards, 2s.
For Maimie's Sake: A Tale of Love and Dynamite. Cr. 8vo, cl. ex., 6s.
In all Shades: A Novel. New and Cheaper Edition. Crown 8vo, cloth extra, 3s. 6d.
The Beckoning Hand, &c. With a Frontispiece by TOWNLEY GREEN. Crown 8vo, cloth extra, 6s.

Architectural Styles, A Handbook of. Translated from the German of A. ROSENGARTEN, by W. COLLETT-SANDARS. Crown 8vo, cloth extra, with 639 Illustrations, 7s. 6d.

Arnold.—Bird Life in England. By EDWIN LESTER ARNOLD. Crown 8vo, cloth extra, 6s.

Artemus Ward :
Artemus Ward's Works: The Works of CHARLES FARRER BROWNE, better known as ARTEMUS WARD. With Portrait and Facsimile. Crown 8vo, cloth extra, 7s. 6d.
The Genial Showman: Life and Adventures of Artemus Ward. By EDWARD P. HINGSTON. With a Frontispiece. Cr. 8vo, cl. extra, 3s. 6d.

Art (The) of Amusing: A Collection of Graceful Arts, Games, Tricks, Puzzles, and Charades. By FRANK BELLEW. With 300 Illustrations. Cr. 8vo cloth extra, 4s. 6d.

Ashton (John), Works by:
Crown 8vo, cloth extra, 7s. 6d. each.

A History of the Chap-Books of the Eighteenth Century. With nearly 400 Illustrations, engraved in facsimile of the originals.

Social Life in the Reign of Queen Anne. From Original Sources. With nearly 100 Illustrations.

Humour, Wit, and Satire of the Seventeenth Century. With nearly 100 Illustrations.

English Caricature and Satire on Napoleon the First. With 120 Illustrations. [*Preparing.*

Bacteria.—A Synopsis of the Bacteria and Yeast Fungi and Allied Species. By W. B. Grove, B.A. With 87 Illusts. Crown 8vo, cl. extra, 3s. 6d.

Bankers, A Handbook of London; together with Lists of Bankers from 1677. By F. G. Hilton Price. Crown 8vo, cloth extra, 7s. 6d.

Bardsley (Rev. C.W.), Works by:
Crown 8vo, cloth extra, 7s. 6d. each.

English Surnames: Their Sources and Significations. Third Ed., revised.

Curiosities of Puritan Nomenclature.

Bartholomew Fair, Memoirs of. By Henry Morley. With 100 Illusts. Crown 8vo, cloth extra, 7s. 6d.

Beaconsfield, Lord: A Biography. By T. P. O'Connor, M.P. Sixth Edition, with a New Preface. Crown 8vo, cloth extra, 7s. 6d.

Beauchamp. — Grantley Grange: A Novel. By Shelsley Beauchamp. Post 8vo, illust. bds., 2s.

Beautiful Pictures by British Artists: A Gathering of Favourites from our Picture Galleries. All engraved on Steel in the highest style of Art. Edited, with Notices of the Artists, by Sydney Armytage, M.A. Imperial 4to, cloth extra gilt and gilt edges 21s.

Bechstein. — As Pretty as Seven, and other German Stories. Collected by Ludwig Bechstein. With Additional Tales by the Brothers Grimm, and 100 Illusts. by Richter. Small 4to, green and gold, 6s. 6d.; gilt edges, 7s. 6d.

Beerbohm. — Wanderings in Patagonia; or, Life among the Ostrich Hunters. By Julius Beerbohm. With Illusts. Crown 8vo, cloth extra, 3s. 6d.

Belgravia. One Shilling Monthly. A New Serial Story by W. Clark Russell, entitled The Frozen Pirate, began in the July Number.—Two New Serial Stories will begin in the Number for January, 1888, and will be continued through the year: Undercurrents, by the Author of " Phyllis ;" and The Blackhall Ghosts, by Sarah Tytler.
*** *Now ready, the Volume for* July *to* October, 1887, *cloth extra, gilt edges,* 7s. 6d.; *Cases for binding Vols.,* 2s. *each.*

Belgravia Holiday Number, 1887. Demy 8vo, with Illustrations, 1s.

Belgravia Annual, 1887 : A Collection of Powerful Short Stories, each complete in itself. With Illustrations. Demy 8vo, 1s. [*Nov.* 10.

Bennett (W.C.,LL.D.),Works by:
Post 8vo, cloth limp, 2s. each.

A Ballad History of England.
Songs for Sailors.

Besant (Walter) and James Rice, Novels by. Crown 8vo, cloth extra, 3s. 6d. each ; post 8vo, illust. boards, 2s. each; cloth limp, 2s. 6d. each.

Ready-Money Mortiboy.
With Harp and Crown.
This Son of Vulcan.
My Little Girl
The Case of Mr. Lucraft.
The Golden Butterfly.
By Celia's Arbour.
The Monks of Thelema.
'Twas in Trafalgar's Bay.
The Seamy Side.
The Ten Years' Tenant.
The Chaplain of the Fleet.

Besant (Walter), Novels by:
Crown 8vo, cloth extra, 3s. 6d. each; post 8vo, illust. boards, 2s. each; cloth limp, 2s. 6d. each.

All Sorts and Conditions of Men: An Impossible Story. With Illustrations by Fred. Barnard.

The Captains' Room, &c. With Frontispiece by E. J. Wheeler.

All in a Garden Fair. With 6 Illusts. by H. Furniss.

Dorothy Forster. With Frontispiece by Charles Green.

Uncle Jack, and other Stories.

BESANT (WALTER), *continued—*
Crown 8vo, cloth extra, 3s. 6d. each.
Children of Gibeon.
The World Went Very Well Then.
With Illustrations by A. FORESTIER.

The Art of Fiction. Demy 8vo, 1s.

**Library Edition of the Novels of
Besant and Rice.**

Messrs. CHATTO & WINDUS *are
now issuing a choicely-printed Library
Edition of the Novels of Messrs.* BESANT
and RICE. *The Volumes (each one containing a Complete Novel) are printed
from a specially-cast fount of type on
a large crown 8vo page, and handsomely
bound in cloth. Price Six Shillings
each. The First Volumes are—*

Ready-Money Mortiboy. With Por-
trait of JAMES RICE, etched by DANIEL
A. WEHRSCHMIDT, and a New Preface
by WALTER BESANT, telling the story
of his literary partnership with JAMES
RICE.
My Little Girl.
With Harp and Crown.
This Son of Vulcan.
The Golden Butterfly. With Etched
Portrait of WALTER BESANT. [*Nov.*
The Monks of Thelema.
By Celia's Arbour.
The Chaplain of the Fleet.
The Seamy Side. &c. &c.

**Betham-Edwards (M.), Novels
by:**
Felicia. Cr. 8vo, cloth extra, 3s. 6d. ;
post 8vo, illust. bds., 2s.
Kitty. Post 8vo, illust. bds., 2s.

Bewick (Thos.) and his Pupils.
By AUSTIN DOBSON. With 95 Illustrations. Square 8vo, cloth extra, 10s. 6d.

Birthday Books:—
The Starry Heavens: A Poetical
Birthday Book. Square 8vo, hand-
somely bound in cloth, 2s. 6d.
Birthday Flowers: Their Language
and Legends. By W. J. GORDON.
Beautifully Illustrated in Colours by
VIOLA BOUGHTON. In illuminated
cover, crown 4to, 6s.
The Lowell Birthday Book. With
Illusts. Small 8vo, cloth extra, 4s. 6d.

**Blackburn's (Henry) Art Hand-
books.** Demy 8vo, Illustrated, uniform in size for binding.
**Academy Notes, separate years, from
1875 to 1886, each 1s.**
Academy Notes, 1887. With numerous Illustrations. 1s.
Academy Notes, 1875-79. Complete
in One Vol., with nearly 600 Illusts. in
Facsimile. Demy 8vo, cloth limp, 6s.

BLACKBURN (HENRY), *continued—*
Academy Notes, 1880-84. Complete
in One Volume, with about 700 Fac-
simile Illustrations. Cloth limp, 6s.
Grosvenor Notes, 1877. 6d.
**Grosvenor Notes, separate years, from
1878 to 1886, each 1s.**
Grosvenor Notes, 1887. With nu-
merous Illusts. 1s.
Grosvenor Notes, Vol. I., 1877-82.
With upwards of 300 Illustrations.
Demy 8vo, cloth limp, 6s.
Grosvenor Notes, Vol. II., 1883-87.
With upwards of 300 Illustrations.
Demy 8vo, cloth limp, 6s.
**The English Pictures at the National
Gallery.** 114 Illustrations. 1s.
**The Old Masters at the National
Gallery.** 128 Illustrations. 1s. 6d.
**A Complete Illustrated Catalogue
to the National Gallery.** With
Notes by H. BLACKBURN, and 242
Illusts. Demy 8vo, cloth limp, 3s.

**Illustrated Catalogue of the Luxem-
bourg Gallery.** Containing about
250 Reproductions after the Original
Drawings of the Artists. Edited by
F. G. DUMAS. Demy 8vo, 3s. 6d.
The Paris Salon, 1887. With about
300 Facsimile Sketches. Demy 8vo, 3s.

Blake (William) : Etchings from
his Works. By W. B. SCOTT. With
descriptive Text. Folio, half-bound
boards, India Proofs, 21s.

Boccaccio's Decameron ; or,
Ten Days' Entertainment. Translated
into English, with an Introduction by
THOMAS WRIGHT, F.S.A. With Portrait
and STOTHARD'S beautiful Copper-
plates. Cr. 8vo, cloth extra, gilt, 7s. 6d.

Bourne (H. R. Fox), Works by :
English Merchants : Memoirs in Illustration of the Progress of British
Commerce. With numerous Illustrations. Cr. 8vo, cloth extra, 7s. 6d.
English Newspapers : Contributions
to the History of Journalism. Two
vols., demy 8vo, cloth extra, 25s.

Bowers'(G.) Hunting Sketches:
Oblong 4to, half-bound boards, 21s. each.
Canters in Crampshire.
Leaves from a Hunting Journal.
Coloured in facsimile of the originals.

Boyle (Frederick), Works by :
Crown 8vo, cloth extra, 3s. 6d. each; post
8vo, illustrated boards, 2s. each.
Camp Notes: Stories of Sport and
Adventure in Asia, Africa, and
America. [*Trotter.*
Savage Life: Adventures of a Globe.

Chronicles of No-Man's Land.
Post 8vo, illust. boards, 2s.

Brand's Observations on Popular Antiquities, chiefly Illustrating the Origin of our Vulgar Customs, Ceremonies, and Superstitions. With the Additions of Sir HENRY ELLIS. Crown 8vo, cloth extra, gilt, with numerous Illustrations, 7s. 6d.

Bret Harte, Works by:

Bret Harte's Collected Works. Arranged and Revised by the Author. Complete in Five Vols., crown 8vo, cloth extra, 6s. each.
Vol. I. COMPLETE POETICAL AND DRAMATIC WORKS. With Steel Portrait, and Introduction by Author.
Vol. II. EARLIER PAPERS—LUCK OF ROARING CAMP, and other Sketches —BOHEMIAN PAPERS — SPANISH AND AMERICAN LEGENDS.
Vol. III. TALES OF THE ARGONAUTS —EASTERN SKETCHES.
Vol. IV. GABRIEL CONROY.
Vol. V. STORIES — CONDENSED NOVELS, &c.

The Select Works of Bret Harte, in Prose and Poetry. With Introductory Essay by J. M. BELLEW, Portrait of the Author, and 50 Illustrations. Crown 8vo cloth extra, 7s. 6d.

Bret Harte's Complete Poetical Works. Author's Copyright Edition. Beautifully printed on hand-made paper and bound in buckram. Cr. 8vo, 4s. 6d.

Gabriel Conroy: A Novel. Post 8vo, illustrated boards, 2s.

An Heiress of Red Dog, and other Stories. Post 8vo, illust. boards, 2s.

The Twins of Table Mountain. Fcap. 8vo, picture cover, 1s.

Luck of Roaring Camp, and other Sketches. Post 8vo, illust. bds., 2s.

Jeff Briggs's Love Story. Fcap. 8vo, picture cover, 1s.   [2s. 6d.

Flip. Post 8vo, illust. bds., 2s. ; cl. limp,

Californian Stories (including THE TWINS OF TABLE MOUNTAIN, JEFF BRIGGS'S LOVE STORY, &c.) Post 8vo, illustrated boards, 2s.

Maruja: A Novel. Post 8vo, illust. boards, 2s. ; cloth limp, 2s. 6d.

The Queen of the Pirate Isle. With 28 original Drawings by KATE GREENAWAY, Reproduced in Colours by EDMUND EVANS. Sm. 4to, bds., 5s.

Brewer (Rev. Dr.), Works by:

The Reader's Handbook of Allusions, References, Plots, and Stories. Fifth Edition, revised throughout, with a New Appendix, containing a COMPLETE ENGLISH BIBLIOGRAPHY. Cr. 8vo, 1,400 pp., cloth extra, 7s. 6d.

Authors and their Works, with the Dates: Being the Appendices to "The Reader's Handbook," separately printed. Cr. 8vo, cloth limp, 2s.

BREWER (REV. DR.), *continued*—

A Dictionary of Miracles: Imitative, Realistic, and Dogmatic. Crown 8vo, cloth extra, 7s. 6d. ; half-bound, 9s.

Brewster (Sir David), Works by:

More Worlds than One: The Creed of the Philosopher and the Hope of the Christian. With Plates. Post 8vo, cloth extra, 4s. 6d.

The Martyrs of Science: Lives of GALILEO, TYCHO BRAHE, and KEPLER. With Portraits. Post 8vo, cloth extra, 4s. 6d.

Letters on Natural Magic. A New Edition, with numerous Illustrations, and Chapters on the Being and Faculties of Man, and Additional Phenomena of Natural Magic, by J. A. SMITH. Post 8vo, cl. ex., 4s. 6d.

Brillat-Savarin.—Gastronomy as a Fine Art. By BRILLAT-SAVARIN. Translated by R. E. ANDERSON, M.A. Post 8vo, cloth limp, 2s. 6d.

Buchanan's (Robert) Works:

Crown 8vo, cloth extra, 6s. each.
Ballads of Life, Love, and Humour. Frontispiece by ARTHUR HUGHES.
Undertones. | London Poems.
The Book of Orm.
White Rose and Red: A Love Story.
Idylls and Legends of Inverburn.
Selected Poems of Robert Buchanan. With a Frontispiece by T. DALZIEL.
The Hebrid Isles: Wanderings in the Land of Lorne and the Outer Hebrides. With Frontispiece by WILLIAM SMALL.
A Poet's Sketch-Book: Selections from the Prose Writings of ROBERT BUCHANAN.
The Earthquake; or, Six Days and a Sabbath.
The City of Dream: An Epic Poem.
[*Immediately.*

Robert Buchanan's Complete Poetical Works. With Steel-plate Portrait. Crown 8vo, cloth extra, 7s. 6d.

Crown 8vo, cloth extra, 3s. 6d. each ; post 8vo, illust. boards, 2s. each.
The Shadow of the Sword.
A Child of Nature. With a Frontispiece.
God and the Man. With Illustrations by FRED. BARNARD.
The Martyrdom of Madeline. With Frontispiece by A. W. COOPER.
Love Me for Ever. With a Frontispiece by P. MACNAB.
Annan Water. | The New Abelard.
Foxglove Manor.
Matt: A Story of a Caravan.
The Master of the Mine.

Bunyan's Pilgrim's Progress.
Edited by Rev. T. SCOTT. With 17 Steel Plates by STOTHARD engraved by GOODALL, and numerous Woodcuts. Crown 8vo, cloth extra, gilt, 7s. 6d.

Burnett (Mrs.), Novels by:
Surly Tim, and other Stories. Post 8vo, illustrated boards, 2s.

Fcap. 8vo, picture cover, 1s. each.
Kathleen Mavourneen.
Lindsay's Luck.
Pretty Polly Pemberton.

Burton (Captain).—The Book of the Sword: Being a History of the Sword and its Use in all Countries, from the Earliest Times. By RICHARD F. BURTON. With over 400 Illustrations. Square 8vo, cloth extra, 32s.

Burton (Robert):
The Anatomy of Melancholy. A New Edition, complete, corrected and enriched by Translations of the Classical Extracts. Demy 8vo, cloth extra, 7s. 6d.

Melancholy Anatomised: Being an Abridgment, for popular use, of BURTON'S ANATOMY OF MELANCHOLY. Post 8vo, cloth limp, 2s. 6d.

Byron (Lord):
Byron's Letters and Journals. With Notices of his Life. By THOMAS MOORE. A Reprint of the Original Edition. Cr. 8vo, cloth extra, 7s. 6d.

Byron's Don Juan. Complete in One Vol., post 8vo, cloth limp, 2s.

Caine (T. Hall), Novels by:
The Shadow of a Crime. Cr. 8vo, cloth extra, 3s. 6d.; post 8vo, illustrated boards, 2s.

A Son of Hagar. New and Cheaper Edition. Crown 8vo, cloth extra, 3s. 6d.

The Deemster: A Romance of the Isle of Man. Three Vols., cr. 8vo.

Cameron (Comdr.).— The Cruise of the "Black Prince" Privateer, Commanded by ROBERT HAWKINS, Master Mariner. By Commander V. LOVETT CAMERON, R.N., C.B., D.C.L. With Frontispiece and Vignette by P. MACNAB. Crown 8vo, cl. ex., 5s.

Cameron (Mrs. H. Lovett), Novels by:
Crown 8vo, cloth extra, 3s. 6d. each post 8vo, illustrated boards, 2s. each.
Juliet's Guardian. | Deceivers Ever.

Carlyle (Thomas):
On the Choice of Books. By THOMAS CARLYLE. With a Life of the Author by R. H. SHEPHERD. New and Revised Edition, post 8vo, cloth extra, Illustrated, 1s. 6d.

The Correspondence of Thomas Carlyle and Ralph Waldo Emerson 1834 to 1872. Edited by CHARLES ELIOT NORTON. With Portraits. Two Vols., crown 8vo, cloth extra, 24s.

Chapman's (George) Works:
Vol. I. contains the Plays complete, including the doubtful ones. Vol. II., the Poems and Minor Translations, with an Introductory Essay by ALGERNON CHARLES SWINBURNE. Vol. III., the Translations of the Iliad and Odyssey. Three Vols., crown 8vo, cloth extra, 18s.; or separately, 6s. each.

Chatto & Jackson.—A Treatise on Wood Engraving, Historical and Practical. By WM. ANDREW CHATTO and JOHN JACKSON. With an Additional Chapter by HENRY G. BOHN; and 450 fine Illustrations. A Reprint of the last Revised Edition. Large 4to, half-bound, 28s.

Chaucer:
Chaucer for Children: A Golden Key. By Mrs. H.R. HAWEIS. With Eight Coloured Pictures and numerous Woodcuts by the Author. New Ed., small 4to, cloth extra, 6s.
Chaucer for Schools. By Mrs. H. R. HAWEIS. Demy 8vo, cloth limp, 2s. 6d.

Chronicle (The) of the Coach: Charing Cross to Ilfracombe. By J. D CHAMPLIN. With 75 Illustrations by EDWARD L. CHICHESTER. Square 8vo, cloth extra, 7s. 6d.

Clodd. — Myths and Dreams. By EDWARD CLODD, F.R.A.S., Author of "The Childhood of Religions," &c. Crown 8vo, cloth extra, 5s.

Cobban.—The Cure of Souls: A Story. By J. MACLAREN COBBAN. Post 8vo, illustrated boards, 2s.

Coleman.—Curly: An Actor's Story. By JOHN COLEMAN. Illustrated by J. C. DOLLMAN. Crown 8vo, 1s.; cloth, 1s. 6d.

Collins (Wilkie), Novels by :
Crown 8vo, cloth extra, Illustrated, 3s.6d. each ; post 8vo, illustrated bds., 2s. each ; cloth limp, 2s. 6d. each.

Antonina. Illust. by Sir JOHN GILBERT.
Basil. Illustrated by Sir JOHN GILBERT and J. MAHONEY.
Hide and Seek. Illustrated by Sir JOHN GILBERT and J. MAHONEY.
The Dead Secret. Illustrated by Sir JOHN GILBERT.
Queen of Hearts. Illustrated by Sir JOHN GILBERT.
My Miscellanies. With a Steel-plate Portrait of WILKIE COLLINS.
The Woman in White. With Illustrations by Sir JOHN GILBERT and F. A. FRASER.
The Moonstone. With Illustrations by G. DU MAURIER and F. A. FRASER.
Man and Wife. Illust. by W. SMALL.
Poor Miss Finch. Illustrated by G. DU MAURIER and EDWARD HUGHES.
Miss or Mrs.? With Illustrations by S. L. FILDES and HENRY WOODS.
The New Magdalen. Illustrated by G. DU MAURIER and C. S. REINHARDT.
The Frozen Deep. Illustrated by G. DU MAURIER and J. MAHONEY.
The Law and the Lady. Illustrated by S. L. FILDES and SYDNEY HALL.
The Two Destinies.
The Haunted Hotel. Illustrated by ARTHUR HOPKINS.
The Fallen Leaves.
Jezebel's Daughter.
The Black Robe.
Heart and Science: A Story of the Present Time.
"I Say No."
The Evil Genius.

Little Novels. Cr. 8vo, cl. ex., 3s. 6d.

Collins (Mortimer), Novels by :
Crown 8vo, cloth extra, 3s. 6d. each ; post 8vo, illustrated boards, 2s. each.

Sweet Anne Page. | Transmigration.
From Midnight to Midnight.

A Fight with Fortune. Post 8vo, illustrated boards, 2s.

Collins (Mortimer & Frances), Novels by :
Crown 8vo, cloth extra, 3s. 6d. each ; post 8vo, illustrated boards, 2s. each.

Blacksmith and Scholar.
The Village Comedy.
You Play Me False.

Post 8vo, illustrated boards, 2s. each.
Sweet and Twenty. | Frances.

Collins (C. Allston).—The Bar Sinister: A Story. By C. ALLSTON COLLINS. Post 8vo, illustrated bds., 2s.

Colman's Humorous Works: "Broad Grins," "My Nightgown and Slippers," and other Humorous Works, Prose and Poetical, of GEORGE COLMAN. With Life by G. B. BUCKSTONE, and Frontispiece by HOGARTH. Crown 8vo cloth extra, gilt, 7s. 6d.

Convalescent Cookery: A Family Handbook. By CATHERINE RYAN. Crown 8vo, 1s. ; cloth, 1s. 6d.

Conway (Moncure D.), Works by :
Demonology and Devil-Lore. Two Vols., royal 8vo, with 65 Illusts., 28s.
A Necklace of Stories. Illustrated by W. J. HENNESSY. Square 8vo, cloth extra, 6s.
Pine and Palm : A Novel. Two Vols., crown 8vo.

Cook (Dutton), Works by :
Crown 8vo, cloth extra, 6s. each.
Hours with the Players. With a Steel Plate Frontispiece.
Nights at the Play : A View of the English Stage.

Leo : A Novel. Post 8vo, illustrated boards, 2s.
Paul Foster's Daughter. crown 8vo, cloth extra, 3s. 6d. ; post 8vo, illustrated boards, 2s.

Copyright. — A Handbook of English and Foreign Copyright in Literary and Dramatic Works. By SIDNEY JERROLD, of the Middle Temple, Esq., Barrister-at-Law. Post 8vo, cloth limp, 2s. 6d.

Cornwall.—Popular Romances of the West of England; or, The Drolls, Traditions, and Superstitions of Old Cornwall. Collected and Edited by ROBERT HUNT, F.R.S. New and Revised Edition, with Additions, and Two Steel-plate Illustrations by GEORGE CRUIKSHANK. Crown 8vo, cloth extra, 7s. 6d.

Craddock. — The Prophet of the Great Smoky Mountains. By CHARLES EGBERT CRADDOCK. Post 8vo, illus. bds., 2s cloth limp, 2s. 6d.

Creasy.—Memoirs of Eminent Etonians : with Notices of the Early History of Eton College. By Sir EDWARD CREASY, Author of "The Fifteen Decisive Battles of the World." Crown 8vo, cloth extra, gilt, with 13 Portraits, 7s. 6d.

Cruikshank (George):

The Comic Almanack. Complete in Two SERIES: The FIRST from 1835 to 1843; the SECOND from 1844 to 1853. A Gathering of the BEST HUMOUR of THACKERAY, HOOD, MAYHEW, ALBERT SMITH, A'BECKETT, ROBERT BROUGH, &c. With 2,000 Woodcuts and Steel Engravings by CRUIKSHANK, HINE, LANDELLS, &c. Crown 8vo, cloth gilt, two very thick volumes, 7s. 6d. each.

The Life of George Cruikshank. By BLANCHARD JERROLD, Author of "The Life of Napoleon III.," &c. With 84 Illustrations. New and Cheaper Edition, enlarged, with Additional Plates, and a very carefully compiled Bibliography. Crown 8vo, cloth extra, 7s. 6d.

Robinson Crusoe. A beautiful reproduction of Major's Edition, with 37 Woodcuts and Two Steel Plates by GEORGE CRUIKSHANK, choicely printed. Crown 8vo, cloth extra, 7s. 6d.

Cumming (C. F. Gordon), Works by:

Demy 8vo, cloth extra, 8s. 6d. each.

In the Hebrides. With Autotype Facsimile and numerous full-page Illustrations.

In the Himalayas and on the Indian Plains. With numerous Illustrations.

Via Cornwall to Egypt. With a Photogravure Frontispiece. Demy 8vo, cloth extra, 7s. 6d.

Cussans.—Handbook of Heraldry;

with Instructions for Tracing Pedigrees and Deciphering Ancient MSS., &c. By JOHN E. CUSSANS. Entirely New and Revised Edition, illustrated with over 400 Woodcuts and Coloured Plates. Crown 8vo, cloth extra, 7s. 6d.

Cyples.—Hearts of Gold: A

Novel. By WILLIAM CYPLES. Crown 8vo, cloth extra, 3s. 6d.; post 8vo, illustrated boards, 2s.

Daniel. — Merrie England in

the Olden Time. By GEORGE DANIEL. With Illustrations by ROBT. CRUIKSHANK. Crown 8vo, cloth extra, 3s. 6d.

Daudet.—The Evangelist; or,

Port Salvation. By ALPHONSE DAUDET. Translated by C. HARRY MELTZER. With Portrait of the Author. Crown 8vo, cloth extra, 3s. 6d.; post 8vo, illust. boards, 2s.

Davies (Dr. N. E.), Works by:

Crown 8vo, 1s. each; cloth limp, 1s. 6d. each.

One Thousand Medical Maxims.
Nursery Hints: A Mother's Guide.

Aids to Long Life. Crown 8vo, 2s.; cloth limp, 2s. 6d.

Davies' (Sir John) Complete

Poetical Works, including Psalms I. to L. in Verse, and other hitherto Unpublished MSS., for the first time Collected and Edited, with Memorial-Introduction and Notes, by the Rev. A. B. GROSART, D.D. Two Vols., crown 8vo, cloth boards, 12s.

De Maistre.—A Journey Round

My Room. By XAVIER DE MAISTRE. Translated by HENRY ATTWELL. Post 8vo, cloth limp, 2s. 6d.

De Mille.—A Castle in Spain:

A Novel. By JAMES DE MILLE. With a Frontispiece. Crown 8vo, cloth extra, 3s. 6d.; post 8vo, illust. bds., 2s.

Derwent (Leith), Novels by:

Crown 8vo, cloth extra, 3s. 6d. each; post 8vo, illustrated boards, 2s. each.

Our Lady of Tears. | **Circe's Lovers.**

Dickens (Charles), Novels by:

Post 8vo, illustrated boards, 2s. each.

Sketches by Boz. | **Nicholas Nickleby.**
Pickwick Papers. | **Oliver Twist.**

The Speeches of Charles Dickens, 1841-1870. With a New Bibliography, revised and enlarged. Edited and Prefaced by RICHARD HERNE SHEPHERD. Cr. 8vo, cloth extra, 6s.—Also a SMALLER EDITION, in the *Mayfair Library.* Post 8vo, cloth limp, 2s. 6d.

About England with Dickens. By ALFRED RIMMER. With 57 Illustrations by C. A. VANDERHOOF, ALFRED RIMMER, and others. Sq. 8vo, cloth extra, 10s. 6d.

Dictionaries:

A Dictionary of Miracles: Imitative, Realistic, and Dogmatic. By the Rev. E. C. BREWER, LL.D. Crown 8vo, cloth extra, 7s. 6d.; hf.-bound, 9s.

The Reader's Handbook of Allusions, References, Plots, and Stories. By the Rev. E. C. BREWER, LL.D. With an Appendix, containing a Complete English Bibliography. Eleventh Thousand. Crown 8vo, 1,400 pages, cloth extra, 7s. 6d.

Authors and their Works, with the Dates. Being the Appendices to "The Reader's Handbook," separately printed. By the Rev. Dr. BREWER. Crown 8vo, cloth limp, 2s.

DICTIONARIES, *continued*—
Familiar Short Sayings of Great Men. With Historical and Explanatory Notes. By SAMUEL A. BENT, M.A. Fifth Edition, revised and enlarged. Cr. 8vo, cloth extra, 7s. 6d.

A Dictionary of the Drama: Being a comprehensive Guide to the Plays, Playwrights, Players, and Playhouses of the United Kingdom and America, from the Earliest to the Present Times. By W. DAVENPORT ADAMS. A thick volume, crown 8vo, half-bound, 12s. 6d. [*In preparation.*]

The Slang Dictionary: Etymological, Historical, and Anecdotal. Crown 8vo, cloth extra, 6s. 6d.

Women of the Day: A Biographical Dictionary. By FRANCES HAYS. Cr. 8vo, cloth extra, 5s.

Words, Facts, and Phrases: A Dictionary of Curious, Quaint, and Out-of-the-Way Matters. By ELIEZER EDWARDS. New and Cheaper Issue. Cr. 8vo, cl. ex., 7s. 6d.; hf.-bd., 9s.

Diderot.—The Paradox of Acting. Translated, with Annotations, from Diderot's "Le Paradoxe sur le Comédien," by WALTER HERRIES POLLOCK. With a Preface by HENRY IRVING. Cr. 8vo, in parchment, 4s. 6d.

Dobson (W. T.), Works by:
Post 8vo, cloth limp, 2s. 6d. each.
Literary Frivolities, Fancies, Follies, and Frolics. [*cities.*]
Poetical Ingenuities and Eccentri-

Doran. — Memories of our Great Towns; with Anecdotic Gleanings concerning their Worthies and their Oddities. By Dr. JOHN DORAN, F.S.A. With 38 Illusts. New and Cheaper Edit. Cr. 8vo, cl. extra, 7s. 6d.

Drama, A Dictionary of the. Being a comprehensive Guide to the Plays, Playwrights, Players, and Playhouses of the United Kingdom and America, from the Earliest to the Present Times. By W. DAVENPORT ADAMS. (Uniform with BREWER's "Reader's Handbook.") Crown 8vo, half-bound, 12s. 6d. [*In preparation.*]

Dramatists, The Old. Cr. 8vo, cl. ex., Vignette Portraits, 6s. per Vol.
Ben Jonson's Works. With Notes Critical and Explanatory, and a Biographical Memoir by WM. GIFFORD. Edit. by Col. CUNNINGHAM. 3 Vols.
Chapman's Works. Complete in Three Vols. Vol. I. contains the Plays complete, including doubtful ones; Vol. II., Poems and Minor Translations, with Introductory Essay by A. C. SWINBURNE; Vol. III., Translations of the Iliad and Odyssey.

DRAMATISTS, THE OLD, *continued*—
Crown 8vo, cloth extra, Vignette Portraits, 6s. per Volume.
Marlowe's Works. Including his Translations. Edited, with Notes and Introduction, by Col. CUNNINGHAM. One Vol.
Massinger's Plays. From the Text of WILLIAM GIFFORD. Edited by Col. CUNNINGHAM. One Vol.

Dyer. — The Folk-Lore of Plants. By Rev. T. F. THISELTON DYER, M.A. Crown 8vo, cloth extra, 7s. 6d. [*In preparation.*]

Early English Poets. Edited, with Introductions and Annotations, by Rev. A. B. GROSART, D.D. Crown 8vo, cloth boards, 6s. per Volume.
Fletcher's (Giles, B.D.) Complete Poems. One Vol.
Davies' (Sir John) Complete Poetical Works. Two Vols.
Herrick's (Robert) Complete Collected Poems. Three Vols.
Sidney's (Sir Philip) Complete Poetical Works. Three Vols.
Herbert (Lord) of Cherbury's Poems. Edit., with Introd., by J. CHURTON COLLINS. Cr. 8vo, parchment, 8s.

Edgcumbe. — Zephyrus: A Holiday in Brazil and on the River Plate. By E. R. PEARCE EDGCUMBE. With 41 Illusts. Cr. 8vo, cl. extra, 5s.

Edwardes (Mrs. A.), Novels by:
A Point of Honour. Post 8vo, illustrated boards, 2s.
Archie Lovell. Crown 8vo, cloth extra, 3s. 6d.; post 8vo, illust. bds., 2s.

Eggleston.—Roxy: A Novel. By EDWARD EGGLESTON. Post 8vo, illust. boards, 2s.

Emanuel.—On Diamonds and Precious Stones: their History, Value, and Properties; with Simple Tests for ascertaining their Reality. By HARRY EMANUEL, F.R.G.S. With numerous Illustrations, tinted and plain. Crown 8vo, cloth extra, gilt, 6s.

Ewald (Alex. Charles, F.S.A.), Works by:
The Life and Times of Prince Charles Stuart, Count of Albany, commonly called the Young Pretender. From the State Papers and other Sources. New and Cheaper Edition, with a Portrait, crown 8vo, cloth extra, 7s. 6d.
Stories from the State Papers. With an Autotype Facsimile. Crown 8vo, cloth extra, 6s.
Studies Re-studied: Historical Sketches from Original Sources. Demy 8vo, cloth extra, 12s.

Eyes, Our: How to Preserve Them from Infancy to Old Age. By JOHN BROWNING, F.R.A.S., &c. Sixth Edition (Eleventh Thousand). With 58 Illustrations. Crown 8vo, cloth, 1s.

Fairholt.—Tobacco: Its History and Associations; with an Account of the Plant and its Manufacture, and its Modes of Use in all Ages and Countries. By F. W. FAIRHOLT, F.S.A. With upwards of 100 Illustrations by the Author. Crown 8vo, cloth extra, 6s.

Familiar Short Sayings of Great Men. By SAMUEL ARTHUR BENT, A.M. Fifth Edition, Revised and Enlarged. Crown 8vo, cloth extra, 7s. 6d.

Faraday (Michael), Works by: Post 8vo, cloth extra, 4s. 6d. each. The Chemical History of a Candle: Lectures delivered before a Juvenile Audience at the Royal Institution. Edited by WILLIAM CROOKES, F.C.S. With numerous Illustrations. On the Various Forces of Nature, and their Relations to each other: Lectures delivered before a Juvenile Audience at the Royal Institution. Edited by WILLIAM CROOKES, F.C.S. With numerous Illustrations.

Farrer (James Anson), Works by: Military Manners and Customs. Crown 8vo, cloth extra, 6s. War: Three Essays, Reprinted from "Military Manners." Crown 8vo, 1s.; cloth, 1s. 6d.

Fin-Bec. — The Cupboard Papers: Observations on the Art of Living and Dining. By FIN-BEC. Post 8vo, cloth limp, 2s. 6d.

Fireworks, The Complete Art of Making; or, The Pyrotechnist's Treasury. By THOMAS KENTISH. With 267 Illustrations. A New Edition, Revised throughout and greatly Enlarged. Crown 8vo, cloth extra, 5s.

Fitzgerald (Percy), Works by: The Recreations of a Literary Man; or, Does Writing Pay? With Recollections of some Literary Men, and a View of a Literary Man's Working Life. Cr. 8vo, cloth extra, 6s. The World Behind the Scenes. Crown 8vo, cloth extra, 3s. 6d. Little Essays: Passages from the Letters of CHARLES LAMB. Post 8vo, cloth limp, 2s. 6d. A Day's Tour: A Journey through France and Belgium. With Sketches in facsimile of the Original Drawings. Crown 4to, picture cover, 1s.

FITZGERALD (PERCY), *continued*— Fatal Zero: A Homburg Diary. Cr. 8vo, cloth extra, 3s. 6d.

Post 8vo, illustrated boards, 2s. each. Bella Donna. | Never Forgotten The Second Mrs. Tillotson. Polly. Seventy-five Brooke Street. The Lady of Brantome.

Fletcher's (Giles, B.D.) Complete Poems: Christ's Victorie in Heaven, Christ's Victorie on Earth, Christ's Triumph over Death, and Minor Poems. With Memorial-Introduction and Notes by the Rev. A. B. GROSART, D.D. Cr. 8vo, cloth bds., 6s.

Fonblanque.—Filthy Lucre: A Novel. By ALBANY DE FONBLANQUE. Post 8vo, illustrated boards, 2s.

Francillon (R. E.), Novels by: Crown 8vo, cloth extra, 3s. 6d. each; post 8vo, illust. boards, 2s. each. One by One. | A Real Queen. Queen Cophetua. | Olympia. Post 8vo, illust. boards, 2s. Esther's Glove. Fcap. 8vo, 1s.

Frederic. — Seth's Brother's Wife: A Novel. By HAROLD FREDERIC. Two Vols., crown 8vo. [*Immediately.*

French Literature, History of By HENRY VAN LAUN. Complete in 3 Vols., demy 8vo, cl. bds., 7s. 6d. each.

Frere.—Pandurang Hari; or, Memoirs of a Hindoo. With a Preface by Sir H. BARTLE FRERE, G.C.S.I., &c. Crown 8vo, cloth extra, 3s. 6d.; post 8vo, illustrated boards, 2s.

Friswell.—One of Two: A Novel. By HAIN FRISWELL. Post 8vo, illustrated boards, 2s.

Frost (Thomas), Works by: Crown 8vo, cloth extra, 3s. 6d. each. Circus Life and Circus Celebrities. The Lives of the Conjurers. The Old Showmen and the Old London Fairs.

Fry's (Herbert) Royal Guide to the London Charities, 1887-8. Showing their Name, Date of Foundation, Objects, Income, Officials, &c. Published Annually. Cr. 8vo, cloth, 1s. 6d.

Gardening Books: Post 8vo, 1s. each; cl. limp, 1s. 6d. each. A Year's Work in Garden and Greenhouse: Practical Advice to Amateur Gardeners as to the Management of the Flower, Fruit, and Frame Garden. By GEORGE GLENNY. Our Kitchen Garden: The Plants we Grow, and How we Cook Them. By TOM JERROLD.

GARDENING BOOKS, *continued*—
Post 8vo, 1s. each ; cl. limp, 1s. 6d. each.
 **Household Horticulture: A Gossip
 about Flowers.** By TOM and JANE
 JERROLD. Illustrated.
The Garden that Paid the Rent.
 By TOM JERROLD.

My Garden Wild, and What I Grew
 there. By F. G. HEATH. Crown 8vo,
 cloth extra, 5s. ; gilt edges, 6s.

Garrett.—The Capel Girls: A
Novel. By EDWARD GARRETT. Cr. 8vo,
cl. ex., 3s. 6d. ; post 8vo, illust. bds., 2s.

Gentleman's Magazine (The).
One Shilling Monthly. In addition to
the Articles upon subjects in Litera-
ture, Science, and Art, for which this
Magazine has so high a reputation,
"Science Notes," by W. MATTIEU
WILLIAMS, F.R.A.S., and "Table Talk,"
by SYLVANUS URBAN, appear monthly.
 ⁎ *Now ready, the Volume for* JANUARY
to JUNE, 1887, *cloth extra, price* 8s. 6d.;
Cases for binding, 2s. *each.*

Gentleman's Annual (The) for
1887. Consisting of one entire Novel,
entitled The Golden Hoop: An After-
Marriage Interlude. By T. W. SPEIGHT,
Author of "The Mysteries of Heron
Dyke." Demy 8vo, picture cover, 1s.
 [Nov. 10.

German Popular Stories. Collected by the Brothers GRIMM, an 1
Translated by EDGAR TAYLOR. Edited,
with an Introduction, by JOHN RUSKIN.
With 22 Illustrations on Steel by
GEORGE CRUIKSHANK. Square 8vo,
cloth extra, 6s. 6d. ; gilt edges, 7s. 6d.

Gibbon (Charles), Novels by :
 Crown 8vo, cloth extra, 3s. 6d. each
 post 8vo, illustrated boards, 2s. each.

Robin Gray.	**Braes of Yarrow.**
What will the World Say ?	**A Heart's Problem.**
In Honour Bound.	**The Golden Shaft.**
Queen of the Meadow.	**Of High Degree.**
	Fancy Free.
The Flower of the Forest.	**Loving a Dream.**
	A Hard Knot.

 Post 8vo, illustrated boards, 2s. each.
 For Lack of Gold.
 For the King. | **In Pastures Green.**
 In Love and War.
 By Mead and Stream.
 Heart's Delight.   *[Preparing.*

Gilbert (William), Novels by :
 Post 8vo, illustrated boards, 2s. each.
 Dr. Austin's Guests.
 The Wizard of the Mountain.
 James Duke, Costermonger.

Gilbert (W. S.), Original Plays
by: In Two Series, each complete in
itself, price 2s. 6d. each.
 The FIRST SERIES contains—The
Wicked World—Pygmalion and Ga-
latea — Charity — The Princess — The
Palace of Truth—Trial by Jury.
 The SECOND SERIES contains—Bro-
ken Hearts—Engaged—Sweethearts—
Gretchen—Dan'l Druce—Tom Cobb—
H.M.S. Pinafore—The Sorcerer—The
Pirates of Penzance.

Eight Original Comic Operas. Writ-
ten by W. S. GILBERT. Containing:
The Sorcerer—H. M.S. "Pinafore"
—The Pirates of Penzance—Iolanthe
— Patience — Princess Ida — The
Mikado—Trial by Jury. Demy 8vo,
cloth limp, 2s. 6d.

Glenny.—A Year's Work in
Garden and Greenhouse: Practical
Advice to Amateur Gardeners as to
the Management of the Flower, Fruit,
and Frame Garden. By GEORGE
GLENNY. Post 8vo, 1s.; cloth, 1s. 6d.

Godwin.—Lives of the Necro-
mancers. By WILLIAM GODWIN.
Post 8vo, limp, 2s.

Golden Library, The :
 Square 16mo (Tauchnitz size), cloth
 limp, 2s. per Volume.
 **Bayard Taylor's Diversions of the
 Echo Club.**
 **Bennett's (Dr. W. C.) Ballad History
 of England.**
 Bennett's (Dr.) Songs for Sailors.
 Byron's Don Juan.
 **Godwin's (William) Lives of the
 Necromancers.**
 **Holmes's Autocrat of the Break-
 fast Table.** Introduction by SALA.
 **Holmes's Professor at the Break-
 fast Table.**
 Hood's Whims and Oddities. Com-
 plete. All the original Illustrations.
 **Irving's (Washington) Tales of a
 Traveller**
 **Jesse's (Edward) Scenes and Oc-
 cupations of a Country Life.**
 Lamb's Essays of Elia. Both Series
 Complete in One Vol.
 **Leigh Hunt's Essays: A Tale for a
 Chimney Corner,** and other Pieces.
 With Portrait, and Introduction by
 EDMUND OLLIER.
 **Mallory's (Sir Thomas) Mort
 d'Arthur: The Stories of King
 Arthur and of the Knights of the
 Round Table.** Edited by B. MONT-
 GOMERIE RANKING.

GOLDEN LIBRARY, THE, *continued—*
Square 16mo, 2s. per Volume.
Pascal's Provincial Letters. A New Translation, with Historical Introduction and Notes, by T. M'CRIE, D.D.
Pope's Poetical Works. Complete.
Rochefoucauld's Maxims and Moral Reflections. With Notes, and Introductory Essay by SAINTE-BEUVE.
St. Pierre's Paul and Virginia, and The Indian Cottage. Edited, with Life, by the Rev. E. CLARKE.

Golden Treasury of Thought,
The: An ENCYCLOPÆDIA OF QUOTATIONS from Writers of all Times and Countries. Selected and Edited by THEODORE TAYLOR. Crown 8vo, cloth gilt and gilt edges, 7s. 6d.

Graham. — The Professor's
Wife: A Story. By LEONARD GRAHAM. Fcap. 8vo, picture cover, 1s.

Greeks and Romans, The Life
of the, Described from Antique Monuments. By ERNST GUHL and W. KONER. Translated from the Third German Edition, and Edited by Dr. F. HUEFFER. 545 Illusts. New and Cheaper Edit., demy 8vo, cl. ex., 7s. 6d.

Greenaway (Kate) and Bret
Harte.—The Queen of the Pirate Isle. By BRET HARTE. With 25 original Drawings by KATE GREENAWAY, Reproduced in Colours by E. EVANS. Sm. 4to, bds., 5s.

Greenwood (James), Works by:
Crown 8vo, cloth extra, 3s. 6d. each.
The Wilds of London.
Low-Life Deeps: An Account of the Strange Fish to be Found There.

Dick Temple: A Novel. Post 8vo, illustrated boards, 2s.

Guyot.—The Earth and Man;
or, Physical Geography in its relation to the History of Mankind. By ARNOLD GUYOT. With Additions by Professors AGASSIZ, PIERCE, and GRAY; 12 Maps and Engravings on Steel, some Coloured, and copious Index. Crown 8vo, cloth extra, gilt, 4s. 6d.

Habberton (John), Author of
"Helen's Babies," Novels by:
Post 8vo, illustrated boards, 2s. each ; cloth limp, 2s. 6d. each.
Brueton's Bayou.
Country Luck.

Hair (The): Its Treatment in
Health, Weakness, and Disease. Translated from the German of Dr. J PINCUS. Crown 8vo, 1s.; cloth, 1s. 6d.

Hake (Dr. Thomas Gordon),
Poems by:
Crown 8vo, cloth extra, 6s. each.
New Symbols.
Legends of the Morrow.
The Serpent Play.

Maiden Ecstasy. Small 4to, cloth extra, 8s.

Hall.—Sketches of Irish Cha-
racter. By Mrs. S. C. HALL. With numerous Illustrations on Steel and Wood by MACLISE, GILBERT, HARVEY, and G. CRUIKSHANK. Medium 8vo, cloth extra, gilt, 7s. 6d.

Halliday.—Every-day Papers.
By ANDREW HALLIDAY. Post 8vo, illustrated boards, 2s.

Handwriting, The Philosophy
of. With over 100 Facsimiles and Explanatory Text. By DON FELIX DE SALAMANCA. Post 8vo, cl. limp, 2s. 6d.

Hanky-Panky: A Collection of
Very Easy Tricks, Very Difficult Tricks, White Magic, Sleight of Hand, &c. Edited by W. H. CREMER. With 200 Illusts. Crown 8vo, cloth extra, 4s. 6d.

Hardy (Lady Duffus). — Paul
Wynter's Sacrifice: A Story. By Lady DUFFUS HARDY. Post 8vo, illust. boards, 2s.

Hardy (Thomas).—Under the
Greenwood Tree. By THOMAS HARDY, Author of "Far from the Madding Crowd." With numerous Illustrations. Crown 8vo, cloth extra, 3s. 6d. ; post 8vo, illustrated boards, 2s.

Harwood.—The Tenth Earl.
By J. BERWICK HARWOOD. Post 8vo, illustrated boards, 2s.

Haweis (Mrs. H. R.), Works by:
The Art of Dress. With numerous Illustrations. Small 8vo, illustrated cover, 1s.; cloth limp, 1s. 6d.
The Art of Beauty. New and Cheaper Edition. Crown 8vo, cloth extra, Coloured Frontispiece and Illusts. 6s.
The Art of Decoration. Square 8vo, handsomely bound and profusely Illustrated, 10s. 6d.
Chaucer for Children: A Golden Key. With Eight Coloured Pictures and numerous Woodcuts. New Edition, small 4to, cloth extra, 6s.
Chaucer for Schools. Demy 8vo, cloth limp, 2s. 6d.

Hawels (Rev. H. R.).—American Humorists. Including WASHINGTON IRVING, OLIVER WENDELL HOLMES, JAMES RUSSELL LOWELL, ARTEMUS WARD, MARK TWAIN, and BRET HARTE. By the Rev. H. R. HAWEIS, M.A. Crown 8vo, cloth extra, 6s.

Hawthorne (Julian), Novels by. Crown 8vo, cloth extra, 3s. 6d. each; post 8vo, illustrated boards, 2s. each.

Garth. | Sebastian Strome.
Ellice Quentin. | Dust.
Prince Saroni's Wife.
Fortune's Fool. | Beatrix Randolph.

Crown 8vo, cloth extra, 3s. 6d. each.
Miss Cadogna.
Love—or a Name.

Mrs. Gainsborough's Diamonds. Fcap. 8vo, illustrated cover, 1s.

Hays.—Women of the Day: A Biographical Dictionary of Notable Contemporaries. By FRANCES HAYS. Crown 8vo, cloth extra, 5s.

Heath (F. G.). — My Garden Wild, and What I Grew There. By FRANCIS GEORGE HEATH, Author of "The Fern World," &c. Crown 8vo, cloth extra, 5s.; cl. gilt, gilt edges, 6s.

Helps (Sir Arthur), Works by: Post 8vo, cloth limp, 2s. 6d. each.
Animals and their Masters.
Social Pressure.

Ivan de Biron: A Novel. Crown 8vo, cloth extra, 3s. 6d.; post 8vo, illustrated boards, 2s.

Herman.—One Traveller Re- turns: A Romance. By HENRY HERMAN and D. CHRISTIE MURRAY. Crown 8vo, cloth extra, 6s.   [*Preparing.*

Herrick's (Robert) Hesperides, Noble Numbers, and Complete Collected Poems. With Memorial-Introduction and Notes by the Rev. A. B. GROSART, D.D., Steel Portrait, Index of First Lines, and Glossarial Index, &c. Three Vols., crown 8vo, cloth, 18s.

Hesse-Wartegg (Chevalier Ernst von), Works by:
Tunis: The Land and the People. With 22 Illustrations. Crown 8vo, cloth extra, 3s. 6d.
The New South-West: Travelling Sketches from Kansas, New Mexico, Arizona, and Northern Mexico. With 100 fine Illustrations and Three Maps. Demy 8vo, cloth extra, 14s.   [*In preparation.*

Herbert.—The Poems of Lord Herbert of Cherbury. Edited, with Introduction, by J. CHURTON COLLINS. Crown 8vo, bound in parchment, 8s.

Hindley (Charles), Works by: Crown 8vo, cloth extra, 3s. 6d. each.
Tavern Anecdotes and Sayings: Including the Origin of Signs, and Reminiscences connected with Taverns, Coffee Houses, Clubs, &c. With Illustrations.
The Life and Adventures of a Cheap Jack. By One of the Fraternity. Edited by CHARLES HINDLEY.

Hoey.—The Lover's Creed. By Mrs. CASHEL HOEY. With Frontispiece by P. MACNAB. Post 8vo, illustrated boards, 2s.

Holmes (O. Wendell), Works by: The Autocrat of the Breakfast-Table. Illustrated by J. GORDON THOMSON. Post 8vo, cloth limp, 2s. 6d.—Another Edition in smaller type, with an Introduction by G. A. SALA. Post 8vo, cloth limp, 2s.
The Professor at the Breakfast-Table; with the Story of Iris. Post 8vo, cloth limp, 2s.

Holmes. — The Science of Voice Production and Voice Preservation: A Popular Manual for the Use of Speakers and Singers. By GORDON HOLMES, M.D. With Illustrations. Crown 8vo, 1s.; cloth, 1s. 6d.

Hood (Thomas): Hood's Choice Works, in Prose and Verse. Including the Cream of the COMIC ANNUALS. With Life of the Author, Portrait, and 200 Illustrations. Crown 8vo, cloth extra, 7s. 6d.
Hood's Whims and Oddities. Complete. With all the original Illustrations. Post 8vo, cloth limp, 2s.

Hood (Tom), Works by: From Nowhere to the North Pole: A Noah's Arkæological Narrative. With 25 Illustrations by W. BRUNTON and E. C. BARNES. Square crown 8vo, cloth extra, gilt edges, 6s.
A Golden Heart: A Novel. Post 8vo, illustrated boards, 2s.

Hook's (Theodore) Choice Hu- morous Works, including his Ludicrous Adventures, Bons Mots, Puns and Hoaxes. With a New Life of the Author, Portraits, Facsimiles, and Illusts. Cr. 8vo, cl. extra, gilt, 7s. 6d.

Hooper.—The House of Raby: A Novel. By Mrs. GEORGE HOOPER. Post 8vo, illustrated boards, 2s.

Hopkins—"'Twixt Love and Duty:" A Novel. By TIGHE HOPKINS. Crown 8vo, cloth extra, 6s.; post 8vo, illustrated boards, 2s.

Horne.—Orion: An Epic Poem, in Three Books. By RICHARD HENGIST HORNE. With Photographic Portrait from a Medallion by SUMMERS. Tenth Edition, crown 8vo, cloth extra, 7s.

Howell.—Conflicts of Capital and Labour, Historically and Economically considered: Being a History and Review of the Trade Unions of Great Britain. By GEO. HOWELL M.P. Crown 8vo, cloth extra, 7s. 6d.

Hunt (Mrs. Alfred), Novels by: Crown 8vo, cloth extra, 3s. 6d. each; post 8vo, illustrated boards, 2s. each.
Thornicroft's Model.
The Leaden Casket.
Self-Condemned.
That other Person.

Hunt.—Essays by Leigh Hunt. A Tale for a Chimney Corner, and other Pieces. With Portrait and Introduction by EDMUND OLLIER. Post 8vo, cloth limp, 2s.

Hydrophobia: an Account of M. PASTEUR'S System. Containing a Translation of all his Communications on the Subject, the Technique of his Method, and the latest Statistical Results. By RENAUD SUZOR, M.B., C.M. Edin., and M.D. Paris, Commissioned by the Government of the Colony of Mauritius to study M. PASTEUR'S new Treatment in Paris. With 7 Illustrations. Crown 8vo, cloth extra, 6s.

Indoor Paupers. By ONE OF THEM. Crown 8vo, 1s.; cloth, 1s. 6d.

Ingelow.—Fated to be Free: A Novel. By JEAN INGELOW. Crown 8vo, cloth extra, 3s. 6d.; post 8vo, illustrated boards, 2s.

Irish Wit and Humour, Songs of. Collected and Edited by A. PERCEVAL GRAVES. Post 8vo, cloth limp, 2s. 6d.

Irving—Tales of a Traveller. By WASHINGTON IRVING. Post 8vo, cloth limp, 2s.

Janvier.—Practical Keramics for Students. By CATHERINE A. JANVIER. Crown 8vo, cloth extra, 6s.

Jay (Harriett), Novels by: Post 8vo, illustrated boards, 2s. each.
The Dark Colleen.
The Queen of Connaught.

Jefferies (Richard), Works by: Crown 8vo, cloth extra, 6s. each.
The Life of the Fields.
The Open Air.

Nature near London. Crown 8vo, cloth extra, 6s.; post 8vo, cloth limp, 2s. 6d.

Jennings (H. J.), Works by:
Curiosities of Criticism. Post 8vo, cloth limp, 2s. 6d.
Lord Tennyson: A Biographical Sketch. With a Photograph-Portrait. Crown 8vo, cloth extra, 6s.

Jerrold (Tom), Works by: Post 8vo, 1s. each; cloth, 1s. 6d. each.
The Garden that Paid the Rent.
Household Horticulture: A Gossip about Flowers. Illustrated.
Our Kitchen Garden: The Plants we Grow, and How we Cook Them.

Jesse.—Scenes and Occupations of a Country Life. By EDWARD JESSE. Post 8vo, cloth limp, 2s.

Jeux d'Esprit. Collected and Edited by HENRY S. LEIGH. Post 8vo, cloth limp, 2s. 6d.

Jones (Wm., F.S.A.), Works by: Crown 8vo, cloth extra, 7s. 6d. each.
Finger-Ring Lore: Historical, Legendary, and Anecdotal. With over Two Hundred Illustrations.
Credulities, Past and Present; including the Sea and Seamen, Miners, Talismans, Word and Letter Divination Exorcising and Blessing of Animals, Birds, Eggs, Luck, &c. With an Etched Frontispiece.
Crowns and Coronations: A History of Regalia in all Times and Countries. With One Hundred Illustrations.

Jonson's (Ben) Works. With Notes Critical and Explanatory, and a Biographical Memoir by WILLIAM GIFFORD. Edited by Colonel CUNNINGHAM. Three Vols., crown 8vo, cloth extra, 18s.; or separately, 6s. each.

Josephus, The Complete Works of. Translated by WHISTON. Containing both "The Antiquities of the Jews" and "The Wars of the Jews." Two Vols., 8vo, with 52 Illustrations and Maps, cloth extra, gilt, 14s.

Kempt.—Pencil and Palette: Chapters on Art and Artists. By ROBERT KEMPT. Post 8vo, cloth limp, 2s. 6d.

Kershaw.—Colonlal Facts and Fictlons: Humorous Sketches. By MARK KERSHAW. Post 8vo, illustrated boards, 2s.; cloth, 2s. 6d.

King (R. Ashe), Novels by:

Crown 8vo, cloth extra, 3s. 6d. each; post 8vo, illustrated boards, 2s. each.

A Drawn Game.

"The Wearlng of the Green."

Kingsley (Henry), Novels by:

Oakshott Castle. Post 8vo, illustrated boards, 2s.

Number Seventeen. Crown 8vo, cloth extra, 3s. 6d.

Knight.—The Patient's Vade Mecum: How to get most Benefit from Medical Advice. By WILLIAM KNIGHT, M.R.C.S., and EDWARD KNIGHT, L.R.C.P. Crown 8vo, 1s.; cloth, 1s. 6d.

Lamb (Charles):

Lamb's Complete Works, in Prose and Verse, reprinted from the Original Editions, with many Pieces hitherto unpublished. Edited, with Notes and Introduction, by R. H. SHEPHERD. With Two Portraits and Facsimile of Page of the "Essay on Roast Pig." Cr. 8vo, cl. extra, 7s. 6d.

The Essays of Ella. Complete Edition. Post 8vo, cloth extra, 2s.

Poetry for Children, and Prince Dorus. By CHARLES LAMB. Carefully reprinted from unique copies. Small 8vo, cloth extra, 5s.

Little Essays: Sketches and Characters. By CHARLES LAMB. Selected from his Letters by PERCY FITZGERALD. Post 8vo, cloth limp, 2s. 6d.

Lane's Arablan Nights, &c.:

The Thousand and One Nights: commonly called, in England, "THE ARABIAN NIGHTS' ENTERTAINMENTS." A New Translation from the Arabic, with copious Notes, by EDWARD WILLIAM LANE. Illustrated by many hundred Engravings on Wood, from Original Designs by WM. HARVEY. A New Edition, from a Copy annotated by the Translator, edited by his Nephew, EDWARD STANLEY POOLE. With a Preface by STANLEY LANE-POOLE. Three Vols., demy 8vo, cloth extra, 7s. 6d. each.

Arablan Soclety in the Middle Ages: Studies from "The Thousand and One Nights." By EDWARD WILLIAM LANE, Author of "The Modern Egyptians," &c. Edited by STANLEY LANE-POOLE. Cr. 8vo, cloth extra, 6s.

Lares and Penates; or, The Background of Life. By FLORENCE CADDY. Crown 8vo, cloth extra, 6s.

Larwood (Jacob), Works by:

The Story of the London Parks. With Illustrations. Crown 8vo, cloth extra, 3s. 6d.

Post 8vo, cloth limp, 2s. 6d. each.
Forensic Anecdotes.
Theatrical Anecdotes.

Life In London; or, The History of Jerry Hawthorn and Corinthian Tom. With the whole of CRUIKSHANK'S Illustrations, in Colours, after the Originals. Crown 8vo, cloth extra, 7s. 6d.

Linskill.—In Exchange for a Soul. By MARY LINSKILL, Author of "The Haven Under the Hill," &c. Three Vols., crown 8vo.

Linton (E. Lynn), Works by:

Post 8vo, cloth limp, 2s. 6d. each.
Witch Storles.
The True Story of Joshua Davldson
Ourselves: Essays on Women.

Crown 8vo, cloth extra, 3s. 6d. each; post 8vo, illustrated boards, 2s. each.
Patricia Kemball.
The Atonement of Leam Dundas.
The World Well Lost.
Under whlch Lord?
With a Sllken Thread.
The Rebel of the Famlly.
"My Love!" | lone.

Longfellow:

Crown 8vo, cloth extra, 7s. 6d. each.
Longfellow's Complete Prose Works. Including "Outre Mer," "Hyperion," "Kavanagh," "The Poets and Poetry of Europe," and "Driftwood." With Portrait and Illustrations by VALENTINE BROMLEY.
Longfellow's Poetical Works. Carefully Reprinted from the Original Editions. With numerous fine Illustrations on Steel and Wood.

Long Life, Alds to: A Medical, Dietetic, and General Guide in Health and Disease. By N. E. DAVIES, L.R.C.P. Crown 8vo, 2s.; cloth limp, 2s. 6d.

Lucy.—Gldeon Fleyce: A Novel. By HENRY W. LUCY. Crown 8vo, cl. ex., 3s. 6d.; post 8vo, illust. bds., 2s.

Luslad (The) of Camoens. Translated into English Spenserian Verse by ROBERT FFRENCH DUFF. Demy 8vo, with Fourteen full-page Plates, cloth boards, 18s.

Macalpine. — Teresa Itasca,
and other Stories. By AVERY MAC-
ALPINE. Crown 8vo, bound in canvas,
2s. 6d.

McCarthy (Justin, M.P.), Works
by :
A History of Our Own Times, from
the Accession of Queen Victoria to
the General Election of 1880. Four
Vols. demy 8vo, cloth extra, 12s.
each.—Also a POPULAR EDITION, in
Four Vols. cr. 8vo, cl. extra, 6s. each.
—And a JUBILEE EDITION, with an
Appendix of Events to the end of
1886, complete in Two Vols., square
8vo, cloth extra, 7s. 6d. each.

A Short History of Our Own Times.
One Vol., crown 8vo, cloth extra, 6s.

History of the Four Georges. Four
Vols. demy 8vo, cloth extra, 12s.
each.   [Vol. I. *now ready.*

Crown 8vo, cloth extra, 3s. 6d. each ;
post 8vo, illustrated boards, 2s. each.
Dear Lady Disdain.
The Waterdale Neighbours.
A Fair Saxon.
Miss Misanthrope.
Donna Quixote.
The Comet of a Season.
Maid of Athens.
Camiola : A Girl with a Fortune.

Post 8vo, illustrated boards, 2s. each.
Linley Rochford.
My Enemy's Daughter.

"The Right Honourable :" A Ro-
mance of Society and Politics. By
JUSTIN MCCARTHY, M.P., and Mrs.
CAMPBELL-PRAED. New and Cheaper
Edition, crown 8vo, cloth extra, 6s.

McCarthy (Justin H., M.P.),
Works by :
An Outline of the History of Ireland,
from the Earliest Times to the Present Day. Cr. 8vo, 1s. ; cloth, 1s. 6d.

Ireland since the Union : Sketches
of Irish History from 1798 to 1886.
Crown 8vo, cloth extra, 6s.

The Case for Home Rule.   Crown
8vo, cloth extra, 5s.

England under Gladstone, 1880-85.
Second Edition, revised.   Crown
8vo, cloth extra, 6s.

Doom ! An Atlantic Episode.   Crown
8vo, 1s. ; cloth, 1s. 6d.

Our Sensation Novel.   Edited by
JUSTIN H. MCCARTHY.   Crown 8vo,
1s. ; cloth, 1s. 6d.

Hafiz in London. Choicely printed.
Small 8vo, gold cloth, 3s. 6d.

MacDonald.—Works of Fancy
and Imagination. By GEORGE MAC-
DONALD, LL.D.   Ten Volumes, in
handsome cloth case, 21s.   Vol. 1.
WITHIN AND WITHOUT. THE HIDDEN
LIFE.—Vol. 2. THE DISCIPLE.   THE
GOSPEL WOMEN. A BOOK OF SONNETS,
ORGAN SONGS.—Vol. 3. VIOLIN SONGS.
SONGS OF THE DAYS AND NIGHTS.
A BOOK OF DREAMS. ROADSIDE POEMS.
POEMS FOR CHILDREN.   Vol. 4. PARA-
BLES.   BALLADS.   SCOTCH SONGS.—
Vols. 5 and 6. PHANTASTES: A Faerie
Romance.—Vol. 7. THE PORTENT.—
Vol. 8. THE LIGHT PRINCESS.   THE
GIANT'S HEART.   SHADOWS.—Vol. 9.
CROSS PURPOSES.   THE GOLDEN KEY.
THE CARASOYN. LITTLE DAYLIGHT.—
Vol. 10. THE CRUEL PAINTER.   THE
WOW O' RIVVEN. THE CASTLE.   THE
BROKEN SWORDS. THE GRAY WOLF.
UNCLE CORNELIUS.
*The Volumes are also sold separately
in Grolier-pattern cloth, 2s. 6d. each.*

Macdonell.—Quaker Cousins:
A Novel.   By AGNES MACDONELL.
Crown 8vo, cloth extra, 3s. 6d. ; post
8vo, illustrated boards, 2s.

Macgregor. — Pastimes and
Players. Notes on Popular Games.
By ROBERT MACGREGOR.   Post 8vo,
cloth limp, 2s. 6d.

Mackay.—Interludes and Un-
dertones ; or, Music at Twilight. By
CHARLES MACKAY, LL.D.   Crown 8vo,
cloth extra, 6s.

Maclise Portrait-Gallery (The)
of Illustrious Literary Characters ;
with Memoirs—Biographical, Critical,
Bibliographical, and Anecdotal—illustrative of the Literature of the former
half of the Present Century. By
WILLIAM BATES, B.A. With 85 Portraits printed on an India Tint. Crown
8vo, cloth extra, 7s. 6d.

Macquoid (Mrs.), Works by :
Square 8vo, cloth extra, 10s. 6d. each.
In the Ardennes. With 50 fine Illustrations by THOMAS R. MACQUOID.
Pictures and Legends from Normandy and Brittany. With numerous Illusts. by THOMAS R. MACQUOID
About Yorkshire. With 67 Illustrations by T. R. MACQUOID.

Crown 8vo, cloth extra, 7s. 6d. each.
Through Normandy. With 90 Illus-
trations by T. R. MACQUOID.
Through Brittany. With numerous
Illustrations by T. R. MACQUOID.

Post 8vo, illustrated boards, 2s. each.
The Evil Eye, and other Stories.
Lost Rose.

Magician's Own Book (The):
Performances with Cups and Balls, Eggs, Hats, Handkerchiefs, &c. All from actual Experience. Edited by W. H. CREMER. With 200 Illustrations. Crown 8vo, cloth extra, 4s. 6d.

Magic Lantern (The), and its Management: including full Practical Directions for producing the Limelight, making Oxygen Gas, and preparing Lantern Slides. By T. C. HEPWORTH. With 10 Illustrations. Crown 8vo, 1s. ; cloth, 1s. 6d.

Magna Charta. An exact Facsimile of the Original in the British Museum, printed on fine plate paper, 3 feet by 2 feet, with Arms and Seals emblazoned in Gold and Colours. 5s.

Mallock (W. H.), Works by:
The New Republic; or, Culture, Faith and Philosophy in an English Country House. Post 8vo, cloth limp, 2s. 6d. ; Cheap Edition, illustrated boards, 2s.
The New Paul and Virginia; or, Positivism on an Island. Post 8vo, cloth limp, 2s. 6d.
Poems. Small 4to, in parchment, 8s.
Is Life worth Living? Crown 8vo, cloth extra, 6s.

Mallory's (Sir Thomas) Mort d'Arthur: The Stories of King Arthur and of the Knights of the Round Table. Edited by B. MONTGOMERIE RANKING. Post 8vo, cloth limp, 2s.

Mark Twain, Works by:
The Choice Works of Mark Twain. Revised and Corrected throughout by the Author. With Life, Portrait, and numerous Illustrations. Crown 8vo, cloth extra, 7s. 6d.
The Innocents Abroad ; or, The New Pilgrim's Progress : Being some Account of the Steamship " Quaker City's " Pleasure Excursion to Europe and the Holy Land. With 234 Illustrations. Crown 8vo, cloth extra, 7s. 6d.—Cheap Edition (under the title of " MARK TWAIN'S PLEASURE TRIP "), post 8vo, illust. boards, 2s.
Roughing It, and The Innocents at Home. With 200 Illustrations by F. A. FRASER. Cr. 8vo, cl. ex., 7s. 6d.
The Gilded Age. By MARK TWAIN and CHARLES DUDLEY WARNER. With 212 Illustrations by T. COPPIN Crown 8vo, cloth extra, 7s. 6d.
The Adventures of Tom Sawyer With 111 Illustrations. Crown 8vo, cloth extra, 7s. 6d.—Cheap Edition post 8vo, illustrated boards, 2s.
The Prince and the Pauper. With nearly 200 Illustrations. Crown 8vo, cloth extra, 7s. 6d.

MARK TWAIN'S WORKS, *continued*—
A Tramp Abroad With 314 Illusts. Cr. 8vo, cloth extra, 7s. 6d.—Cheap Edition, post 8vo, illust. bds., 2s.
The Stolen White Elephant, &c. Crown 8vo, cloth extra, 6s.; post 8vo, illustrated boards, 2s.
Life on the Mississippi. With about 300 Original Illustrations. Crown 8vo, cloth extra, 7s. 6d.—Cheap Edition, post 8vo, illustrated boards, 2s.
The Adventures of Huckleberry Finn. With 174 Illustrations by E. W. KEMBLE. Crown 8vo, cloth extra, 7s. 6d.—Cheap Edition, post 8vo, illustrated boards, 2s.
Mark Twain's Library of Humour. With numerous Illustrations. Crown 8vo, cloth extra, 7s. 6d. [*Preparing.*

Marlowe's Works. Including his Translations. Edited, with Notes and Introductions, by Col. CUNNINGHAM. Crown 8vo, cloth extra, 6s.

Marryat (Florence), Novels by:
Crown 8vo, cloth extra, 3s. 6d. each; post 8vo, illustrated boards, 2s. each.
Open ! Sesame ! | Written in Fire.

Post 8vo, illustrated boards, 2s. each.
A Harvest of Wild Oats.
A Little Stepson.
Fighting the Air.

Massinger's Plays. From the Text of WILLIAM GIFFORD. Edited by Col. CUNNINGHAM. Crown 8vo, cloth extra, 6s.

Masterman.—Half a Dozen Daughters: A Novel. By J. MASTERMAN. Post 8vo, illustrated boards, 2s.

Matthews.—A Secret of the Sea, &c. By BRANDER MATTHEWS. Post 8vo, illustrated boards, 2s ; cloth, 2s. 6d.

Mayfair Library, The :
Post 8vo, cloth limp, 2s. 6d. per Volume.
A Journey Round My Room. By XAVIER DE MAISTRE. Translated by HENRY ATTWELL.
Quips and Quiddities. Selected by W. DAVENPORT ADAMS.
The Agony Column of " The Times," from 1800 to 1870. Edited, with an Introduction, by ALICE CLAY.
Melancholy Anatomised: A Popular Abridgment of " Burton's Anatomy of Melancholy."
Gastronomy as a Fine Art. By BRILLAT-SAVARIN.
The Speeches of Charles Dickens.
Literary Frivolities, Fancies, Follies, and Frolics. By W. T. DOBSON.
Poetical Ingenuities and Eccentricities. Selected and Edited by W. T. DOBSON.

MAYFAIR LIBRARY, *continued*—
Post 8vo, cloth limp, 2s. 6d. per Vol.

The Cupboard Papers. By FIN-BEC.

Original Plays by W. S. GILBERT. FIRST SERIES. Containing: The Wicked World — Pygmalion and Galatea—Charity—The Princess—The Palace of Truth—Trial by Jury.

Original Plays by W. S. GILBERT. SECOND SERIES. Containing: Broken Hearts — Engaged — Sweethearts—Gretchen—Dan'l Druce—Tom Cobb—H.M.S. Pinafore — The Sorcerer —The Pirates of Penzance.

Songs of Irish Wit and Humour. Collected and Edited by A. PERCEVAL GRAVES.

Animals and their Masters. By Sir ARTHUR HELPS.

Social Pressure. By Sir A. HELPS.

Curiosities of Criticism. By HENRY J. JENNINGS.

The Autocrat of the Breakfast-Table By OLIVER WENDELL HOLMES. Illustrated by J. GORDON THOMSON.

Pencil and Palette. By ROBERT KEMPT.

Little Essays: Sketches and Characters. By CHAS. LAMB. Selected from his Letters by PERCY FITZGERALD.

Forensic Anecdotes; or, Humour and Curiosities of the Law and Men of Law. By JACOB LARWOOD.

Theatrical Anecdotes. By JACOB LARWOOD.

Jeux d'Esprit. Edited by HENRY S. LEIGH.

True History of Joshua Davidson. By E. LYNN LINTON.

Witch Stories. By E. LYNN LINTON.

Ourselves: Essays on Women. By E. LYNN LINTON.

Pastimes and Players. By ROBERT MACGREGOR.

The New Paul and Virginia. By W. H. MALLOCK.

New Republic. By W. H. MALLOCK.

Puck on Pegasus. By H. CHOLMONDE-LEY-PENNELL.

Pegasus Re-Saddled. By H. CHOL-MONDELEY-PENNELL. Illustrated by GEORGE DU MAURIER.

Muses of Mayfair. Edited by H. CHOLMONDELEY-PENNELL.

Thoreau: His Life and Aims. By H. A. PAGE.

Puniana. By the Hon. HUGH ROWLEY.

More Puniana. By the Hon. HUGH ROWLEY.

The Philosophy of Handwriting. By DON FELIX DE SALAMANCA.

By Stream and Sea. By WILLIAM SENIOR.

Old Stories Re-told. By WALTER THORNBURY.

Leaves from a Naturalist's Note-Book. By Dr. ANDREW WILSON.

Mayhew.—London Characters and the Humorous Side of London Life. By HENRY MAYHEW. With numerous Illustrations. Crown 8vo, cloth extra, 3s. 6d.

Medicine, Family.—One Thousand Medical Maxims and Surgical Hints, for Infancy, Adult Life, Middle Age, and Old Age. By N. E. DAVIES, L.R.C.P. Lond. Cr. 8vo, 1s.; cl., 1s. 6d.

Merry Circle (The): A Book of New Intellectual Games and Amusements. By CLARA BELLEW. With numerous Illustrations. Crown 8vo, cloth extra, 4s. 6d.

Mexican Mustang (On a), through Texas, from the Gulf to the Rio Grande. A New Book of American Humour. By ALEX. E. SWEET and J. ARMOY KNOX, Editors of "Texas Siftings." With 265 Illusts. Cr. 8vo, cloth extra, 7s. 6d.

Middlemass (Jean), Novels by. Post 8vo, illustrated boards, 2s. each. Touch and Go. | Mr. Dorillion.

Miller. — Physiology for the Young; or, The House of Life: Human Physiology, with its application to the Preservation of Health. For Classes and Popular Reading. With numerous Illusts. By Mrs. F. FENWICK MILLER. Small 8vo, cloth limp, 2s. 6d.

Milton (J. L.), Works by: Sm. 8vo, 1s. each; cloth ex., 1s. 6d. each.

The Hygiene of the Skin. A Concise Set of Rules for the Management of the Skin; with Directions for Diet, Wines, Soaps, Baths, &c.

The Bath in Diseases of the Skin.

The Laws of Life, and their Relation to Diseases of the Skin.

Molesworth (Mrs.).—Hather- court Rectory. By Mrs. MOLESWORTH, Author of "The Cuckoo Clock," &c. Cr. 8vo, cl. extra, 4s. 6d.

Moncrieff.—The Abdication; or, Time Tries All. An Historical Drama. By W. D. SCOTT-MONCRIEFF. With Seven Etchings by JOHN PETTIE, R.A., W. Q. ORCHARDSON, R.A., J. MACWHIRTER, A.R.A., COLIN HUNTER, A.R.A., R. MACBETH, A.R.A., and TOM GRAHAM, R.S.A. Large 4to, bound in buckram, 21s.

Murray (D. Christie), Novels by. Crown 8vo, cloth extra, 3s. 6d. each; post 8vo, illustrated boards, 2s. each.
A Life's Atonement. | A Model Father.
Joseph's Coat. | Coals of Fire.
By the Gate of the Sea.
Val Strange. | Hearts.

Murray (D. C.), *continued*—
Crown 8vo, cloth extra, 3s. 6d.; post 8vo,
    illustrated boards, 2s. each.
  The Way of the World.
  A Bit of Human Nature.
  First Person Singular.
  Cynic Fortune.

  Old Blazer's Hero. With Three Illus-
    trations by A. McCormick. Crown
    8vo, cloth extra, 6s.
  One Traveller Returns. . By D.
    Christie Murray and Henry Her-
    man. Cr. 8vo, cl. ex., 6s.   [*Dec.* 1.

North Italian Folk. By Mrs.
Comyns Carr. Illust. by Randolph
Caldecott. Sq. 8vo, cl. ex., 7s. 6d.

Novelists. — Half-Hours with
the Best Novelists of the Century:
Choice Readings from the finest Novels.
Edited, with Critical and Biographical
Notes, by H. T. Mackenzie Bell.
Crown 8vo, cl. ex., 3s. 6d. [*Preparing*.

Nursery Hints: A Mother's
Guide in Health and Disease. By N. E.
Davies, L.R.C.P. Cr.8vo, 1s.; cl., 1s.6d.

O'Connor.—Lord Beaconsfield:
A Biography. By T. P. O'Connor, M.P.
Sixth Edition, with a New Preface,
bringing the work down to the Death
of Lord Beaconsfield. Crown 8vo,
cloth extra, 7s. 6d.

O'Hanlon. — The Unforeseen:
A Novel. By Alice O'Hanlon. New
and Cheaper Edition. Post 8vo, illustrated boards, 2s.

Oliphant (Mrs.) Novels by:
  Whiteladies. With Illustrations by
    Arthur Hopkins and H. Woods.
    Crown 8vo, cloth extra, 3s. 6d.;
    post 8vo, illustrated boards, 2s.
  Crown 8vo, cloth extra, 4s. 6d. each.
  The Primrose Path.
  The Greatest Heiress in England.

O'Reilly.—Phœbe's Fortunes:
A Novel. With Illustrations by Henry
Tuck. Post 8vo, illustrated boards, 2s.

O'Shaughnessy (A.), Works by:
  Songs of a Worker. Fcap. 8vo, cloth
    extra, 7s. 6d.
  Music and Moonlight. Fcap. 8vo,
    cloth extra, 7s. 6d.
  Lays of France. Cr.8vo, cl. ex.,10s. 6d.

Ouida, Novels by. Crown 8vo,
cloth extra, 5s. each; post 8vo, illustrated boards, 2s. each.

Held in Bondage.	**Tricotrin.**
Strathmore.	**Puck.**
Chandos.	**Folle Farine.**
Under Two Flags.	**Two Little Wooden**
Cecil Castle-	**Shoes.**
maine's Gage.	**A Dog of Flanders.**
Idalia	**Pascarel.**

Ouida, *continued*—
Crown 8vo, cloth extra, 5s. each; post
    8vo, illustrated boards, 2s. each.

Signa.	**Ariadne.**	**A Village Com-**
In a Winter City.		**mune.**
Friendship.		**Wanda.**
Moths.	**Bimbi.**	**Frescoes.** [Ine.
Pipistrello.		**Princess Naprax-**
In Maremma.		**Othmar.**

  Wisdom, Wit, and Pathos, selected
    from the Works of Ouida by F.
    Sydney Morris. Sm.cr.8vo,cl.ex.,5s.

Page (H. A.), Works by:
  Thoreau: His Life and Aims: A Study.
    With Portrait. Post 8vo,cl.limp, 2s.6d.
  Lights on the Way: Some Tales with-
    in a Tale. By the late J. H. Alex-
    ander, B.A. Edited by H. A. Page.
    Crown 8vo, cloth extra, 6s.
  Animal Anecdotes. Arranged on a
    New Principle. Cr. 8vo, cl. extra, 5s.

Parliamentary Elections and
Electioneering in the Old Days (A
History of). Showing the State of
Political Parties and Party Warfare at
the Hustings and in the House of
Commons from the Stuarts to Queen
Victoria. Illustrated from the original
Political Squibs, Lampoons, Pictorial
Satires, and Popular Caricatures of
the Time. By Joseph Grego, Author
of "Rowlandson and his Works,"
"The Life of Gillray," &c. A New
Edition, crown 8vo, cloth extra, with
Coloured Frontispiece and 100 Illus-
trations, 7s. 6d.   [*Preparing*.

Pascal's Provincial Letters. A
New Translation, with Historical In-
troduction and Notes, by T. M'Crie,
D.D. Post 8vo, cloth limp, 2s.

Patient's (The) Vade Mecum:
How to get most Benefit from Medical
Advice. By W. Knight, M.R.O.S., and
E. Knight, L.R.C.P. Cr.8vo, 1s.; cl. 1/6.

Paul Ferroll:
  Post 8vo, illustrated boards, 2s. each.
  Paul Ferroll: A Novel.
  Why Paul Ferroll Killed his Wife.

Payn (James), Novels by.
Crown 8vo, cloth extra, 3s. 6d. each;
post 8vo, illustrated boards, 2s. each.
  Lost Sir Massingberd.
  The Best of Husbands.
  Walter's Word.
  Less Black than we're Painted.
  By Proxy. | **High Spirits.**
  Under One Roof.
  A Confidential Agent.
  Some Private Views.
  A Grape from a Thorn.
  For Cash Only. | **From Exile.**
  The Canon's Ward.
  The Talk of the Town.
  Glow-worm Tales.   [*Shortly*.

PAYN (JAMES), *continued—*
Post 8vo, illustrated boards, 2s. each.
Kit: A Memory. | Carlyon's Year.
A Perfect Treasure.
Bentinck's Tutor.|Murphy's Master.
What He Cost Her.
Fallen Fortunes. | Halves.
A County Family. | At Her Mercy.
A Woman's Vengeance.
Cecil's Tryst.
The Clyffards of Clyffe.
The Family Scapegrace.
The Foster Brothers.| Found Dead.
Gwendoline's Harvest.
Humorous Stories.
Like Father, Like Son.
A Marine Residence.
Married Beneath Him.
Mirk Abbey. | Not Wooed, but Won.
Two Hundred Pounds Reward.

In Peril and Privation: Stories of Marine Adventure Re-told. A Book for Boys. With numerous Illustrations. Crown 8vo, cloth gilt, 6s.
Holiday Tasks: Being Essays written in Vacation Time. Crown 8vo, cloth extra, 6s.

Paul.—Gentle and Simple. By MARGARET AGNES PAUL. With a Frontispiece by HELEN PATERSON. Cr. 8vo, cloth extra, 3s. 6d.; post 8vo, illustrated boards, 2s.

Pears.—The Present Depression in Trade: Its Causes and Remedies. Being the "Pears" Prize Essays (of One Hundred Guineas). By EDWIN GOADBY and WILLIAM WATT. With an Introductory Paper by Prof. LEONE LEVI, F.S.A., F.S.S. Demy 8vo, 1s.

Pennell (H. Cholmondeley), Works by:
Post 8vo, cloth limp, 2s. 6d. each.
Puck on Pegasus. With Illustrations.
Pegasus Re-Saddled. With Ten full-page Illusts. by G. DU MAURIER.
The Muses of Mayfair. Vers de Société, Selected and Edited by H. C. PENNELL.

Phelps (E. Stuart), Works by:
Post 8vo, 1s. each; cl. limp, 1s. 6d. each.
Beyond the Gates. By the Author of "The Gates Ajar."
An Old Maid's Paradise.
Burglars in Paradise.

Jack the Fisherman. With Twenty-two Illustrations by C. W. REED. Cr. 8vo, picture cover, 1s.; cl. 1s. 6d.

Pirkis (Mrs. C. L.), Novels by:
Trooping with Crows. Fcap. 8vo, picture cover, 1s.
Lady Lovelace. Post 8vo, illustrated boards, 2s.   *[Preparing.*

Planché (J. R.), Works by:
The Pursuivant of Arms; or, Heraldry Founded upon Facts. With Coloured Frontispiece and 200 Illustrations. Cr. 8vo, cloth extra, 7s. 6d.
Songs and Poems, from 1819 to 1879. Edited, with an Introduction, by his Daughter, Mrs. MACKARNESS. Crown 8vo, cloth extra, 6s.

Plutarch's Lives of Illustrious Men. Translated from the Greek, with Notes Critical and Historical, and a Life of Plutarch, by JOHN and WILLIAM LANGHORNE. Two Vols., 8vo, cloth extra, with Portraits, 10s. 6d.

Poe (Edgar Allan):—
The Choice Works, in Prose and Poetry, of EDGAR ALLAN POE. With an Introductory Essay by CHARLES BAUDELAIRE, Portrait and Fac-similes. Crown 8vo, cl. extra, 7s. 6d.
The Mystery of Marie Roget, and other Stories. Post 8vo, illust.bds.,2s.

Pope's Poetical Works. Complete in One Vol. Post 8vo, cl. limp, 2s.

Praed (Mrs. Campbell-).—"The Right Honourable:" A Romance of Society and Politics. By Mrs. CAMPBELL-PRAED and JUSTIN MCCARTHY, M.P. Cr. 8vo, cloth extra, 6s.

Price (E. C.), Novels by:
Crown 8vo, cloth extra, 3s. 6d. each; post 8vo, illustrated boards, 2s. each.
Valentina. | The Foreigners.
Mrs. Lancaster's Rival.
Gerald. Post 8vo, illust. boards, 2s.

Princess Olga—Radna; or, The Great Conspiracy of 1881. By the Princess OLGA. Cr. 8vo, cl. ex., 6s.

Proctor (Richd. A.), Works by:
Flowers of the Sky. With 55 Illusts. Small crown 8vo, cloth extra, 4s. 6d.
Easy Star Lessons. With Star Maps for Every Night in the Year, Drawings of the Constellations, &c. Crown 8vo, cloth extra, 6s.
Familiar Science Studies. Crown 8vo, cloth extra, 7s. 6d.
Saturn and its System. New and Revised Edition, with 13 Steel Plates. Demy 8vo, cloth extra, 10s. 6d.
The Great Pyramid: Observatory, Tomb, and Temple. With Illustrations. Crown 8vo, cloth extra, 6s.
Mysteries of Time and Space. With Illusts. Cr. 8vo, cloth extra, 7s. 6d.
The Universe of Suns, and other Science Gleanings. With numerous Illusts. Cr. 8vo, cloth extra, 7s. 6d.
Wages and Wants of Science Workers. Crown 8vo, 1s. 6d.

Rabelais' Works. Faithfully Translated from the French, with variorum Notes, and numerous characteristic Illustrations by GUSTAVE DORÉ. Crown 8vo, cloth extra, 7s. 6d.

Rambosson.—Popular Astronomy. By J. RAMBOSSON, Laureate of the Institute of France. Translated by C. B. PITMAN. Crown 8vo, cloth gilt, numerous Illusts., and a beautifully executed Chart of Spectra, 7s. 6d.

Reade (Charles), Novels by :

Cr. 8vo, cloth extra, illustrated, 3s. 6d. each ; post 8vo, illust. bds., 2s. each.

Peg Woffington. Illustrated by S. L. FILDES, A.R.A.

Christie Johnstone. Illustrated by WILLIAM SMALL.

It is Never Too Late to Mend. Illustrated by G. J. PINWELL.

The Course of True Love Never did run Smooth. Illustrated by HELEN PATERSON.

The Autobiography of a Thief; Jack of all Trades; and James Lambert. Illustrated by MATT STRETCH.

Love me Little, Love me Long. Illustrated by M. ELLEN EDWARDS.

The Double Marriage. Illust. by Sir JOHN GILBERT, R.A., and C. KEENE.

The Cloister and the Hearth. Illustrated by CHARLES KEENE.

Hard Cash. Illust. by F. W. LAWSON.

Griffith Gaunt. Illustrated by S. L. FILDES, A.R.A., and WM. SMALL.

Foul Play. Illust. by DU MAURIER.

Put Yourself in His Place. Illustrated by ROBERT BARNES.

A Terrible Temptation. Illustrated by EDW. HUGHES and A. W. COOPER.

The Wandering Heir. Illustrated by H. PATERSON, S. L. FILDES, A.R.A., C. GREEN, and H. WOODS, A.R.A.

A Simpleton. Illustrated by KATE CRAUFORD.   [COULDERY.

A Woman-Hater. Illust. by THOS.

Singleheart and Doubleface: A Matter-of-fact Romance. Illustrated by P. MACNAB.

Good Stories of Men and other Animals. Illustrated by E. A. ABBEY, PERCY MACQUOID, and JOSEPH NASH.

The Jilt, and other Stories. Illustrated by JOSEPH NASH.

Readiana. With a Steel-plate Portrait of CHARLES READE.

Reader's Handbook (The) of Allusions, References, Plots, and Stories. By the Rev. Dr. BREWER. Fifth Edition, revised throughout, with a New Appendix, containing a COMPLETE ENGLISH BIBLIOGRAPHY. Cr. 8vo, 1,400 pages, cloth extra, 7s. 6d.

Red Spider : A Romance. By the Author of "John Herring," &c. Cr. 8vo, cloth extra. 3s. 6d.   [*Shortly.*

Rice (Portrait of James).— Specially etched by DANIEL A. WEHRSCHMIDT for the New Library Edition of BESANT and RICE's Novels. A few Proofs before Letters have been taken on Japanese paper, size 15¾×10 in. Price 6s. each.

Richardson. — A Ministry of Health, and other Papers. By BENJAMIN WARD RICHARDSON, M.D., &c. Crown 8vo, cloth extra, 6s.

Riddell (Mrs. J. H.), Novels by :

Crown 8vo, cloth extra, 3s. 6d. each ; post 8vo, illustrated boards, 2s. each.

Her Mother's Darling.

The Prince of Wales's Garden Party

Weird Stories.

Post 8vo, illustrated boards, 2s. each.

The Uninhabited House.

Fairy Water.

The Mystery in Palace Gardens.

Rimmer (Alfred), Works by :

Square 8vo, cloth gilt, 10s. 6d. each.

Our Old Country Towns. With over 50 Illustrations.

Rambles Round Eton and Harrow. With 50 Illustrations.

About England with Dickens. With 58 Illustrations by ALFRED RIMMER and C. A. VANDERHOOF.

Robinson Crusoe : A beautiful reproduction of Major's Edition, with 37 Woodcuts and Two Steel Plates by GEORGE CRUIKSHANK, choicely printed. Crown 8vo, cloth extra, 7s. 6d.

Robinson (F. W.), Novels by :

Crown 8vo, cloth extra, 3s. 6d. each ; post 8vo, illustrated boards, 2s. each.

Women are Strange.

The Hands of Justice.

Robinson (Phil), Works by :

Crown 8vo, cloth extra, 7s. 6d. each.

The Poets' Birds.

The Poets' Beasts.

The Poets and Nature: Reptiles, Fishes and Insects.   [*Preparing.*

Rochefoucauld's Maxims and Moral Reflections. With Notes, and an Introductory Essay by SAINTE-BEUVE. Post 8vo, cloth limp, 2s.

Roll of Battle Abbey, The ; or, A List of the Principal Warriors who came over from Normandy with William the Conqueror, and Settled in this Country, A.D. 1066-7. With the principal Arms emblazoned in Gold and Colours. Handsomely printed, 5s.

Rowley (Hon. Hugh), Works by:
Post 8vo, cloth limp, **2s. 6d.** each.
Puniana: Riddles and Jokes. With numerous Illustrations.
More Puniana. Profusely Illustrated.

Runciman (James), Stories by:
Post 8vo, illustrated boards, **2s.** each; cloth limp, **2s. 6d.** each.
Skippers and Shellbacks.
Grace Balmaign's Sweetheart.
Schools and Scholars.

Russell (W. Clark), Works by:
Crown 8vo, cloth extra, **6s.** each; post 8vo, illustrated boards, **2s.** each.
Round the Galley-Fire.
On the Fo'k'sle Head.
In the Middle Watch.
Crown 8vo, cloth extra, **6s.** each.
A Voyage to the Cape.
A Book for the Hammock.
The Frozen Pirate, the New Serial Novel by W. CLARK RUSSELL, Author of "The Wreck of the *Grosvenor*," began in "Belgravia" for July, and will be continued till January next. One Shilling, Monthly. Illustrated.

Sala.—Gaslight and Daylight.
By GEORGE AUGUSTUS SALA. Post 8vo, illustrated boards, **2s.**

Sanson.—Seven Generations of Executioners: Memoirs of the Sanson Family (1688 to 1847). Edited by HENRY SANSON. Cr.8vo,cl.ex.**3s.6d.**

Saunders (John), Novels by:
Crown 8vo, cloth extra, **3s. 6d.** each; post 8vo, illustrated boards, **2s.** each.
Bound to the Wheel
Guy Waterman. | Lion in the Path.
The Two Dreamers.
One Against the World. Post 8vo, illustrated boards, **2s.**

Saunders (Katharine), Novels by. Cr. 8vo, cloth extra, **3s. 6d.** each; post 8vo, illustrated boards, **2s.** each.
Joan Merryweather.
Margaret and Elizabeth.
The High Mills.
Heart Salvage. | Sebastian.
Gideon's Rock. Crown 8vo, cloth extra, **3s. 6d.**

Science Gossip: An Illustrated Medium of Interchange for Students and Lovers of Nature. Edited by J. E. TAYLOR, F.L.S., &c. Devoted to Geology, Botany, Physiology, Chemistry, Zoology, Microscopy, Telescopy, Physiography, &c. Price **4d.** Monthly; or **5s.** per year, post free. Vols. I. to XIV. may be had at **7s. 6d.** each; and Vols. XV. to XXII. (1886), at **5s.** each. Cases for Binding, **1s. 6d.** each.

"Secret Out" Series, The:
Cr. 8vo, cl. ex., Illusts., **4s. 6d.** each.
The Secret Out: One Thousand Tricks with Cards, and other Recreations; with Entertaining Experiments in Drawing-room or "White Magic." By W. H. CREMER. 300 Illusts.
The Art of Amusing: A Collection of Graceful Arts, Games, Tricks, Puzzles, and Charades By FRANK BELLEW. With 300 Illustrations.
Hanky-Panky: Very Easy Tricks Very Difficult Tricks, White Magic Sleight of Hand. Edited by W. H. CREMER. With 200 Illustrations.
The Merry Circle: A Book of New Intellectual Games and Amusements. By CLARA BELLEW. Many Illusts.
Magician's Own Book: Performances with Cups and Balls, Eggs, Hats, Handkerchiefs, &c. All from actual Experience. Edited by W. H. CREMER. 200 Illustrations.

Senior.—By Stream and Sea.
By W. SENIOR. Post 8vo, cl. limp, **2s. 6d.**

Seven Sagas (The) of Prehistoric Man. By JAMES H. STODDART, Author of "The Village Life." Crown 8vo, cloth extra, **6s.**

Shakespeare:
The First Folio Shakespeare.—MR. WILLIAM SHAKESPEARE's Comedies, Histories, and Tragedies. Published according to the true Originall Copies. London, Printed by ISAAC IAGGARD and ED. BLOUNT. 1623.—A Reproduction of the extremely rare original, in reduced facsimile, by a photographic process—ensuring the strictest accuracy in every detail. Small 8vo, half-Roxburghe, **7s. 6d.**
The Lansdowne Shakespeare. Beautifully printed in red and black, in small but very clear type. With engraved facsimile of DROESHOUT's Portrait. Post 8vo, cloth extra, **7s. 6d.**
Shakespeare for Children: Tales from Shakespeare. By CHARLES and MARY LAMB. With numerous Illustrations, coloured and plain, by J. MOYR SMITH. Cr. 4to, cl. gilt, **6s.**
The Handbook of Shakespeare Music. Being an Account of 350 Pieces of Music, set to Words taken from the Plays and Poems of Shakespeare, the compositions ranging from the Elizabethan Age to the Present Time. By ALFRED ROFFE. 4to, half-Roxburghe, **7s.**
A Study of Shakespeare. By ALGERNON CHARLES SWINBURNE. Crown 8vo, cloth extra, **8s.**

Shelley.—The Complete Works
In Verse and Prose of Percy Bysshe Shelley. Edited, Prefaced and Annotated by RICHARD HERNE SHEPHERD. Five Vols., crown 8vo, cloth boards, 3s. 6d. each.

Poetical Works, in Three Vols.

Vol. I. An Introduction by the Editor; The Posthumous Fragments of Margaret Nicholson; Shelley's Correspondence with Stockdale; The Wandering Jew (the only complete version); Queen Mab, with the Notes; Alastor, and other Poems; Rosalind and Helen; Prometheus Unbound; Adonais, &c.

Vol. II. Laon and Cythna (as originally published, instead of the emasculated "Revolt of Islam"); The Cenci; Julian and Maddalo (from Shelley's manuscript); Swellfoot the Tyrant (from the copy in the Dyce Library at South Kensington); The Witch of Atlas; Epipsychidion; Hellas.

Vol. III. Posthumous Poems, published by Mrs. SHELLEY in 1824 and 1839; The Masque of Anarchy (from Shelley's manuscript); and other Pieces not brought together in the ordinary editions.

Prose Works, in Two Vols.

Vol. I. The Two Romances of Zastrozzi and St. Irvyne; the Dublin and Marlow Pamphlets; A Refutation of Deism; Letters to Leigh Hunt, and some Minor Writings and Fragments.

Vol. II. The Essays; Letters from Abroad; Translations and Fragments, Edited by Mrs. SHELLEY, and first published in 1840, with the addition of some Minor Pieces of great interest and rarity, including one recently discovered by Professor DOWDEN. With a Bibliography of Shelley, and an exhaustive Index of the Prose Works.

. Also a LARGE-PAPER EDITION, to be had in SETS only, at 52s. 6d. for the Five Volumes.

Sheridan :—

Sheridan's Complete Works, with Life and Anecdotes. Including his Dramatic Writings, printed from the Original Editions, his Works in Prose and Poetry, Translations, Speeches, Jokes, Puns, &c. With a Collection of Sheridaniana. Crown 8vo, cloth extra, gilt, with 10 full-page Tinted Illustrations, 7s. 6d.

Sheridan's Comedies: The Rivals, and The School for Scandal. Edited, with an Introduction and Notes to each Play, and a Biographical Sketch of Sheridan, by BRANDER MATTHEWS. With Decorative Vignettes and 10 full-page Illusts. Demy 8vo, half-parchment, 12s. 6d.

Sidney's (Sir Philip) Complete
Poetical Works, including all those in "Arcadia." With Portrait, Memorial-Introduction, Notes, &c., by the Rev. A. B. GROSART, D.D. Three Vols., crown 8vo, cloth boards, 18s.

Signboards: Their   History.
With Anecdotes of Famous Taverns and Remarkable Characters. By JACOB LARWOOD and JOHN CAMDEN HOTTEN. Crown 8vo, cloth extra, with 100 Illustrations, 7s. 6d.

Sims (George R.), Works by :
How the Poor Live. With 60 Illusts. by FRED. BARNARD. Large 4to, 1s.
Post 8vo, illustrated boards, 2s. each; cloth limp, 2s. 6d. each.
Rogues and Vagabonds.
The Ring o' Bells.
Mary Jane's Memoirs.

Sister Dora : A Biography. By MARGARET LONSDALE. Popular Edition, Revised, with additional Chapter, a New Dedication and Preface, and Four Illustrations. Sq. 8vo, picture cover, 4d.; cloth, 6d.

Sketchley.—A Match in the
Dark. By ARTHUR SKETCHLEY. Post 8vo, illustrated boards, 2s.

Slang Dictionary, The : Etymological, Historical, and Anecdotal. Crown 8vo, cloth extra, gilt, 6s. 6d.

Smith (J. Moyr), Works by :
The Prince of Argolis: A Story of the Old Greek Fairy Time. Small 8vo, cloth extra, with 130 Illusts., 3s. 6d.
Tales of Old Thule. With numerous Illustrations. Cr. 8vo, cloth gilt, 6s.
The Wooing of the Water Witch: A Northern Oddity. With numerous Illustrations. Small 8vo, cl. ex., 6s.

Society in London. By A FOREIGN RESIDENT. Crown 8vo, 1s.; cloth, 1s. 6d.

Society in Paris: The Upper Ten Thousand. By Count PAUL VASILI. Trans. by RAPHAEL LEDOS DE BEAUFORT. Cr. 8vo, cl. ex., 6s. [*Preparing*.

Spalding.—Elizabethan Demonology : An Essay in Illustration of the Belief in the Existence of Devils, and the Powers possessed by Them. By T. A. SPALDING, LL.B. Cr. 8vo, cl. ex., 5s.

Spanish Legendary Tales. By Mrs. S. G. C. MIDDLEMORE, Author of "Round a Posada Fire." Crown 8vo, cloth extra, 6s.

Speight (T. W.), Novels by :
The Mysteries of Heron Dyke. With a Frontispiece by M. ELLEN EDWARDS. Crown 8vo, cloth extra, 3s. 6d.; post 8vo, illustrated bds., 2s.
A Barren Title. Cr. 8vo, 1s.; cl., 1s. 6d.
Wife or No Wife? Cr. 8vo, picture cover, 1s.; cloth, 1s. 6d.
The Golden Hoop. Demy 8vo, 1s.
[*Nov.* 10.

Spenser for Children. By M. H. TOWRY. With Illustrations by WALTER J. MORGAN. Crown 4to, with Coloured Illustrations, cloth gilt, **6s.**

Starting in Life: Hints for Parents on the Choice of a Profession for their Sons. By FRANCIS DAVENANT, M.A. Post 8vo, 1s.; cloth limp, 1s. 6d.

Staunton.—Laws and Practice of Chess; Together with an Analysis of the Openings, and a Treatise on End Games. By HOWARD STAUNTON. Edited by ROBERT B. WORMALD. New Edition, small cr. 8vo, cloth extra, **5s.**

Stedman (E. C.), Works by:

Victorian Poets. Thirteenth Edition, revised and enlarged. Crown 8vo, cloth extra, **9s.**

The Poets of America. Crown 8vo, cloth extra, **9s.**

Sterndale.—The Afghan Knife: A Novel. By ROBERT ARMITAGE STERNDALE. Cr. 8vo, cloth extra, 3s. 6d.; post 8vo, illustrated boards, **2s.**

Stevenson (R. Louis), Works by:

Travels with a Donkey in the Cevennes. Sixth Ed. Frontispiece by W. CRANE. Post 8vo, cl. limp, **2s. 6d.**

An Inland Voyage. With Front. by W. CRANE. Post 8vo, cl. lp., **2s. 6d.**

Familiar Studies of Men and Books. Second Edit. Crown 8vo, cl. ex., **6s.**

New Arabian Nights. Crown 8vo, cl. extra, 6s.; post 8vo, illust. bds., **2s.**

The Silverado Squatters. With Frontispiece. Cr. 8vo, cloth extra, 6s. Cheap Edition, post 8vo, picture cover, 1s.; cloth, **1s. 6d.**

Prince Otto: A Romance. Fourth Edition. Crown 8vo, cloth extra, 6s.; post 8vo, illustrated boards, **2s.**

The Merry Men, and other Tales and Fables. Cr. 8vo, cl. ex., **6s.**

Underwoods: Poems. Post 8vo, cl. ex. **6s.**

Memories and Portraits. Fcap. 8vo, buckram extra, **6s.**

Virginibus Puerisque, and other Papers. A New Edition, Revised. Fcap. 8vo, buckram extra, **6s.**

St. John.—A Levantine Family. By BAYLE ST. JOHN. Post 8vo, illustrated boards, **2s.**

Stoddard.—Summer Cruising in the South Seas. By CHARLES WARREN STODDARD. Illust. by WALLIS MACKAY. Crown 8vo, cl. extra, **3s. 6d.**

Stories from Foreign Novelists. With Notices of their Lives and Writings. By HELEN and ALICE ZIMMERN. Frontispiece. Crown 8vo, cloth extra, 3s. 6d.; post 8vo, illust. bds., **2s.**

St. Pierre.—Paul and Virginia, and The Indian Cottage. By BERNARDIN ST. PIERRE. Edited, with Life, by Rev. E. CLARKE. Post 8vo, cl. lp., **2s.**

Strutt's Sports and Pastimes of the People of England; including the Rural and Domestic Recreations, May Games, Mummeries, Shows, &c., from the Earliest Period to the Present Time. With 140 Illustrations. Edited by WM. HONE. Cr. 8vo, cl. extra, **7s. 6d.**

Suburban Homes (The) of London: A Residential Guide to Favourite London Localities, their Society, Celebrities, and Associations. With Notes on their Rental, Rates, and House Accommodation. With Map of Suburban London. Cr. 8vo, cl. ex., **7s. 6d.**

Swift's Choice Works, in Prose and Verse. With Memoir, Portrait, and Facsimiles of the Maps in the Original Edition of "Gulliver's Travels." Cr. 8vo, cloth extra, **7s. 6d.**

Swinburne (Algernon C.), Works by:

Selections from the Poetical Works of Algernon Charles Swinburne. Fcap. 8vo, cloth extra, **6s.**

Atalanta in Calydon. Crown 8vo, **6s.**

Chastelard. A Tragedy. Cr. 8vo, **7s.**

Poems and Ballads. FIRST SERIES. Fcap. 8vo, 9s. Cr. 8vo, same price.

Poems and Ballads. SECOND SERIES. Fcap. 8vo, 9s. Cr. 8vo, same price.

Notes on Poems and Reviews. 8vo, **1s.**

Songs before Sunrise. Cr. 8vo, **10s. 6d.**

Bothwell: A Tragedy. Cr. 8vo, **12s. 6d.**

George Chapman: An Essay. Cr. 8vo, **7s.**

Songs of Two Nations. Cr. 8vo, **6s.**

Essays and Studies. Crown 8vo, **12s.**

Erechtheus: A Tragedy. Cr. 8vo, **6s.**

Note of an English Republican on the Muscovite Crusade. 8vo, **1s.**

Note on Charlotte Bronte. Cr. 8vo, **6s.**

A Study of Shakespeare. Cr. 8vo, **8s.**

Songs of the Springtides. Cr. 8vo, **6s.**

Studies in Song. Crown 8vo, **7s.**

Mary Stuart: A Tragedy. Cr. 8vo, **8s.**

Tristram of Lyonesse, and other Poems. Crown 8vo, **9s.**

A Century of Roundels. Small 4to, **8s.**

A Midsummer Holiday, and other Poems. Crown 8vo, **7s.**

Marino Faliero: A Tragedy. Cr. 8vo, **6s.**

A Study of Victor Hugo. Cr. 8vo, **6s.**

Miscellanies. Crown 8vo, **12s.**

Locrine: A Tragedy. Crown 8vo, **6s.**

Symonds.—Wine, Women, and Song: Mediæval Latin Students' Songs. Now first translated into English Verse, with Essay by J. ADDINGTON SYMONDS. Small 8vo, parchment, 6s.

Syntax's (Dr.) Three Tours: In Search of the Picturesque, in Search of Consolation, and in Search of a Wife. With the whole of ROWLANDSON's droll page Illustrations in Colours and a Life of the Author by J. C. HOTTEN. Med. 8vo, cloth extra, 7s. 6d.

Taine's History of English Literature. Translated by HENRY VAN LAUN. Four Vols., small 8vo, cloth boards, 30s.—POPULAR EDITION, Two Vols., crown 8vo, cloth extra, 15s.

Taylor's (Bayard) Diversions of the Echo Club: Burlesques of Modern Writers. Post 8vo, cl. limp, 2s.

Taylor (Dr. J. E., F.L.S.), Works by. Crown 8vo, cloth ex., 7s. 6d. each.
The Sagacity and Morality of Plants: A Sketch of the Life and Conduct of the Vegetable Kingdom. Coloured Frontispiece and 100 Illust.
Our Common British Fossils, and Where to Find Them: A Handbook for Students. With 331 Illustrations.
The Playtime Naturalist : A Book for every Home. With about 300 Illustrations. Crown 8vo, cloth extra, 6s.
[Preparing.

Taylor's (Tom) Historical Dramas: "Clancarty," "Jeanne Darc," "'Twixt Axe and Crown," "The Fool's Revenge," "Arkwright's Wife," "Anne Boleyn," "Plot and Passion." One Vol., cr. 8vo, cloth extra, 7s. 6d.
⁂ The Plays may also be had separately, at 1s. each.

Tennyson (Lord): A Biographical Sketch. By H. J. JENNINGS. With a Photograph-Portrait. Crown 8vo, cloth extra, 6s.

Thackerayana; Notes and Anecdotes. Illustrated by Hundreds of Sketches by WILLIAM MAKEPEACE THACKERAY, depicting Humorous Incidents in his School-life, and Favourite Characters in the books of his every-day reading. With Coloured Frontispiece. Cr. 8vo, cl. extra, 7s. 6d.

Thomas (Bertha), Novels by: Crown 8vo, cloth extra, 3s. 6d. each post 8vo, illustrated boards, 2s. each.
Cressida. | Proud Maisie.
The Violin-Player.

Thomas (M.).—A Fight for Life: A Novel. By W. MOY THOMAS. Post 8vo, illustrated boards, 2s.

Thomson's Seasons and Castle of Indolence. With a Biographical and Critical Introduction by ALLAN CUNNINGHAM, and over 50 fine Illustrations on Steel and Wood. Crown 8vo, cloth extra, gilt edges, 7s. 6d.

Thornbury (Walter), Works by
Haunted London. Edited by EDWARD WALFORD, M.A. With Illustrations by F. W. FAIRHOLT, F.S.A. Crown 8vo, cloth extra, 7s. 6d.
The Life and Correspondence of J. M. W. Turner. Founded upon Letters and Papers furnished by his Friends and fellow Academicians. With numerous Illusts. in Colours, facsimiled from Turner's Original Drawings. Cr. 8vo, cl. extra, 7s. 6d.
Old Stories Re-told. Post 8vo, cloth limp, 2s. 6d.
Tales for the Marines. Post 8vo, illustrated boards, 2s.

Timbs (John), Works by: Crown 8vo, cloth extra, 7s. 6d. each.
The History of Clubs and Club Life in London. With Anecdotes of its Famous Coffee-houses, Hostelries, and Taverns. With many Illusts.
English Eccentrics and Eccentricities: Stories of Wealth and Fashion, Delusions, Impostures, and Fanatic Missions, Strange Sights and Sporting Scenes, Eccentric Artists, Theatrical Folk, Men of Letters, &c. With nearly 50 Illusts.

Trollope (Anthony), Novels by: Crown 8vo, cloth extra, 3s. 6d. each; post 8vo, illustrated boards, 2s. each.
The Way We Live Now.
Kept in the Dark.
Frau Frohmann. | Marion Fay.
Mr. Scarborough's Family.
The Land-Leaguers.
Post 8vo, illustrated boards, 2s. each.
The Golden Lion of Granpere.
John Caldigate. | American Senator

Trollope (Frances E.), Novels by Crown 8vo, cloth extra, 3s. 6d. each; post 8vo, illustrated boards, 2s. each.
Like Ships upon the Sea.
Mabel's Progress. | Anne Furness.

Trollope (T. A.).—Diamond Cut Diamond, and other Stories. By T. ADOLPHUS TROLLOPE. Post 8vo, illustrated boards, 2s.

Trowbridge.—Farnell's Folly: A Novel. By J. T. TROWBRIDGE. Post 8vo, illustrated boards, 2s.

Turgenieff. — Stories from Foreign Novelists. By IVAN TURGENIEFF, and others. Cr. 8vo, cloth extra, 3s. 6d.; post 8vo, illustrated boards, 2s.

Tytler (C. C. Fraser-). — Mistress Judith: A Novel. By C. C. FRASER-TYTLER. Cr. 8vo, cloth extra, 3s. 6d.; post 8vo, illust. boards, 2s.

Tytler (Sarah), Novels by:
Crown 8vo, cloth extra, 3s. 6d. each; post 8vo, illustrated boards, 2s. each.
What She Came Through.
The Bride's Pass.
Saint Mungo's City.
Beauty and the Beast.
Noblesse Oblige.
Lady Bell.

Crown 8vo, cloth extra, 3s. 6d. each.
Citoyenne Jacqueline. Illustrated by A. B. HOUGHTON.
The Huguenot Family. With Illusts.
Buried Diamonds.

Disappeared. With Six Illustrations by P. MACNAB. Crown 8vo, cloth extra, 6s.

Van Laun.—History of French Literature. By H. VAN LAUN. Three Vols., demy 8vo, cl. bds., 7s. 6d. each.

Villari.— A Double Bond: A Story. By LINDA VILLARI. Fcap. 8vo, picture cover, 1s.

Walford (Edw., M.A.), Works by:
The County Families of the United Kingdom. Containing Notices of the Descent, Birth, Marriage, Education, &c., of more than 12000, distinguished Heads of Families, their Heirs Apparent or Presumptive, the Offices they hold or have held, their Town and Country Addresses, Clubs, &c. Twenty-seventh Annual Edition, for 1887, cloth gilt, 50s.

The Shilling Peerage (1887). Containing an Alphabetical List of the House of Lords, Dates of Creation, Lists of Scotch and Irish Peers, Addresses, &c. 32mo, cloth, 1s. Published annually.

The Shilling Baronetage (1887). Containing an Alphabetical List of the Baronets of the United Kingdom, short Biographical Notices, Dates of Creation, Addresses, &c. 32mo, cloth, 1s.

The Shilling Knightage (1887). Containing an Alphabetical List of the Knights of the United Kingdom, short Biographical Notices, Dates of Creation, Addresses, &c. 32mo, cl., 1s.

The Shilling House of Commons (1887). Containing a List of all the Members of Parliament, their Town and Country Addresses, &c. New Edition, embodying the results of the recent General Election. 32mo, cloth, 1s. Published annually.

Walford's (Edw.) Works, *continued—*
The Complete Peerage, Baronetage, Knightage, and House of Commons (1887). In One Volume, royal 32mo, cloth extra, gilt edges, 5s.
Haunted London. By WALTER THORNBURY. Edited by EDWARD WALFORD, M.A. With Illustrations by F. W. FAIRHOLT, F.S.A. Crown 8vo, cloth extra, 7s. 6d.

Walton and Cotton's Complete Angler; or, The Contemplative Man's Recreation; being a Discourse of Rivers, Fishponds, Fish and Fishing, written by IZAAK WALTON; and Instructions how to Angle for a Trout or Grayling in a clear Stream, by CHARLES COTTON. With Original Memoirs and Notes by Sir HARRIS NICOLAS, and 61 Copperplate Illustrations. Large crown 8vo, cloth antique, 7s. 6d.

Walt Whitman, Poems by. Selected and edited, with an Introduction, by WILLIAM M. ROSSETTI. A New Edition, with a Steel Plate Portrait. Crown 8vo, printed on hand-made paper and bound in buckram, 6s.

Wanderer's Library, The:
Crown 8vo, cloth extra, 3s. 6d. each.
Wanderings in Patagonia; or, Life among the Ostrich-Hunters. By JULIUS BEERBOHM. Illustrated.
Camp Notes: Stories of Sport and Adventure in Asia, Africa, and America. By FREDERICK BOYLE.
Savage Life. By FREDERICK BOYLE.
Merrie England in the Olden Time. By GEORGE DANIEL. With Illustrations by ROBT. CRUIKSHANK.
Circus Life and Circus Celebrities. By THOMAS FROST.
The Lives of the Conjurers. By THOMAS FROST.
The Old Showmen and the Old London Fairs. By THOMAS FROST.
Low-Life Deeps. An Account of the Strange Fish to be found there. By JAMES GREENWOOD.
The Wilds of London. By JAMES GREENWOOD.
Tunis: The Land and the People. By the Chevalier de HESSE-WARTEGG. With 22 Illustrations.
The Life and Adventures of a Cheap Jack. By One of the Fraternity. Edited by CHARLES HINDLEY.
The World Behind the Scenes. By PERCY FITZGERALD.
Tavern Anecdotes and Sayings: Including the Origin of Signs, and Reminiscences connected with Taverns, Coffee Houses, Clubs, &c. By CHARLES HINDLEY. With Illusts.
The Genial Showman: Life and Adventures of Artemus Ward. By E. P. HINGSTON. With a Frontispiece.

WANDERER'S LIBRARY, THE, *continued*—
The Story of the London Parks
By JACOB LARWOOD. With Illusts.
London Characters. By HENRY MAY-
HEW. Illustrated.
Seven Generations of Executioners:
Memoirs of the Sanson Family (1688
to 1847). Edited by HENRY SANSON.
Summer Cruising in the South
Seas. By C. WARREN STODDARD.
Illustrated by WALLIS MACKAY.

Warner.—A Roundabout Jour-
ney. By CHARLES DUDLEY WARNER,
Author of "My Summer in a Garden."
Crown 8vo, cloth extra, 6s.

Warrants, &c. :—
Warrant to Execute Charles I. An
exact Facsimile, with the Fifty-nine
Signatures, and corresponding Seals.
Carefully printed on paper to imitate
the Original, 22 in. by 14 in. Price 2s.
Warrant to Execute Mary Queen of
Scots. An exact Facsimile, including the Signature of Queen Elizabeth, and a Facsimile of the Great
Seal. Beautifully printed on paper
to imitate the Original MS. Price 2s.
Magna Charta. An exact Facsimile
of the Original Document in the
British Museum, printed on fine
plate paper, nearly 3 feet long by 2
feet wide, with the Arms and Seals
emblazoned in Gold and Colours. 5s.
The Roll of Battle Abbey; or, A List
of the Principal Warriors who came
over from Normandy with William
the Conqueror, and Settled in this
Country, A.D. 1066-7. With the
principal Arms emblazoned in Gold
and Colours. Price 5s.

Wayfarer, The : Journal of the
Society of Cyclists. Published Quar-
terly. Price 1s. Number I., for OCTO-
BER 1886, Number II., for JANUARY
1887, and Number III., for May, are
now ready.

Weather, How to Foretell the,
with the Pocket Spectroscope. By
F. W. CORY, M.R.C.S. Eng., F.R.Met.
Soc., &c. With 10 Illustrations. Crown
8vo, 1s.; cloth, 1s. 6d.

Westropp.—Handbook of Pot-
tery and Porcelain; or, History of
those Arts from the Earliest Period.
By HODDER M. WESTROPP. With numerous Illustrations, and a List of
Marks. Crown 8vo, cloth limp, 4s. 6d.

Whist. — How to Play Solo
Whist: Its Method and Principles
Explained, and its Practice Demon-
strated. With Illustrative Specimen
Hands, and a Revised and Augmented
Code of Laws. By ABRAHAM S. WILKS
and CHARLES F. PARDON. Crown 8vo,
cloth extra, 3s. 6d.　　　　　[*Shortly.*

Whistler's (Mr.) "Ten o'Clock.'
Uniform with his "Whistler *v.* Ruskin:
Art and Art Critics." Cr.8vo,1s.[*Shortly.*

Williams (W. Mattieu, F.R.A.S.),
Works by:
Science Notes. See the GENTLEMAN'S
MAGAZINE. 1s. Monthly.
Science in Short Chapters. Crown
8vo, cloth extra, 7s. 6d.
A Simple Treatise on Heat. Crown
8vo, cloth limp, with Illusts., 2s. 6d.
The Chemistry of Cookery. Crown
8vo, cloth extra, 6s.

Wilson (Dr. Andrew, F.R.S.E.),
Works by:
Chapters on Evolution: A Popular
History of Darwinian and Allied
Theories of Development. 3rd ed.
Cr. 8vo, cl. ex.,with 259 Illusts., 7s. 6d.
Leaves from a Naturalist's Note-
book. Post 8vo, cloth limp, 2s. 6d.
Leisure-Time Studies, chiefly Bio-
logical. Third Edit., with New Pre-
face. Cr. 8vo, cl. ex., with Illusts., 6s.
Studies in Life and Sense. With
numerous Illusts. Cr. 8vo, cl. ex., 6s.
Common Accidents, and How to
Treat them. By Dr. ANDREW WIL-
SON and others. With numerous Il-
lusts. Cr. 8vo, 1s.; cl. limp, 1s. 6d.

Winter (J. S.), Stories by :
Cavalry Life. Post 8vo, illust. bds., 2s.
Regimental Legends. Cr. 8vo, cl. ex.,
3s. 6d.; post 8vo, illust. bds., 2s.

Women of the Day : A Biogra-
phical Dictionary of Notable Contemporaries. By FRANCES HAYS. Crown
8vo, cloth extra, 5s.

Wood.—Sabina : A Novel. By
Lady WOOD. Post 8vo, illust. bds., 2s.

Wood (H. F.)—The Passenger
from Scotland Yard: A Detective
Story By H. F. WOOD. Crown 8vo,
cloth, 6s.　　　　　　　　　[*Shortly.*

Words, Facts, and Phrases :
A Dictionary of Curious, Quaint, and
Out-of-the-Way Matters. By ELIEZER
EDWARDS. New and cheaper issue,
cr. 8vo, cl. ex., 7s. 6d.; half-bound, 9s.

Wright (Thomas), Works by :
Crown 8vo, cloth extra, 7s. 6d. each.
Caricature History of the Georges
(The House of Hanover.) With 400
Pictures, Caricatures, Squibs, Broad
sides, Window Pictures, &c.
History of Caricature and of the
Grotesque in Art, Literature
Sculpture, and Painting. Profusely
Illustrated by F.W. FAIRHOLT, F.S.A

Yates (Edmund), Novels by :
Post 8vo, illustrated boards, 2s. each.
Castaway. | The Forlorn Hope
Land at Last.

NEW NOVELS.

MISS LINSKILL'S NEW NOVEL.
In Exchange for a Soul. By MARY LINSKILL, Author of "The Haven under the Hill," &c. 3 Vols., cr. 8vo.

HALL CAINE'S NEW NOVEL.
The Deemster: A Romance of the Isle of Man. By HALL CAINE, Author of "A Son of Hagar," &c. 3 vols., cr. 8vo.

NEW RUSSIAN NOVEL.
Radna; or, The Great Conspiracy of 1881. By the Princess OLGA. Crown 8vo, cloth extra, 6s.

CHRISTIE MURRAY'S NEW NOVEL
Old Blazer's Hero. By D. CHRISTIE MURRAY. Crown 8vo, cloth extra, 6s.

M. CONWAY'S NEW NOVEL.
Pine and Palm. By MONCURE D. CONWAY. 2 Vols., crown 8vo.

NEW STORY OF ADVENTURE.
One Traveller Returns. By D. CHRISTIE MURRAY and HENRY HERMAN. Crown 8vo, cloth, 6s. [*Dec. 1*

A NEW DETECTIVE STORY.
The Passenger from Scotland Yard. By H. F. WOOD. Crown 8vo, cloth, 6s. [*Preparing.*

NEW AMERICAN NOVEL.
Seth's Brother's Wife. By HAROLD FREDERIC. 2 Vols., cr. 8vo. [*Immediately.*

THE PICCADILLY NOVELS.

Popular Stories by the Best Authors. LIBRARY EDITIONS, many Illustrated, crown 8vo, cloth extra, 3s. 6d. each.

BY GRANT ALLEN.
Philistia.
In all Shades.

BY THE AUTHOR OF "JOHN HERRING."
Red Spider.

BY W. BESANT & JAMES RICE.
Ready-Money Mortiboy.
My Little Girl.
The Case of Mr. Lucraft.
This Son of Vulcan.
With Harp and Crown
The Golden Butterfly.
By Celia's Arbour.
The Monks of Thelema.
'Twas in Trafalgar's Bay.
The Seamy Side.
The Ten Years' Tenant.
The Chaplain of the Fleet.

BY WALTER BESANT.
All Sorts and Conditions of Men.
The Captains' Room.
All in a Garden Fair.
Dorothy Forster. | Uncle Jack.
Children of Gibeon.
The World Went Very Well Then.

BY ROBERT BUCHANAN.
Child of Nature.
God and the Man.
The Shadow of the Sword.
The Martyrdom of Madeline.
Love Me for Ever.
Annan Water. | The New Abelard.
Matt. | Foxglove Manor.
The Master of the Mine.

BY HALL CAINE.
The Shadow of a Crime.
A Son of Hagar.

BY MRS. H. LOVETT CAMERON.
Deceivers Ever. | Juliet's Guardian.

BY MORTIMER COLLINS.
Sweet Anne Page. | Transmigration.
From Midnight to Midnight.

MORTIMER & FRANCES COLLINS.
Blacksmith and Scholar
The Village Comedy.
You Play me False.

BY WILKIE COLLINS.
Antonina.
Basil.
Hide and Seek.
The Dead Secret.
Queen of Hearts.
My Miscellanies.
Woman in White.
The Moonstone.
Man and Wife.
Poor Miss Finch.
Miss or Mrs. ?
New Magdalen.
The Frozen Deep.
The Law and the Lady.
The Two Destinies
Haunted Hotel.
The Fallen Leaves
Jezebel's Daughter
The Black Robe.
Heart and Science
"I Say No."
Little Novels.

BY DUTTON COOK.
Paul Foster's Daughter.

BY WILLIAM CYPLES.
Hearts of Gold.

BY ALPHONSE DAUDET.
The Evangelist; or, Port Salvation.

BY JAMES DE MILLE.
A Castle in Spain.

BY J. LEITH DERWENT.
Our Lady of Tears.
Circe's Lovers.

BY M. BETHAM-EDWARDS.
Felicia.

BY MRS. ANNIE EDWARDES.
Archie Lovell.

BY PERCY FITZGERALD.
Fatal Zero.

BY R. E. FRANCILLON.
Queen Cophetua.
One by One.
A Real Queen.

Prefaced by Sir BARTLE FRERE.
Pandurang Hari.

BY EDWARD GARRETT.
The Capel Girls.

PICCADILLY NOVELS, *continued—*

BY CHARLES GIBBON.

Robin Gray.
What will the World Say?
In Honour Bound.
Queen of the Meadow.
The Flower of the Forest.
A Heart's Problem.
The Braes of Yarrow.
The Golden Shaft.
Fancy Free.
Of High Degree.
Loving a Dream.
A Hard Knot.

BY THOMAS HARDY.

Under the Greenwood Tree.

BY JULIAN HAWTHORNE.

Garth.
Ellice Quentin.
Sebastian Strome.
Prince Saroni's Wife
Dust.
Fortune's Fool.
Beatrix Randolph.
Miss Cadogna.
Love—or a Name.

BY SIR A. HELPS.

Ivan de Biron.

BY MRS. ALFRED HUNT.

Thornicroft's Model.
The Leaden Casket.
Self-Condemned.
That other Person.

BY JEAN INGELOW.

Fated to be Free.

BY R. ASHE KING.

A Drawn Game.
"The Wearing of the Green."

BY HENRY KINGSLEY.

Number Seventeen.

BY E. LYNN LINTON.

Patricia Kemball.
Atonement of Leam Dundas.
The World Well Lost.
Under which Lord?
With a Silken Thread.
The Rebel of the Family
"My Love!" | Ione.

BY HENRY W. LUCY.

Gideon Fleyce.

BY JUSTIN McCARTHY.

The Waterdale Neighbours.
A Fair Saxon.
Dear Lady Disdain.
Miss Misanthrope.
Donna Quixote.
The Comet of a Season.
Maid of Athens.
Camiola.

BY MRS. MACDONELL

Quaker Cousins.

PICCADILLY NOVELS, *continued—*

BY FLORENCE MARRYAT.

Open! Sesame! | Written In Fire.

BY D. CHRISTIE MURRAY.

Life's Atonement. | Coals of Fire.
Joseph's Coat. | Val Strange.
A Model Father. | Hearts.
By the Gate of the Sea
The Way of the World.
A Bit of Human Nature.
First Person Singular.
Cynic Fortune.

BY MRS. OLIPHANT.

Whiteladies.

BY MARGARET A. PAUL.

Gentle and Simple.

BY JAMES PAYN.

Lost Sir Massing- | From Exile.
   berd. | A Grape from a
Best of Husbands | Thorn.
Walter's Word. | For Cash Only.
Less Black than | Some   Private
   We're Painted. | Views.
By Proxy | The   Canon's
High Spirits. | Ward
Under One Roof. | Talk of the Town.
A   Confidential | Glow-worm Tales.
   Agent. |

BY E. C. PRICE.

Valentina. | The Foreigners.
Mrs. Lancaster's Rival.

BY CHARLES READE.

It is Never Too Late to Mend.
Hard Cash.
Peg Woffington.
Christie Johnstone.
Griffith Gaunt. | Foul Play.
The Double Marriage.
Love Me Little, Love Me Long.
The Cloister and the Hearth.
The Course of True Love.
The Autobiography of a Thief.
Put Yourself in His Place.
A Terrible Temptation.
The Wandering Heir. | A Simpleton
A Woman-Hater. | Readiana.
Singleheart and Doubleface.
The Jilt.
Good Stories of Men and other
   Animals.

BY MRS. J. H. RIDDELL.

Her Mother's Darling.
Prince of Wales's Garden-Party
Weird Stories.

BY F. W. ROBINSON.

Women are Strange.
The Hands of Justice.

BY JOHN SAUNDERS.

Bound to the Wheel.
Guy Waterman.
Two Dreamers.
The Lion in the Path.

PICCADILLY NOVELS, *continued—*

BY KATHARINE SAUNDERS.
Joan Merryweather.
Margaret and Elizabeth.
Gideon's Rock. | Heart Salvage.
The High Mills. | Sebastian.

BY T. W. SPEIGHT.
The Mysteries of Heron Dyke.

BY R. A. STERNDALE.
The Afghan Knife.

BY BERTHA THOMAS.
Proud Maisie. | Cressida.
The Violin-Player.

BY ANTHONY TROLLOPE.
The Way we Live Now.
Frau Frohmann. | Marion Fay.
Kept in the Dark.
Mr. Scarborough's Family.
The Land-Leaguers.

PICCADILLY NOVELS, *continued—*

BY FRANCES E. TROLLOPE.
Like Ships upon the Sea.
Anne Furness.
Mabel's Progress.

BY IVAN TURGENIEFF, &c.
Stories from Foreign Novelists.

BY SARAH TYTLER.
What She Came Through.
The Bride's Pass.
Saint Mungo's City.
Beauty and the Beast.
Noblesse Oblige.
Citoyenne Jacqueline.
The Huguenot Family.
Lady Bell.
Buried Diamonds.

BY C. C. FRASER-TYTLER.
Mistress Judith.

BY J. S. WINTER.
Regimental Legends.

CHEAP EDITIONS OF POPULAR NOVELS.

Post 8vo, illustrated boards, 2s. each.

BY EDMOND ABOUT.
The Fellah.

BY HAMILTON AÏDÉ.
Carr of Carrlyon. | Confidences.

BY MRS. ALEXANDER.
Maid, Wife, or Widow?
Valerie's Fate.

BY GRANT ALLEN.
Strange Stories.
Philistia.
Babylon.

BY SHELSLEY BEAUCHAMP
Grantley Grange.

BY W. BESANT & JAMES RICE.
Ready-Money Mortiboy.
With Harp and Crown.
This Son of Vulcan. | My Little Girl.
The Case of Mr. Lucraft.
The Golden Butterfly.
By Celia's Arbour.
The Monks of Thelema.
'Twas in Trafalgar's Bay.
The Seamy Side.
The Ten Years' Tenant.
The Chaplain of the Fleet.

BY WALTER BESANT.
All Sorts and Conditions of Men.
The Captains' Room.
All in a Garden Fair.
Dorothy Forster.
Uncle Jack

BY FREDERICK BOYLE.
Camp Notes. | Savage Life.
Chronicles of No-man's Land.

BY BRET HARTE.
An Heiress of Red Dog.
The Luck of Roaring Camp.
Californian Stories.
Gabriel Conroy. | Flip.
Maruja.

BY ROBERT BUCHANAN.
The Shadow of the Sword.
A Child of Nature.
God and the Man.
Love Me for Ever.
Foxglove Manor.
The Master of the Mine.
The Martyrdom of Madeline.
Annan Water.
The New Abelard.
Matt.

BY MRS. BURNETT.
Surly Tim.

BY HALL CAINE.
The Shadow of a Crime.

BY MRS. LOVETT CAMERON
Deceivers Ever. | Juliet's Guardian.

BY MACLAREN COBBAN.
The Cure of Souls.

BY C. ALLSTON COLLINS.
The Bar Sinister.

BY WILKIE COLLINS.
Antonina.
Basil.
Hide and Seek.
The Dead Secret.
Queen of Hearts.
My Miscellanies.
Woman in White.
The Moonstone.

CHEAP POPULAR NOVELS, *continued*—
E. LYNN LINTON, *continued*—
The World Well Lost.
Under which Lord ?
With a Silken Thread.
The Rebel of the Family.
"My Love." | Ione.

BY HENRY W. LUCY.
Gideon Fleyce.

BY JUSTIN McCARTHY.
Dear Lady Disdain | Miss Misanthrope
The Waterdale | Donna Quixote.
Neighbours. | The Comet of a
My Enemy's | Season.
Daughter. | Maid of Athens.
A Fair Saxon. | Camiola.
Linley Rochford.

BY MRS. MACDONELL.
Quaker Cousins.

BY KATHARINE S. MACQUOID.
The Evil Eye. | Lost Rose.

BY W. H. MALLOCK.
The New Republic.

BY FLORENCE MARRYAT.
Open! Sesame | A Little Stepson.
A Harvest of Wild | Fighting the Air.
Oats. | Written in Fire.

BY J. MASTERMAN.
Half-a-dozen Daughters.

BY BRANDER MATTHEWS.
A Secret of the Sea.

BY JEAN MIDDLEMASS.
Touch and Go. | Mr. Dorillion.

BY D. CHRISTIE MURRAY.
A Life's Atonement | Hearts.
A Model Father. | Way of the World.
Joseph's Coat. | A Bit of Human
Coals of Fire. | Nature.
By the Gate of the | First Person Sin-
Sea. | gular.
Val Strange. | Cynic Fortune.

BY ALICE O'HANLON.
The Unforeseen.

BY MRS. OLIPHANT.
Whiteladies.

BY MRS. ROBERT O'REILLY.
Phœbe's Fortunes.

BY OUIDA.
Held in Bondage. | Two Little Wooden
Strathmore. | Shoes.
Chandos. | In a Winter City.
Under Two Flags. | Ariadne.
Idalia. | Friendship.
Cecil Castle- | Motha.
maine's Gage. | Pipiatrello.
Tricotrin. | A Village Com-
Puck. | mune.
Folle Farine. | Bimbi.
A Dog of Flanders. | Wanda.
Pascarel. | Frescoes.
Signa. [Ine. | In Maremma.
Princess Naprax- | Othmar.

CHEAP POPULAR NOVELS, *continued*—
BY MARGARET AGNES PAUL.
Gentle and Simple.

BY JAMES PAYN.
Lost Sir Massing- | Like Father, Like
berd. | Son.
A Perfect Trea- | Marine Residence.
sure. | Married Beneath
Bentinck's Tutor. | Him.
Murphy's Master. | Mirk Abbey.
A County Family. | Not Wooed, but
At Her Mercy. | Won.
A Woman's Ven- | Less Black than
geance. | We're Painted.
Cecil's Tryst. | By Proxy.
Clyffards of Clyffe | Under One Roof.
The Family Scape- | High Spirits.
grace. | Carlyon's Year.
Foster Brothers. | A Confidential
Found Dead. | Agent.
Best of Husbands. | Some Private
Walter's Word. | Views.
Halves. | From Exile.
Fallen Fortunes. | A Grape from a
What He Cost Her | Thorn.
Humorous Stories | For Cash Only.
Gwendoline's Har- | Kit: A Memory.
vest. | The Canon's Ward
£200 Reward. | Talk of the Town.

BY MRS. PIRKIS.
Lady Lovelace.

BY EDGAR A. POE.
The Mystery of Marie Roget.

BY E. C. PRICE.
Valentina. | The Foreigners.
Mrs. Lancaster's Rival.
Gerald.

BY CHARLES READE.
It is Never Too Late to Mend.
Hard Cash. | Peg Woffington.
Christie Johnstone.
Griffith Gaunt.
Put Yourself in His Place.
The Double Marriage.
Love Me Little, Love Me Long.
Foul Play.
The Cloister and the Hearth.
The Course of True Love.
Autobiography of a Thief.
A Terrible Temptation.
The Wandering Heir.
A Simpleton. | A Woman-Hater.
Readiana. | The Jilt.
Singleheart and Doubleface.
Good Stories of Men and other
Animals.

BY MRS. J. H. RIDDELL.
Her Mother's Darling.
Prince of Wales's Garden Party.
Weird Stories. | Fairy Water.
The Uninhabited House.
The Mystery in Palace Gardens.

BY F. W. ROBINSON
Women are Strange.
The Hands of Justice.

CHEAP POPULAR NOVELS, *continued*—

BY JAMES RUNCIMAN.
Skippers and Shellbacks.
Grace Balmaign's Sweetheart.
Schools and Scholars.

BY W. CLARK RUSSELL.
Round the Galley Fire.
On the Fo'k'sle Head.
In the Middle Watch.

BY BAYLE ST. JOHN.
A Levantine Family.

BY GEORGE AUGUSTUS SALA.
Gaslight and Daylight.

BY JOHN SAUNDERS.
Bound to the Wheel.
One Against the World.
Guy Waterman.
The Lion in the Path.
Two Dreamers.

BY KATHARINE SAUNDERS.
Joan Merryweather.
Margaret and Elizabeth.
The High Mills.
Heart Salvage. | Sebastian.

BY GEORGE R. SIMS.
Rogues and Vagabonds.
The Ring o' Bells.
Mary Jane's Memoirs.

BY ARTHUR SKETCHLEY.
A Match in the Dark.

BY T. W. SPEIGHT.
The Mysteries of Heron Dyke.

BY R. A. STERNDALE.
The Afghan Knife.

BY R. LOUIS STEVENSON.
New Arabian Nights. | Prince Otto.

BY BERTHA THOMAS.
Cressida. | Proud Maisie.
The Violin-Player.

BY W. MOY THOMAS.
A Fight for Life.

BY WALTER THORNBURY.
Tales for the Marines.

BY T. ADOLPHUS TROLLOPE.
Diamond Cut Diamond.

BY ANTHONY TROLLOPE.
The Way We Live Now.
The American Senator.
Frau Frohmann.
Marion Fay.
Kept in the Dark.
Mr. Scarborough's Family.
The Land-Leaguers.
The Golden Lion of Granpere.
John Caldigate.

By FRANCES ELEANOR TROLLOPE
Like Ships upon the Sea.
Anne Furness. | Mabel's Progress.

BY J. T. TROWBRIDGE.
Farnell's Folly.

BY IVAN TURGENIEFF, &c.
Stories from Foreign Novelists.

CHEAP POPULAR NOVELS, *continued*—

BY MARK TWAIN.
Tom Sawyer.
A Pleasure Trip on the Continent
of Europe.
A Tramp Abroad.
The Stolen White Elephant.
Huckleberry Finn.
Life on the Mississippi.

BY C. C. FRASER-TYTLER.
Mistress Judith.

BY SARAH TYTLER.
What She Came Through.
The Bride's Pass.
Saint Mungo's City.
Beauty and the Beast.

BY J. S. WINTER.
Cavalry Life. | Regimental Legends.

BY LADY WOOD.
Sabina.

BY EDMUND YATES.
Castaway. | The Forlorn Hope.
Land at Last.

ANONYMOUS.
Paul Ferroll.
Why Paul Ferroll Killed his Wife.

POPULAR SHILLING BOOKS.

Jeff Briggs's Love Story. By BRET
HARTE.
The Twins of Table Mountain. By
BRET HARTE.
Mrs. Gainsborough's Diamonds. By
JULIAN HAWTHORNE.
Kathleen Mavourneen. By Author
of "That Lass o' Lowrie's."
Lindsay's Luck. By the Author of
"That Lass o' Lowrie's."
Pretty Polly Pemberton. By the
Author of "That Lass o' Lowrie's."
Trooping with Crows. By Mrs. PIRKIS
The Professor's Wife. By LEONARD
GRAHAM.
A Double Bond. By LINDA VILLARI.
Esther's Glove. By R. E. FRANCILLON.
The Garden that Paid the Rent.
By TOM JERROLD.
Curly. By JOHN COLEMAN. Illus-
trated by J. C. DOLLMAN.
Beyond the Gates. By E. S. PHELPS.
Old Maid's Paradise. By E. S. PHELPS.
Burglars in Paradise. By E.S.PHELPS.
Jack the Fisherman. By E. S.
PHELPS.
Doom: An Atlantic Episode. By
JUSTIN H. MACCARTHY, M.P.
Our Sensation Novel. Edited by
JUSTIN H. MACCARTHY, M.P.
A Barren Title. By T. W. SPEIGHT.
Wife or No Wife? By T. W. SPEIGHT.
How the Poor Live. By G. R. SIMS.
A Day's Tour. By PERCY FITZGERALD.
The Silverado Squatters. By R.
LOUIS STEVENSON.

J. OGDEN AND CO. LIMITED, PRINTERS, GREAT SAFFRON HILL, E.C.